IT MAY BE YEARS
BEFORE WE SEE EACH OTHER
AGAIN . . .

"Can I write you?" Ruth asked. "Can we be in touch?"

"No," he answered quickly. "I think it would really be much harder if we were."

Tears were streaming down her cheeks. "Don't you care?"

He turned her head around to face him. "Don't you ever say that. I can't imagine getting out of this bed and getting in my car and driving away. But at noon, I have to do it. Now . . . we can lie here feeling sorry for ourselves or we can do something happy in the five hours we have left.

"But Ruth—don't expect me to be brave all by myself. If you want to lie here and cry, I'll lie right beside you and cry just as hard.

"But don't put the burden for being strong on my shoulders, because, my sweet Ruth, I don't feel so strong. Like the rest of our love, we'll have to do it together."

❧ HEART ❧

Susan Ross

BANTAM BOOKS
TORONTO · NEW YORK · LONDON · SYDNEY

HEART

A Bantam Book / April 1982

ISBN 0-553-20411-4

Published simultaneously in the United States and Canada

Bantam Books are published by Bantam Books, Inc. Its trademark, consisting of the words "Bantam Books" and the por-
trayal of a rooster, is Registered in U.S. Patent and Trademark
Office and in other countries. Marca Registrada. Bantam
Books, Inc., 666 Fifth Avenue, New York, New York 10103.

PRINTED IN THE UNITED STATES OF AMERICA

0 9 8 7 6 5 4 3 2 1

Heart
is dedicated
with love
to the believers!

CONTENTS

❧ PROLOGUE ❧

She stopped walking and eased herself down on a bed of pine needles, close to the edge of the crystal blue lake. It was hard to get comfortable; her stomach was beginning to get in the way. She leaned back against the rough brown bark and closed her eyes.

Please, God . . . please, let him write.

She wanted not to hope. She wanted not to count on him. She tried to be worldly-wise and independent. Instead she was herself. She had changed over the years, certainly. It was almost impossible to imagine that she had once been so young and naive. But she had not really changed at heart.

And look where it had gotten her.

She opened her eyes. This had to be the most tranquilly beautiful countryside in all the world. Perhaps Hawaii was more lush and warm; perhaps Kenya was more exotic—but surely the Swiss Alps were the cleanest, crispest beauty available to man. Air that straightens spines and strengthens steps.

She loved these sky-pushing trees, the scent of energy and vitality that permeates the air and the people. Green trees and white mountains.

But, my God, what it took to get here. How far away, Pittsburgh, PA. How distant the innocence, the security of college.

Only yesterday, she had laughed in class. The day after yesterday she had sat in her black veil and cried real tears. Other yesterdays, she had wiggled her toes in warm Italian sands, experienced the exhilaration of sports cars which traveled beyond all limits, dined with prime ministers and poets . . .

Poets. Oh, dear God! where was he?

The baby moved deep in her womb and gave its mother one of those tender tantalizing teases which later develops into a kick, but which now was merely the reassurance of life. New life. If only she knew where she would lead and nourish that new life.

If only he would write. . . .

She sat up straight, looking out at the ice blue lake, and laughed aloud in remembrance.

Nine years ago she had waited for another letter. How *that* letter had changed the flow of her life. Would she have done it—would she have accepted the challenge if she had known what lay ahead? Would she have had the heart? How trusting she had been, how completely unprepared.

She closed tear-swollen lids over eyes as blue as the lake, and leaned her head back against the sheltering tree.

She had all morning. She would just sit here and remember.

The sunlight streamed through the evergreens, highlighting the golden threads in her long hair, creating a quilt of the happiness and heartache she had known. From deep within she heard the rhythm mounting, the rhythm of her sentimental journey . . . the beat of her heart. . . .

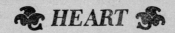

HEART

PART I

Akron, Ohio: Spring 1971

1

Her right hand holding aloft the letter, Ruth Tyack retucked her unpolished toes and her left shoulder under the froth of Herbal Garden Bubbling Bath Oil. Chris had given her the bath oil for Christmas, and now in early April she was using it for the first time. Unaccustomed to the luxury of a bubble bath, she kept finding herself sitting up straight in the tub, elbows on knees, only her bottom and feet getting oiled. She reminded herself to sink back under and relax. That was the whole purpose, after all; a bath like this was supposed to relieve the tensions of the day. There was just one problem: today she loved the tension, had never felt better in her life. She could barely comprehend it or contain her excitement. They had actually offered her the job!

She decided to read the letter one more time. This would only be the sixteenth reading; that didn't seem excessive.

The American School of Rome
76 Via Americanna
APO, New York 09852

Miss Ruth Tyack
46 Rhodes Avenue
Akron, Ohio 44330

Dear Miss Tyack,

We are pleased to inform you that of the seventy-three applications for the one English position we have to fill, our committee has selected you as the best applicant, and we are, therefore, writing to offer

3

you the job beginning in September, 1971, at the salary of $7,000 per year.

While your grades were not the highest of any applicant and you have less classroom experience than some of the other applicants, we were very impressed with the wide range of courses you have completed and were also swayed by the warmth and respect shown to you and the confidence shown in you in the references we received.

We will be in touch concerning your exact teaching assignment and the calendar for the school year. In the meantime, we would appreciate if you would advise us by return mail whether or not you will be accepting the job. If so, please sign the enclosed contract.

Hoping to be working with you in the near future.

Angelina Fabrosi, Head
English Department

Every sentence caught her up in a tumult of thoughts: the corny address; the fact that *she* was chosen out of seventy-three applicants; the good recommendations from the faculty and from her high school English teacher; and the total unbelievability that the job was being offered to her! To be going to Rome—motherless little Ruth Tyack from Pittsburgh. Imagine! Not Rome, New York, or Rome, Georgia, but Rome, Italy. The real Rome: the Colosseum, the Pantheon, St. Peter's.

She reached over and put the letter on the toilet cover, pushed herself back down in the tub, and drew in a big breath. She couldn't believe it.

She had walked into the building today unsuspecting, feeling good but with no premonition of great happenings. Then she had spotted the letter in her mailbox and had felt almost instant depression. She was not usually a defeatist, but she had mailed fifteen letters of application and so far had received six rejections. The American School of Rome, she supposed, was the longest shot of all.

In fact, so sure was she of a rejection that she had carried the unopened letter upstairs and stretched out on the green plaid sofa to call Harry's Pizza and drown her sorrows in tomato sauce and mushrooms. The line was busy. So she opened the letter. She knew that they wanted her as soon as she saw that it was two pages long. It doesn't take that long to say no.

She straightened up on the sofa, blue eyes glistening the color of the water around the Isle of Capri. She had the job! She actually had gotten the job! Rome! Sexy Italian men! Tomato sauce and mushrooms? No, she needed something fancier than a lonely pizza tonight. She would call Chris.

As she dialed the phone, she noticed the dust on the coffee table, made obvious by the April sunshine streaming through her yellow curtains. She wiped it off with her sweater sleeve. He answered after only one ring.

"Chris Wilson." His bass voice always sounded assured.

"Ruth Tyack." Her contralto sounded uneven.

"Hiya, kiddo. What's up?"

She heard the chair squeak as he leaned back.

"Well, how about coming over for steak?"

"Tonight? We never do anything on Thursday nights." She could see the puzzled frown; Chris never veered from his patterns. "You have that eight o'clock discussion class Friday mornings."

"I know. But this is special," she said, gloating.

"Okay. I'll bite. What's so special?"

"A job." She tried to sound calm.

"Hey, that's great! I told you somebody'd want you—besides me, that is," he added quietly.

"Yeah, but you won't believe who it is." She was bursting with pride.

"Let me guess. Fallsview State Mental Hospital."

"Very funny." She was hurt. He was making fun of the most exciting thing that had ever happened to her. "Just for that, your curiosity can kill you until you get here."

"That'll serve me right." He didn't sound very tortured.

"Sure will," she said, disappointed by his lack of interest.

"Shall I bring some champagne?" he asked, reinstating himself in Ruth's good graces.

"Oh, Chris, that would be really nice."

"Okay. See you later, kiddo."

Smiling, she replaced the receiver and crossed the living room to her tiny brown kitchen. What had prompted her to buy that steak yesterday? She put it out on the counter to thaw. Steak and champagne—that was almost a complete meal. She would make a salad and that good garlic dressing—and bread! She got down the box of natural cereal she had bought and hated. There was a bread recipe on the side of the box. Maybe it could be palatable yet.

Shortly, the smell of dates, raisins, and nuts baking in flour teased her senses, and she wondered what Rome would smell like. She started planning: she'd have to spend every minute all week on her schoolwork so that as soon as the kids were excused on Fridays she could become a tourist. Seven thousand dollars was not all that much to live on. But there must be a lot of things to do that were free. Rome on five dollars a day—it had to be possible. The hell with clothes and food. One of the advantages of being a teacher was that at noon every day she could eat a starchy, filling meal. Now if she could just find a cheap, convenient room. . . . Goodbye, Ohio; hello, Rome!

Ohio . . . she had to get the themes graded to hand back to the discussion class tomorrow! No wonder Chris was shocked to get a call on a Thursday. Always before it was, "Not Thursday night—I have that early discussion class on Friday." A teaching assistant at Eastern Ohio University in the spring of 1971; a teacher of sophomore and junior English at the American School of Rome in the fall of 1971. "Not an insignificant improvement," as Howard Cosell would say.

Ruth forced herself to concentrate on another batch of inane, half-baked analyses of George Orwell's 1984. Why couldn't they assign something different? Although she had only taught the class for five terms, already she had heard every idea one hundred times. Wasn't there an original thinker in all of Akron? Maybe they put tranquilizers in the water.

Somehow the themes got graded, and the bread formed more peaks than valleys, and the salad got tossed and the table set. But she didn't know how. Ruth Tyack dreamed away that late Thursday afternoon in April, envisioning lions devouring Christians and coins splashing in Trevi Fountain.

She was just emerging from the bathtub when she heard Chris's special drumroll on the door. "Coming." She wrapped herself in a nubby pink towel and, dripping, dashed across the living room. Carefully positioned behind the door, she opened it only enough for Chris to enter. All he could see was the trail of wet footprints. "Close your eyes," Ruth commanded from behind the imitation oak panel.

He obliged, closing the door with his foot as he did so. She tried to hurry past, but, eyes still shut, he reached out with the hand not holding the champagne and pulled her toward him for a chaste but affectionate kiss.

"Welcome to the working force of America, Miss Tyack." His right hand squeezed her bare shoulder, his left pushed the champagne bottle into her back. She was oblivious.

"Oh, Chris, I got the most wonderful job!"

He opened his eyes, smiled, and pushed her away a bit to get a better look at the white skin outside the pink towel. He had never seen so much of her body before; nor had he ever seen her radiating so much energy and excitement. Her shoulder-length blond hair was damp around the ends and curled instead of waving—Little Orphan Annie hair. The exposed body . . . the wide, trusting blue eyes stirred a protectiveness in Chris that brought a lump to his throat.

"Much as I like the view, I'm afraid you're going to freeze if I hear about it before you get dried off."

"Okay. I'll be right back." She left the bedroom door ajar and hollered back to him, "I'm sorry. I don't know how I got so late. I finished the themes for tomorrow and took a bath. That's about all I did all afternoon."

Chris walked across to the kitchen. "You also did whatever this is on the counter." He leaned over to sniff. "Smells good."

"Oh, the natural bread."

"I figured you had enough class not to serve artificial bread with champagne." He put the champagne on its side in the refrigerator, then took off his coat and tie and sprawled on the sofa, rolling the sleeves of his shirt. Chris was tall and lean and constantly tanned. He spent two evenings a week working out at a health club and jogged for a half-hour every morning before work. He wasn't handsome—his face was too angular, his hair too receding and his lips had the thin stretch of a perfectionist. Yet his good physical condition gave him an aura of vitality that was almost better than good looks. His trained singing voice added a resonant, melodic quality to his speech that made him pleasant to listen to.

"Would you like to hear the song that's been running through my head since you opened the door?"

"No."

Undaunted, he sang in his bass voice, "'You'd be so-o-o nice to come home to...'"

Her head appeared around the door. "I thought we had an understanding, Chris."

"Yeah, well, guess what, baby?" He grinned at her, hands behind his head. "I'm looking for a gainfully employed wife who is willing to support me in the style to which I intend to become accustomed." She disappeared into the bedroom, and he had to raise his voice. "You are going to have some gain from your employment, aren't you?"

"Seven thou."

"Okay for a start, for sure. Together we'd be making a nice little sum of money—enough for a house."

"Chris..." Ruth emerged in a powder-blue skirt and a blue-and-white-striped sweater. She was carrying a hairbrush in her hand. "The champagne is for my new job, not for a proposition. I don't hear any wedding bells; I have too much to do, too many places to see. When the two cities you have lived in are steely Pittsburgh and rubbery

Akron, you really do not have a fair representation of life."

"Okay, okay, I surrender. Now tell me about your job and how being a high school teacher is going to give you a fairer representation of life."

"Guess where I'm going to teach."

"Copley? Here in Akron? Ravenna? Cleveland? Pittsburgh? Mingo Junction?"

Each guess was greeted by a negative shake of Ruth's head. She had perched on the sofa arm near his feet, smiling with her secret knowledge, brushing her hair.

"I give up."

"Rome."

"I never heard of it. Where is it?"

"In Italy."

"Come on, smart mouth. Where is it?"

He sounded tense, and she sensed trouble.

"Honestly, Chris, the job's in Rome, Italy. The American School of Rome."

"Ruth, you are kidding, aren't you?" Chris was no longer slouched on the couch but sitting up straight, hands on knees, head tilted in disbelief.

"I'm sorry, Chris, but I'm not kidding," she said quietly.

"Ruth, I've been trying to tell you for months that I want you to marry me."

"I thought that was just sort of a joke."

"Well, the joke's on me, isn't it?" He sounded like a petulant child.

"Chris . . ."

He stood up, rolling down and rebuttoning his sleeves. "Listen, I think I'll go; I've suddenly lost my appetite."

"Chris, wait, please." She stood beside him, trying to get him to look at her. "I'm really sorry. I see now that I should at least have warned you that this was possible. I really didn't expect to get the job. I thought it was such a lark that if it did come through, it would be fun to surprise you."

"Some surprise—the woman I love is leaving the country."

"Nothing is final. I only got the job offer this afternoon.

Even if I do sign it, the contract is only for a year." She had tears in her eyes as she reached a hand out to him in entreaty. "Please don't spoil it. I'm so happy."

"Well, your happiness and mine seem for the moment to be in conflict, since your happiness means you leave and my happiness means you stay."

"Why don't you come along?"

"Sure—maybe I could sell some of Goodyear's trade secrets to Pirelli or somebody."

His angry sarcasm left her speechless. She merely watched, wide-eyed, as he tightened his tie and replaced his jacket. Once again immaculate, he crossed to the door, calling over his shoulder, "Enjoy your steak. Since you've chosen the solitary life, you may as well begin getting used to it. Call me when you wake up."

Apparently that last barb was supposed to bring her crawling back. Instead, she sat feeling as though someone had pulled the plug. All the joy was gone.

She sat quietly for long minutes after the door had slammed, thinking, not thinking. And then she rose decisively, slipped on her loafers and a sweater, and walked out of the apartment.

She spent the evening eating popcorn in the village theater, watching a Walt Disney movie. She'd had worse evenings.

The next day, though, Ruth still felt leaden. After her eight o'clock class, she met Jill for coffee as usual. But Jill was bubbling over about Dave, her new lover. Ruth couldn't handle it. She mumbled an excuse and made her escape.

Ruth left the student union and started walking aimlessly, her spirits sagging. As she always did when she was truly sad, she started thinking about her mother. Annie had been nineteen when she died in childbirth. It didn't sound like something that could happen in 1948; 1848, maybe, but not 1948. But it had happened. Ruth could never believe it as a little girl. She had imagined her mother to be a famous Broadway actress who would one day drive up Parkview Avenue in Squirrel Hill, Pennsylvania, proclaiming to the world, like the duke of Windsor, that she could no longer live or act without the support of the child she loved. A vicious agent had forced her to leave her family, but she now realized how wrong she had been, and she had come home to beg her husband and little girl to forgive her. She would settle down and bake chocolate chip cookies and be a mother and bandage Ruth's knees and rock her back to sleep when she had bad dreams.

Finally, Ruth's father had started taking Ruth to the cemetery to try to make Annie's death real. Ruth loved having her father's complete attention, for usually he was engrossed in his reading and studying. He taught biology, and he collected European stamps. Quiet, shy, and reserved, he was a good, moral man, but Ruth had always thought of him as ineffectual. He had a weak heart, had always had, and never took the risk of becoming involved in anything. The only daring thing he had done in his life was to elope to Elkton, Maryland, with eighteen-year-old Anne Maria Himmel. The Biology Department at the University of Pittsburgh lost its new secretary, and Benjamin Harrison Tyack gained fifteen months of happiness.

"Hey, blondie, ya wanna ride?"

Ruth looked up, surprised, and tried to smile at the truck driver stopped for the light. "No, thanks."

"Okay, blondie, if you're sure. Take care of those pretty legs now, ya hear?"

"Right. Thanks." Ruth laughed in relief and pleasure as he pulled away. *He liked my legs*, she thought. *Funny how a chance comment from a stranger can cheer you up. How we need to be noticed!*

Ruth wasn't surprised to find that her "pretty legs" had transported her to 10 South Main. The one thing guaranteed to bring her out of her doldrums was a visit with Tilly. Bertilla Ludding lived in a one-room apartment on the sixteenth floor of 10 South Main. That is, if you could call what Bertilla did living. For forty years Bertilla had made the salads for Akron's famous Tea Garden Buffet. One night a drunk driver had hit her as she crossed the street, and now Tilly lay legless and half-blind in Apartment 1608. Her mattress was on the floor, as was a basin that she used for a toilet. Her whole life was lived on a low level, but Tilly was one of those gutsy, ornery people whose spirit would not be conquered.

Ruth was sure she was going to get mugged someday in the creaky gray elevator or the long pea-soup green hall. The building depressed even her.

"Tilly?" Ruth knocked and called.

"Come you in." The smell was so overpoweringly bad that it was difficult for Ruth to force herself to enter.

"How are you, Tilly?"

"Be it Ruth?"

"Yes, Tilly, hi."

"Well, Ruthie, you be heaven-sent. How'd you know I was just a dyin' for a cuppa water and was too dang lazy to git it myself? An in you struts just on the moment."

"Tilly, you make me feel so good. I'm always glad when I come to see you."

"You brang lunch?"

"No—I only do Mobile Meals one Thursday a month, and this is Friday."

"Well, still you can git me some water."

"Can I get you something else, Tilly? Do you have anything I could make for you—some coffee or tea or some breakfast of some sort?"

"You can scout in the frigerator, honey, but I'm afraid Ma Hubbard's cupboards is bare." Her big tummy shook with silent laughter. She was wearing the ugliest yellow nightgown Ruth had ever seen.

"There's an orange in here, Tilly. How would that taste?"

"Ooh, I be dead an' in heaven."

"How do you ever use this sink, Tilly?" Ruth cut the orange in sections, removing seeds and rind, surreptitiously cleaning the filthy sink at the same time.

"I can git myself up on that chair there, Ruthie, but I ain't too graceful, and it ain't too sturdy. I's taken a tumble or three."

"Tilly, tell me about your husband. Does it make you sad to talk about him?" Ruth knew it didn't.

"My Preston is my happiest thing of all to talk on. What you wanna know, honey?"

"Did you know right away when you met him that he was the man for you?"

"Aw, honey, no—twern't like that nohow. We's growed up together. And I been seein' Preston since we's started to school." For the first time Ruth noticed that Tilly had a truly attractive face.

"Well, when did it change? When did you know?"

"Aw, honey." She sighed in anticipation and smiled with her broken teeth. "Well, Preston were always a military man. We lived here in Akron—our daddies was friends at the Goodyear. So my daddy tells me when his buddy's boy goes off to what they used to call boot camp. And sure nuff, bout two, three month later, Saturday night it were, up on the porch struts Mr. Preston Dale Ludding, and he says to my daddy, 'Mr. Davis, sir, I wants to ast if I kin marry your daughter, Bertilla.' And my daddy, he sits up straight and tall, and he says, 'Why, Bertilla ain't only but seventeen, Mr. Ludding, and here you is a military man of the world!'

" 'Yes, sir,' says Preston, 'that be the gospel truth, sir, but I gots me no interest in some used woman. I wants my own woman to teach her how I wants her to be, so she be only mine and allus waitin'.' And my daddy, he looks that Preston up and down, and that Preston, he looks straight at my daddy. And my mama and me, we ain't breathin' *at all*. Then my daddy, he says, 'You plannin' to treat my Tilly real nice, ain't ya, boy?' And Preston, he looks over to me, and he tries to smile, but it just won't come, and he looks back at my daddy, and he says, 'I sure nuff am, Mr. Davis, sir, I sure nuff am plannin' to be some fine husband.'

"So my daddy, he sort a nods his head, an' Preston, he holds out his hand to me, and I goes to him, and we just sorta floats off the porch, and we's halfway to Youngstown, walkin' and just sort a gettin' the rhythm of each other. And then I sees somethin' I ain't seen before in the whole sitiation, and I says, 'Yous takin' mighty lot for granted,

Preston Dale Ludding, thinkin' 'I'd be marryin' you.' And he stops right there, right in the middle of the walkway, and he swings me off my feet, Ruth, absolutely off my feet, and he gives me the gawd dangest kiss I ever had in my whole life, and it's long, and it's so awful sweet, and then still holdin' me off my feet, he looks me in my eyes, and he says, 'Tilly, honey, I am your man, and you is my woman, and let there be no mistakin' 'bout that, not now nor never.' And I gots my eyes full of tears and my throat full of cotton, and my heart is poundin' 'bout triple, and I just croaks, real meeklike, 'Yes, Preston.' "

Sitting there in that shit-colored-smelling hole with that now sexless creature, Ruth could see it, she could see it all. She could see the seventeen-year-old Tilly minus forty pounds, plus two legs, hair in neat corn rows instead of flying four-inch fuzz, and she thanked God that at some point in her life—because it sure as hell wasn't now—Tilly had known happiness.

Ruth and Tilly sat in silence.

"Aw, Ruthie, that orange were the best thing I been eatin' for some long time. Thank you, honey, for fixin' it so nice."

"How do you do it, Tilly? How do you keep going?"

"Aw, honey, there ain't nothin' to it. I's jus bidin'. I been bidin' since the day the telegram came 'bout Preston. Made it all the way through World War II he did, and then he gets kilt in Korea. I told him he were too old for that fightin' stuff, an' he just laughs. He were some real hero, Ruthie. Gets kilt savin' some young kid who starts doin' dumb things—kid gets plumb scart crazy. So Preston marches in to git the kid out—and he gits hit from behind. But he allus felt 'sponsible for his men. He's allus sayin' that: 'my men.' He was a sergeant—all that time, he was allus a sergeant." Tilly sighed at the injustice. "Good Lordy, he be good. An he's waitin'. Gonna carry me around through eternity, he is. Just knows it. So I's just bidin'."

"Tilly, you are some special lady. I mean that," Ruth's voice was choked.

"Honey, I's as ordinary as a closet broom."

14

"I have to go, Tilly; I have a class to teach. But I wanted to stop and say hello."

"Well, I thanks ya, honey-chile, I sure does. You gives me some right rare treat, astin' bout my Preston like you does. Now I'll just spend the day out thinkin' about them happy times. My, but we had some purty little red house. Every time it was time to paint it I said to Preston, 'How bouts we paints it white or green or blue or somethin' this time?' No. He allus said no. Red. He wanted it the same. So he'd know when he was home."

"What happened to your home, Tilly?"

"Well, now, of course that there drunken fella that hit me didn't have no insurance. So I has to pay to have my legs took off and to go part blind. Ain't that just the most? But, don't matter, honey—ain't nothin to worry. Cause I's just bidin'. Now you has a happy day, Ruthie. An you comes back, ya hear? Cause you surely does know how to make dis ole body happy."

"Thank you, Tilly." Ruth was trying hard to fight back the tears. "I'll be back." It didn't sound like her own voice. She rushed out the door and ran down the hall. In the elevator she collapsed against the wall and sobbed. Then she grabbed her sunglasses from her bag, jutted her chin toward the sunshine, and started walking back to school.

The twelve o'clock discussion class went beautifully. The kids were lively and expressed much more interesting ideas in class than they had in their papers. She felt good when she returned to the faculty dining room and stood, tray balanced in front of her, looking for an empty table or a familiar face. Her eye was caught by a middle-aged black man whom Ruth remembered taught African history. He motioned to the other seat at his window table, and Ruth walked across the room anticipating a good conversation.

"Thank you. Most of the time when you're standing there looking for a seat and you catch someone's eye, they look right through you as if you're the invisible man or something." Ruth put down her tray and held out her hand. "I'm Ruth Tyack. English."

"Lionel Grant. History."

"You have a fine reputation. I've heard students say

good things—tough but fair. That's the best thing to have them say, I think."

"Thank you." He gave her a wonderfully honest smile. "Music to my tired ears. I often think that one problem with college teaching is the lack of feedback. I taught high school for a few years before I had any advanced degrees, and you get a lot more encouragement there. Of course, maybe you would at a smaller university, too. But anyhow, thanks. Few people will tell you something nice like that."

"You know, I read this crazy poem once—it was really bad poetry, but the thought has always stuck with me. 'Don't bother putting flowers on the grave—hand them over when the person is alive.' That was the idea. So there now, you have been duly warned. I do not intend putting flowers on your grave."

"In that case, I'm not inviting you to the funeral."

They laughed.

"I was just talking about death this morning with this amazing lady; her name's Bertilla Ludding. She's half-blind and legless, and do you know what she said? She said her husband, an army sergeant who died in Korea, is going to carry her around through eternity. Isn't that beautiful? I can't get that out of my mind. She says she's just biding and waiting for Preston to carry her away. Gosh, I'm starting again." She brushed away a tear that ran down her cheek.

"It's wonderful to feel things deeply enough to cry."

Ruth smiled through her tears.

Lionel Grant sighed. "The last time I cried was during the movie *Friendly Persuasion*."

"I don't remember crying then, but I probably did. I almost always cry."

"Tell me more about your friend Bertilla."

"She lives down on Main in the worst condition of any human being I ever saw. She has one room, with a mattress on the floor because of her legs, I guess—or her lack of legs. Tiny refrigerator, usually empty. Today she had one orange and about half a pie someone brought her—you could tell she just ate it right out of the pie plate—and a quart of milk and a bunch of carrots. I should have peeled the carrots for her; I didn't think of it. I think she'd be better off institutionalized. Maybe she doesn't want that; I don't know. Her mind is fine. She has a tiny black and white TV she listens to a lot; it's almost always on when I go in there. I met her because I do Mobile Meals, and she was on my route one day, and I just admired her spunk. But the room smells so bad. It absolutely stinks! And the sheets always look dirty—sometimes bloody from the sores on her stumps. She's in a pathetic state."

"She is black." It wasn't a question—he just wanted confirmation.

"Yes."

"I'll ask around at church. Sounds like she needs looking after. Maybe some lonely Baptist soul will feel the spirit move them." His eyes twinkled. He seemed quite an extraordinary man.

"That would be so good, if you would do that," Ruth said. "And if you want to go see her sometime, I'd be glad to go with you."

"I'll see what I can do at church or through some of the agencies we're involved with, and then maybe we can go see her together with some good news."

"I'm so glad I sat down at your table."

"Me, too." That honest look flashed between them again. "I have to head off; I have a one forty-five appointment, but I'll be in touch with you regarding the biding lady. Maybe we can see to it she can bide in a more comfortable state."

"Thank you, Dr. Grant. I knew you were a good teacher, but I had no idea what a good person you were, too."

A fatherly black hand reached over and patted her on the cheek. "I didn't know they made 'em like you anymore, Ruth Tyack. And for heaven's sake, call me Lionel. If we are going to endure Bertilla's room together, we'd better be on a first-name basis."

"Thank you, Lionel."

"So long."

Ruth looked down at her half-eaten lasagna. "God," she mumbled, "if I believed in You, I would certainly wonder if this was You working in Your mysterious ways. Of course, Dr. Grant may not really be able to do anything, but, then, maybe he will."

A deep voice interrupted her whispered monologue. "Is this a private conversation, or can anyone join in?"

Ruth jumped.

"Hey, I didn't mean to scare you. I'm sorry." Dr. Fielding, one of her English professors, put his hand out, as if to quiet a skittish horse, then sat down opposite her.

"Was I talking out loud?"

"Ruth, don't worry about it. I understand it's a common characteristic of senility."

Ruth flashed him a Ruth-smile—an open, warm, a dazzling smile that transformed her face and made her suddenly beautiful.

He smiled back, then looked at her plate, and said, "You eat all that and you're going to fall asleep in Chaucer."

"Dr. Fielding, how could I possibly fall asleep in one of your classes?" For seventeen years he had reigned as the most boring professor in the English Department.

"Good question."

"Besides," she added, "we're doing the Miller's Tale today, and *no one* could fall asleep during the Miller's Tale."

"True, true." He nodded his bald head solemnly.

"That's a funny class, isn't it?" Ruth wanted him to talk so she could eat.

"There's a good cross-section of attitude and opinion in there—when I can get a discussion going. It's certainly a strange class in that way; not many of my classes are so reticent."

"Well, everybody in there just seems to have such problems right now. Gary's wife just lost a baby; Jenny's father is scheduled to have open-heart surgery; Helen didn't get her thesis proposal accepted; and you know Arnold's wife went home to mama with their little boy in tow. Now that doesn't leave very many happy people in that room."

"Good grief." His cloudy gray eyes focused on her in astonishment. "It sounds like a soap opera."

"Don't you think that's what makes soap operas so popular—how closely they hit home to so many people?"

"I always thought they were so outlandish."

Ruth knew it was pointless to argue. "Dr. Fielding, we're going to be late for your Chaucer class if we don't hurry."

"True, true, my dear. Off we go."

As usual Ruth and one or two others did most of the talking. All of her life Ruth had felt an obligation to keep things going for people. She dropped money in the Salvation Army pot when others were passing by; she sat in front rows and smiled encouragingly at ministers, pianists, shaky vocalists, and youngsters learning to dance; and in classes she felt constrained to break the awkward silences that resulted when teachers posed questions and students possessed no answers. She often did it to her own detriment, giving answers that she knew were inadequate, rather than enduring the tension of waiting. So it went in Chaucer class. She spoke even more than usual, and the reason was, to Ruth herself, hilarious. She seemed to be the only person in the room who could bring herself to say the word fart. It was such an easy word to say—like bark or duck—but nobody else was able to pronounce it. In a discussion of the Miller's Tale somebody needed to be able to say fart.

So Ruth went home laughing and heard the phone ringing as she walked in the door of her apartment.

"Hello."

"Where the hell have you been all day?" Chris demanded. "I thought you were going to call me."

Ruth very quietly put the receiver back on the base of the phone and walked into the bathroom and turned on the shower. From time to time she heard the phone ringing, but she kept on shampooing her hair and shaving her legs, doing everything she could think of to stay under the spray. When she got out of the shower, the phone was ringing again, and she answered it.

"Hello."

"I'm sorry, honey. I was just worried."

"I'm sorry I didn't get to phone. It was really a full day."

"Dinner tonight as usual?"

"That'd be great." Ruth sighed, relieved that he seemed to have gotten over his anger at her job. She wanted to keep their friendship intact.

"Where would you like to go?"

"How about somewhere where there's some jazz in the background?"

"Do you really like that? I like my music and my food kept separate. But if you'd like that, I'll see what I can do."

"Whatever you feel like, Chris. It's your Friday night, too."

"About seven-thirty?"

"Good. See you then."

So they went to Fat Fred's and heard Tommy Mack caress his piano like a tender lover while they ate broiled scallops. Ruth, who had been very tired, felt more alive with each new set; Chris, who had felt great when they walked in, was now feeling grumpy, tired, and bored. And sick. When Jill and Dave waved from across the room, Chris said, "Go ask them if you can have a ride home. I think I'm going to be sick." He headed for the bathroom. About ten minutes later he reappeared, looking decidedly green.

Ruth grabbed his arm. "Come on. I paid the bill. I'll drive you home."

He didn't have the strength to argue.

She had to stop once on the way home, but the fresh air seemed to revive him, and he didn't throw up. He wanted her to drop him off and take his car to her apartment, but she wanted to see him safely tucked into bed before she went. So together they went to his apartment on Fir Hill, and while he crawled into bed and fell asleep almost immediately, Ruth sat at the kitchen table. She drank successive cups of tea, lost on a sea of thoughts and dreams, plans and feelings. After about an hour and a half, she tiptoed into the bedroom and stole the other pillow. She found a blanket in the bathroom closet and settled down for the night on Chris's couch. She slept deeply and soundly.

They had a lovely Saturday morning. Chris woke up feeling healthy, hungry, and disproportionately happy to see that Ruth had spent the night. He shaved, singing songs from *Showboat*, and they ate grapefruit and waffles and drank tea. Chris took her home around ten so she could take a shower and change her clothes before they went grocery shopping.

They made plans to have supper together Sunday night, as they often did. Otherwise, they spent the weekend involved in their own activities. In the weeks that followed, their relationship reverted to its previous casual course —which was a relief to Ruth. Neither of them mentioned Rome.

About two weeks after her chance lunch with Lionel Grant, the good man himself called her to say he had found a lonely widow, Virginia White, who wanted to meet Tilly. The next Tuesday Lionel and Ruth took Virginia to Tilly's apartment; and before they left, plans had been made to move Tilly's "bidin'" place. In the elevator Virginia swooped both man and woman under her wings and said, "Thank God we were able to do something about *that*."

With the warm glow of Tilly's resettlement outweighing the uncertainty of her relationship with Chris, Ruth tried to concentrate on teaching and studying.

She had two more courses to take. She had finished her master's thesis, and it was typed and approved; so all that remained was to pass Twentieth Century American Drama and a Milton seminar, and she would possess a master's degree. Since there was no assistantship available in the summer, she found a parttime job at Arnold's Ice Cream Parlor. In addition to gaining ten pounds that summer, she also made enough money to pay the rent and buy some of Fazio's Hi-Pro Mix, which is what poor people eat instead of hamburger.

Between spring and summer sessions, she drove home to Pittsburgh for a week. Her father always seemed glad to have her home but was somewhat lost as to what he should do with her. Their visits were awkward and unaffectionate. Neither of them seemed capable of doing anything to change that, yet they both seemed to need the companionship and sense of family.

She returned to Akron for summer school and knowing herself to be at the end of her student days, immersed herself completely in scholarship, reading extra background material and writing the best papers she had ever written. She felt like a miler on the last lap.

It was on July 11, 1971, a quite ordinary day, that, in the most unexpected and unheralded way, Ruth experienced the happiest, most exciting sixteen hours of her twenty-three years of life.

2

The poet was arriving on the 5:15 from Buffalo—United 122. Ruth Tyack stood resignedly at the end of the escalator in the Akron-Canton airport scrutinizing the arriving passengers. She rejected, of course, the women and children, the men who were too old or too young, and anyone who was being met. After six years in Akron, she recognized the rubber company executives by their strutlike walks and the austerity of their dark suits and white shirts. She rejected them, too. She also discarded the men who looked too straight. A poet would not look like that. He would be self-conscious and have too much hair, either on his head or on his face or, save all else, on his body. Somehow the hair went with the uncertainty of the profession, the added hair a security blanket.

Ruth stood in plain sight, smiling tentative smiles, holding a discreet gray tablet-back on which she had printed TOM JEFFERS. Poets liked to see their names in print; she wondered if this would count. The line of travelers was dwindling. Damn it! She really didn't need this frustration. All because she happened to be hanging around the graduate student bullpen at four o'clock. That would teach her to work at school. The secretary had simply sauntered in and said, "Ruth, Dr. Brickhouse would like to see you in his office."

"Ruth!" Dr. Brickhouse always sounded as if you were the only person in the world he could possibly want to talk to. He motioned her to an institutional black vinyl chair and then leaned back against his desk, towering over her.

"Ruth, I really need your help. My wife just called, and she's at the hospital with our son. He broke his arm on his bike today—somehow." He sounded exasperated. "Now, I've got to get over there and calm them both down. To be frank, Ruth, you're the only one around. You know this man Jeffers is coming for the poetry reading tonight? I need you to meet him at the airport." Dr. Brickhouse frequently stroked his prematurely white beard as he talked; Ruth thought it looked like a form of masturbation. Today he was so flustered he was simply clutching the white hairs in his left hand. "Here's twenty dollars, Ruth." He held it out with his right hand. "Please go meet Jeffers, take him out to dinner, and have him at the auditorium by eight. Okay? Thanks, Ruth. I really appreciate your help." Then he was gone, still clutching.

"Sure, Dr. Brickhouse. Never mind my own plans—the department first, of course." *Damn. And he's probably a jerk. I'll have the burden of conversation all night. And he'll talk about nothing but his poetry.*

"Ah, pardon me, miss." She looked up in surprise; she hadn't even seen him approach. "Just what are you planning to do with this, ah"—he studied the cardboard to be sure of the name—"Tom Jeffers, when you find him? If you don't mind my asking?" She saw wide, sexy lips under laughing gray eyes, and short, curly, cocoa-brown hair. It couldn't be him. Not enough hair! Ruth laughed back at the laughing eyes.

"Well, actually I was going to take him out to dinner and then to a motel, although I'm hesitant to admit that that was what I had in mind. But, he hasn't appeared, so I'll have to think of some more respectable way to spend the evening." He smiled at her story and made no move either to leave or to continue the conversation. "Were you on the plane from Buffalo?" she asked.

"Sure was."

"You didn't see any nice, hairy, insecure poets, did you?"

The gray eyes above the forty-regular tan summer suit moved from her face, taking in her teacher's skirt and vest and her loafers. He threw back his head to howl a low, delicious laugh.

"Prepare to have your delusions smashed." He extracted

a wallet from his pants pocket and pulled out a license with a three-year-old picture of an even-then, short-haired creature with the label *Thomas Paul Jeffers*.

"Oh, no." Her face turned red. She pulled herself together enough to smile an apology. "I'm afraid this is not an auspicious beginning."

"Not at all." He sketched a bow of forgiveness. "You are not, I take it, Dr. Brickhouse. When I talked to him on the phone, I heard a distinct New York accent, which you do not have. So you are undoubtedly a substitute, roped in at the last minute when Dr. Brickhouse's wife acquired a headache."

"Son broke his arm."

"Oh, yeah. You're a graduate student in the English department"—she nodded yes—"and if a friend wants to hail you on the street he shouts, 'Hey, Francine.'"

She laughed in astonishment at the idea of Francine and looked to see if he was teasing. She saw only kindness in his eyes. "Prepare to have *your* delusions smashed—Ruth."

"Ruth." He stared at her, assimilating the information. This blue-eyed blond in front of him, pretty (but not a knockout), probably should have been Carol or Sandy or something more upbeat. Ruths were brown and gentle. What he saw were slightly off-balance eyes, a nose too long, and a chin that could be stubborn. But you'd have to look hard to notice the flaws—the happy blue eyes caught you up and carried you to the smiling mouth so that you saw a radiant enthusiasm.

"Ruth." He put his hand inside her arm, and they started walking, looking at each other, eyes locked. He was about four inches taller than Ruth. Even walking, they seemed to fit. Then he broke the spell. "Now, as you know from standing there holding a sign with the almost name, Tom Jeffers—everyone thinking you got lazy and just didn't add the O-N—I am in no position to be critical of names. In fact, mine has an ironic twist. When I was old enough to demand an explanation for what they had done to me, my mom said they just never realized. Thomas was her father's name, and if my parents had a boy they were going to name him Thomas—they never practiced putting it together with Jeffers, so they never realized it was so nearly Thomas Jefferson. How about Ruth?"

"Just from the Bible. My mother died having me, and my father picked a good, nonfrivolous name to give him strength and me courage, I guess. There are times when I like it. There are times when I hate it. It seems so disgustingly solid and dependable." He laughed at her disgust, dismissing it, making her feel anything but solid and dependable.

They headed for the baggage claim area, where he took the last remaining piece of luggage, a fairly small tan leather suitcase, and followed her out to her yellow Corvair. She was suddenly ashamed that it was dirty. When she hesitated with the keys in her hand, he merely took them, opened the trunk, and put his suitcase in, then opened the passenger door and put Ruth in, all with great assurance.

"Are you a good driver?" She was teasing; she felt unaccountable trust.

"At over two miles an hour I'm excellent. I really should let you back out of the parking space—it's the only danger we'll experience. I'm dynamite on freeways. Where to?"

"How about Virginia Beach for a week of sun and sand?" God! Had she really said that?

But he looked at her in admiration before starting the car. The little tilt of his head and the half-smile made her flush with pleasure. And when his choice was north on 77 toward Akron or east on 76 toward Pittsburgh (and Virginia Beach), he actually got in the eastbound lane.

She put her hand on the wheel and said, "North, please—duty first." He took her hand off the wheel and held it in his, on his leg. She was trembling, but she couldn't stop smiling at him.

His voice broke the silence like the crash of cymbals. "God, you have a beautiful smile."

"I hate to be unoriginal, but so do you. Does anyone ever call you T.J.?"

"Not before you."

"How old are you?" She turned toward him, afire with

questions. "What do you teach? You aren't in the English Department, are you?"

"Forty-one—marketing—no." He laughed.

"Do I sound like the Spanish Inquisition?"

"No, you don't. You sound like Ruth asking reasonable questions." He squeezed her hand. His hands weren't much bigger than hers, but they were strong. She felt him flowing into her and tightened the pressure of her own hand in the clasp.

"Would you mind directing me to the motel?" He added swiftly, "I'd really like a quick shower and a clean shirt before we go out to dinner."

"I would have been glad to do the hospitable thing and cook for you, but I didn't know until four o'clock that I was going to get any more intimate with you than to smile at you from the fourth row and laugh at the funny lines in your poems tonight."

"Are we going to get intimate?" he teased.

She tried to withdraw her hand, but he held on too tightly. She was befuddled completely by her racing thoughts, his laughing eyes, his caressing baritone voice, and his life-giving grasp. She felt out of control. "I don't know," she mumbled.

He just squeezed her hand again.

"Turn here and head for that green and gold Holiday Inn sign." It was a relief to be impersonal.

"I'll go get the key." He parked the car in the swing-around and strolled in, returning in a moment with the key and a smile.

"We're around back." As he drove behind the building, he kept mumbling, "Two thirty-eight...two thirty-eight."

Ruth spotted it first, deliberately trying not to think what he meant by "we're."

"Your eyes are functional as well as decorative, eh? Come on up and holler at me through the bathroom door while I wash off the sweat of my morning classes and the airports." He had taken hold of her hand again. Again that warm flow from him into her, as he led the way down an interminable motel walkway. Her body followed his; her mind raced. What was happening?

"Room service is going to bring us some wine. Just pour it out when it comes, okay?" He took his shaving kit and disappeared into the bathroom.

She sat on the edge of a chair and looked around, concentrating on the decor. It was a pretty room—Mediterranean furniture with red carpet, drapes, and spread. A worthy room, she thought, and then tried to figure out what it was worthy of.

A fist on the door announced the wine. She poured it out as instructed, then wondered whether to knock on the bathroom door with a glass for him. Nervously, she took a long drink from her own glass, refilled it (so he wouldn't be able to tell), and knocked on the door and called, "Shall I set a glass of wine out here for you?" Damn! She sounded so nervous.

He opened the door. He was stripped to the waist, cream over half of his face; the other half was closely shaven.

"You're shaving." She didn't know what she thought he was doing, but she hadn't thought he'd be shaving. He raised his eyebrows.

"It may look like ordinary shaving to you, but actually it's the Zambigadan Festival Ritual."

"The Zambigadan Festival Ritual," Ruth repeated, leaning on the door edge.

"Yes. If you'd care to come have a seat"—he pointed with his chin to the toilet—"I'd be willing to let you watch the second half of the ritual. If you prove yourself to be a good observer, I may even sing you the ritual chant that accompanies the performance."

She hurried to the toilet seat and sat, primly, legs tightly together. She held her wine, put his on the sink.

"I—I wouldn't dream of missing anything so rare and unique." Maybe it was the wine, but suddenly, she didn't feel nervous at all. "No, this is the life for sure, a comfortable seat, a glass of wine, and the—" she couldn't remember the name.

"Zambigadan Festival Ritual." He sounded out of patience with her.

"Pardon me. I don't know how it could have slipped my

mind." She tried to sound contrite. "Of course, the Zambigadan Festival Ritual."

"Are you ready for the music?"

"I doubt it."

She pursed her lips, trying unsuccessfully to keep from smiling, as well as to prepare herself for the opening strains of an Italian aria, or some such. But he started singing, almost under his breath, something that Ruth thought might be Gregorian chant. It was hauntingly lovely.

Then he put down the razor, splashed cold water on his face, dried it on a towel, and patted on St. James' Lime After-Shave. *His face is so right*, she thought. Not handsome: his nose and lips were too broad, his eyes maybe too far apart. His forehead and cheeks were lined, as if he'd been squinting in the sun, or laughing. His skin was warm bronze. . . . She forced herself to stop thinking. "Was that Gregorian chant?"

"My dear lady"—he stood erect and stern—"you are making me very sorry I ever decided to let you watch. That was the traditional chant of the Zambigadan Festival Ritual. You must take this a little more seriously. Ah, poor me, another frivolous feminist."

As Ruth's foot reached out to kick him, he disappeared into the shower.

"You can't go in there with your pants on! Wait—I'll leave." But she didn't—she couldn't; she was mesmerized.

Handing out his pants around the white vinyl shower curtain, he said, "Stay put—unless you want to miss another part of the ritual." He turned on the water and chanted some more. Ruth pulled her feet up on the seat, tucking her knees inside the circle of her arms, closing her eyes to listen. In a few minutes he stepped out with a towel wrapped around his waist.

"That felt great."

"That's what I should have done." Her head turned on her knees to look at him. "I should have dropped you off and gone home and gotten cleaned up myself. I don't know why I'm so lethargic. Is it the effect of the ritual and the chant and everything?"

"Hop in the shower. I'll go get a robe for you." He walked out, returning with a soft old robe and the bottle of wine. Much to her amazement her glass was empty, so he filled it. "There ya are, Francine—clothes and wine. Don't say I never gave ya nothin'," and he half-patted, half-stroked her cheek.

She laughed at his retreating back, then wrapped her hair in the one remaining dry towel, tried to keep the water below her neck, and enjoyed completely the massaging wetness. When she came out of the bathroom, enveloped in the blue terry robe, he patted the bed beside him. He was sitting up, wearing only a pair of slacks, a pillow behind his back, papers spread out before him. His chest looked warm and inviting, the brown curls just as soft as those on the top of his head.

"I just want to make a substitution in my readings tonight."

He went back to his piles of poetry as Ruth sat on the edge of the bed, gingerly at first. Then as he, apparently oblivious to her, scribbled some notes, she carefully lay back against the pillow. She felt so relaxed. The wine and the shower, the easiness of being with him were all acting like a Valium. So good . . .

When she opened her eyes, he was lying on his side, facing her, his own eyes closed, one hand barely tucked under her. The papers were gone. She looked at her watch.

"My God, Tom, it's twenty of eight. Hurry up. We'll hardly make it."

She was sitting now, trying to wake up, her heart pounding. He grabbed her around the waist and pulled her back beside him. His eyes were still closed.

"That is absolutely the worst job of waking someone up that anyone has ever done in the history of mankind." Then he opened his eyes, looking at her so furiously that she had to laugh.

"I'm sorry." She bit her lip. "I was just so shocked to see what time it was. How did we fall asleep, anyhow? Oh, well, now I can say I slept with a famous poet."

He gave her a funny, soul-searching look before he said, "Yeah."

She kept saying all these crazy things! Why was everything so full of sexual innuendo?

And then he moved his hands up her body, from her waist to her neck, as he very slowly brought his mouth to hers in an intricately arousing kiss. He pulled away gently, his eyes suddenly sad. "Now we'd better get ready."

She leaped off the bed. "I forgot again. I'm usually so responsible. Did you drug the wine?"

"Just your heart."

It was her turn to look questioningly at him and to swallow the lump in her throat before replying, "I believe that."

In silence, never taking their eyes from each other, they dressed.

The poetry reading, it was agreed in whispers down the rows, was the best they had ever heard at Eastern Ohio University. "He's good." Ruth gasped at the short, short one called "Room 238."

> I was so old and stodgy
> and the minute I saw you,
> so clean and new,
> I wanted to be young again, too.
>
> So I was.

After the reading a group from the English Department carried them off to the artsy Tradito to drink and talk poetry. Around ten-thirty the ordinarily resilient Dr. Jeffers started yawning the most obvious yawns, and finally Ruth said, "Are you ready to leave?"

"Yeah. This is very pleasant, but"—he smiled around the table—"I'm sorry not to have more partying in me. Planes always seem to sap all my energy."

But as soon as they were out the door, he grabbed Ruth's hand and started running, demanding, "Keys!" She had a hard time digging them out of the bottom of her purse while running, but she did, and he handed her into the car, locked her door, and ran around to his side, collapsing against the back of the seat, laughing.

"I was going crazy. I couldn't wait to get out of there." When he had caught his breath, he put his arm around her and pulled her over to him.

She looked up at him in confusion. "I thought we were being chased by a mugger or something."

"No," he replied, stroking her face with his fingers, "we were running from the thieves who were trying to steal our time."

He *is* a poet, she thought, as they leaned in to kiss. Then he sat her back up in the seat and started the car.

"We'd better get something to eat, but I hate to spend the time sitting in public somewhere."

"How about a pizza to go?"

So they went to Trecatino's and ordered a large pizza with everything "to go," and drank Cokes and ate an antipasto while waiting. They returned to Room 238 and sat cross-legged on the bed, the pizza between them, Cokes and ice from the machines on the nightstand.

They didn't talk about their lives apart. From little things he revealed, she knew without being told, that he was married and a father. She believed that what was happening between them was as unique to him as it was to her. He didn't ask if she had lovers or was engaged; he knew men had and would love her. This night was simply a separate entity in their lives. In the days to come they would both thank God that they had the sense to see what this night offered them. They didn't bring their pasts to bed with them; they didn't hold up future worries or checklists. They simply accepted with joy what was happening.

Ruth was extolling John Updike's poetry when she stopped in mid-sentence to receive a kiss. And they both knew that the time had come. Wordlessly she went into the bathroom. Tom turned on some music and turned off the lights and opened the drapes. She returned, carrying her loafers and stockings. The moonlight showed him sitting on the edge of the bed, bent over, untying his brown oxfords.

He held out his hand. When she came, trustingly, he tugged her down beside him.

"Ruth. I don't know what to say. I know you have never done this before. You may find it hard to believe, but I haven't either. We barely know each other. But it's so strong." He practically groaned as he said the word strong. "I've never felt anything like this. Do you know what I mean?"

She nodded. They clutched hands like drowning people.

"I'm no out-of-control young man, Ruth. We can go anywhere with this you want to go—or nowhere. Just stay. I will just hold you in my arms all night. We'll do what you want. But stay."

She was stunned by the vulnerability he revealed. She swallowed convulsively to try to regain her voice.

"T.J. This is the craziest thing I have ever said in my life—but I love you. I have never felt so . . . turned on. For the first time that expression makes sense. Suddenly I don't care about anything—that you're married, that I'm not, that we never will be, that this is forbidden. All I know is what I feel. You. Good with you. Right with you. I want to be together with you as I have never been together with anyone in my life. Do you know what?" She disengaged her hands from his, then put a hand on either side of his face. "I wouldn't be surprised if I never felt this strongly about anyone or anything again in my life. God couldn't let people walk around feeling this good—nobody'd ever work or—"

Ruth never finished her sentence. T.J. stood her up and with great and gentle enthusiasm peeled her out of her clothes until she stood naked before him. He didn't touch her, but his eyes fastened on her breasts and never left them as she undressed him. When he stood naked before her, she looked at his body in awe: the curls on chest and lower; the strong, sustaining muscles.

Reverently he leaned over to take a breast in his mouth.

But passion tore at the gentleness, and he put his hands under her soft, round bottom and lifted her in the air, lips fastened to sweet plum nipple. The tension as bodies aligned, thigh against thigh, penis stretching at the contact with the moist blond hair between Ruth's legs, caused her to cry, "Oh, Tom."

He laid her on the bed, mouth pouring kisses on breasts and navel. His hands were on her legs, caressing inside and outside her thighs. She rolled toward him, her whole body clamoring for his attention. She felt herself dripping moisture, so ready was she to pull him into her. But he stopped, pushed her flat on her back, and knelt over her legs. Their eyes locked as he cupped her hands around his penis. He slid his thumbs along the edges of her vagina and then, softly, inside. Her hips rose up to entice him, and her hands guided his throbbing body until, ceremoniously, his hands held her open to receive him, and hand-against-hand they held themselves and each other while they became one. Slowly, and not entirely comfortably, his hard penis slid into her until she was sure he must be touching her lungs.

Tom slid his whole body over her, and clutching her tightly, he rolled over, pulling her on top. For long, sweet minutes they lay like that. He could feel her tears against his cheek, and he lifted her hand to his own eyes so her fingers could feel his tears. In amazement she raised her head, and then he moved his hands to cradle her head and draw her lips down on his. Joined at lips and everywhere they lay, savoring the feeling of union.

Subtly the kiss changed until they were no longer content to be still. Once more they rolled over, and with her legs and arms molded to his body, Ruth met and answered each thrust. He came, too quickly for her, but she had never experienced, or even imagined, the passion she had aroused in him, and she was quite content that he lay exhausted and fulfilled at her side.

"Ruth, I'm sorry. It went too fast for you."

"I loved it." She stroked his face while they looked at each other. "To feel you in me is like being at the bottom of the ocean."

"It'll get better for you. We'll figure out how to make it great for you, too, I promise." He kissed her and then leaned back against the pillow, his eyes all over her. "Ruth, you have the most sensational body." He propped himself up on an elbow for a better view. "Just look at those beautiful breasts." His free hand reached out to hold a breast at its fullness. He looked back to her eyes, and she was aglow, but looking at him. "Look at yourself," he insisted. She finally did. "Aren't you gorgeous?" All she could do was laugh. "No wonder you walk like a queen. If I had a body like this, I'd walk like royalty, too."

"You have a fantastic body, T.J. I love your chest."

"Just my chest? Is that all you love?" he teased.

"I've never really looked at the rest before."

"Well look. Explore. Touch me. I love you. My God, Ruth, I honestly love you."

For hours they became acquainted with the intricacies of physical desire and delight. He memorized her breasts. She knew his body by heart. Many more times she traveled to the ocean depths, and finally with his hands, rubbing her, teasing her, twice Tom took her to the stars. She breathed too fast; she couldn't breathe; and then she felt the explosion. The world stopped.

"T.J. I don't understand. I don't believe this. Will you please explain this to me?" She was curled into a ball in his left arm.

"If I could explain this, I'd retire tomorrow." He paused. "Ruth." Tom's voice was so low and serious it scared her. "You realize that there is nowhere we can go with this. Tomorrow you'll have to return to your life, and I'll have to return to mine. I'd better not see either of us sitting around moping for what-ifs and might-have-beens. We have tonight. And I am so grateful for tonight. Grateful to you. Grateful to whomever gave us this unearned, unexpected gift." His voice changed, charged with emotion. "You'll be all right, won't you? Please tell me you will." His arms held her so tightly that it hurt.

"I will. I will be all right. I will be better, always, for this. I'll keep tucked in my heart the knowledge that you—most special you—would choose me, and that together we could work magic. Since we have only tonight, let's really *be* tonight."

And they were. The locked doors to private thoughts and dreams, to secret longings and goals were thrust open, and they talked constantly, with words and with hands and with eyes and with bodies. At three in the morning Tom went out and purchased four cold drinks from the machine; they were parched from the passion and the closeness. At six they ordered a huge breakfast from room service, and naked, they fed each other every bite. In between, they explored the niches and crevices of mind and soul and body. Like refugees leaving on pilgrimage, they packed carefully, filling their minutes with precious memories and priceless trust. They cried, and they laughed.

At nine that morning she drove him to the airport to catch United 417 to Buffalo. At the last moment they both were so busy saying thank you for such a multitude of different things, looks and words and gifts of poetry, that they started laughing. Their final view of each other, as he ran for his plane, was a smile. Since it was Thursday, the only day of the week when Ruth didn't have classes, she went home and crawled into bed and cried herself to sleep. When she woke up, at six Friday morning, she knew she would live and move onward, but she thought of him constantly and only—seeing, needing, and wanting no one else for weeks.

She felt so damned powerful and impotent at the same time. There was a heaviness in her heart that had never been there before. Somehow she knew, with new sensitivity and intuitiveness, that when United 122 had arrived she was still a girl, and when United 417 had departed, she was a woman. She could thank a poet for that.

The rest of the summer passed in drudgery and anticlimax. There were days when Ruth wondered if the rest of her life wasn't going to be anticlimactic. She studied Eugene O'Neill and Tennessee Williams and found sad after sad life devoid of even a few hours of happiness, and she determined to be simply grateful. She spent days and nights smiling and listening to her new recording of Gregorian chant.

She would see lovers strolling hand in hand, and all her resolve would gush out in a torrent of tears. Twice she made reservations on a flight to Buffalo, and one of those times she packed her bags and drove to the airport. But when she got there, the only empty parking space was the same space she had used when she had picked him up, two weeks before, and the sadness of it immobilized her. She could hear his voice saying, "And I'd better not see either of us sitting around moping." So the sunglasses came out, and the chin came up, and she drove back to Akron and cleaned her apartment.

A million times she thanked God that she had the trip to Rome to look forward to. On good days she pored over travelers' guides to Rome, Florence, and Ostia Antica and read any novel she could get her hands on that was set in Italy. On bad days she read Emily Dickinson and Sylvia Plath and tortured herself with Elizabeth Barrett Browning.

Finally, suddenly, it was over. She had passed her Twentieth Century American Drama exam with the highest grade in the class and squeaked through the Milton course with an A-, finding Milton not quite as dry as she had expected—but pretty near. She had listened to her last discussion of whether to have a butterscotch or a hot fudge sundae. Working at Arnold's had been just what she needed to get her through the summer because it had exhausted her physically. School had exhausted her mentally. And a minor American poet named Tom Jeffers had exhausted her emotionally.

It must have been a hundred degrees on August 18, 1971, in the Rubber City. And the people heat factor drove the temperature up even higher inside Quint Hall Gymnasium on that Sunday afternoon of summer commencement. Five women and two men fainted in their rented black gowns. Ruth's father didn't make it to commencement. She hadn't expected him to, but still, she was disappointed. Chris was her only guest. Their relationship now was polite, pleasant, and impersonal. They had exchanged no more than closed-mouth kisses in the past four months. Although they weren't to each other what Chris wished they would be, both he and Ruth needed the friendship, and they both worked hard at keeping it alive.

They went out for dinner after graduation exercises with Jill and Dave. Jill had received her master's degree three months pregnant. Dave, a policeman, marched across the stage to accept an associate degree in criminal justice. They spent most of the dinner explaining their wedding plans to Ruth and Chris, stirring up feelings the not-to-be-marrieds would more happily have left repressed.

Ruth was planning to drive to Pittsburgh the next day, and she suspected she and Chris were due for a scene before she left. Veteran of two psychology courses, she decided the best defense was a good offense. Ruth launched her plan when they were alone in her apartment after teary farewells with Jill. Ruth had already taken the precaution of having clothing strewn across the bed and boxes cluttering the sofa.

"How would you like to come to Rome for Christmas?"

"How would you like to come to Akron for Christmas? We could get married while you're here."

"Chris, we are not going to get married." So much for well-laid plans.

"That sounds pretty definite."

"It is. Be realistic. We are friends. Friends are friends, not mates."

"Well! I have tried to be patient these last few months to give you time to sort things out. But I really didn't think you were going to persist in this madness. You should not be going to Rome alone, for any number of very good reasons. One of which happens to be that you are turning down the best offer you are ever likely to have. By next year I'll probably be making twenty thousand. We could build a house and have kids. You could teach or do whatever you wanted to. You know I've always loved you."

He was close to tears, and Ruth was astonished and embarrassed. Had he thought she wouldn't go through with it? "Chris, I'm so sorry. I have to do this. I can't marry you. I'm all wrong for you. You don't want an independent freethinker like me. I'd probably drive you to drink or drugs or gambling or something. But I really care about you. I can never thank you enough for all the good times we've had. I really needed your friendship, and you never let me down."

By now tears were streaming down Ruth's cheeks, and Chris seemed to be back in command. "I guess I hoped too much." He pulled her onto his lap then, and they just held onto each other for a very long time.

After awhile they managed an awkward goodbye, and as Chris was running down the steps of the apartment building, Ruth was flinging herself on her clothes-strewn bed. She cried, hating the close of another chapter.

It was eight o'clock the next morning when the phone woke her.

"Hello."

"Ruthie, honey? You still sleepin'?"

"Tilly! What a pleasant surprise! How are you?"

"Honey, I is just fine. You said you was leavin' today, and I wants to say a nice goodbye afore you takes off. So Virginia, she say it be better if I be callin' real early."

"Oh, Tilly. It's so good to hear from you. Are you and Virginia having good days?"

"Honey, we havin' a ball. And you know what happened? This here Grace of Christ Baptist Church done got me a wheelchair. And them two strong boys next door just pops over in the mornin' and plunks me in my chair an' then pops on back in the evenin' and plunks me in my bed, and the day long I just toots around, sittin' so purty. . . . Oh, we doin' just so fine, Ruthie, just so fine. An' I tells the Good Lord maybe a hundred times the day just what I thinks of my Ruthie who done this for me."

Tilly paused for breath and heard Ruth making strange noises.

"Is you cryin', honey-girl? What be the matter, Ruthie?"

"I needed you to call me this morning and tell me I did something good. Thank you, Tilly, thank you very much for thinking about that."

"Aw, honey, I doesn't know what coulda happen to you, but I gots one thing I wants you allus to remember. Now, Tilly say this, so you know it true."

"Okay." Ruth was smiling, back in check.

"You not only a *good* girl, you the *best*. You got that? You the best."

"Got it. And I know if Tilly says it, it must be true."

"Say that."

"Now, what would you like from Rome?"

"Aw, honey, might be one thing you *could* do for Tilly. I's so glad you ast. They gots that fountain there, the one they say's for lovers. Well, you git yourself to that ole fountain and throw in a penny, ya hear? You throws in the penny for me an' my Preston. That be somethin' I really been hopin' you do for Tilly."

"Tilly, it's the first thing I'll do in Rome," Ruth promised, her voice breaking.

"Aw, Ruthie, that's gonna make me so glad that you's doin' that lucky thing for me an' my man."

"It's going to make me feel good to do it, too, Tilly."

"Now, these boys of mine just comes in to put me in my chair. So I gots to git. You be one real happy girl now, ya hear?"

"Oh, I will, Tilly. Thank you."

"I thanks you, honey, I surely does. Bye-bye, Ruthie."

"Bye-bye, Tilly."

With a lightness of spirit Ruth took the last shower of her life in Akron, Ohio, packed the rest of her clothes, stuffed everything in her car, and drove without stopping to Parkview Avenue, Squirrel Hill, Pennsylvania.

❧ 3 ❧

Tom Jeffers sat at his desk in his office, looking as if he were trying to decide how to improve his channel strategy lecture or whether or not to recommend Dr. Terry for tenure. He frowned in deep concentration at the single sheet of paper on his blotter. Before him was a copy of the poem he had written for Ruth, and he reread it now, imagining what her reaction would be.

"Possession"

I never could believe in the flimsy sentimentalism
of love at first sight—of seeing and coming and
    conquering—
of a life changed by a few hours—of joy so intensely
    potent
that the rest of life is thereafter filtered.

I never could believe in the power of Goodness and
    God
to the extent that I could love and leave—that I could
    live
contentedly with the knowledge of my one brief,
    brilliant moment
and feel more gratitude than grief.

I never could believe that things belong to those
who most appreciate and understand them—that the
    poor man
who comprehendingly adores the masterpiece
owns it more surely than the rich man on whose wall
    it hangs.

And I never shall believe that in sixteen hours
you eradicated forty-one years of cynicism
and that we loved at first sight, we parted in faith,
and we shall possess each other always.

He thought she would like it. He also thought she'd like
the single rose he'd enclosed in the envelope. And he
knew she'd appreciate the fact that he broke down in the
note. He hadn't kept a copy of that—it would be too dangerous. He closed his eyes, and he could see from memory
the hand-typed sheet of yellow legal paper.

Ruth,
    If you have gotten things back on an even keel,
please throw this away without reading it. Because
herein, after only a month, I give up the fight, throw
in the towel, proclaim defeat. I want to see you. I
decided to have this waiting for you at home—you
said you had a couple of weeks before you left for
Rome. I thought that that way, if you were interested,
too, I at least wouldn't be interfering with your
summer school. I can stand only so much guilt. It's
one thing to corrupt you morally. To corrupt you
academically as well would be too much for this old
teacher to bear.
    I imagine you have good days and bad days. I
certainly have. Every time the phone rings or the
door opens I hope both that it is and isn't you. I
thought it would get easier as the days turned into
weeks, but somehow the opposite is true.
    The office number is listed at the bottom of the
page. If you want to get together (Freudian, but not a
slip), call. It may take a couple of tries to catch me.
But I'm running real slow these days.

                                                    Tom

Eyes still closed, he brought her face into view. He felt
like a teenager in love for the first time. He was hopeless.
For a month he had stewed about Ruth: he had handled it
wrong; he should never have touched her; he should have

moved her to Buffalo and installed her in an apartment in Liberty Square; he should have been sophisticated about it—he was wrong to have allowed himself to get so emotionally involved. He tortured himself twenty-four hours a day.

He accomplished nothing. During these weeks he had been merely treading water, making no forward progress. *Good God, Jeffers . . . forty-one-year-old men don't act like this. Get your shit together. Get your ass in gear. Get out of here and get something done this afternoon. It's Monday, August nineteenth. She's forgotten all about you. She's just a kid. She was just flattered that an old gopher like you would pay any attention. Now get it in gear before anyone discovers what a jerk you've been.*

He tried to heed his own advice—and ended up walking aimlessly out to the secretary's desk. The phone rang just as he got there, and since Lynn was busy filing, he waved her off and answered it himself in the middle of the second ring.

"Marketing—Jeffers."

"Tom?"

He was silent, stunned; she waited, uncertain. His heart actually stopped beating for a second and then started again, double time, as if to make up for the beat it had missed. But when he spoke, it was his usual calm voice that said, "Hold the line a minute, please," and to Lynn, "I'll take this call in my office." She turned from her filing and smiled after him as he half-skipped, half-sprinted to his office and closed his door. It was never dull working for Dr. Jeffers.

"Ruth?" He was scared, sweating like a fighter awaiting the decision.

"Hi."

"Hi, yourself." *I love you. Please tell me what I want to hear.*

Ruth got right to the point. "Yes, please, as soon as possible for as long as possible."

"Can you get away this weekend?" He was eager.

"Absolutely." So was she.

"I'll make some plans and call you back. Would you

mind driving partway up here? We could meet in the middle somewhere."

"That'd be fine."

"I have in mind a friend with a cabin on the Pennsy-New York line."

"That'd be great because I don't have a cent."

"Yeah. It would save some explanations here, too."

"Tom, there's one thing. See if you can get some sort of phone number. If the cabin doesn't have a phone, then a neighbor or something. I always have to leave a number with my dad—because of his heart."

"Sure thing. Now give me a number where I can reach you. Can I call anytime or just during the day?"

"Anytime. I always answer the phone when I'm home. If a man answers, hang up, because it means I'm at the store or somewhere. Pittsburgh's area code is 412. The number is 934-9234."

"Got it."

"Tom?"

"Hm?" He ran his hand through his curls.

"I have a feeling it's not going to work."

"Are you worried about it?" Her concern communicated itself.

"I'm only worried that something will prevent its happening."

Then he understood. "Has it been bad?" he asked softly.

"I made plane reservations to Buffalo twice."

"Oh, Ruth." He sounded so pleased.

"And I wrote you two letters. But I didn't send them."

"Mail them here to the office, please. I really want to read them."

"Okay. Oh, I love my rose. Thank you." He could hear her moving, and he wondered if she were getting situated on the floor.

"You're welcome. Thank you for calling."

"You're welcome. Thank you for writing."

"Here we go again," he said, laughing.

"At least our little repartee kept me from crying until I got to the car."

44

"You are crying a lot these days, aren't you?" Somehow he knew.

"Yes, I really am. You know how van Gogh had all those different periods? Well, when they write about me, they will call this my emotional period."

"I thought all women got emotional during their periods."

"Not that kind of a period, you!"

"You aren't having that kind of a period this weekend, are you?"

"No, I just had that kind."

"Oh, great. That means you'll be just ripe to get pregnant. That would solve all our problems."

"Don't even mention it."

"The thought never crossed my mind. And don't think I'm only after your body. I'm not."

"No, I know. The sex we can take or leave, right?"

"Yeah."

"Then we might as well just talk on the phone this weekend instead of getting together." He envisioned her gesturing with the phone cord, grinning as she teased. He could actually see her smiling.

"Except that it's so much easier to have a meaningful conversation when you can look someone in the eye."

"I guess you're right." She allowed herself to be persuaded. "Maybe we should get together after all."

"Yes, I think a little social intercourse would be exhilarating." His eyes crinkled, the smile was in his voice.

"Are you nuts?" Ruth asked.

"About you, yes. Yes." He decided to share his doubts. "I'm afraid this must be my middle-aged impetuous period: man tries to recapture fleeting youth."

"That's not what it is."

"That's what the popular judgment would be."

She had to get that depressed sound out of Tom's voice.

"Let them judge what and where they may. They didn't feel what we did. And it was no middle-aged desperation."

"I'm feeling guilty, Ruth."

"I know; I'm feeling guilty for you."

"Do you have trouble with it morally?"

"For me, no. And actually, I don't have trouble with the morality of it for you, either. I think there's a special special dispensation for us. How's that for situational ethics?"

"Now look in your supply and see if you can find some rationale for you and me running away together for the next forty years."

There was a slight pause; he could hear her changing position. "That's what I feel guilty about—I want to do it."

"Me, too." His chair squeaked as he sat up. "That's precisely the point. It's this desire to throw caution and responsibility back in everybody's faces and say, 'The hell with everything but you.' Because I never felt so good and right and strong."

"Me, too. And maybe we'll only make it harder by seeing each other."

"That could be. Do you want to forget it?"

"No." She was half afraid to ask. "You?"

"No. Even if that makes it harder still?" he persisted.

"Even if it makes it harder still."

"Then we are in agreement?" His tone was lighter already.

"We are of one mind."

"And we shall be of one body." He was going to have a lot of trouble standing up.

Ruth's voice was low and slow. "I'm afraid I love you."

"Yeah, this is no passing fancy."

"Oh, T.J."

"Put those letters in the mail right away, okay?"

"Yes, this afternoon. Will you call me back?"

"Yeah, let's make it tomorrow morning; by then I can have some definite plans for you, for us."

"Tom, thank you."

"Thank you, Ruth." There was a long pause. "I can't even hang up the damn phone." That got them laughing. "I'll call you in the morning, love."

"Good-bye, T.J."

"Bye."

Tom called Ruth on Tuesday morning, and they finalized

plans for meeting at a little country inn in Wellsville, New York, around ten o'clock Friday night.

With that Tom began flying. In the next four days he accomplished the work that had piled up for the last six weeks. He felt strong and whole again. He read and made insightful comments on the two thesis proposals that had been sitting on his desk for weeks. He was able to devise quite quickly a promotional strategy for the Buffalo-based bicycle company, E. M. Anders, a freelance project that had stumped him for the last month. And he cleaned up and sent off the four mournful poems that his six sad weeks had produced.

It was Thursday morning before Tom received "Ruth's Laments" in the mail. He read them over and over, that day and throughout the years. They were written on small white note sheets in girlish penmanship. He loved them.

Lament #1

You have upset my serenity—and I hunger for more. I need reassurance. Did it really all happen? Was that spontaneity as electrically charged as I think it was? How will I keep the faith? How will that sustain me?

Where are you? You said you had another reading in Montreal. Are you in the Main? Will you come back? Is the motel room closing in on you? Is your mind in turmoil? Your heart? Your body?

I read some pornography tonight. Now I want to try it. With you. On you. Such excitement lies ahead. New voyages and adventures. You make me feel primitive and lovely and sophisticated and innocent and woman. It was a miracle—a chance, a lucky one-in-a-million bingo. Aren't you going crazy? Don't your hands ache? And your legs? Aren't you hungry? There's so much I wanted to say and didn't, couldn't. Now it's eating me up, my sins of omission. Please reassure me. Please call. Please come.

But know how scared I am. It is much more powerful than I.

Tom leaned back in his chair. *It is much more powerful than the both of us, Ruth. I wonder where this love will take us.* Then he turned the page.

Lament #2

My dear—the pain is receding; now more of the smiles and laughs and lines are surfacing. Good God, I don't believe it. What audacity. Where were our minds, our common sense? Adults can't throw caution to the wind like that—not responsible people like us. We didn't exactly attain our "positions" on impulses like those. But how liberating it feels—to know we can *feel*. And so strongly.

I am still much more bothered by what we didn't do than by what we did do. We should have told each other more—but we were concerned about disloyalty. I was in a state of shock—I guess I didn't believe my own reactions.

I am trying to write this so that anyone who happens on it will not know when or where or how or what. Only you will know what I am really saying.

The words were all so right—we just needed more of them—more feelings.

Maybe you should have walked away, really early on, when you realized my plans for you. If you're smart, you won't come back.

I'm tingling again. Damn you.

With the laments in his pocket he drove to Wellsville, New York, arriving at the Green Country Inn at about nine-thirty Friday night. There he found her message.

Dad in hospital—suspected appendix—critical because of heart. Sorry doesn't begin to cover it.

He canceled the reservation and got back in the car. He stopped three times for coffee—he was that tired. When he got into Pittsburgh, he pulled into a gas station that had a pay phone and started calling hospitals.

He was lucky, considering the number of hospitals in

Pittsburgh. The third hospital he tried had a Benjamin Harrison Tyack. He found the Sisters of Mercy Hospital in a section of Pittsburgh called Squirrel Hill. He had stopped at two all-night gas stations for directions and had lost almost an hour traversing the unfamiliar city. At the hospital he encountered another obstacle: he found the intensive care unit on the third floor, but Ruth was nowhere to be seen. A grandma sitting in the waiting room, wanting to think about someone else's problems instead of her husband's kidney stones asked Tom, as he stood indecisively, if he was by any chance looking for "that sweet blond girl." She directed him to the basement coffee shop.

At 4:00 A.M. on a Saturday in August, the Sisters of Mercy Coffee Shoppe was not crowded. Ruth was sitting with her back to the door, her head in her hands. Everyone but Ruth looked up as Tom walked into the room. And then Tom Jeffers lightened the hearts of the nine people there by walking over to Ruth's table, sitting down beside her, and lifting her onto his lap. Never before in her life, and never again, would Ruth feel heartaches melt as they did at that moment in Tom's arms. When she had stopped crying, he put her back in her own chair so he could look at her and talk to her. They sat knee to knee, arms holding arms, heads together. They both looked white and tight and tired.

Ruth reached a hand up to stroke the hair back from his forehead where a few curls roamed free.

"Are you real? Are you really here?"

He just smiled in answer.

"I will never again doubt the power of prayer."

"Why? What were you praying?"

"For dad—and for me: that he would go on living and that I would go on wanting to."

His hands were moving up and down her arms. Their eyes locked on each other's.

"Let's go get the most recent report on dad, and then we can plan some rest."

Nine heads turned to smile at them as, arms around each other's waists, they walked out of the coffee shop. They saw no one.

As soon as the elevator doors closed, Tom wrapped his arms around Ruth, and their lips met in a painfully sweet kiss. Her head fell on his shoulder in exhausted gratitude.

The intensive care nurses reported no change in Dr. Tyack's condition. Ruth and Tom sat on a cushioned bench in the waiting room and held each other. For a few minutes Ruth's head rested on Tom's shoulder, but soon she felt him swaying in sleep, so she sat up straight, moving to the far side of the bench, pulling his head down on her lap. For almost two hours she sat, wide awake, watching him sleep, smoothing his hair, touching his arms.

At seven the shift changed, and a new head nurse came to tell Ruth that they felt her father had stabilized and was resting comfortably. If Ruth would like to leave a telephone number, it was probably safe for her to go home now.

They left Tom's car in the hospital lot, and Ruth drove him the few blocks to 239 Parkview Avenue.

"I'm surprised," he said. "There really is a view of the park, and it really is an avenue."

"In Pittsburgh, Pennsylvania, we name our streets honestly."

That was all the talking they did in the car. When they got inside, Tom went to shower and shave while Ruth called her father's sister to tell her the news and to say that she was now going to bed. She did not mention that she wasn't going to bed alone. She told her aunt she would call again later. Then she made a big breakfast of bacon and eggs and coffee and toasted muffins. They were both yawning uncontrollably by the time they finished their second cups of coffee. Hand-in-hand they climbed the stairs.

They had talked little. What they seemed to need was to touch. Upstairs Ruth went to the windows of her room and pulled down the familiar shades. It was almost nine o'clock in the morning. Luckily her father had installed window air conditioners, so there was a cool hum in the semi-dusky light as they undressed. Their eyes devoured each other while clothes fell about their feet. In unison they pulled off the covers and sank down on the sheet.

Tom slid over to the middle of the bed on his back, reaching for Ruth as he went, so that she simply got into bed on top of him. From lips to toes their bodies were aligned, and for a minute or two they just lay like that, letting the passion mount, until, roughly, Tom rolled her over and with a cry of need sucked her breasts until she didn't know or care if what she felt was pleasure or pain. While he clung to her, her legs closed over his tanned back, and she rubbed herself up and down against his soft-skinned stomach. She was teasing the brown-gray curls with her own moist blondness, driving him wild with the feel of her wet, caressing warmth.

His mouth needed to taste that creamy moistness, and he slid his head between her legs, and she came, hard and fast and crying out to him. Quickly he spun, thrusting his legs over her head, positioning himself, so that for the first time, without thought of shyness or aversion, she found herself with a man in her mouth, and, like her, he came tumultuously. He spun again and imprisoned her lips.

They moaned against each other in an agony of release. She thought they might fall asleep now. But within minutes she felt him hardening against her thigh. He slid himself inside her, bodies realigned, oiled. With legs and arms she held him, as with seemingly tireless energy he drove deeper and deeper, passionately insane, until simultaneously they breathed each other's names. For long minutes they shuddered and grabbed at each other, unable to believe or comprehend what they had just experienced. Finally they quieted enough to roll on their sides, and, still one, intricately intertwined, Ruth snuggled her head between Tom's jaw and shoulder.

The catharsis was complete. Fear and doubt and loneliness were abolished. They ached with love. They were physically exhausted, as they had been emotionally and spiritually exhausted, and for six hours, holding each other, shifting from position to position, sometimes awakening to be reassured that the other was truly there, they slept.

By four-thirty that afternoon they had showered, together, and were back at the hospital. Ruth's father was conscious and doing well in intensive care. There had been no problem with the actual operation, but his heart had stopped momentarily during the surgery, and so he was to remain in intensive care, with the monitoring systems, for forty-eight hours. It would be Monday morning before he would be in a regular room. The intensive care visiting schedule allowed one visitor for five minutes every hour, so from 5:00 until 5:05, from 6:00 until 6:05, and from 7:00 until 7:05 Ruth sat with her father. He was groggy and sedated; he looked terrible. But when she was leaving at 7:05, he managed to smile at her and tell her to go home now, he'd see her tomorrow. The nurses seemed to agree. They thought he'd sleep through the night without any problems.

Ruth and Tom spent the remaining fifty-five minutes of each hour walking and talking. Mostly they talked about themselves. They were trying to understand what they felt and how to handle it. It seemed both the best and the worst thing that they had ever had to deal with.

They continued talking as they fixed supper. Ruth had taken two steaks out of the freezer around four o'clock, and now Tom started some charcoal in the outdoor grill. After Ruth had sliced some tomatoes and started some beans cooking, she walked out to Tom with two drinks in her hand.

"Bourbon and ginger, sir?"

"You remembered."

He kissed her hair for her memory. Then they sat down on a glider on the back porch. The neighbors had just finished mowing the grass, and it smelled fertile and fresh.

"I've been drinking this ever since I tasted yours at the Tradito. You know what? I really didn't want to taste your drink—I just wanted the closeness of drinking out of your glass." She grinned sheepishly. "I didn't realize we were going back to the motel together."

"You didn't?"

"No—did you?"

"It had to be. How could it have been otherwise? I wouldn't have been able to say that we were absolutely going to bed together—but I knew we were going to spend our time together. That kiss! Couldn't you tell from that kiss?"

"Yes. I just didn't believe my senses. I didn't believe it was the same for you. I still have trouble with that. I feel like you are just doing this for me."

He looked at her in amazement. "I'm glad to do it for you. But I happen to be loving every minute of it myself."

Ruth leaned over to kiss him, and he caught her to him with a groan, and in a moment they were both struggling for self-control.

"I'll go get the steaks."

"Yeah. We better be careful, or we won't be eating."

"At least not steak."

"At least not charcoal broiled."

"You win. That was very good."

From the safe distance of the doorway, she called, "I love you, nonhairy poet."

And he ran after her and picked her up in his arms. "I came to get my steak."

She knew what he meant but wanted to hear him say it.

"It's there on the counter."

"It's here in my arms."

And they kissed, softly, gently.

"But it *is* a meaty steak." He put her down.

"I know. I gained ten pounds since I saw you last. I always gain weight when I'm unhappy."

They exchanged a long look—they had each endured bad days. Without answering, Tom walked out of the room.

Ruth put some rolls in the oven and then followed him outside. The steaks were starting to sizzle. Tom was sitting, head down, on a low wall, flanked by petunias, roses, and snapdragons. As she approached he held open his arms, and she came to sit on his lap.

Silently they hugged, and she pressed his head against her chest.

"I'm too heavy," Ruth said as she slid off to sit close beside him.

"You're not too heavy, but I have to let you go, or I

won't be able to say what I have to say. When you're that close, I don't feel like talking."

They stared ravenously at each other.

"I'm married. She is a supportive wife. Even if she weren't, I don't know that I'd be able to leave her. But it would seem incredibly selfish to do so when she is doing her part. With Helen I don't feel, have never felt, what I feel with you. This is totally different. It's like something from another planet. There is such intensity, Ruth. Do you believe the intensity?"

She shook her head no; she didn't believe it, either.

"But the main reason that I am so helpless, that I have to stay where I am, is Tommy. He's sixteen now—has a mental age of three or four, and it will never change much. Ten years ago I told Helen that we would do what *she* wanted to do about Tommy and that I would help her. She decided she wanted to take care of him herself. You wouldn't believe what it has taken out of her. But I intend to go on supporting her. I have no choice. It has made Helen and me dependent on each other."

"I'm so sorry, Tom. I understand. And I didn't mean to pressure you in any way. I don't expect any commitment of any kind. I'm sorry that I haven't been better about this."

"Oh, honey." He pulled her head on his shoulder. "I wasn't criticizing you. You've been very brave." He gave her a big squeeze. "Here, let me turn the steaks."

Her eyes never left him.

"Ruth, I think we both want to be together. I want to just get in a car with you and drive and drive and leave everything behind. I've thought a lot about doing just that. But I simply can't. Maybe I'm a coward. Maybe I'm too stodgy. But I don't understand how men can throw twenty or thirty years of marriage and family and obligations out the window." He walked over and sat down in front of Ruth, taking her hands in his. "I want you, and I believe you want me." He paused, trying himself to understand. "I can go to bed with you. I can come to you like this. A good man wouldn't be able to do that."

"Tom, if you aren't a good man, then I don't know who is."

But he sat there unconvinced, so she tried to verbalize some of her thoughts.

"What we feel—it's so strong. It feels so right to be together—to love each other so givingly. Where do feelings like that come from if they aren't God-given?"

"I think they are God-given. I agree it's God in our hearts that gives us the capacity to love."

"Why would he give us feelings like that if he didn't want us to use them? Are we just supposed to love each other mentally and spiritually? Is there some magic about not loving each other physically? Does that prove what great self-sacrificers we are, if we draw the line on hopping into bed? Rubbish! That's hypocritical! You love, or you don't love. What the hell difference what form it takes!"

"*D'accordo.* Either we should never have stopped and smiled and talked in the first place, or we have to accept the inevitability of some emotional involvement—we have to expect that sometimes our feelings for each other will run deep and strong. As you cannot have failed to notice, sweet lady, my feelings for you so run."

"Kind sir, you do me great honor."

"Bat those baby blues at your own risk, love. Only the smell of these cooked-to-perfection steaks is keeping me from dragging you into the snapdragons and having my way with you."

"I'll go get the rest of the dinner."

She had set the table in the dining room, and after she carried in the rolls, beans, and sliced tomatoes, she lit the candles. Then she took a plate out to Tom for the steaks. He was rather too hearty in praising the cooking, and he put his arm around her in an impersonal way as they walked inside. But when he saw the candlelight, he said in a choked voice, "Beautiful."

They sat down; they got that far. In fact, they got some food on their plates. But neither of them tasted anything. They happened to pause, forks in hand, and their eyes met. He reached out a hand to her, but instead of answering with her hand, she got up. They met at the middle of the table and lips locked, sank down on the soft blue dining room carpet. There in the candlelight, oblivious to the cooling dinner, they very slowly and lovingly undressed each other and made gentle love.

They lay for a long time, senseless with contentment. Then they brought the candles and the food down on the floor, and, wearing nothing, they enjoyed immensely a late-night cold dinner.

When they were done eating, they washed the day's dishes together. Ruth called the hospital for an up-to-date report; then she called her aunt again. Tom was waiting in the living room for her and for a few minutes cradled her head in his lap, but they were so tired they went to bed.

They slept fitfully, the unfamiliar feel of naked love in their arms, and awoke with the sun.

"What time must you leave?"

"Noon."

"How can we?"

"What?"

"Separate?"

He lay on his side, head propped on an elbow, fingers smoothing her hair back from her face. "Ruth, we have no choice. We will do it because we have no choice. Friday you leave for Rome. It may be years before we see each other again. Let's face it. It will hurt less if we look at the worst."

Tears were streaming down her cheeks; he seemed so heartless. "Don't you care?"

He grabbed her chin in his hand and jerked her head around to face him. "Don't you ever say that."

She saw that his eyes, too, were filled with tears. "Oh, T.J., I'm sorry. I know you care. It just hurts so much."

"Listen, Ruth. If you had one chance to go to the Louvre, would you pass it up because you might never get there again?"

It took her a minute to see what he meant. Then she smiled. "No, of course not."

"Okay. Now let's try to be sensible about this. It hurts like hell. It is physically painful. I can't imagine getting out of this bed and getting dressed and getting in my car and driving for ten hours. But at noon I'm going to do it.

Now . . . we can spend the five hours between now and then lying here feeling sorry for ourselves, or we can do something happy in the five hours we have left. But I'll tell you something, Ruth—don't expect me to be brave all by myself. If you want to lie here and cry, I'll lie right beside you and cry just as hard. If you want to get up and do something or lie here and make love for five hours or anything else, I'll do it with you. But don't put the burden for being strong on my shoulders, because, my sweet Ruth, I don't feel so strong. Like the rest of our love, we'll have to do it together."

"I feel like I just had a lecture from Professor Jeffers." He smiled with mouth and eyes. "You did."

"Okay. I'm ready to be partners again. Like our night in Akron, right? We make it as full and happy as we can."

"Right." Tom sat up against the headboard and pulled Ruth on his legs. They punctuated sentences with kisses and strokes.

"Can I write to you? Can we be in touch?"

"No." He answered so quickly she knew he had already thought it through. "I think it would really make it much harder if we were. We are simply not in a position to be dependent on each other—and I think it would be a mistake to try. Don't misunderstand me. It would be a bright day when I heard from you. Too bright. That's the problem. Every other day, every day when I didn't hear from you would be lifeless by comparison. Do you know what I mean?"

"Yes, but you're thinking about me, aren't you?" She somehow read it in his eyes. "You're thinking I won't give anyone or anything else a try if I have you in my life?"

"How did you come up with that?"

"I'm right, T.J., aren't I?" She grabbed his face between her hands.

"Yes, you're right." He begrudged her having figured it out. "You're twenty-three, for God's sake. You have no idea how young that is. I refuse to steal your youth by tying up your heart."

"But how will I know where to find you if I need you?"

"I'll give you my agent's name in New York, okay?"

"Okay. And you have the address here. Don't hesitate to use it—no matter what the circumstances."

"Ruth, I really want to impress upon you how strongly I believe the outcome of our love is up to us. We could easily let it destroy us or others. Or we can commit ourselves to making it enriching, instead."

"I agree."

"Now." He held her away from him so he could get the full benefit of her nakedness. "Do you know what I would really like to do this morning?"

"What?" She leaned forward to kiss him and rub her breasts against his chest.

"Go to church."

"Go to church?" Her voice had risen two octaves. She fell back in mock shock.

"Go to church," he repeated. "Wouldn't you like to feel that we've somehow been 'blessed'." She nodded. "And wouldn't you like a little 'watch-between-thee-and-me-while-we-be-parted'?"

They stared at each other in admiration. Then Ruth started to smile. "Let's go to early church so we can come home and go to bed once more before noon."

"A flawless plan, Miss Tyack, flawless. While you shower and get fixed up, I'll make you some T.J. flapjacks."

"If I may amend your plan . . . let's shower together. Then I'll sit and sip tea while you make my breakfast."

"If we shower together, we may need to do it twice."

"I can accept setbacks."

"You're a staunch soldier. Plan accepted."

The T.J. flapjacks were surprisingly good—and he wouldn't tell her how to make them. "The only way to get T.J. flapjacks is to get T.J."

Church was emotional but sustaining. They felt as if they were meant to go. The sermon was on Jesus' greatest commandment: "Love one another." They were able to interpret the sermon as a blessing.

At quarter to eleven they were back in bed.

It was almost one when they pulled up beside Tom's car in the hospital parking lot. Tom turned off Ruth's car and then turned in the seat to face her.

"Ruth, do you believe we will be together again?"

"I have to, T.J. I don't think I could live through this parting if I didn't. I just have to believe it. Do you believe?"

"Ruth." His voice was a caress; he took her face in his hands with utmost tenderness and made her look him in the eye. "I guarantee we will be together again."

She suspected a trick. "In this life?"

"In this life!"

They simply stared at each other, unable to get their fill.

"Maybe your car won't start," she said hopefully.

"Maybe an earthquake will wipe us out right now, and we can die in each other's arms."

"Tom, at the moment death with you sounds much preferable to life without you."

"I know. It does to me, too, Ruth. I love you. You are the most beautiful woman in the world to me. I have never met anyone with whom I feel so good."

"Oh, T.J. I love you. You taught me so many things. Thank you for teaching me about love."

His mind had raced ahead. "Let's make a pact, Ruth; let's pour ourselves in."

"Okay." She sat up straight, eyes glistening. "I like it. Pour ourselves into teaching?"

"Yes, and sightseeing for you."

"And poetry for you."

"Let's learn as much as we can before we meet again— and then we'll have all that much more to give to each other."

They leaned together and kissed.

"Come on. I want to see you walk into the hospital before I drive away."

"So I won't sit here and cry—oh, T.J., you're always thinking about me."

"More than you'll ever know, my love."

They got out of the car, transferred Tom's luggage to his car, locked Ruth's car, and opened Tom's.

"I love you, Ruth."

"I love you, T.J. Thank you."

"Thank you."

She walked away, never knowing how she did it. When she got to the door of the hospital, she turned back, but she couldn't smile, and she couldn't wave. She just looked. He was looking at her. Ruth stood transfixed, as though she had used all her strength getting that far and she could go no further. And then Tom Jeffers got into his car and drove away.

❧ PART II ❧
Rome, Italy:
Fall 1971–1972

❧ 4 ❧

The Leonardo da Vinci International Airport was under construction. At least that was Ruth Tyack's first impression as she emerged from the dim gray interior of the airplane into the blinding yellow Italian sunshine. It would not be until her third arrival in Italy, four years hence, that Ruth would understand that the da Vinci was *always* under construction. But this first time, as she stepped out into the stifling, heavy air, her eye was immediately caught by the scaffolding, ladders, and general mess. Her heart lurched with a strong sense of misgiving. Now was the moment of truth: could she stand on her own two feet in a strange new land, or couldn't she?

The flight itself had been a flight of fancy, an interlude of fantasy. She had dined on white wine and lobster Newburg and chocolate petit fours—three of them—and had read half of a new John D. MacDonald before sleeping the night away. Ruth's seatmate was Sister Anne, of the round pink cheeks and the ever-present smile. During the entire flight Ruth had that unique euphoria that comes from doing something dangerous in the presence of one of God's chosen few.

But now the flight was behind her, the ocean crossed, her bridges truly burned. She had made a daring choice. She wondered if she was woman enough to carry it off. Could she withstand the culture shock, the loneliness, the lack of money, the lack of support—on top of her father's illness and T.J.'s return to his family? She shivered in the heat and started down the steps.

The sunshine at nine that morning was so startlingly bright that she missed the second last step and was caught midair by the Italian steward standing at the foot of the stairs. That's how she got her first feel of Italy, or, more precisely, her first Italian feel. The young man in the snappy gray uniform very gallantly grabbed Ruth around the waist to help her gain her balance. When she thanked him for his assistance with a smile instead of a haughty glance, he ran his hand on down over her hips. She walked away a wiser woman. At least he hadn't pinched.

Nervously Ruth handed the brass-buttoned guard her passport. He looked over the passport and her, approved both with an austere, officious nod. Ruth followed the crowd to the baggage claim, where she got her first taste of Italian efficiency: forty-five minutes later she got her bags. By that time she had missed two limousines into the center of Rome and had to wait forty minutes for another.

Ruth sat on a curb under a two-foot, shaded overhang and looked around. It was so hot! No wonder so many American tourists found Italians frustratingly unhurried. Who could be quick and energetic in weather like this? Sitting in the shade, she shivered as the perspiration trickled between her breasts. You could smell the dried human juices in the air—pungent, too sweet, too strong.

Dirt! The whole place was so littered and dusty. Half-eaten pieces of fruit fought with paper and cans and broken glass for space in the gutter. Rome had to be better than this, she thought as she sat and watched and tried not to be pulled under by the stink and the mess. She counted the cigarette butts and sniffed daintily as the sweat-drenched workers sauntered by, and still she sat waiting, fearing, losing control. Her head sank down on her knees.

"T.J. I can't do it. I'm too scared. And so lonely. It's just no use without you. Come rescue me!"

"Ruth, you know you can do it. You're talented and capable. Surely you can stand an hour's loneliness in an airport. Look what you have ahead of you: the new teaching experience, seeing the world—"

"But, T.J., you are my world!"

"Ah, Ruth, but what happened to pouring ourselves in?"

"I forgot, T.J. We have to pour ourselves in, don't we, so we have more to bring to each other."

The daydream straightened Ruth's spine. She pushed the dampness back inside her eyes and tried to notice more positive things. *Look in the gutters, Ruth, and you're bound to see trash. Look at the people instead.* So she studied the unfamiliar breed before her. There seemed to be no intermediate emotions here. Either one was deliriously happy or furiously angry: a manic-aggressive society. Everything was done in excess! For the one person arriving, seven or eight would be greeters, the men and the women obviously separated. And the women seemed to be more strictly uniformed than Catholic schoolchildren: black dresses, single strand pearls, black low-heeled shoes, gloves. Gloves! All the women were wearing gloves on a Saturday morning to an airport.

Finally the decrepit black airport limousine jerked to a halt in front of Ruth, and she smiled when she saw the other eight passengers, all Orientals—Japanese, she thought. Short bodies and round faces were wrapped in smiles. Sophisticated-looking cameras swung from each neck. Her fellow travelers nodded and bowed to her, and then they turned in to each other, chattering their singsong.

The thirty-five-minute drive into Rome renewed Ruth's hopes and started to confirm her expectations: Rome was going to be great after all. When the taxi left the motorway, the cobblestone roads over which they bounced and jostled, the piles of stones beside the road, and the ancient gates and walls all looked so historic—so authentic. Nearer town the limousine banged and rattled through a lovely, large residential section, broad tree-lined boulevards bringing cool shade in the late August heat. More cobblestone roads, again, and then, amazingly, just like the pictures: the Colosseum . . . white, crumbling, gigantically proportioned. One side only soared toward the sky. Ruth craned her neck to keep the timeless wonder in sight. Then her attention was captured by the fountains— fountains everywhere. What a city for lovers! But then, what city is not for lovers?

Ruth debarked on shaky legs at the Grand Hotel, bowed and nodded eight times to her Oriental companions, repossessed her two shabby red suitcases, and found a fairly new-looking taxi: the school had made a reservation for her at a *pensione* where she might live relatively cheaply until she found an apartment.

The taxi driver got out from behind the wheel and opened the door—Ruth thought for her. When she got in, however, he shoved her suitcases in the backseat beside her, pinching her thigh with their weight. He had intended no gallantry but was merely trying to get underway.

Reinstated behind the wheel, he revved the engine and grinned leeringly at her in the rear-view mirror.

"*Prego*, signorina?" he asked condescendingly.

"*Sei*"—she held up six fingers—"*quattro*"—she reduced the number of fingers to four—"Via Cordova," she enunciated very distinctly.

"*Si. Pensione Lydia.*"

She felt deflated and stupid. Why hadn't she just said the name to begin with? "*Prego,*" she said, with as much dignity as she could muster and turned to stare out the window. She had no more than a fleeting impression of narrow brick streets and bright flower stalls before the taxi came to an abrupt halt. She gave the driver the five hundred lire his meter registered and one hundred lire for a tip. He smiled, showing two prominent gold teeth, tossed her suitcases out beside her, and drove off in a literal cloud of dust.

"*Oh, T.J., I don't know.*"
"*You can do it, Ruth.*"

She squared her shoulders. *Pensione Lydia* appeared from the outside as if Lydia should pay people to live there. Pushing open the huge oak door, Ruth was greeted by a long, dim hall. In front of her stood a very untrustworthy-looking elevator. *Pensione Lydia*, she remembered from the address, was on the third floor. Walk up three flights of dingy Roman steps with two heavy suitcases or take the chance on getting stuck in the pre-World War II elevator? As Ruth pushed the button a distinguished gray-haired gentleman entered the building and joined Ruth in front of the elevator.

The elevator squeaked to a halt before them, and when the doors crawled open, the man nodded and gestured with his hand for Ruth to precede him into the conveyance.

"*Prego*, signorina?"

"*Tre, grazie*," she replied, practically exhausting her Italian vocabulary. She wasn't even sure that he had asked what floor, but it seemed reasonable. He pushed seven, she saw, the highest floor shown, and pushed three for her, and they rode to the third floor without incident.

She offered a casual "*Ciao*," as she got out, but he surprised her by lifting off the second suitcase for her and setting it in front of Lydia's door before nodding, saying *ciao*, and getting back on the elevator.

Feeling good she rang the bell, and the door was almost immediately thrown wide. Before her eyes stood the brightest sight Ruth had seen for many a day. Lydia must have been fifty-five or sixty, had bleached blond hair, weighed about two hundred pounds (a conservative estimate), wore a bright blue and green print housedress with lots of bosom and bra showing, and topped off the outfit—or bottomed it out, more accurately—with gold sandals. This resplendent creature took one look at Ruth and her suitcases, promptly swallowed her up in a big hug, calling over her shoulder, "Stephano, Stephano . . . come, come."

On cue appeared Stephano, the all-American boy. He grinned as he was pulled in under Lydia's other wing.

"You must be Ruth." He smiled across Lydia's ample bosom.

"Stephano?" Ruth asked, trying to put all the clues together.

"Steve to you."

"Come, come. You have a cool drink and some cheese and fruit." Lydia clip-clopped down the hall in her sandals, mama bird guiding her babies. "After that plane ride always one needs much sleep, quick. Stephano—you take Ruth, yes? I bring *vino*."

Lydia lovingly shoved Stephano and Ruth into each other's arms, and it was clear that, although the landlady was probably Catholic instead of Jewish, she had the instincts of a matchmaker.

As soon as Lydia had clip-clopped out of sight, Ruth disentangled her arm from Steve's and held out her hand.

"Ruth Tyack," she said, with a formality that might not have been necessary.

Steve smiled and shook her hand. "Steve Armstrong. Hello. Welcome." He had a melodic baritone voice and seductive baby blue eyes.

"Thank you. That was quite a greeting."

"She must have taken an instant shine to you. I've seen her greet two others, and neither of them got a hug or anything."

"I'll bet *you* did." Ruth teasingly pointed her finger at him.

Steve had the good grace to blush. "She seems to like me." He shuffled in place.

"I'd say so," Ruth responded dryly. "How long have you been here?"

"I got here yesterday."

Ruth took a step back and raked her gaze over him assessingly. "You came *yesterday*, and she treats you like the heir apparent?"

"Yeah, well, we kind of hit it off," he explained humbly.

They had edged down the hall with starts and stops until finally Steve opened a door. "Well, this is it." It was dark in the room with the shutters closed, but cool. "I'll open the shutters so you can get a real look at it."

After he did so, Ruth said, "I think maybe it looked better in the dark." The corners of her mouth drooped a little. Well, it was clean. The furniture consisted of a dresser, a desk, and a single bed covered with a pale lavender spread. The walls were light green. There were no drapes, and the wood floor was bare.

"Where's the bathroom?" she asked, trying to mask her disappointment.

"Down the hall." Steve pointed out the door.

"You're kidding." Her voice wobbled.

"Lydia has some rooms with private baths, but they're all full at the moment. I'm on the waiting list."

"I think I'll see what else I can find."

"On the salary we're getting paid?" He perched on the edge of the desk.

"You're a teacher, too?" Ruth asked. "What subject?"

"Guess." His blue eyes sparkled, one brown loafer swung back and forth from his perch.

"Phys. ed.?" She sat on the wide windowsill.

"Thanks a lot."

"Well, you look like a jock." He was a gorgeous specimen: about six two, one ninety, rippling muscles, Robert Redford hair and eyes. "Let's see—physics?"

"No, you were right the first time—phys. ed. They want the kids over here to learn American sports and sportsmanship."

They laughed.

"Have you found a ride into school?" The problem had been preying on her mind.

"I've only been out of the *pensione* once, and it wasn't to find a ride to school."

Ruth smiled her first smile at him. "What was it for?"

"To get a breath of fresh air." He grinned.

"Oh."

They were still smiling at each other when Lydia bustled in carrying a small woven tray holding four different kinds of fruit. On an ornate blue plate sat two crusty rolls and a generous slab of cheese. Beside the plate lay a knife, fork, and a white linen napkin rolled in a silver napkin ring. A carafe of wine and a glass goblet completed the offering.

"Oh, Lydia. This looks perfect. Could I just bother you for one more thing?"

"Certo, bambina, certo. What you would like?" Lydia looked up and smiled as she deposited the tray on the desk beside Stephano.

"Some water and some ice."

"Oh, no, Ruth." The old blond head wagged. "Is not good for you. The *vino* is cool—was in icebox. But no ice. When you hot, ice do bad thing to you. No ice, *bambina*. You listen to Lydia—you not be sorry. I keep you healthy."

Feeling as if she would die without something really

69

cold to quench her thirst, Ruth found it hard to smile and acquiesce. But Ruth had a suspicion that this lady did not like to be crossed—and Ruth was not about to get off to a bad start.

"Okay, Lydia." She yawned. "Oh, excuse me," she said for the yawn. "I'll be glad to listen to you."

"You are good girl—I tell to look. I send somebody to wake you for supper if you sleep long. Now you have good food and good sleep, eh? Come, Stephano, come." She tucked her hand under his arm, and obediently Stephano departed, waving.

Left alone Ruth took her snack to the window and ate and drank leaning over the sill to watch the traffic zoom around the corner. Rome! She was actually in Rome! She was also very tired. And with food in her stomach she was finally content. *I'll worry about the bathroom and all that stuff later.* She kicked off her shoes and laid down on the bed. Her last thought was that a week ago Saturday at this time she was in bed with T.J. She fell asleep with tears in her eyes and a lump in her throat.

They woke her for dinner as promised, and Ruth sat at Lydia's white-draped round table with the six other guests of the moment and savored every bite of her first truly Italian meal. Lydia, like boardinghouse cooks the world over, was a master of stretching, and so dinner that first night consisted of a cold rice salad, bread with prosciutto, and fruit. Lydia even unbent enough to provide two ice cubes for Ruth's wine. Ruth was quiet during the meal, mainly because she was having trouble waking up. But, she was enjoying the camaraderie of the others at the table. Growing up in a single-parent, single-child home, Ruth loved and yet was awed by clans.

"So, what are you going to do tonight?" asked Ricardo of the sexy mustache.

"Go to the Trevi Fountain."

"Oh, no—you'll just be disappointed. Go to Castle Saint Angelo first," advised the chic Sophia.

"No. She should start with Saint Peter's," architect Raphael suggested.

"First the Colosseum," Andrea countered.

"You are all crazy," boomed Giorgio. "First the Pantheon."

For five full minutes the argument raged. When the dust settled, Lydia asked, "So who do you believe, eh? Where do you go first?"

Ruth smiled her "Ruth smile" and said, "To the Trevi Fountain."

Six people turned to her and asked, "Why?"

She answered truthfully. "Because I promised a friend that that was the first thing I would do in Rome."

"Ah, a lover," Ricardo teased.

"Well, actually, no. A fifty-five-year-old blind black woman with no legs."

There ensued the longest conversational pause Ruth was ever to experience in Italy. Lydia's pensioners reassessed Ruth Tyack.

Steve broke the silence. "Would you like some company?"

"I think I'd like to go alone to Trevi—but I'd love your company for sightseeing any other time."

"Great. Maybe we can make a day of it tomorrow."

Dinner over, Ruth got directions from Lydia and set off on foot to Trevi Fountain, her sentimental journey for Tilly and Preston.

She walked slowly and with pleasure down the narrow streets. The uneven cobblestones made for rough going, but it was a warm, sun-kissed evening, and she was, after all, walking down the streets of Rome. On this late August Saturday night, the city was flooded with tourists. Seeing the cars bumper to bumper, all going much too fast, Ruth wondered if she would ever have the nerve to drive in Italy. Twice she passed spacious squares, each resplendent with fountains, the music of the water counterpoint to the street noises. The shops looked enticing. Everything in America seemed to be synthetic. Not so in Italy. There were real leather shoes and bags, silk shirts and underwear, dresses of marvelous soft materials.

Ruth rounded yet another corner just as the evening sun was covered by clouds. She checked the street signs and then walked forward into the square in shock. This was Trevi? This dingy, skinny, four-sided break in the city? It was the smallest, least cared-for, shabbiest fountain she'd seen in Rome. The statuary was all tarnished. There were only a few people; she could tell why. What a disappointment. Shocked, she sat down on the low wall of the fountain called Trevi.

And then the sun came out. Suddenly Trevi Fountain looked different. The water glittered and shimmered in the sun, and the drab statuary seemed to regain some luster. The fountain was poorly placed, it was right up against a building. Why in the world had they done that? The other fountains she had seen were in the midst of wide, clear spaces, catching the light from all angles and sides. Yet, this was more intimate. The other fountains were so public. Trevi was a private fountain, she decided. - Ruth looked around. There were two couples, in various degrees of intertwinement; there was a German family, children in lederhosen; four Orientals were taking pictures; and most interestingly there was a woman who appeared to be an Italian grandmother and her granddaughter. They, like Ruth, were seated on the wall, and for the first time Ruth wished she were able to speak and understand Italian. She could tell from the rapt expression on the girl's face that the grandma in the black dress and pearls was telling a wonderful story.

Ruth dug in her shoulder bag for some American pennies, and one by one she threw them in. The first two were easy: one penny for Preston and Tilly. May you indeed be carried through eternity, dear Tilly. Thank God you are out of that room! A second penny for Tom. Not for Tom and Ruth or Tom and anyone—just for beautiful T.J. A penny for the love in T.J.'s heart. She looked at the third penny in her hand and decided to throw it in for her father and his Annie. Who knows what the future holds—the really big future. She sat there feeling strong. She was twenty-three, for God's sake. Someone had recently pointed that out. This was a time for beginnings, not endings, for finding love, not giving up on love. She loved T.J. Maybe she would never love anyone more. But she would love others. She could not believe that there was only one man for one woman. There was Tom. There would always be Tom. But love wasn't some static quantity that could be spent entirely. Surely it was expandable, elastic—surely a person could love and love and never run out of love. If there were six kids in a family, did they only get one-sixth of the love an only child would receive?

Too philosophical, she thought and dug in her purse for a fourth penny. She tossed it over her shoulder, and instead of wishing to come back to Rome, which was what you were supposed to wish for at Trevi Fountain, she wished for a heart full of love. *May my supply never be depleted.*

She noticed a couple arriving. A stocky young man got out of an expensive green sports car and then went around to open his girlfriend's door. Only the girlfriend was an old woman, gray-haired, plain. Ruth smiled to see them, arm in arm crossing the street to sit by the fountain. They seemed so serene and contented with each other, this mother and son visiting Trevi.

Sighing, Ruth rose and retraced her steps to Lydia's. Finding everyone out she stole four ice cubes and a bottle of Apollinaris mineral water from the refrigerator. Then she went to bed with John D. MacDonald.

At eight the next morning the symphony of church bells played their first movement. Ruth had grown up in a city, and she was used to the noises and smells of a city, but never in Pittsburgh, Pennsylvania, did the bells chime and peel with such abandon. Rome was one of those places that was "too"—it was too loud, too hot, too slow, too crowded, and she imagined after only one day that she could get "too" attached to it. Ruth was beginning to believe that she loved quickly and deeply or not at all.

When she woke again it was ten-thirty, and she wondered how she'd slept through the bells of nine and ten. She put on her robe, preparing to trek to the bathroom, and found Steve's note on the floor under the door: "Ready when you are. Steve." She had forgotten that they had agreed to spend the day together sightseeing. Right now she was dreading it.

Shampoo, soap, and toothpaste in hand, she passed by Steve's room, and there he sat, chair tilted back precariously, feet propped on the desk, a newspaper in his hands. He peered over the paper and smiled a smile sure to stop any female in her tracks. "Shake a leg, there, cutie. All Rome waits for us, and you remain abed. Under other circumstances I wouldn't complain about your wanting to stay in bed, but . . ."

She grinned and interrupted. "A half hour. I'll be all set in half an hour."

"Okay. I've got a stopwatch on you. Thirty minutes." His head ducked back down behind *The Rome Daily American,* and Ruth sped toward the bathroom.

Steve was impressed that twenty-six minutes later they were on their way. Since it was Sunday, they thought it fitting to begin their sightseeing with the most famous church in Rome. Taxis being the one bargain available in Italy, they took a cab across the Tiber to Saint Peter's Square.

"It's so big, Steve. I can't believe it's so big." It was also wildly chaotic. There seemed to be no specific place for cars or pedestrians—both were intermingled. It was a life-risking proposition to get across the square. She grabbed Steve's arm and then was sorry she had done so, for he looked down at her with an intimate smile. She tried to pull her hand back, but he tightened his grip and led her on across the streams of traffic. "You have to be an athlete to climb the steps of Saint Peter's," Ruth complained to Steve. Twice, she tugged at him to slow down.

Inside, they both stopped, awestruck. She had heard of its beauty. She hadn't heard about its startling purity—the whole church gigantic in its gold and whiteness.

They explored—simultaneous masses were in progress in small chapels flanking the main church, each chapel large enough to hold a few hundred people, and each having its own masterpiece of art. They walked slowly, stopping at last in front of Michelangelo's *Pietà*. They were held captive by the sorrow in Mary's face as she embraces the body of her dead son.

"Can you believe the beauty?" Ruth asked Steve softly.
"I can't believe the artist!"

Later, Steve and Ruth joined a tour that was going
"below stairs." There, in the coolness, were small sanctuaries,
each the tomb of a former pope, each personality somehow reflected in the surroundings. The nicest, to Ruth's
eyes, was the room for Pope John XXIII. She had read
The Journey of a Soul and remembered the great humani-
tarian. His tranquillity pervaded the chamber. The room
was freshly white, decked in flowers; she wasn't the only
one who remembered him.

The tour progressed to a subbasement and, in the cold,
damp stone depths, the guide explained some of the
excavations under Saint Peter's. Archaeologists were trying
to authenticate, among other things, if this was indeed
where Simon Peter had been laid to rest.

They finished their tour at the Sistine Chapel.

"It's so little," Ruth said. "Steve, didn't you get a
different impression from the pictures?"

"Yeah, I really did. It looked bigger and brighter in
books."

"I'm disappointed."

They just stood there staring as God and Adam reached
out to each other.

"Let's sit down," she whispered.

"Where?" he hissed back.

In answer she tugged him down on the floor. Now,
shoulder to shoulder, they studied the ceiling from the
floor.

"This looks more like it. I think the photographers must
have been flat on their backs to get some of the pictures
we've seen."

"It really does look better from here." But Steve's
attention wandered faster than Ruth's. "Hey—look at this
floor."

"Oh, Steve, you're right. What lovely mosaics." She
rewarded his discovery with a smile. He winked at her.

They visited four other churches that August Sunday,
although their internal sightseeing clocks did not seem to

be synchronized. Ruth ended up feeling rushed; Steve felt like he had spent more time in church that Sunday than he would have needed to spend in church in a year.

They enjoyed each other. They were of the same vintage. They had been to the same movies, had read the same books, had been brought up in the postwar niceness of America: people were nice, houses were nice, cars were nice, clothes were nice, Dr. Spock even advocated treating your children nicely. They remembered the honor code of the Lone Ranger and the shameful disgrace of the "$64,000 Question." Back home the similarities would have been overshadowed by the differences. But transported to a strange land with a foreign language, culture shock magnified the likenesses to a level of comfortable familiarity.

They ate dinner at a small *ristorante* on Via Fiumiaino—and Ruth had a rude awakening. In Italy spaghetti is not a main course. First one eats a cold antipasto, followed by spaghetti or linguini or ravioli or whatever, and then the main course. On this particular Sunday evening in this particular *trattoria*, the specialties were *ossobuco* and *anquilla*.

Feeling adventuresome, Ruth ordered *ossobuco*, and Steve ordered *capitone*. They also ordered a six-hundred-lire bottle of Chianti and, for about a dollar, received a half gallon of wine. They were doing remarkably well draining their bottle with the cold tuna salad and the spaghetti bolognese. Unfortunately they were unprepared for the main course.

With a flourish the maitre d' set down before the young American couple two plates. Ruth's contained marrow-bone veal stew, which smelled herbal and hearty. Steve's *capitone* turned out to be marinated eel, which not only reeked of the ocean, but looked like it was still moving. As Ruth glanced up from the gently sloshing eel into Steve's perfectly white face, she giggled.

To her surprise, he did not laugh; he didn't even smile. He went into a rage. "What the hell are you laughing about?" he snapped. "Do something helpful! What am I supposed to do with this?" he asked, surreptitiously backing his chair away from the eel.

Ruth sobered instantly. She reached under the table for her big navy blue bag, dug a one-thousand-lire note out of her wallet, and put it by her plate.

"Do whatever you want to do." She stood up. "And thank you—I had a lovely day." Then at a fast walk she left the *ristorante*. As if on cue there was a cab cruising the street, and she hailed it and got in, giving merely the name of the *pensione*.

T.J. would have thought that was funny. He would have laughed me under the table. It was funny.

Oh, T.J. Why aren't you here with me? I bet Helen would get upset with marinated eel, too. Only you and I would sit there laughing. T.J.—I miss you.

With relatively minimal honking of horn, the taxi arrived at Lydia's. Ruth trusted herself to the elevator, got through Lydia's parlor and into her room without being seen, and, fully dressed, lay down on the bed and cried herself to sleep. She didn't hear Steve knock on her door or see him slip the thousand lire under the door. She awoke the next morning, feeling considerably wiser and sadder. Steve was in the kitchen, sitting at the big wooden table, eating some of Lydia's rolls and drinking coffee.

"Ruth—I'm sorry. What happened? Where did you go?"

"Good morning. I'm the one who owes you an apology."

Except for the two of them, the big, sunny kitchen was empty. Ruth poured herself some coffee from the pot on the stove and sat down across from Steve. Then she smiled at him and asked him how he had resolved things last night.

"Well, you had me so worried, I just threw down some more money and followed you outside—only to see a taxi disappearing down the hill. Was that you?"

"Yes. I'm sorry. I just needed to get away by myself all of a sudden."

"Were you sick?"

"Yes. I really was." *Emotional sickness should count for as much as physical sickness.*

"Are you okay now?" He thought her eyes looked funny.

"Yes. Thank you. I guess I was just overtired."

Ruth started buttering a second roll. She was touched

by his concern: he looked so cute this morning. But white chinos and a yellow-check seersucker shirt do not a man make. No, he was a man, but . . . he was a very *young* man. But he could be a good friend. Ruth smiled up at him over the strawberry jam.

"Are you planning on staying here at Lydia's when school starts?"

"Yeah. She really needs boarders in the winter, and the price she quoted me is about as cheap as I'm going to find anywhere. Why don't you stay here, too? We could figure out a way into school together. Maybe go together to buy a really cheap *cinquecento*—each use it every other weekend, or something."

"Stephano! That is an inspired idea!"

He grinned at the praise and leaned back in his chair.

"Why are you calling me Stephano this morning?" he asked.

"I don't know." Ruth studied him, her head cocked to one side. "I just think maybe Lydia is right—you are more Stephano than Steve."

"Is that good or bad?"

"I think that's probably good," she said, smiling.

They were washing their breakfast plates and cups when Lydia came into the kitchen.

"*Buon giorno*, Ruth."

"*Buon giorno*, Lydia."

"Ah, Stephano." He got a big hug and a kiss on the cheek.

"*Buon giorno*, Lydia." He blushed his all-American blush. "We have two questions, Lydia." She beamed at them. Today she sparkled in a pink plaid housedress and her regulation gold sandals. "Do you have room for Ruth this year, too?"

"*Si, si*. But of course Ruth will live here this year."

"At the same rate as me?"

"Ah, Stephano, you drive the hard bargain." She appeared to look him over, maybe considering if she wanted him enough to have Ruth also.

"*Bene, bene*. Ruth, too, at the same *cheap* rate as you."
By now all three of them were beaming.

"Secondly, where can we buy a good, not expensive, used car?"

"You want a car?"

"Yes, Ruth and I thought we could share a car and that way have transportation to school all the time."

"A car, eh? You wait. I see. I call my cousin's nephew—I think maybe we have car for you. You wait. I tell you at lunchtime, eh? You and Ruth be here for lunch today? In Italy, Ruth, you eat big meal at lunchtime. You here today, Stephano, no? I make *scaloppine di vitello al marsala. Delizioso!*" She kissed her fingertips in that classic Italian gesture. They laughed and assured Lydia they would indeed be back for lunch; they would not consider eating anywhere else. The matchmaker smiled smugly as she set off to clean the rooms.

Steve and Ruth set out to see more sights. They left sunny Lydia's sunny kitchen for the still brighter streets of Rome and passed a quick three hours exploring the neighborhood. The Spanish Steps were only about two blocks away, so they headed there, observing and commenting on all the Italianism along the way: the greengrocer's shop, the chicken store, the bottles of milk sitting out in the sunlight at what appeared to be a neighborhood grocery store.

The Spanish Steps were simply concrete steps, lots of them; Rome's florists seemed to congregate there to peddle their wares. The steps were festooned with color—buds and blooms garnished each landing with rainbows. It seemed as though every imaginable species and strain of flower was represented, from perfect yellow roses to mammoth red gladiolas and virginal white carnations.

Ruth and Steve sauntered past Keats's house, up the steps and on to the Via Veneto, where they walked about three blocks, up one side and down the other, on one of the world's most famous streets. Harry's Bar, Doney's, the Paris Café: these were places you read about in books;

these were places where the famous of fashion and the arts congregated. Ruth sighed, thinking of poets, and then walked on, trying not to think.

With each passing hour Ruth felt less and less sure. She was trying to "pour herself in," but something was going wrong. The void that had been in her heart since she and T.J. had parted at the hospital seemed to have spread throughout the rest of her body. She had read about out-of-body experiences in which a person who was injured and unconscious could see his own body, see the firemen pull him from the car, watch the ambulance attendants put him in the ambulance, observe the doctors bending over to examine, the whole thing seen from a distance. That's how she felt—as if she were somehow outside herself, watching Ruth Tyack sightsee, listening to Ruth Tyack talk. She saw everything, but she was uninvolved.

She watched Ruth Tyack eat Lydia's fantastic veal with Marsala. She heard Ruth Tyack laugh at all the right places and ask some of the right conversational questions. But it was almost scary how detached she was. Later in life she would learn that the human mechanism has marvelous shock absorbers, that in order to bear pain, the mind will simply detach itself from the body. But as late August turned into early September in Rome, Ruth only knew that at that time in her life, she felt numb—anesthetized.

Monday night Lydia produced a cousin's nephew who had a "magnifico" cinquecento for the young Americans. It was white, rusted, and berattled, but it ran. So Tuesday and Wednesday Steve and Ruth went sightseeing by car. Tuesday morning, the Forum; Tuesday afternoon, Ostia Antica, Wednesday, the Colosseum, the Pantheon, and three more churches..They had spent four entire days sightseeing and had barely scratched the surface of Rome's treasures.

Thursday they were due at school. Thursday and Friday were staff orientation days, Monday was Labor Day, (the Rome-American School celebrated all US *and* Italian holidays), and on Tuesday the students would come. At 8:30

A.M. Steve and Ruth set off for their first trip to the
school, which was run by the Department of Defense for
the Army brats, the diplomacy bums, and the children
of assorted American businessmen living in and around
Rome.

"It's lovely," Ruth cried. "It looks like a little piece of
Americana transplanted to Italy. Don't you love it?" She
pounded on Steve's arm as he tried to steer the uncooperative
little car.

"The little red brick schoolhouse?" he teased.

It really *was* pretty, this out-of-place piece of colonial
America. The two-story red brick building was flanked
with trees and bushes and topped with waving Stars and
Stripes. The grass lawn was the greenest she had seen
since leaving Pennsylvania. She felt a definite pang, as if
she should stand up and sing the national anthem, or at
least put her hand on her chest. She realized that for the
first time in almost two weeks she felt happy. These kids
had a nice school, and it was going to be a good experience to teach here—she felt she was where she belonged.
The stupor began to lift. It was a sensation she was to
experience almost every morning when she arrived at
school, but it would never be as strong as it was that first
day.

"Oh, Steve, doesn't it make you feel good—that the
school is so nice?"

"Yeah. And look—they even have an athletic field. This
might not be such a fiasco after all."

"Were you wondering, too, if you had made a bad
decision?"

"Yeah, I sure was," he said honestly. "We *are* awfully far
from Bloomington, Indiana."

They got out of the car, not locking it. The passenger
door was permanently locked, so you could never get in or
out that side—you had to slide over from the driver's seat.
The driver's door, on the other hand *never* locked, the
lock was broken, unrepairable, but "molto" unnecessary in
Italy, the cousin's nephew had assured them. Ruth slid
under the steering wheel and as she got out grabbed
Steve's hand.

"Come on, teach. This is going to be a good year, I feel it in my bones." She did a quick two-step on the gravel parking lot.

"Oh, pretty lady, I hope you're right."

5

"Seems like only yesterday we were walking in here for the first time."

"Stephano!" Ruth swung around from her poetry bulletin board to see Steve leaning against the doorjamb, grinning at her. She dashed across the classroom to be swept off her feet in a bear hug. There were tears in her eyes at the sight of his familiar face.

"If I'd known you were going to miss me so much, I would have married you instead of Maria." Ruth had the good manners to refrain from saying that it was Maria, not she, who had been pregnant. In the two months of summer holidays, she had indeed missed him. He leaned forward and gave her a kiss on each cheek.

"Steve—can you believe we are about to start our second year here?"

He perched on the edge of one of the children's desks, and Ruth leaned on another across the aisle from him. He just shook his head in answer to her question—he was busy studying the changes in Ruth since he had last seen her. Except for her eyes she looked fine: tanned and fashionably slim, she was dressed with a new chic that was definitely European. Only her eyes revealed some of the old sadness and longing—she never quite smiled all the way. It had been November of the previous year when she had finally told him about T.J. Now he reached out for her hand and said, "How are you doing?"

"Better." She smiled at him and squeezed his arm. "I'm really doing better. Every once in a while I'll go for a couple hours and not think of him at all. Some of the time now it's more like I'm a widow—I get some comfort from the memories, instead of always just being haunted by them."

"Did you go home this summer?" Steve asked.

"No." Ruth smiled a melancholy smile. "I just couldn't trust myself. I was afraid I'd try to get in touch with Tom. I think maybe I'll go at Christmas. Dad and I usually go to my aunt's farm, and there is lots of activity. I'd be really busy, and, of course, a married man can't very well desert his family at Christmas, so I would be spared the temptation of asking him to. It's such a relief to me that you know all about him—it's good to be able to have someone understand, to have someone to share it with."

She sighed and looked down at her ever-present brown loafers for a minute in order to pull her mind off her thoughts. "So, anyhow, how's the old married man?" She punched him in the gut.

"Good. It seems good so far. Maria was really down in the dumps this morning when it was time for me to leave for school and she couldn't come too. I haven't met the new Italian teacher yet, but he's going to have some big shoes to fill. She and the kids got along great."

"It is just asinine that they won't let her keep on teaching."

"Yeah. Good grief, it's not like the kids never saw a pregnant lady before or anything." Steve gestured wildly with his hands, and Ruth wondered if the influence of living with Maria's family was showing. "Anyway, I guess we should get down to the meeting." Steve stood up and stretched, as if he weren't quite awake.

"Yes. And for heaven's sake, come see Lydia. She asks me every day when Stephano is going to come 'home'"— Ruth clutched her hands to her heart—"to see her. She is pining away for you, Romeo."

"Dear Lydia." He smiled broadly. "How is the old girl?"

"Up to her usual tricks. She tried to bribe me out of the corner room—she had found a young architect who would pay her twice what I'm paying."

"How'd you fight that?" Steve looked at Ruth in awe.

"I told her if I got mad and left she'd have no way of

keeping tabs on you"—she patted his cheek—"so she
better treat me nicely."

Ruth was looking forward to this year flying by the way
last year had. She had been *so* busy. High school teaching
was a revelation. Not only did she work all day, her
non-classroom time filled with study halls and lunchroom
duty, but all night, too, trying to keep ahead of the kids,
reading what they read and correcting what they wrote.
She loved it.

She remembered the first day last year, how uncertain
she and Steve had been as they walked into the building.
She knew that now, as they walked into the faculty meeting, waving at familiar faces, they both looked poised and
confident.

She and Steve had stayed at Lydia's, sticking to their
plan to drive back and forth together. Weekends they went
their own way. Steve started dating Maria, so Ruth would
set off either with some other single female from school or
by herself: by the end of that first year, she knew the area
around Rome better than most Italians did.

She had spent the summer traveling in a much wider
scope with Frances, a young woman who had been at the
American School for two years and was going home at the
end of August to marry her young doctor. On Eur-rail
passes they toured France, the Netherlands, Belgium, and
took a ferry to England, returning to Rome via Germany
and Austria. They came home happy, exhilarated, exhausted,
and literally penniless. Ruth was grateful that Lydia was
willing to let Ruth live at the *pensione* on credit until her
first paycheck. It no doubt helped that Ruth had brought
her numerous presents, including some Belgian lace nap-
kins for her supper table and a lovely pink (Lydia's favorite
color) wool shawl from England.

The vacation had refreshed Ruth. She had been leery of
setting out, but she thought of T.J. and decided to pour
herself in. She spent ten hours in the Louvre and smiled
to think how pleased Tom would be. She attended a
concert in Brussels Grand Place because she thought Tom

would expect it of her, even though she felt like staying in the hotel that night. She took extra walks, spent extra time, devoted extra energy—at first, doing it for T.J., and then, later, just doing it. Pouring herself in became a way of life.

When the meeting broke for lunch, Ruth was joined by Sally, the British home economics teacher who had married an Italian businessman and settled in Rome for good.

"Ruth, I think you're just the person I need. You play bridge, don't you?"

"Sally, I love bridge. It's the best thing I learned in the girl's dorm—after the sex education, of course."

Sally laughed. "Of course, that's the main thing we all learn as undergrads—except I'm afraid these kids today are getting so knowledgeable that they'll have nothing left to learn when they get to college."

"But, in any case," Sally went on, "Nick and I are having a bridge party tomorrow night, and he invited a young—well, thirtyish, I guess—accountant, and I need an extra female. It won't be a date or anything"—she could sense Ruth prickling at the idea of being fixed-up— "because we'll be playing bridge and moving around, changing partners all night. You will come, won't you? I really need you."

"Oh, Sally, for you, I suppose...."

Nevertheless, as she dressed for Sally and Nick's party, Ruth felt a sweet sense of anticipation. She hadn't done anything really social since the senior prom last May when she had spent the night fending off that amorous Italian biology teacher—thank God he wasn't back at school this year.

Nick greeted Ruth at the door by whistling at her, making her feel young and pretty in her new blue silk, sleeveless A-line. Then he led her across the room to meet the accountant. It was an acutely disappointing moment: he was so damned ordinary. He was stocky, only a few inches taller than Ruth and had unremarkable brown hair, unremarkable brown eyes; and a rather unremarkable smile.

"Ruth Tyack, I'd like you to meet Bruno Sevini."

"Bruno, this is Ruth, who teaches with Sally. Bruno has

done some consulting for us, Ruth—and he's an old friend."

Nick hurried away, leaving them stranded with each other. They each smiled rather halfheartedly; he seemed no more impressed than she. Childishly, she felt cheated.

"Would you like a drink, Ruth? Nick set up a bar over here so we could help ourselves."

He had a nice voice—very soft, yet not hesitant—a soothing voice.

"Yes, I need a little Dutch courage to help my bidding."

"Dutch courage? I never heard that. That means the drink makes you brave so you bid more courageously?"

"Yes." She was reluctant to grant that he had figured it out.

"I'll have to tell my mother," he said seriously. "She'll enjoy knowing that. Her mother, my grandmother, was American, and she loves to keep abreast of the colloquialisms."

"That explains your excellent English, doesn't it." She smiled rather smugly.

"Well," he hesitated, "I don't know that my English is excellent, but I suppose it explains my ease with the language. My mother was brought up to be bilingual, and she tried to do me the same favor. And I'm grateful. It has really been a help to me in business. Often I get the better assignments because they demand someone who can speak English."

She looked at him quizzically, trying to decide if that was false or actual modesty. He no doubt got good assignments because he was a good accountant.

"What do you wonder?" he asked.

He was perceptive, she thought. "Well, quite honestly, I was wondering if you were asking for a compliment."

He looked at her without smiling—his eyes held a sadness.

"No, I wasn't asking for a compliment. I do not usually seek the approval," he said very slowly and seriously, "of my fellowmen—or women. So, no, I was not seeking compliments from you."

Ruth was puzzled. He didn't seem angry or hurt, more disappointed, and she felt, inexplicably, that she had let him down. She was silent and embarrassed and ashamed of herself. It wasn't like her to be cruel, and yet she felt she had been.

They played the first round as partners, and although Ruth didn't think she could meet his eyes, she was forced to by their need to communicate their bids. He answered her looks with placidly peaceful smiles, and the awkward moment passed. Her bidding was atrocious. All four times she landed them in the wrong suit or at the wrong level. The three times that he played the hand he made her crazy bids anyhow, usually right on the nose. The one time that she played, she went down three tricks—a humiliating experience.

They moved on, playing with different partners. Ruth found herself looking at him frequently, trying to analyze why, suddenly, she felt drawn to him. She had the strongest urge to put her head on his shoulder and let him rub all the pain away. But though he'd answer her with a smile when he felt her eyes on him, she never found him watching her, and when it was time for a break for supper, it was she who sought him out. He was polite, asked her questions to keep her talking, and laughed in all the right places. But he didn't seem the least bit sorry to leave her when the game resumed. Well, at least he would be taking her home. They were the only single man and woman in the group.

But when the evening was over, he simply left. She saw him at the door saying goodbye to Sally and Nick and to her mortification saw all three turn and look at her. Then he was gone. She felt abandoned.

Who the hell did he think he was, treating her like that? Ignoring her? Not even offering to take her home? Man, she hoped he'd call for a date sometime—she'd really let him have it!

She was so mad she could have walked all the way home on anger. But then Sally asked her to help clean up, and for almost an hour she and Sally and Nick put away food and washed dishes.

"Come on, let's polish off this cake," Sally said at last,

and the three of them sat down at the kitchen table with cake and milk.

When the doorbell rang, Ruth said, "Somebody must have forgotten something," which Sally and Nick inexplicably found hilarious. A moment later Nick ushered in Bruno, and Ruth knew why her remark had been so funny.

He joined them at the table, explaining that he had had to drive his mother home from her bridge game. Sally put on a pot of coffee, and still they sat, the other three talking and Ruth trying to sort out her feelings. She had experienced the strangest sensation when Bruno walked back in the room—a warm flood of relief, a release from pain, and the certainty that everything would be all right now. But it was a totally unaccountable reaction, and she was troubled by the power he seemed to have over her.

It was after three when they finally left Sally and Nick—and Ruth had a shock when she got outside. The only car in sight was a magnificent green sports car—a Maserati, she was to learn—and it was elegant. It was low-slung, a sexy, exciting automobile, and it seemed totally out of character for a soft-spoken, serious accountant. More strangely still, the car looked familiar to Ruth, and she wondered where she'd seen it before.

"Would you like to go for a ride?" he asked as he opened the door for her.

"Yes, please." She felt ridiculously grateful.

They drove in silence through the dark night. After twenty minutes or so, they had escaped the lights of Rome and were on the road to Ostia Antica and the sea. She could smell it before they saw it—that salty, briny smell of adventure. Bruno stopped the car when they neared the beach. He got out his side and came around the car, taking her hand to help her, and then just holding on to it.

"This is the smoothest beach around, but you have to cross the rocks here before you get to the sand."

When they had traversed the rough ground, he dropped her hand, and she stopped walking, captured by the beauty of the white sand and the dark blue water, the small waves breaking white from blue, the yellow light of the half-moon, the smell of life.

"Bruno, can I take off my shoes?"

"Of course." He smiled.

He did the same, and they moved together to the edge of the surf.

"Shall we walk?" he invited.

She nodded her head and held out her hand. He took her fingers securely in his. Ever so slowly they moved, the sand caressing their toes, their hands tightly clasped.

"Oh, Bruno. I needed this so badly." She turned to look at him, and he saw naked pain.

"I know you needed this. That's why I brought you here. I have never brought any other woman to the beach in the middle of the night. But I knew this was where you needed to be."

"How did you know that?"

"I could feel the tension and the unhappiness inside you. And the ocean is wonderful for both things."

He pulled her down on the sand, and they sat on the starlit beach in utter silence and stillness. The sand was still warm from the day's sunshine, and Ruth's right hand sifted the grains while her left hand stayed clasped firmly in Bruno's strong fingers.

She had never been with anyone with whom she was so comfortable while pulling into herself. She would learn later that this was a gift Bruno gave freely but that he expected the same gift to be given to him—the right to retreat inside one's own soul. It was a gift much easier to receive, than to give, Ruth would discover. But this night it was something that she very much needed.

The mournful little roll of the waves at her feet seemed to seep into her heart, remove particles of doubt and despair, and carry them away with each return of the tide. When she shivered, Bruno put her left hand into his left hand and draped his warm right arm over her shoulders, shifting a bit so their bodies were tightly touching.

After a while he pulled her to her feet, and they walked. She felt she could have walked all the way down to Naples, it felt so good.

"Bruno." She stopped him in mid-stride. "You know how you go to the dentist and get your teeth cleaned? How fresh and tingling your mouth feels? You just can't stop running your tongue over your teeth, and you feel like smiling at everyone you meet and saying, 'See me. I feel great.' Well, I feel like you are doing that for me—for my—soul, I guess. Does that make any sense to you?"

"Of course it does."

He tightened his arm around her shoulders, and they walked on. For two hours they alternately walked and rested. And then it started: they sat on the warm, crusty sand, watching in awe as the colorless streak of light built and exploded, reflected over the sea, changing the color of the water, dancing patterns on the waves.

Ruth became aware, surprised, at how intertwined their bodies were, his arm on her shoulders, her arms resting on his upright knees, his face gentle against her hair.

She turned and kissed him on the cheek.

He pulled her head down and kissed the top of her hair.

"Shall we go get some breakfast?" His eyes were asking more than his words indicated.

She smiled broadly, brushing sand from her skirt. "I feel like I haven't eaten for a year."

He smiled back; her world felt complete.

They stopped to put their shoes on, and she hesitated with the panty hose she had tucked into her sandals. He just shook his head and reached out for them, stuffing them in his pocket.

On the way to the restaurant she turned toward him in the car and tried to tell him. "Bruno, that was such a fantastic experience. I feel so new."

"Good," was all he replied, but she felt he understood.

They devoured a huge Italian breakfast of fresh fruit, cheese omelets, dark brown bread, and many harmonious smiles. She fell asleep on the way back to Rome, her head against the backrest, and he woke her when he had pulled up in front of *Pensione Lydia*.

"Ruth, we're back." He gently rubbed her arm.

She had trouble getting her eyes to focus.

"I think maybe you better go in by yourself," Bruno

counseled. "It would only make things worse if your Lydia saw the man who brought you home the next morning."

"Lydia!" Ruth was shocked into wakefulness. "I forgot all about Lydia." She looked down at her wrinkled dress and reached a hand up to her hair.

"Maybe I can sneak in," she said desperately. "Stop laughing"—she punched his leg—"and tell me what time it is."

"Seven-thirty." She watched the corners of his mouth trying to straighten, the lines around his eyes still crinkled. Finally, she had to laugh, too.

"You're right," she said. "I think I'll just brazen it out. What the heck. A night like that was worth anything."

"Anything?" he asked quietly.

"Anything." She felt so sure.

They smiled warmly at each other.

"Thank you very much," she said prettily.

"It was my pleasure," he replied gallantly.

She put her hand on the door handle.

"Ruth, may I call you?" His voice was deceptively casual.

She turned back for a last smile. "Please do, so I can let you know how Lydia takes the scandal."

"Okay. *Ciao.*"

"*Ciao*, Bruno."

Ruth could easily have avoided Lydia, who was puttering in the kitchen, but mischievously she walked into the kitchen smiling her sweetest smile, poured herself a cup of coffee, said "Good morning, Lydia," and with a jaunty wave headed for her room and bed. Lydia stared at her, aghast and speechless. As Ruth walked down the hall, she heard the young architect saying, "Here, Lydia, come sit down. You look a little pale."

Ruth sat in bed drinking her coffee, looking at the morning copy of *The Rome Daily American*, until she again felt sleepy. Then she slept until four o'clock.

She spent her first weekend "in." As if Lydia hadn't had enough shocks. First, that innocent young American girl who rarely went out not only *went* out, but *stayed* out all night. Then that innocent young American girl who spent every weekend on the go, sightseeing, didn't leave the *pensione* all weekend. Lydia didn't know, and Ruth didn't explain, that she was waiting for a phone call. It never came.

Ruth was waiting in the home ec room when Sally walked in on Monday morning, but it was clear that Sally knew nothing of Bruno's plans, so Ruth retreated to her room to sulk the day away. Tuesday she was so mad at him that she wouldn't have talked to him if he had called. By Wednesday she had decided that he was never going to call, and then at five o'clock he did. Ruth had only been home for a few minutes when Lydia knocked on her door to say she had a phone call. She had given up expecting him, but his "Ruth?" was all it took to put the expectation back in her life.

"Hi," she answered softly.

There were no preliminaries, no small talk.

"I'm leaving tonight for Orvieto, I have to work there Thursday and Friday, and I spent Monday and Tuesday in Hamburg—just got back in this morning. This has been a really upside-down week. How have you been?"

"Not very good." She wasn't going to indulge in small talk, either.

"Why?"

"Because I didn't hear from you," she admitted.

He gave a great sigh of satisfaction. "I'm glad you realized you wanted to hear from me."

"Yes, I was a little slow on the draw, wasn't I?"

"You can be as slow as you want to if you keep coming up with the right answers." That dear soft, sexy voice of his!

"Bruno?" She just wanted to say his name and establish the reality of him on the other end of the line.

"Yes?"

"I don't know. Just talk to me."

He gave a little chuckle. "Shall we go to the beach this weekend?" he asked casually.

"Yes!" Her voice broke in her eager, quick response.

"Saturday?"

"Whenever it works out best for you. I have no other

plans." If Bruno wanted her humble, she was willing to be totally humble.

"Well, then, let's spend the weekend. I'll pick you up Saturday morning, and if the weather is nice, we'll just stay until late Sunday afternoon."

"That sounds great. I would really like that." She pressed a hand against her forehead to try to hold herself back.

"Okay. Eleven o'clock?"

"How about ten?" Her hand hadn't helped much.

"Ten-thirty," he compromised.

"Okay. But I'm not anxious to see you."

"That's good. Then you won't have any trouble waiting until Saturday," he said teasingly.

"No. None at all," she assured him, laughing. Then she decided to turn the tables. "How about you? Will you have any trouble waiting?"

"No. Of course not. I will merely be concentrating on the finances of this little pottery business in Orvieto. I will have no thoughts of sitting in the moonlight, watching the waves, resting my cheek on a head of soft golden hair."

Ruth was touched by his romantic remark. "Bruno. That was a beautiful thing to say."

There was a lengthy pause.

"I will see you Saturday morning at ten-thirty."

"I'll be ready. I'm so glad you called."

"Ciao."

"Ciao."

She was waiting for him, an overnight bag and a beach bag in hand, when he pulled up at 10:25 Saturday morning. He put her bags in the car, handed her into her seat, and pulled out into the traffic all without saying a word. Then he picked up her hand from where it lay in her lap, kissed her fingers, and said, "Hello."

"Hi." She turned in the seat to smile a greeting.

"How are you doing?" he asked seriously.

"Great," she enthused.

They passed smiles back and forth, and then Bruno put her hand back in her lap and concentrated on his driving. Most of the trip was spent in silence. Ruth just leaned her head back and basked in the strange new feeling of contentment. She felt so safe with him. She looked over to study his face. His nose was too big to be aesthetically correct, but it was aristocratic. The hair right beside his ears was graying. She reached out to touch it, but he caught her hand in mid-flight.

"What do you reach for, signorina?"

"I wanted to touch your gray hair and see if it was real," she said solemnly.

He gave a quiet laugh. Even though his laughter was contained, Ruth felt strangely triumphant that she had made him laugh. He was such a serious person. It would feel good to add some fun to his life. Without saying anything he just put her hand back in her lap, giving it a few taps, as if to say, "Keep your hands where they belong."

Ruth put her head back against the seat and closed her eyes, a smile on her face. When she opened her eyes again, she turned to look at Bruno. His lips were moving, but no sound was coming out.

"What are you mumbling about?" she asked. "Or were you singing?"

Bruno didn't answer but looked at her with a crooked smile and raised his eyebrows like a stern teacher. "We're feeling very feisty and full of it this morning, aren't we, Miss Tyack?"

"Yes, Mr. Sevini." Ruth smiled at him, but her eyes misted suddenly. "We are feeling wonderful and very much alive this morning."

"Don't we always feel alive in the morning, Miss Tyack?" Bruno was trying to keep the lightness in the conversation. But Ruth looked at him with utter seriousness, and he could see again the pain there. "It has been a long time, Bruno, since I have felt this good."

"Well, we'll see what we can do. We may have to increase the length of the treatments or the number of treatments given. Right now the doctor orders a big Italian lunch. I'm hungry, are you?"

"Yes. I was starving. I'm so glad you came along." Her words had double meanings; she thought he sensed what she was trying to say.

"I, also," he answered very quietly.

Their one weekend at the beach turned into two weekends at the beach and then three and then four—until it was October and getting cooler and they switched to riding boats around Capri and stomping the ruins at Pompeii. Ruth worried about the finances.

"Bruno, I am costing you a fortune."

"I don't have a fortune, but I can support you for a few more weekends. So where would you like to go next?"

The first weekend in November he was away, staying in England on a two-week job. Then he was back, and they spent the following weekend in Assisi, paying homage to Saint Francis and the lovely pottery in his town. The next weekend Bruno was scheduled to be away on a two-week stint in Paris. Thursday night he cabled her a ticket to come join him for the weekend. So it went. They were together more and more. At first he would call only once a week so they could make plans. Then he called twice a week—and then every night. In November, after the trip to England, he took her to his apartment, and together they cooked dinner and spent the evening on their separate work, and then he returned her to Lydia. By December they were spending every free minute together, almost always at Bruno's apartment.

But they had not slept together. Every weekend it was separate rooms. They had kissed, some long, very passionate kisses. Beyond that he wouldn't go. He had held her when she needed to be held; and sometimes she held his head in her lap while they read or watched TV.

When Ruth mentioned going back to the states for Christmas, he was positively enthusiastic. She almost thought he had a wife and children tucked away somewhere and had to return to them for the holiday. And then slowly it dawned on her. A couple of times she had tried to tell him about T.J. He would never let her go on. "Ruth, I don't want to know. You just work it out as well as you can. Anything else I'll be happy to help with. Just tell me when that chapter is closed. I don't want any part of it."

She was hurt. But she guessed it was self-preservation on his part, rather than lack of concern. Slowly the pieces fell together in her mind. His refusal to discuss any past relationships on her part, his refusal to touch her physically. He was waiting, waiting for her to be free enough to come to him without any shadows and ghosts between them. She wondered how he had ever known. But then he always seemed to know. She was coming to depend on it.

She thought she realized why he wanted her to go home. He was hoping that she would come back a free person. She knew she had a choice: she could keep T. J. alive and between them, she could—just as he had warned—allow T. J. to steal her heart and her youth; or she could try to really tie that all up and come back to Bruno's love.

She was to arrive home on the thirteenth of December and was scheduled to stay until the twenty-eighth. Bruno had made her reservations for her. He was shocked and disappointed in her that she had not been home to see her father since she had come to Italy, and he felt it was high time she made a visit. Yet she didn't want to be away from Bruno for so long. She cried when he gave her her ticket, but he was adamant. He said something that she was later to remember. "Who knows, Ruth, sometime you may have to learn to live without me entirely." She cried some more. He would not change the plans. "You give fifteen days to the lonely old man in the United States who loves you, and then you come back here, if you want to, and give the rest of your days to me."

He refused to tell her he loved her. Just as he refused to love her physically. Numerous times she had tried to undress him or herself, and always he had stopped her.

"Bruno, why not, for God's sake?" She was angry and hurt.

"Because it isn't time yet," he argued patiently.

"When, when will it be time?" she asked huffily.

"I don't know exactly. But we'll know. It will be time, and it will be right. I'm a patient man."

"Well, I'm not a patient woman."

"Then go somewhere where you can get what you want."

"What I want is right here."

"Then you'll just have to learn to be patient, too, won't you?" And she would storm out of the room, only to return a few minutes later, sedate and contrite. The scene was played and replayed and replayed some more. Ruth knew she was being childish. She imagined Bruno felt sorely tried. Sometimes he would say, "I said no, Ruth," and he'd barricade himself behind his desk and his paperwork—or he'd quite literally lock himself in the bathroom and take a cold shower.

She couldn't know how relieved he felt when she got on the plane. He had been strong enough for the role he had assigned himself. She would have smiled if she could have heard him, because as the plane lifted off the ground, he had a rare moment of doubt, and he looked heavenward and said, "God, you wouldn't have offered me this only to tease me, would you?" But just then the sun came out from behind the clouds, and Bruno sighed: "Thank you." For fifteen days he simply kept the faith.

Ruth enjoyed her visit home. She felt like she and her father were able to reestablish a warmth they hadn't experienced since Ruth was a very young girl. Perhaps, in their case, absence did make the heart grow fonder, and their separation had allowed each of them to reassess and revalue the other. They Christmas shopped together, buying gifts for the whole family at the farm, and Ben sat in the kitchen, smoking his pipe and talking while Ruth cooked a stockpile of his favorite foods to have on hand in the freezer.

Two days before Christmas they journeyed through the hills outside Pittsburgh to the old family farm, where Ben's sister Agnes and her husband, along with their children and grandchildren, were all gathered together.

The children always looked forward to seeing Aunt Ruth. Aunt Ruth was fun. She'd make fudge for you or take walks with you or in the summer, be the lifeguard so you could swim in the creek, or, when your mother said positively no more cookies, it was Aunt Ruth who would slip you one and stem the flow of tears.

This Christmas was no different. For one thing, Aunt

Ruth cooked, all by herself, for twenty-four people, a real Italian meal. The day before Christmas, when everyone was feeling frantic, Aunt Ruth piled the eight children in the largest station wagon available and drove them into the nearest town to a department store, where the little ones sat on Santa's knee, and the big ones roamed for a whole hour in the toy department with never one warning of "Don't touch."

Christmas eve, Uncle Mike, the high school music teacher, sat at the piano and played and led the singing of every carol and Christmas song the family could remember. Then they made the traditional warm, salty popcorn and spicy, mulled cider. Christmas morning it was Aunt Ruth who was dragged out of bed at six, and for two hours she tried to keep the early birds quiet and happy as they ate hot cereal and guessed the contents of package after package. The biggest excitement of Christmas day was the call for Ruth from Rome. They couldn't know how exciting it was for the man on the other end of the line to hear twenty-four people say, almost in unison, "Merry Christmas, Bruno."

The day after Christmas they started clearing out, treasures and memories stored away, and Ben and Ruth were among the first to go. Aware of the new closeness, they were anxious to get back home and spend their last two days together. And when the time came, Ben felt good to put on the plane a happy and newly serene daughter.

Ruth was ecstatic. She had made it. She had slept in the bed she and T.J. had shared. She had used the telephone they had talked on. She had been within a reasonable distance of him and had not written or called or gone to see him. She wasn't even sure where he was now. She had survived it all! Still, she knew she had been right, that never again would she experience a love as perfect as she had shared with T.J. She loved Bruno, but it was a quiet love. She knew it would be good; she would flourish and grow under that sheltering love. She was anxious to return to his arms. And that's just what she did.

She saw him from maybe a hundred feet away, standing way in back of the crowd, and she disengaged herself from the throng to race into his arms. He seemed shocked—he was apparently expecting a more dignified greeting—but he recovered quickly and held her, feeling her need, knowing she had truly come back to him.

Wordlessly they retrieved Ruth's bags and walked out to the car. Once settled in their seats Bruno put the key in the ignition, but Ruth stopped him with her hand on his. She leaned over in front of him.

"Now, really say hello to me."

"Hello." He looked straight ahead.

"Try again," she demanded softly.

He grabbed her and kissed her with a passion that he had previously kept under tight control. His tongue probed the deep, moist corners of her mouth, and his hand caressed a taut breast under her coat. Her legs moved a little, convulsively, wanting his hardness between them. She reached a hand over on his crotch and felt an explosive response.

"Have you ever been raped in an airport parking lot?" he asked hoarsely.

"I don't think you call it rape when the woman is an active and willing participant." She moved in closer.

"Anyway, let's see . . . if I can remember the way home. I'm warning you, *bambina*, don't touch me again, or we won't make it home."

"Yes, sir," Ruth said, smiling, sitting up straight in her seat, making a business of fastening her seat belt.

"Now tell me about Christmas. It sounded as if all of Pittsburgh was there."

On the way to Bruno's apartment she chattered. She named all the children and discussed the presents they had made each other and described the mulled cider and the carol sing.

Once inside the door, Ruth kicked off her shoes, dropped her coat on the floor, and flung herself into Bruno's arms. Kissing her, he led her over to the couch and laid her down, kneeling on the floor beside her. He might have been consumed with passion but he was a man who knew how to get a button out of a buttonhole; then he had her blouse open and had pulled down the straps of her slip and bra. Cradling one firm white breast in his hand, the other in his mouth, he kissed and caressed. She felt the passion flowing in her. Then, to her amazement, he pulled her bra and slip back in place and rested his head on her breasts for a minute before explaining.

"Ruth—I have to leave in about two hours. We have waited four months—we can wait a few more hours; this is one thing we don't want to rush. Right? I have to spend the next two days in Naples. I should have left early this morning or even last night. But I just had to wait and meet your plane. I was gambling, hoping that you would come back to me—not just come back, you understand, but come back to me. And you did, didn't you?" he asked seriously. She nodded her head yes. "As it is, I'll be trying to cram a three-day job into two days. But I may be able to do it in two hours now that I know what is waiting for me when I return to Rome. You will be waiting for me?"

"You know I will, Bruno. I'm glad, too, that you were there to meet the plane. That was important! I understand." She did, too, though she was aching with desire. "What can I do for you while you're gone?"

"What a woman you are." He kissed her forehead in tribute. "I'm glad you can understand why I did it the way I did. Ruth, I would like it very much if you and my mother started getting acquainted. I know she'll be home all day tomorrow. I think you will love each other. I pray you will. I'll be home on New Year's Eve day. My mother wants us to come have dinner with her around noon—and we are invited to Sally and Nick's for a party in the evening. But that's all on Friday. Then we would have the rest of the weekend to ourselves." His hands were busy stroking her cheeks and arms and shoulders.

"It sounds wonderful"—she sat up to kiss him—"the rest of the weekend to ourselves. Do you think we could tell anyone who asks that we are going away and then just snuggle in here?"

He was buttoning her blouse back up and stopped, surprised and delighted. "Maybe we can even leave the party before midnight and usher the new year in in our own way," he said rather tentatively.

She looked at him uncertainly. "I'm not sure—but I hope that was an indecent proposal!"

"What can I say or do that will make you sure?"

"Have the bed turned down when we arrive?" Her fingers rubbed his wrists at the edge of his sweater sleeves.

"Anything else?" His voice was husky again.

"Well, you could kiss me a few more times like you have for the past hour, but I'm afraid if you do we may not make the new year, so maybe I should just take your word for it and get up and make you some supper so you can be on your way to Naples." She started to rise, but he stopped her.

"I'll bring you a present from Naples. What would you like?"

"Some wine for our New Year's celebration."

"Done." Sealed with a kiss.

Ruth fixed him French toast and sausage, and they ate and talked and laughed, but when they got back to *Pensione Lydia*, she felt sudden fear for him traveling: "Please take care of yourself."

"I'll pick you up around noon on Friday. Believe me, *cara*, nothing could stop me from getting back."

He carried her suitcases up, smiled charmingly at Lydia, and was gone. Ruth went to bed and slept for almost fourteen hours.

Late Wednesday morning, to please Bruno, Ruth walked the few short blocks to his mother's apartment. It was a brisk December day. Ruth's cheeks were pink when she arrived.

"Ruth, come in."

"Hello."

"Hello. Let me take your coat." Nona Sevini just stood and looked at Ruth for a moment. "Bruno told me how lovely you are. I didn't know exactly what he meant. Come —I just took some cookies from the oven."

Ruth followed her into the kitchen. Nona looked familiar. Why? It was a totally unremarkable face. Why would Ruth remember it? When could she have seen this woman before?

"You have known my son only a few months..." Nona began, gesturing for Ruth to sit in one of the chairs at the round wooden table.

"Yes," Ruth agreed, "but we have had wonderful times. Has he told you of all the trips we took?"

"Oh, yes. He loves being your guide. It's so... invigorating to see one's own country through the eyes of someone from another country. You notice things you've never seen before."

"Your English is so good, Signora Sevini."

"Oh, please, Ruth, call me Nona. I'm sure Bruno told you that my mother was American."

"Yes, that's right, he did. I'd almost forgotten."

"She died very young—of cancer, I think they would call it today—but she had a profound influence on my life."

"You were close to her?"

"Yes, very." Nona seemed for a moment to drift into her memories, and then she pulled herself back. "And your mother?"

"She died at my birth. I've always felt a terrific void." *But I've never before admitted it to a stranger,* Ruth thought.

"I'm sure you have. Perhaps when you marry, your husband's mother..."

"That would be very nice for me."

"I'm sure it would be nice for her, too. Women need other women."

"Yes, that's true."

Nona produced a pot of tea and some tangy lemon cookies. They sipped and munched, talking of inconsequential things, but drawing conclusions that would have profound consequences on both their lives.

They were almost immediately at ease with each other, but it went deeper than that. Ruth had been looking for a mother all her life; Nona hungered for a return of youth and vitality in her life.

To Ruth, Nona was a wish granted. She had imagined a woman like this, or known her in another life, or known she was to meet her in this life, or something. Nona was a mother—that combination of guidance and support, of standards and of unswerving love.

Ruth, to Nona, seemed fresh and fragile. And very much in need of her. Nona was drawn by her need.

Two lonely women felt pulled to each other—and they had a common bond: Bruno.

When Bruno returned on Friday, the three of them shared a delightful American meal. Ruth was astonished by Nona's pork and sauerkraut and mashed potatoes: "Anyone who can cook American this well has to be dynamite cooking Italian!"

Bruno basked in the warmth between the women, while they both waited on him by turns. Bruno and Ruth had brought their party clothes along, and all three showered and dressed for the evening out. It was Friday, and Nona's Friday night bridge group was meeting as usual—except that those four women in their sixties had decided to have a slumber party in honor of the New Year. Ruth thought they sounded like a rare and lively breed.

Bruno and Ruth were a little late to Sally and Nick's; people were just lining up for the buffet supper. Afterward, chairs were pushed back and rugs rolled aside for dancing. Around eleven, in the middle of a slow dance, Bruno pulled Ruth close against him, his one leg extended between hers in what might have been a new dance step, but they both knew wasn't.

She hugged him hard and whispered in his ear, "Let's go."

Pretending to go to the kitchen for a drink, they sauntered casually from the room, sneaking out the back door and down to the ground floor on the service elevator. Hand and hand they ran to the car, jumped in, and sped away.

In Bruno's apartment they stood for a moment staring rather shyly at each other. Then, almost reverently, Bruno took her hand and led her to the bedroom door. She smiled and kissed him on the cheek: he had remembered to turn down the covers. Then she saw the jeweler's box on the pillow.

"Bruno." She almost resented that he had felt it necessary.

He tilted her chin up and said, "Ruth, I wanted to do it for you. I want it all to be right and good for you."

She was astonished, and a bit afraid, then, as he said, "Ruth, will you marry me?"

She kissed him full on the mouth, her hands moving slowly on his shoulders, as she answered, "I will."

He pushed her away gently. "Go open your present and see if you like it, while I get the wine I brought you from Naples." The ring was beautiful, and she knew that when he put it on her finger she would never take it off. It was a round diamond, not very big, set with a sapphire on one side and an emerald on the other. She knew without being told that this was a family heirloom. She stared down at it. . . .

"Oh, Tom. Does this mean you are out of my life forever? Marriage to Bruno seems to . . . cut you out. I want to marry him; I love him. But I couldn't accept the fact that I'll never see you again."

"Maybe it'll just be different, Ruth. Maybe there is a new way that we will find to show our love for each other. Marrying Bruno doesn't mean never seeing each other again. How could it? Nothing is impossible for a willing heart."

"Is he going to realize I'm not a virgin? What do you think he'll think?"

"Ruth! You are really underestimating this man. It is you he loves, not your virginity. He wants your love, Ruth. Give it to him. Your supply will never be depleted."

When Bruno walked back into the bedroom with the wine and two glasses, Ruth was sitting cross-legged on the bed, slowly revolving the ring to catch the light. She held it out in the palm of her hand. "I waited for you to put it on, please."

"Of course." He stared, as if stunned by the depth of his feeling for this woman. Then, as he slipped the ring on her finger, they kissed. He lay back on the pillows, pulling her on top of him, feasting his eyes on her.

"You are such a pretty little girl." He looked at her face but touched the blue wool covering her breasts.

"You are so good." She snuggled her cheek against his.

"I'll be good to you," he whispered in her ear.

She put her head up to look him in the eye. "I know. I love you, Bruno."

He smiled as she brought her lips down on his, her tongue tracing the outline of his mouth. As they kissed she felt his hands trailing the zipper down her back, and it felt so right to have him slip the dress off her shoulders. With her dress and slip, down around her waist, Bruno removed her bra, then pulled her up over him so that her breasts were aligned with his hungry mouth. She felt stirrings of maternal feelings she had never felt before, her breasts dangling, enticing, nourishing. He couldn't get his fill. He kissed and licked the smooth white skin, sucked on the nipples. His fingers kneaded and caressed and tickled.

Then he rolled her over in the bed and pulled her dress and slip off the rest of the way. Starting with her toes he kissed every inch of one leg with her stockings on. Then when he got to her waist, he pulled her panty hose down, then kissed every inch of the other leg.

When he stood up and started stripping off his own clothes, Ruth just lay on the bed, smiling. She felt content to the point of lethargy. She stretched out her arms, and as he got into bed, she opened her legs to envelop him. Without preamble he entered her moist, warm sanctuary and almost instantly found release.

For a short eternity they lay thus, his weight almost stealing the life from her, but she supported him physically as he had supported her emotionally for the last four months. Then he slipped off beside her, and his hand slid to the damp hair between her legs, and tirelessly he rubbed and coaxed until finally she groaned, "Yes, Bruno, yes. Right there." Lightning flashed from her center to the outer limits of her body, a delicious warmth stealing over her. She threw her body against him, and he held her as if he would never let her go.

Then his hands began moving over her back and buttocks. Finally she begged him to enter her again, and this time slowly, ever so slowly, he teased and taunted and explored. He didn't come again until he was sure the world had stopped and the stars had exploded for her. Much much later they got up and drank the forgotten wine, and he fed her cheese and crackers and prosciutto and ripe olives. Still later they went back to bed, and Bruno fell asleep cradling Ruth in his arms.

But it was a while before Ruth slept. First she had to ask T.J. one more question. He assured her that she was not being disloyal to him by loving Bruno, that, in fact, she had better love Bruno well and truly. Confident at last that T.J. understood and approved, she slept.

❧ 6 ❧

Christmas that year was particularly bad for Tom Jeffers. Northwestern University had invited him to lecture and critique a two-week pre-Christmas poetry workshop. Initially, he turned it down. He hated to leave Helen and Tommy alone the two weeks preceding Christmas. Then they offered him five thousand dollars for his services for those fourteen days. *That* he couldn't turn down. He had the strongest, most uncanny feeling that someday he was going to need all the money he could get his hands on. So he took off for Evanston, leaving his wife and son busy making Christmas cookies and wrapping presents.

Tuesday of the second week, during a lecture, he was called to the phone.

"Jeffers here."

"Tom? Bill Wallace." said the familiar tenor. He sounded like he was calling from next door.

Bill Wallace was Tommy's doctor, but he was also a good friend of long standing. "Bill! Are you in Chicago?" Tom was pleased to hear from him.

"No. Tom, listen. Helen didn't want me to call"—Tom's panic buttons sounded the alarm—"but I really think you should be here. Has she talked to you at all?"

Tom's sweat glands started producing their salty secretion, and he turned his back to the open office door. He was staring at a poster of a cat, dangling precariously by its claws from a windowsill. The poster read: "Hang in there, baby." Tom answered Bill's question. "I haven't talked to her for a couple of days, Bill. What happened? Last I knew he had a cold."

"We brought him in yesterday. It's a very bad case of

pneumonia. I'm sorry, Tom, but it's *very* bad—I mean touch and go. We've got him on respirators and drugs, but so far his body is not responding. I'm so sorry, Tom. And I hated going over Helen's head—but she is not acting like herself at all." There was an awkward pause. "I'm afraid, Tom, that this has been the last straw for her. She is held together by the thinnest thread right now."

"It's my fault, Bill." His right hand clenched into a fist that silently pounded the wall. "I shouldn't have accepted this workshop—I've felt her falling apart."

"Tom!" The doctor was exasperated. "It's nobody's fault, for Christ's sake." Calm Bill Wallace was practically shouting. "Listen, if you're just going to join your wife on a guilt trip, you can stay in Chicago. I need some help around here, not another walking zombie in sackcloth and ashes."

Tom was about to start yelling back, when he had a flash of his usual sensitivity. He laughed, instead, pleasing Bill Wallace no end. "Okay, your shock tactics worked. I'll be home on the next plane. And thanks, Bill. I'm sure Helen would have collapsed long ago if it hadn't been for you. I'll see you tonight or in the morning at the hospital." He hung up the phone and sank down in the desk chair, closing his eyes, thinking.

Home. Buffalo, New York. He had spent fifteen years of his life in Buffalo, New York. Why? Buffalo had a good, non-live-in school for children like Tommy. He didn't mind—it was as good a reason as any for where to live. They had a lovely home, set on a hill, a long winding driveway, guaranteeing seclusion. It was safe for Tommy, who could feel free without being in danger, particularly of jeers and sneers. And now the boy was lying in a hospital bed, scarcely breathing. Tom ran a hand through his curly hair.

I will never comprehend the way these things happen. One minute everything is fine, and the next minute the roof falls in. One minute all is blah, and the next minute something so wonderful happens that you can hardly bear it. Such as meeting Ruth. . . . Where are you, Ruth Tyack? What are you doing? Have you forgotten? A year and a half! It seems forever. I wish you were here so I could bury my face in your beautiful breasts and sob like a baby. He passed a hand across his eyes and found them actually wet. *Instead, I'll go explain why I'm leaving the workshop*.

Six hours later he was walking into Buffalo's famous Children's Hospital. He felt he had steeled himself for what lay ahead, but he was wrong. He was totally unprepared.

When he entered the room, he found a bleached-out-looking Tommy asleep in an oxygen tent, monitoring systems humming and beeping gently in the background. Helen was asleep, too, her head on the bed, one arm draped over Tommy's feet. He stood for a moment looking at them, trying to shift gears. A few hours ago he had been the expert—126 pairs of eyes and ears were attuned to every nuance of his speech and gesture. Now he was helpless—his son's life on the line, his wife's sanity in doubt. Tom went up behind Helen and gently put his arms around her shoulders. She bolted upright in her chair, crashing the hard top of her head into his not so hard chin.

"Jesus," he mumbled, cupping his chin with both his hands.

She swung around and focused her eyes on him. He was struck dumb by the hate he saw emanating from her fixed glaze.

"Get out," she hissed like a cornered cat.

A violent shiver ran through his body; he took a step backward.

"How dare you come in here? How dare you come be the savior again?" Her voice was low and loaded. "You think he's going to get better now that his dear daddy is here. Well, I have news for you. I killed him. Do you hear me? I killed him!"

He was shocked and appalled, but not so much so that he didn't realize that they needed to get out of Tommy's room—fast. He kept walking backward, heading for the door. She followed, dogging his steps.

"You bastard." He had never heard her swear before—in almost twenty years of marriage she had never even said damn. "You despicable bastard. Come to forgive me, have you? Just like you've been forgiving me for the last eighteen years. Well, I don't want it. Understand? I don't want your generous forgiveness." She was a snake writhing after him, slithering, attacking with poisoned tongue that darted in and out.

By now they were in the hall. For that he was grateful. Thank God that if Tommy was conscious at least he wouldn't hear "Mommy mad." Those were always Tommy's words for it, if and when Helen did raise her voice at either of them.

The nurse from the station was watching them now. Tom had talked to her just a few minutes before to get the late reports and the number of Tommy's room. Dr. Wallace had left word that Tom was to be expected. Now the nurse watched in amazement as his wife rounded on him. Helen gestured violently, leaning forward, a wild animal on the attack.

"I hate you, Mister Poet Jeffers. Is that clear enough for you? Will you please leave my monster son and me alone to die in peace? Go back to your normal people, and don't you ever mouth your hypocrisies at me again. We both know damn well why Tommy is like he is. We both know damn well whose fault it is. I did this to him. And I'm fed up with you being brave about it. I've had it with your patience. You don't love him. No one could love him." He had watched the nurse move around behind them, and now he breathed a sigh of relief as she closed the door to Tommy's room.

"I don't love him," Helen continued. "I've never seen such an unlovable freak in all my life." He saw the nurse run soundlessly back to the nurses' station and lift the phone. He prayed she was calling for help. He was totally incapacitated by the depth and dimension of Helen's hate. All he could do was stand there and watch twenty years of his life blow up in his face.

Helen pinned him against a wall and started punctuating her speech with slaps at his arms and chest. He just stood there, arms at his sides; he had neither the strength nor the desire to fend her off. Every once in a while he would murmur, "Helen." She seemed not to hear.

Another nurse came running soundlessly around the corner, a doctor at her side. The second nurse walked into the station and apparently started watching the monitors. The first nurse and the doctor walked up behind Helen. The nurse had a pad of paper in her hand and a Magic Marker. On it she quickly wrote in heavy black strokes, "She have doctor?" It took a minute before she was able to get Tom's attention, and then he just nodded. "Who?" she scribbled. After a bit Tom unobtrusively splayed his fingers to show the number eight. Sally Maye Floyd tried to think as quickly as she could. He couldn't know the doctor's call numbers. There was no eighth floor on the hospital. She thought perhaps he meant a telephone number beginning with the number 8. And then it came to her: the eighth letter of the alphabet. She turned the tablet over and wrote a big H. After a minute, without ever seeming to look at the tablet, Tom solemnly nodded his head. Her mind raced as she tried to think of the doctors whose names began with H. She thought of Hayworth, an obstetrician, but when she wrote it down, the man jerked his head to the side. The doctor standing beside her, seeing what she was doing, whispered "Holmes," the name of a staff psychiatrist. She wrote it down, and they received an affirmative nod. "Bring along ten milligrams of Valium," the doctor whispered. The nurse raced off to the station. Young Dr. Williams stood watching, appalled, helplessly listening.

The nurse raced back holding a hypo, and in the background they heard "Dr. Holmes, paging Dr. Holmes—red alert, on five. Please respond immediately, Dr. Holmes. Dr. Holmes, red alert on five."

Helen was as unaware of the paging as she was of what was going on around her. A third nurse had appeared and was walking quickly down the hall, closing the doors of patients' rooms. The doctor standing behind Helen had held up the hypo for Tom to see but had received a negative shake of the head. So they waited. And she recounted every time Tom had failed to take out the garbage and every time he had been impotent. She pounded on his chest and arms as she named the cities where Tom had spoken or read his poetry when she hadn't gone along. She scratched his face as she named women with whom she suspected he had had affairs. And she stomped her feet while explaining to him that that dumb retard lying in there wasn't even *his son*.

Twenty minutes too late Dr. Holmes rounded the corner. He stood and observed Helen for only a few seconds before he called out, "Stretcher—restrainers." Walking up behind Helen, he firmly took her arm. She turned violently into him, slapping him with her free hand. Then she focused on him and screamed, "And you! You think I'm crazy!"

He didn't even try to talk to her. Over her shoulder he said to Dr. Williams, standing beside him, "What's in that?"

"Ten milligrams of Valium."

"In the arm I'm holding, please. Nurse, help keep this arm immobile." Sally Maye leaned her healthy, country-girl hip into the side of Helen's thin frame. Doctor and nurse trapped her body between them. All the while Helen screamed abuse and fought and kicked. But Dr. Williams had heard enough, and he rammed the needle home, none too gently.

By this time an orderly was hurrying down the hall with a stretcher. The drug took almost immediate effect, and Helen had stopped kicking by the time Drs. Williams and Holmes lifted her onto the stretcher. The orderly fastened the restraints. As he wheeled her away, Dr. Holmes walked alongside, talking quietly to her and holding her hand. But he called over his shoulder, "I'll be back, Tom."

They had forgotten about Tom. He had simply slid down the wall and was sitting in a crumpled heap on the floor, arms hugging himself, face bleeding. He was shivering convulsively, and both Williams and Sally Maye correctly surmised he was in shock. They each took an arm to lift him, and Sally Maye suggested, "Staff kitchen."

When they got there, Dr. Williams left to get some more Valium. Sally Maye sat Tom down in a chair at the table and then watched as his head fell forward on his arms and he sat deadly still. Tentatively she did the only thing she could think to do: she leaned over him and put her arms around him, holding him securely. After a minute or so of this position, her back felt like it was breaking, but she could feel him beginning to relax, so she tightened her hold, increasing the warmth. She was beginning to think she would have to walk stooped over for the rest of her life, but he finally grunted. She loosened her grasp to see what he was trying to say, and he pulled her around in front of him, unceremoniously yanking her down on his lap, burying his face against her chest. Once again she held on tightly. It was the least sexual embrace in which she had ever participated. It was also the best.

Dr. Williams stuck his head in the door, saw them holding each other, heard her murmuring softly to him, and retreated. For almost ten minutes he stood watch at the door, making sure no one stumbled in on them. Sally Maye sat on Tom's lap, stroking his back, his head, until she could feel the tension easing. She felt him sigh, so she gently pulled his face up with her hands and said, "If I don't soon get my one hundred and fifty pounds off your lap, you'll never walk again." She was relieved to see that he was able to give her a crooked smile before he noticed the blood all over the front of her uniform. Surprised, he reached his hands up to his face and felt the mutilated skin.

Sally Maye pulled his face back again for another instant, a last hug. Then she got to her feet and went across to the sink to get a wet washcloth.

"Here. Just hold this to your face while I get some antiseptic."

She walked out, crashing into Dr. Williams. They nodded solemnly to each other, the changing of the guard, and she walked down to the nurses station while he went in with some elixir of Phenobarbital. Sally Maye returned as Dr. Williams was trying to persuade Tom to drink it. When she looked him in the eye and said, "Yes, please, Dr. Jeffers," he nodded his head in acceptance. Sally Maye set down a cup of sweet black coffee and smiled at him encouragingly to drink that, too. Tom obligingly took a big sip and choked on it.

"It's so sweet."

"Sugar for shock," Sally Maye explained.

"Shock." He tested the word. "Yes. Shock."

"She's never done anything like this before?" Dr. Williams asked curiously. He had just sat down at the table as had Sally Maye. She immediately kicked him—hard. He mumbled under his breath and looked at her, annoyed, but she was talking to Dr. Jeffers.

"I've heard you're a poet. You just came back from a lecture or something, right?"

"Yeah. Chicago. I was giving a seminar in Chicago; Bill Wallace called this afternoon."

"Would you like to stay at the hospital tonight to be with Tommy?" Sally Maye asked. She wanted to get him talking and thinking about the future instead of simply reliving the dreadful last hour.

"Could I do that?" He looked up at the chubby, brown-haired young woman as if she were an angel. "Could I stay here with Tommy? I'd be glad to just sit in the chair in his room."

"Oh, I think we can find a cot somewhere." She smiled warmly at him. "I'm sure it won't be comfortable, but maybe just for a night or two until Tommy gets out of the woods."

"You think he's going to get better?" Tom desperately needed some reassurance.

"Oh, yes, I really do," she nodded confidently. "Children have such a marvelous ability to bounce back."

Dr. Williams listened, amazed at the rapport between the scholar and this plain, little hillbilly, and the devil made him want to show her up. "You mean resilience."

She just smiled at him, deflating him.

"Tom, there you are!" Dr. Holmes burst through the door and sat down at the table with Tom, Sally Maye, and Dr. Williams.

"Dr. Holmes," Sally Maye said quickly, "Dr. Jeffers has had some phenobarb and a cup of sweet black coffee. Now Dr. Williams and I will go see about a cot so he can stay with his son for the night."

She stood up and glared at Fred Williams until, reluctantly, he followed her out the door, carefully closing it behind him. They could hear Dr. Holmes saying, "My God, Tom, I am so sorry."

Sally Maye tried to rush down the hall, but Fred Williams caught her arm and demanded, "Who put you in charge all of a sudden?"

"Dr. Williams"—she looked up at him like a wounded puppy—"I apologize. I don't know what made me take over like that. It was just as if I knew exactly what he needed."

Tall, gaunt Fred Williams looked down his aristocratic nose at the West Virginia farmgirl and found it impossible to be angry. He was only an intern, but he had learned that sometimes the best medicine is compassion—that there is no substitute for emotional support—and Sally Maye had offered that.

"Okay, West Virginia, let's go get that cot set up. Jeffers shouldn't be on his feet much longer, once the phenobarb starts its work."

Together, wordlessly, they set up the cot, got some bedding arranged, and then went back to the staff kitchen. Tom Jeffers was asleep, his head on his arms. Dr. Holmes was sitting beside him, lost in thought. The two doctors half carried, half walked Tom across to Tommy's room. When they left, having removed his shoes and thrown a blanket over him, Sally Maye went into the room, wrestled him out of his pants and shirt, and tucked him tightly into a cocoon of bedding. Then she kissed him on the forehead and tiptoed out.

For the next nine days Tom left the hospital only once a day for less than an hour each time, making the trip to the empty house to shave and change his clothes. Otherwise, he sat at Tommy's bedside or slept in the cot. For hours every day Tom talked to the boy, telling him and retelling him his favorite stories, detailing what fun they would have in the future, reliving aloud the various adventures they had had in the past. The morning of the ninth day Tommy's fever broke, and once his temperature was stabilized, everything else seemed to follow—the fluid drained from his lungs, his head stopped hurting, his appetite returned, and his energy came flooding back with the regeneration of youth.

Helen had been moved from the hospital to the Bethel Hope Nursing Home. Since coming out of the tranquilizing drug, she had not spoken or eaten. Every day she seemed to sink further into herself. Dr. Holmes was not encouraged and was not encouraging to Tom. He felt it was a self-induced state of retreat, and he was not hopeful that they would be able to do anything to pull her out of it. She had decided to give up. They were keeping her alive by intravenous feedings and constant surveillance. She herself showed no will to live.

There was only one bright spot in the traumatic days that followed Tom's return from Chicago: Sally Maye. Every evening she came to collect him from Tommy's room and lead him down to supper. She picked out what he would eat and cajoled him into eating it. At night, before she went home, she brought him a glass of milk, spiked the first two nights with chlorohydrate. She rewarded him for drinking it by giving him a back rub. Then she would somehow talk him into lying down on the cot "for a few minutes." He would awaken the next morning.

They talked. Sally Maye had seen him emotionally naked, and so there was no sense in his holding back anything. He recounted the years of marriage and Helen's deterioration. He told her about his love for, his appreciation of Tommy. He even talked about Ruth.

Later he asked, "What's a nice West Virginia girl like you doing way up north here?" So Sally Maye told him about her daddy dying of black lung disease and she and her mom just heading off on the first bus.

Sixteen days after The Scene, as he came to think of it, Tom was able to take Tommy home.

"Where's mommy?"

Until they walked in the door of the house, Tommy had said nothing about her, almost as if he weren't surprised to have only Tom visiting and sitting by his bed.

"Mommy's in the hospital." Tom busied himself putting their jackets away in the hall closet. "Remember how you were sick and Dr. Wallace put you in the hospital and gave you that nice bed and took real good care of you? Well, that happened to mommy, too."

Tommy, 5'8", 130 pounds, stared at Tom with Helen's clear brown eyes. You could almost see his brain working, trying to absorb and sort the data.

"Did I make mommy sick? Did she catch my cold?" His voice broke with concern.

"No, son. She has something very different wrong with her," Tom explained soothingly.

"She's not neezing?" Tommy asked, kicking off his boots.

"No, son, she's not sneezing."

"Oh, I'm glad she didn't get my cold. She told me not to neeze on her. But I did onest, by accident."

"It's okay, Tommy. I'm sure mommy didn't mind." Tom reassuringly placed an arm around Tommy's shoulder.

"No, she did," he contradicted. "She got real mad and wailed me."

"Well, she was getting sick herself and didn't feel good, Tommy. That's the only reason she spanked you, I'm sure."

They were standing in the hall, both of them immobilized by the lack of Helen to greet and direct them.

"Tommy," Tom said with artificial brightness, "now here's the plan." He gave his arm a squeeze. "We're going to go upstairs and have a little nap. When we wake up, what do you say we get out all the Fisher-Price toys and make a village?"

"Gee, dad, could we?" Making a village was a long, involved cluttery game that Helen detested. They took over the entire den floor with gas stations and hospitals and cars and trucks each performing specific duties, going special places.

"Yeah, Tommy, we really can. *If* you take a good nap first."

When Tommy looked disappointed, Tom tightened his arm around the boy and walked him up the steps saying, "How about if we lie down together?"

"Okay, daddy." Tommy's bright brown eyes glistened trustingly.

Side by side they walked into Helen's room, the only

double bed in the house. It was a relaxing room—beige and brown and serenely restful, just the way Tom had always pictured Helen. From opposite sides of the bed, they pulled down the spread and snuggled under the covers. Tommy fell asleep almost immediately. Tom lay still, trying to talk himself into getting up, but he didn't know what to do if he did get up, so he simply remained in bed.

Two hours later Tommy started tossing and turning, and Tom realized that at some point he, too, must have fallen asleep.

"Dad?"

"Hm?"

"Can we get up now and go play?"

"Sure thing, Tommy, but I think we better have some supper before we play, don't you think so?"

They each swung their feet over the side of the bed and sat up.

"Can we have hot dogs and milkshakes?"

"Hot dogs and milkshakes?" Tom stared at his son, pretending absorption in the menu, really engrossed with the phenomenon of this strange man-child. There he was, looking like he should be asking for the keys to the car and instead . . .

How am I going to deal with this? School starts next week! How am I going to teach and write and be a full-time single parent? I won't have anything left over for this child. Helen . . . what the hell happened? Will she ever come back? Could I face her if she did? Could anyone ever forget an assault like that?

"Daddy?" The brown eyes were puppy puzzled; Tommy patted Tom's arm.

"Tommy, do you know what? You are really a handsome boy."

"Handsome?" Tommy looked confused by the unfamiliar word.

"Pretty, Tommy," said Tom sadly; "you're a pretty boy." Tommy glowed at the compliment, and Tom reached out to give him a hug.

"Okay, sport, let's head for the kitchen." They set off

down the steps, two men in their stocking feet. Tom watched Tommy lead the way. He was so physically perfect, although slight and somewhat effeminate: he was gentle and childlike, his skin was smooth, translucent and pale. He trod loudly and energetically down the steps, and like a small child he tripped often and was klutzy. His brown hair was as straight as Helen's, not curly like Tom's. *"He's not your . . ."* Tom pushed away the vindictive echoes.

"Hot dogs and milkshakes, huh?" said the dad.

"Hot dogs and milkshakes!" replied the son, loving the game.

Tom found hot dogs and buns in the freezer. He put the frozen hot dogs in a pot, added water, and put them on the stove to cook. Then he opened the refrigerator. For the last sixteen days he had had nothing at home but a cup of instant coffee while he shaved, or a quick bourbon before heading back to the hospital. The refrigerator was littered with spoilage. Over two weeks since Tommy had gotten sick! Maybe longer. Helen had probably not paid any attention to the food situation once he was ill.

Tom opened the milk and cautiously sniffed. Overpoweringly sour. No doubt about the milk. Tom glanced over his shoulder and saw Tommy sitting expectantly at the kitchen table.

"Hey, Tommy, bring me a garbage bag." Tommy sprang happily out of his chair. "We have to get rid of this stuff. Some of this food spoiled while we were in the hospital."

Tommy walked over triumphantly with a brown grocery bag.

"No, son, a garbage bag—a plastic bag."

Tears immediately formed in his eyes, although Tom's voice hadn't been particularly harsh.

"I don't know where them are, daddy."

So Tom got up from his stooped inspection of the rot in the refrigerator and sought out the plastic bags. Then he had Tommy hold the bag while he filled it with a half head of spoiled cabbage, three rotten tomatoes, molded cheese, and bread. The milk had to go, as did the orange juice. The Kool-Aid and the iced tea went down the drain. The cottage cheese and the sour cream, black with fuzzy mold, went into Tommy's bag.

"Okay, Tommy, now you check and see if there is any ice cream in the freezer while I take this bag out to the garage."

When Tom returned, Tommy had removed from the freezer three TV dinners and two cans of orange juice.

"What are you doing?" Tom demanded.

Again the tears appeared. "I'm looking for the ice cream."

Tom sighed. *Oh, Lord. I'm never going to have the patience for this.* "Tommy, you don't have to take everything out to see if there is ice cream in here. Let me show you." He put his arm around the boy's shoulder and pulled him close. "Now, you just look from one shelf to the next. Start with the top shelf and see if you see a big rectangular box like an ice cream box. Do you see a box on the first shelf?"

It took the boy a long time before he said, "No."

"Good. Okay, now what about on the second shelf?"

Again the interminable wait. "No!" triumphantly.

"The third shelf, Tommy?"

Quickly, "Yes, daddy. It's on that one." He was so delighted with himself for this trivial achievement.

Tom removed the ice cream box and peered inside. It looked horrible, all grainy and congealed, as if someone had tried to freeze a flour and salt combination. "It's no good, Tommy. The ice cream's too old. And there's no milk. We'll have to have something else to drink, okay?"

Tommy tried to nod, but his lip was quivering. Everything was so different. In the hospital he got everything he wanted. And at home there was always mommy. Now she was in the hospital getting everything she wanted, and she hadn't even left him any ice cream.

"I've got it!" Tom knew he had to act fast to prevent a fall-apart. "What do you say we get bundled up and go down to the store and buy some new ice cream and some good, fresh milk and maybe even a surprise for Tommy—like some raisins or some oranges or something? How does that sound?"

"Could I have some balloons, daddy? Huh?" he asked with innocent enthusiasm.

"If we can find some." At that point Tom would gladly have promised him a new sled.

It was five-thirty. Dark in Buffalo. A ten-degree winter day.

Tom slipped on his ski jacket and went out to start the car. Then he came back into the house to help Tommy bundle up, and he buttoned his own coat more snugly and pulled on a hat. Thus armed, they set off for their adventure. He was pleased with himself that he even remembered to turn down the flame under the hot dogs. They would just whip out for some milk and ice cream; the hot dogs would be ready when they got back home.

Tom thought the Acme would be quickest, but it was closed. Surely the Dawn to Dusk store. It was closed, too. What the hell? Was this Sunday? He decided to get a paper and pulled into the parking lot of the L and K restaurant where he got a paper from the machine. "Jesus," Tom said aloud. "December thirty-first. Tonight is fucking New Year's Eve." He composed his face and plastered on a smile before he got back in the car. Tommy was chattering brightly, enjoying his ride, pleased to see something other than the walls of the hospital room.

Tom knew immediately where to go and headed for the Beer Drive-Thru. They had no ice cream, but they had something in a can that advertised itself as a milkshake. Tom bought two cans, as well as some Coke, some milk, and some ginger ale. Much to Tommy's delight the Beer Drive-Thru, on their party rack, displayed balloons. Tom bought one pack of each of the three sizes available.

They drove back to their house, and father and son sat in the kitchen, each eating their hot dogs and drinking their milkshakes from a can. Tom turned on Helen's little kitchen TV—Helen's—and he and Tommy broke one of the cardinal rules of the house: they watched TV while they ate. Tommy was enthralled with this new treat. The local station played Tom and Jerry reruns over the dinner hour, and they laughed together.

"Now can we make the village, daddy?" Tommy asked

as the mouse triumphantly grinned the conclusion of the show.

"Sure, son."

Tom was more than ready to get out of Helen's green and white kitchen. He had never realized before how sterile it was—such a cold room. How could he not have noticed sooner?

"Daddy, look!" Tommy called from the den. Tom rushed in. There in a corner of the room was a huge stack of presents. Huge! *Christmas. My God, we missed Christmas. Last weekend was Christmas.*

"Daddy, can I open them? I know which ones are for me. Can I open them, huh, can I, daddy, huh, can I open my presents now? Oh, boy! This is really neat. Huh, can I, daddy?"

Tommy was trying to break through, but Tom just stood, cemented to the entranceway of the den, unable to fathom the fact that Christmas had come and gone and he had not even realized it. He had heard people saying "Merry Christmas" in the hospital, but it just hadn't sunk in. Christmas. Helen had done all this, and now she was gone. Maybe forever. The horror of it hit him, and he started shivering. He slipped down the door frame and sat on the floor, face devoid of expression, mind refusing to function. He simply couldn't grasp it.

He didn't know how long he sat there shaking before he was aware of the hand gently patting his arm, the small voice softly saying, "It's all right, daddy. We're going to have lots of fun. We'll go on picnics and walks, and we'll find some new playgrounds. We may even go to a new place to live, a place by the big water, maybe." The voice went on gently, the boy caressing Tom as Tom had caressed the boy. All the love and hope that Tom had spoken, Tommy now returned, multiplied. It was hard to know who comforted who. When Tom pulled Tommy's head down on his lap, the young voice continued its soft recital while the strong father-hands stroked silken brown hair.

"We will, Tommy, we'll do all of those things. But we can't move until this summer. You and I have to finish school, okay? Then this summer we'll see about moving."

Tom got out his handkerchief and dried both wet faces. "Now, what do you say we open a few of those presents? You find four that are for you, and you may open them tonight. The rest we'll save for another time." Tommy opened an artist's tablet and chalk set, a Parcheesi game, a pair of brown boots lined in white fur, and some blue-striped flannel pajamas. Wearing the pajamas and boots, Tommy played three games of Parcheesi with Tom, who finally managed to maneuver a win for the boy on the third game. Then they filled ten sheets of the artist's paper with their renditions of suns, moons, trees, houses, horses, dogs, racing cars, and stick people. Finally Tom made some hot chocolate, gave Tommy his medicine, and put him to bed.

When he walked back into the den, it was ten o'clock and he decided to do something immediately about that stack of presents. So he sorted out all the ones for Tommy and put them under the glass-topped coffee table. Tommy could open one a day until they ran out. Then he went through the rest. There were presents for grandparents (who lived in Florida) and presents for neighbors and presents for babysitters and presents for milkmen and mailmen, and finally there was one present for him: a new thesaurus. A new thesaurus! He couldn't believe it. There must have been four hundred dollars worth of stuff in that pile, and she had spent only ten or so on him for a new thesaurus. Not even a tie or a shirt. A new thesaurus—as if his language weren't already his best feature. His head hurt. He grabbed the non-Tommy presents and stacked them on the top shelf of the hall closet. Then he telephoned his parents in Florida to try to explain what had happened. They were nice, ever-kind, but detached. They had been this way ever since moving, ten years ago, from Syracuse to Sarasota. Once they were living in the constant sunshine, all aspects of their former life seemed to become unrealistic—even their only son had lost his prominence.

When the polite and impersonal call was over, Tom sat staring at the phone. There was no one to call for Helen—except Janice. No parents, no brothers or sisters, no family at all, just the one good friend. He dialed Janice's number. A strange woman answered, and he heard the sounds of a party in the background. He hung up.

Fucking New Year's Eve. He had forgotten again. Stupidest holiday of the year. Even Halloween seemed sane and well-thought-out by comparison.

He went out to the kitchen and fixed himself a large bourbon and ginger. Returning to the den he put a Cat Stevens record on the stereo and read the paper and two old *Time* magazines from cover to cover. He was just coming downstairs from checking on Tommy—the thought of going to bed was repulsive—when he heard a gentle knock on the door.

He opened it to Sally Maye, resplendent in white uniform and winter-chilled cheeks, a bottle of Chianti in her hand.

They just smiled at each other, and then she rushed in out of the cold. He closed the door and turned around to lean against it. She had taken him quite by surprise. They had said goodbye just last night, and now here she stood.

"My date for the evening got summoned to emergency surgery, and I found myself with a bottle of wine and no corkscrew."

"And you knew I'd be depressed as hell to be here in an empty house with a sick child and no one to hold my hand on New Year's Eve."

She blushed.

"Sally Maye." He put his arms on her shoulders, "Get the hell out of here."

She just stared at him, a slight smile on her lips, and then she ducked out from under his hands, set down the bottle of wine on the hall table, and slipped off her coat, throwing it on the nearby chair. She held out her hand. Tom just looked at her. Did she have any idea what she was doing?

She smiled again. "Come on," she said silkily.

He went.

She could tell from the lights which room he had been in, and she led him back to the den, sitting at the end of the sofa, pulling him down so his head rested in her lap. She got him talking. He listed the shocks and frustrations of the evening. They opened her wine and drained the bottle, both talking now, pouring out hurts and sorrows with the grape nectar.

"Could you light me a fire?"

Her question took him by surprise. "Sure."

"Okay. You light a fire, and I'll go check Tommy." She was gone.

A full ten minutes later she came back, wearing an old robe of Tom's, carrying two quilts. He stared at her from his chair by the fire.

"I thought we could relax here by the fire for a little bit."

He was instantly serious, felt incredibly old. "Sally Maye, listen to me for a minute!"

"No. You listen to me. We are just passing through each other's lives. I know that. I understand that. I accept that. I want nothing from you, Tom Jeffers, except a return of the comfort and the friendship that I am offering you. I have no expectations. I want no commitments. This is just for now. So, lie down and I'll give you a back rub."

"Sally Maye, I can't take another thing from you. I've taken too much already. You are a marvelously sensitive, giving girl. I feel like I'm using you."

"Okay, you give me a back rub." She spread out the quilts and lay down on the double thickness of blanket, face turned toward the fire, eyes shut.

After a minute of hesitation, Tom sat down beside her and began fumblingly rubbing her back.

"Wait." She sat up and shrugged herself out of the robe, the whole thing riding along her waist, then lay back down. The play of firelight on her skin was fascinating to Tom, totally seductive. His hands were on her sides and on her buttocks and soon, despite his resolve, he had rolled her over, all semblance of a back rub forgotten. He lost himself in her body. He never even got his pants off. She simply unzipped his zipper and pulled him inside her, and he came. It was so basic. So humanly basic and necessary. He couldn't keep his hands off her body, and for an hour he rubbed her here and kissed her there, and like a contented kitten she lay and purred. He fell asleep, one hand between her legs.

When he awoke he was under a blanket, the fire had died, and Sally Maye had gone. On his way up to bed he found the note on the hall table:

Dear Tom:
   Thank you for all the fires you lit. I'll be back.
                                              S.M.

The bedside clock said 5:23 when he crawled under the covers. In no time at all the electric blanket had him toasty warm, but he was deeply asleep.

Mrs. Mott was the first person to answer Tom's ad for a housekeeper/babysitter. He hired her on the spot because she came from Pittsburgh and she had "kind" white hair. It was almost a month later when his suspicions were confirmed that he had made a sad mistake. It was nothing obvious, nothing overt; rather, it was subtle and insidious. Mrs. Mott was condescending; she treated Tommy as though he were helpless. Throughout the month Tom noticed Tommy doing less and less. It wasn't that Mrs. Mott said to the boy, "You can't do that." That might have brought Tommy's back up, and he might have tried harder. Rather her harmful, well-meaning approach was, "Here, sweetheart, let me do that for you." Or, "No, no, darling, this is the way we color." Or, "Now don't wander around alone outside. We wouldn't want anything to happen to our sweet Tommy."

Tom watched and listened for a few days after he had first begun to realize what was happening: he wanted to be very sure before he took any action. Mrs. Mott was a nice woman, and Tom guessed that this was merely her way. She would do whatever she could for whomever she could. For Tommy, Tom thought, that was very bad. Tommy was easily discouraged, easily intimidated, and thanks to Helen's eighteen years of martyrdom, he was happy to sit around and be waited on.

Tom took the coward's way out.

"Mrs. Mott," he said on the last Friday night in January, "I have just had good news in this morning's mail, but I'm afraid it is news that puts you out of a job. A dear friend of my wife's and mine, a cousin of ours, in fact, is coming on a prolonged visit to take care of Tommy and me. I want to give you two weeks extra pay, of course, and this afternoon, after I read the mail, I wrote up this recommendation for you, which I'm sure will help you to find another position quickly."

"Why, Dr. Jeffers, I'm shocked, just plain shocked. Naturally I'm very happy for you and Tommy that there will be someone here with you, but I had grown quite fond, quite fond of Tommy. Such a dear, sweet little thing he is. I was quite happy taking care of him and shall miss him sorely. I just had no idea. Well, but then neither did you, or you would have warned me, I'm sure. But I'm quite sad and shocked."

And on she went, quite on, and Tom quite let her go and also quite got her out of the house. "It really would be better if you didn't say goodbye to Tommy. I know you'd like to, but these transitions in life are so hard for him to cope with, it would be in his best interests. You do understand, Mrs. Mott."

"Quite."

Later that evening, after he and Tommy had played five games of Candyland, Tom wrote a funny little poem entitled "Quite." If Mrs. Mott ever read it, she would surely recognize herself, but then the chances of Mrs. Mott reading his poetry were slim, at best. Quite slim.

Sally Maye had been coming once a week and hadn't come this week, yet, and so Tom stayed up and kept the lights burning. By eleven-thirty, she still hadn't arrived, and he tried not to feel hurt that she had apparently forgotten him. Then there she was. He opened the door and gathered her into his arms in one continuous motion. He lifted her off the ground with the embrace, and as she slid back down to earth, the slow, strong friction of their bodies worked the ancient sexual magic. Their mouths met, open and hot and wet, and he pulled off her coat, and it dropped to the floor, as did her purse. Still kissing, trying to keep their bodies together and walk at the same time, they stumbled into the den. Tom closed the door and locked it—they were ever conscious of Tommy sleeping upstairs—and they fell to the floor before the roaring fire and devoured each other.

They had been together four or five times before, and it had been straight and basic and warm and comfortable. Tonight, they tried everything they could think of, and they tried two things Tom had never heard of. He discovered a shockingly delightful new fact: Sally Maye loved to fuck. There was just no other word for it—Sally Maye and screwing were meant to go together. Apparently Sally Maye had just been waiting to be swept off her feet, because all of a sudden it was there. There was nothing maternal about her tonight.

He had never learned so much so quickly with so much pleasure. If all teachers could teach like this. . . . She was in charge, she was the coach calling the plays—and they were varied and imaginative and exciting. With hands and mouth and hair and toes and shimmering, fire-kissed skin, she awoke in him nerve endings and muscles, sensations and feelings, he had not known existed. With hands and mouth and legs and head she maneuvered him from one position to the next, and his common sense and imagination took care of the rest. Under his arms, behind her knees, within her hair, at the base of his back. . . . His mind was whirling, he felt like he'd been electrocuted—he pictured himself the cat on the cartoon who had just touched the live wire. He was so loose, fluid, floating. He was at the same time ice and steam, and all he could hope was the right parts were ice and the right parts were steam at the right times.

Around four in the morning, one body rolled off the other and sighed, and Tom realized he missed the warm, wet receptacle that had pillowed and cushioned his head. His tongue was so swollen and tired he didn't think he could talk, so he just groaned. She sat up, completely refreshed and full of vitality, then rolled him on his back and straddled his body, aligning pelvises. She took her weight on her own knees but playfully rubbed herself over him. "Think you can get it up again?" she asked, as she might have asked if he wanted a second helping of beef stew.

He opened his eyes the tiniest bit and groaned again. Voice slurred, drunken, he rasped, "I don't think I'll ever get it up again in my whole life."

"Nonsense," she said, in her best nurse voice. "We aren't feeling tired today, are we, Dr. Jeffers? Come, come, we are only as impotent as we think we are."

"Impotent!" he shouted as he tumbled her off his stomach and rolled her over pinning her to the ground, body trapping body. "Impotent!" And then he collapsed on top of her, laughing, "You bet your sweet ass I'm impotent. You just got all I had to give for the rest of my life. That was my quotient for the next twenty years—squandered, used up by a sex-starved, insatiable"—his voice changed—"sensitive, all-knowing, healing, loving friend. You are really beautiful, do you know that?" Gray eyes spoke through brown eyes, soul to soul. "You are so good for me. Just what the doctor ordered." He was holding her head in his hands, gazing down at her in gratitude.

"That was just some of the loving you've been storing up for the last twenty years," she said gently. "You're a passionate person who has been living a nonpassionate existence. I was just lucky enough to come along at a time when we both needed a loving, passionate friend. But now I'm cold. Let's get dressed and have a drink."

He leaned down and kissed her with all the sweetness and tenderness that lay in his heart, and then they got dressed, talking all the while, and she went to fix a pot of coffee while he stoked the fire.

When Tommy came downstairs at seven the next morning, he heard voices and rushed into the kitchen calling, "Mommy, mommy." He stopped dead in his tracks when he realized it was the nurse he called Sam instead of Mommy. She was standing at the stove, pouring more coffee for Tom. She pretended not to notice the tears well up in his eyes. She calmly walked over to him, ruffled his hair, gave him a hug and a kiss on the forehead, and said, "You look to me like a boy who would like to have some waffles for breakfast, is that right?"

"Sure," rather unenthusiastically. "I'll go watch cartoons until they're ready."

"Tommy," Tom called out to him, voice tight. But just as he was about to reprimand Tommy for his lack of manners, he saw Sally Maye shaking her head. He decided probably she was right, so he said instead, "I'll be in in a minute to watch with you."

Tommy smiled for the first time that morning. "Okay, daddy."

As he walked away Sally Maye said softly, "It was a shock for him, Tom."

"Yeah, you're right. He's going to have another shock, too." He told her about Mrs. Mott and the reasons why he felt he had to fire her. Sally Maye set the coffee down on the table before Tom and then went to the counter to start the waffles.

"You know, I think I have just the person for you. You want someone who will encourage Tommy to the point of pushing him, right? To get him to do everything he's capable of?"

"Exactly. I never realized before what an injustice Helen did him, by doing so much for him. I'm sure he's competent to do much more than he's doing now."

"I agree. I think he should be stimulated and encouraged. I should probably have him out here making his own waffles." She smiled at Tom over her shoulder.

"Do you know of someone who might be interested in this kind of work? What I need is someone who can be here when Tommy comes home from school, stay with him and make some kind of supper, if possible. But I'm much more interested in the taking care of Tommy than I am in any housework or cooking or anything."

"What time does he get home from school?"

"Four o'clock—sometimes five before or five after, but around four."

"Do you trust my judgment to find someone for you?"

"Absolutely."

"Oh, damn." Sally Maye had been turning around to talk with Tom and trying to make the waffle batter at the same time, and she had managed to miss the dish with her cracked egg.

Tom, enjoying seeing a woman do something klutzy in the kitchen, immediately started to laugh. Sally Maye looked at him so indignantly that he laughed even harder, and then to the amazement of them both, she scooped the egg off the counter and threw it at him. She was aiming for his face, but it landed squarely in his lap, which sobered him immediately. Then *she* started laughing at the strange sight of a spreading yellow stain in the middle front of his pants.

The irate teacher ordered, "You better come over here and tell me you're sorry." Meekly, trustingly, she bent over him to kiss him sorry. Even when she felt his hand pulling on her panties, she trusted him. Then she felt his other hand run down over her backside, leaving a film of egg behind it, and she opened her mouth wide and drove her tongue deeply into his mouth. She lost her balance, ending up straddling his legs, his hand still in her pants, both of them barely conscious of anything except the strong sexual pull that made them want to continue what they had started. But something snapped in Sally Maye's mind, and she practically leaped off his lap.

Then she leaned over for a last sweet kiss. "God, I never knew eggs were so damn sexy."

"Me, either." His eyes had a sensual film.

"Actually it feels fantastic now, but by the time I get these waffles made, it'll be hard to navigate."

Tom walked up behind her and patted her on the egg. "You go on up and take a shower. I'm perfectly capable of making us all some waffles for breakfast. Just throw a dry pair of pants down the steps for me, please."

"Okay." She smiled and set down the other egg she was about to break into the dish of dry ingredients. "Add the egg and a cup and a half of milk to that—and you've got it."

He heard her prance up the steps, then heard the soft thud of his pants. Once the restraint of the drying egg had been removed from his crotch, he burst into action, starting a fresh pot of coffee, setting the table in the kitchen, getting the waffles underway, putting some frozen blueberries under the cold running water in the strainer, frying some bacon. Sally Maye returned to the beautiful picture of Tommy carefully carrying the dishes of blueberries topped with ice cream across to the table and Tom singing as he drained the bacon.

Breakfast was fun, both adults feeling so good about themselves that they could devote their energies to helping Tommy feel good about himself. Sally Maye left after breakfast, and they didn't see her for the rest of the weekend. But Tom had given her a spare key to the back door, and she had promised that she would have someone there Monday when Tommy came home from school. She called Sunday night to tell Tom that everything had worked out perfectly: a young woman with a nursing background and a healthy philosophy about "special children" would be waiting when Tommy got off the bus on Monday.

Trusting her, Tom arrived home around quarter of six Monday night and walked in the house. Sally Maye answered his hello with "We're in the kitchen."

"Hi, you two." Tom walked in, found them at the kitchen table playing cards, leaned over to give each of them a kiss on the head, Tommy first, and then demanded, "What happened, couldn't she come?"

"She's here. Me. I was going on days today anyhow, so I figured it would work out perfectly. I have no ties. If you have a business trip or anything, I can stay overnight. I'm a nurse, was Tommy's nurse, who's to question that? Normally, I go home after supper or when Tommy's in bed, unless you have a meeting at night or something. Okay?"

"Sally Maye..."

"You are dripping all over the kitchen floor! Will you please go get those wet things off and come take my rummy hand so I can finish supper." She nodded her head in Tommy's direction, as if to say, "We'll talk about this later."

They had a happy, playful night. It was clear Tommy

had chosen the menu—spaghetti, applesauce, and chocolate cake—in much the same way that he chose the evening's entertainment: they built a village, the three of them down on the floor on their hands and knees, laughing, talking, taking the roles of the Fisher-Price gas station attendant and the Fisher-Price mommy, bringing the 7:20 express rattling through town, staging a bank robbery with the cowboys-turned-bad-guys.

Sally left while Tom was putting Tommy to bed, so he decided they could let it ride this one night. But the one night turned into two, and that two flowed into two months, and still the system continued.

The sex surfaced spontaneously but seldom. Once when Sally Maye had lost a favorite patient to leukemia, he held her and cuddled her until the fire flared. Then one night Dr. Holmes called to tell Tom how hopeless he thought Helen's case was—she had simply withdrawn from the world. Tom had been visiting her every few days, so he was well aware that she was not reacting to anything around her. Dr. Holmes thought Tom should stop the self-torture of the visits. The night of Dr. Holmes's phone call, Sally Maye stayed until dawn, until it was time to get ready for her seven o'clock shift, and she reported to the hospital that day without having slept a wink, although her head had from time to time touched the pillow.

They disagreed about Tommy, what time was bedtime, whether or not he should have an extra Coke, how much he should be pushed to try. They fought about her salary, or lack thereof—he wanting to pay her enormous wages; she, knowing what Helen's sanatorium cost, wanting to do this out of affection for the two Toms. They tussled over whether or not she should stay all night, each taking different sides of the argument on different days, depending who was feeling sexy or lonely or sad.

Nonetheless, it was the most tension-free period of his life. Never before had he been helped as Sally Maye helped him to function, without having to worry constantly about the condition of the helper. For her it was paradise, and she treasured every moment of it. She knew she would never again meet and be loved by a man of Tom's special character; he was so gentle with her, so kind—so absolutely kind. And she knew it was a temporary situation.

She was not unduly surprised when he came home that Thursday in late March and told her his spur-of-the-moment decision. The new contracts had been distributed that day, and he had just stared at his. In the mail that morning had come a letter from his publisher asking him to please spend more time on poetry and wanting him to write some introductions for some other books. That afternoon he had been to see the unresponsive Helen and had had another long conversation with Dr. Holmes on the improbability of her ever returning from her self-imposed exile. And suddenly everything came together in his mind: he and Tommy would move. They would go off by themselves somewhere, and he would be a fulltime poet and a fulltime friend for Tommy.

He was afraid of Sally Maye's reaction. He shouldn't have been—she had been steeling herself for just such news for months and was more than prepared with a smile and good wishes. It was fine with her—she had had a good offer from a San Francisco Children's Hospital specializing in burns, and she felt she would accept the job, which started, coincidentally, in June. It was all pure fabrication, but Tom was convinced. That night they went to bed together and made love for the last time. From then on they worked at establishing more emotional distance. The relationship stayed friendly, but they both knew it was dangerous for it to be anything else. In fact, as a part of Sally Maye's withdrawal, she started dating Dr. Williams, and two weeks after Tom and Tommy left Buffalo, Sally Maye Floyd and Frederick P. Williams, M.D., were married.

PART III

Rome, Italy: Spring 1977

7

Ruth Tyack Sevini sat stiffly in the driver's seat of her green Maserati. Unconsciously her thumbs rubbed the yellow leather steering wheel of the car that had come to mean so much. This elegant car had been Bruno's wedding present to her. It was the feminine counterpart of his own green Maserati, and she had always loved it. More so somehow, now that Bruno was gone.

"Ruth." Nona interrupted her thoughts.

"*Ciao*, Nona," Ruth said sadly. She was so upset with her mother-in-law, that she couldn't wait to get her out of the car. Nona had committed Ruth to a weekend visit that she was simply dreading.

"Oh, Ruth, I can't let you go like this."

The Maserati hugged the curb in front of Morelli's Guanteria. In a moment Nona would enter the glove shop, and Ruth would drive off. But Nona was too worried to let Ruth leave in this mood of martyrdom and resignation.

"*Carissima*," Nona pleaded. She had to make a final attempt to get Ruth to talk. Nona turned in the seat and covered one of Ruth's hands as it caressed the yellow circle. "I know it is the last minute, but maybe you should tell me before you go. I think you've tried to tell me before. What happened between you and Peter? He is my nephew, Ruth, but you are my daughter."

Nona's loving statement was so sincere it shattered Ruth's well-guarded defenses. The blond head came forward, and Nona felt tears on her hand. Perhaps a minute passed. Nona stared out at the street, thinking that the customers were waiting and she really should get the shop opened. She pushed the thought to the back of her mind and tried to concentrate on helping Ruth. This sweet young woman was so dear to her. If only Bruno were still alive—he had always been able to bring peace to Ruth. But alas, her sainted boy was dead. Now Nona felt she must make other arrangements for Ruth. That was what this weekend was all about.

Ruth straightened in her seat, blew her nose on the beige lace hankie Nona offered, and turned to look Nona in the eye. "Nona, it was a nightmare," she stated flatly, remembering back. Bruno had died in October of 1975 and Ruth had gone home to the States with her father after the funeral. Then in March she had returned to Rome to be with Nona. "I had been back for about a week," she continued, now reminiscing out loud. "I came on a Sunday. Remember how the sun shone and what a lovely day it was? It felt so good to be here with you again." Young blue eyes smiled into older, wiser blue eyes, and Ruth halted her story momentarily, swept up in a tide of remembrance and love for the lady beside her.

Ruth looked Nona up and down, as if trying to memorize her face and body, trying to capture this moment in time. There she sat with her usual serenity, the gray hair short and rather unfashionable, the skin wrinkled with age, no makeup. She was dressed in severe black, adorned only by a patterned scarf and pin at her neck; she wore serviceable black shoes. Except for her small, smooth, feminine hands and her lovely, compassionate blue eyes, she was plain. But not on the inside. Ruth loved her deeply.

"About Peter," Nona prompted.

"Oh," Ruth focused back on the time and place. "That first Friday night you went to play bridge as usual. You had been gone about half an hour when I heard a knock on the door. It was Peter. I had just gotten out of the tub and was in a nightie and robe. He said he knew you had bridge and wondered if I wanted some company. He took me completely by surprise. I just nodded my head and opened the door wider and motioned him in. Then I closed the door and stood there, like an imbecile, speechless, staring at him as if he were an apparition.

"Nona, do you *know* what Peter looks like?" She peered closely at her mother-in-law to see if she had understood the question.

"Certainly he is very pleasing to the eye," Nona answered.

Ruth snorted. "Pleasing to the eye! He is a god, Nona. He is an absolutely perfect specimen of a man. Six feet tall, black hair you could get your fingers stuck in, broad shoulders, that devilish grin. Now, granted, there is a lot about his looks that money has bought—thirty-dollar hair-cuts and two-hundred dollar sport coats certainly help make the man look attractive. But however the result is attained, still the result is the same. He is absolutely breathtaking, Nona. At least," she added softly, "he always takes my breath away." She sighed and forced a light note into her voice. It came out brittle.

"Well, add to that the fact that he was obviously nervous. Some of his polish was missing, which made him more dear than ever. Peter Morelli, nervous! Imagine! Well, somehow we arrived in the living room, he in his navy wool blazer and me in my nightie, and he took off his jacket and rolled up his sleeves, appearing for all the world as if he were planning on staying a while, and we sort of sneaked glances at each other and managed to ask each other how we were—to which both of us brilliantly responded, 'Fine.' Then we just stared at each other. Meanwhile, the tension was building, the sparks just flying out of each of us, landing on the other." Ruth shifted in her seat, looking away from Nona, trying hard not to shock her.

"There is just no way for me to put this delicately, Nona. I mean 'bodies.' We looked at each other and it—it was fireworks, Nona. The Fourth of July for bodies. Well, we sat and mumbled at each other, each on our own separate loveseat, and finally Peter couldn't stand it anymore, and he rose and said, 'Ruth?' And like the brave person I am, I said, 'I think I'll go make some coffee.' And I *ran* out to the kitchen, and I leaned over the coffeemaker . . . I couldn't breathe—I mean, Nona, you know, I don't even *like* coffee! Why in the world had I offered this man coffee? I don't even know if *he* likes coffee. Well, there I was. And then I heard him coming. I froze, stiff as a board. He walked into the kitchen, and he came up behind me." Her voice dropped. "Very gently he put his hands on my shoulders. I spun around, smack into his chest, and I just stayed there. I mean I wouldn't have moved for anything. But he put his hand under my chin and forced my head up, and I absolutely drowned in those black eyes. And then . . . he kissed me, Nona. And with that touch we both just went wild. Nona, it was like . . . I don't know . . . like someone opened the door of a cage. We couldn't stop touching, we couldn't stop kissing, we couldn't get close enough. We were peeling each other's clothes off. We walked toward the bedroom, still kissing, both of us ready and—

"Then I saw the bed." Her voice was shaky, remembering. "Bruno's bed. And the guilt hit me, it was a *physical* pain. I doubled over like I'd been punched in the stomach. I couldn't talk to Peter; I couldn't explain. He was reaching for me to try to just hold me, to say it was all right, and I just kept backing away, saying 'Get out.'" Ruth was almost whispering now, shamed by the recollection. "And then I started screaming at him."

Ruth looked pleadingly at her mother-in-law. "Oh, Nona, how can he ever forgive me? How can he ever forget something like that?" A tear rolled down Ruth's cheek, and Nona reached over with her hand to brush it aside. "I haven't heard from him since. And now you want me to drive to Orvieto, to *his* home, to see him on this pretext of store business."

Nona smiled a sweet smile at Ruth. "*Carissima*, I think it is about time you faced him and exorcised these demons. You have carried this guilt for long enough."

"But you see why I'm scared to go? I want to go. I want to see him. There is definitely something simpatico with us." Ruth smiled wryly. "But I'm so afraid. Maybe he won't be able to forgive me—or won't want to. I'm afraid that one disastrous hour ruined our chances of ever having anything."

"Ruth, *he* asked that you come. Who is to say why? As for the business, just give him all the forms and receipts; tell him business is fine. And reassure him that we don't believe in those rumors of his mistreating his employees and disobeying government safety standards," Nona said derisively. "What rubbish!

"And now listen: if he wants something else from you, besides the business report, that is up to you. I hope you have enough faith in me"—Nona squeezed Ruth's hand—"to know that whatever is good for you will make me happy." Nona leaned over and kissed Ruth on the cheek. "Now, I put the papers in the briefcase, and I put the briefcase in the trunk. You packed your swimming suit, right? He was insistent that you bring a suit—and it took enough trouble to choose, eh? I know it will be all right, Ruth." Nona patted her daughter-in-law's hand. "Have some faith, now."

"Thank you, Nona." Ruth felt much calmer as Nona climbed out of the car. "I'll drive carefully. See you Sunday night. *Ciao*."

Ruth waited until Nona had unlocked the iron gate in front of the store. Then she drove down the narrow Via Condotti. As she dead-ended at the Piazza di Spagna, chapel bells rang four o'clock. God, she would never tire of the sight of all the flowers flanking the Spanish Steps. The abundance of color, the excess and opulence of it, the unrestrained glory of it was so Italian. The pastel pinks to the vivid reds looked like a Prince Matchabelli lipstick chart.

Predictably a horn honked behind her and, intimidated as usual, she tried to beat an oncoming cinquecento, causing his horn and a fist out the window. "Oh, stuff it." If only Bruno had lived long enough to teach her to swear in Italian. Swearing was one of the few cultural intricacies his mother hadn't realized she wanted to learn. That was because Nona didn't drive.

As Ruth waited to turn left onto the Via Veneto, her eye was caught by the sparkle of sunlight on the spray of the

American Embassy fountains, then the striped awning of Doney, whose *cappuccino* Bruno had loved. She drove past the wall, through the Etruscan Gate, and onto the Etruscan Way. The same bricks that she now drove over had been put in place by slaves thousands of years before. She wondered again if this was the road along which Spartacus had hung. The last scene of that movie flashed through her mind: the hope in the eyes of the martyred Spartacus as he stared down from his cross to see his pregnant wife riding to freedom over these bricks. Usually she could lose herself for hours in historical daydreams. Today, though, the present blocked her escape to the past.

Ten after four. She should be in Orvieto between five-thirty and six. The town was well known for its pottery. Why would a walled city high on a mountain specialize in pottery? Of course, what else would a walled city high on a mountain specialize in?

"Oh, Bruno," Ruth said aloud, "at least I don't hate you anymore." For a year she had absolutely despised him. How could he have died? How could he have left her? He had wrecked her life. Somehow, even in her deepest grief for herself, she could never grieve very much for him. He had not been at all frightened of death. He was a person who was comfortable anywhere, and she knew he would be as accepting of death as he had been of life. When he had talked about death, he had sounded knowledgeable. His faith in God was so sure; he had really known God. And the knowledge had given him the serenity that had been his most attractive feature. To rest in his arms became the ultimate peaceful sensation of her life. They had had such a comfortable love.

She turned north onto the Autostrada del Sole and smiled as the three cars behind her pulled simultaneously into the left lane to pass her. Every road was a racetrack, every driver Mario Andretti. As they passed, they invariably frowned at the enigma of this chic girl driving a Maserati so conservatively and nonaggressively. She had loved that inconsistency in Bruno, the solid, dependable accountant, becoming the wild, macho daredevil behind the wheel. She had loved it until it had killed him.

A car slowed to keep pace beside her, and as she looked over, the driver mouthed *"bellissima"* and raised his eyebrows in invitation. She smiled and raised her left hand to show the wedding band. He saluted and sped off. Bruno had been dead almost eighteen months, but she couldn't take off the ring. Not so much from sentiment or love did she wear it, she realized, but because she could hide, as she had just done, behind the hands-off status of a married woman. When a woman looked like she did on the outside, it helped to be labeled unapproachable.

Not that she was beautiful. There was nothing about her that was just right, no striking feature. But she was a blue-eyed blond, and in Italy that was remarkable. She looked confident, but unfinished. She wore no makeup, and her nails were merely neatly bitten. She had a good clothes sense, but what set her apart was that she possessed the poise of the classroom and the assurance she had gained from being Mrs. Bruno Sevini. And compared to Italian women, she was well educated.

Bruno had always liked that. He was so proud of her mind. He had really enjoyed talking with her. *Oh, Bruno. Why did you leave me?* She missed her friend. There had been no great passion between them, but she had been committed and contented.

T.J., T.J., I'm so lonely I could die. Bruno leaves me, you send me away. Isn't there someone who wants me? I yearn so for fulfillment. I really enjoyed being married. Of course, I'm lucky I'm not totally alone. There is Nona....

For the last year, Ruth's most strongly felt commitment had been to Bruno's mother. Perhaps because in the last year she had come to know herself through Nona. Perhaps, too, because she had come to know God through Nona. "Would you like to come to mass with me," was an invitation, not a sermon. Nona was no saint, but when a moral, ethical, or spiritual question arose, Nona simply stepped out to meet it. "I just knew, Ruth, that I couldn't feel right about myself if I didn't do this." Or, "I choose to simply accept, Ruth, because I have always been convinced that God knows what he is doing." Nona's attitudes and beliefs were revealed gradually and unpretentiously, like pearls dropped one by one. It was up to Ruth to assemble the pearls. And she did; she made a rosary out of them. Nona felt that the discipline and order of Catholicism were instrumental to her peace. When Ruth met Nona's God, saw him meet Nona's needs, she embraced him herself. She didn't convert to Catholicism, but she began to rely on God for the first time in her life.

Fifteen minutes past five. She would have to steel herself for meeting Peter. She didn't understand the powerful chemistry between them. Before the disastrous night in Nona's apartment, Ruth had only seen him twice in her life—at the wedding and at the funeral. From the moment she had first noticed him at the wedding reception, she had been intensely aware of him. And he of her. They couldn't tear their eyes from each other. There are people for whom one feels instant antagonism and people with whom one feels instant security. Like Bruno. With Peter, she felt instant excitement: they wanted each other. He had asked her to dance three times. The first time, toward the end of the song, she finally forced herself to say, "We'd better talk."

He had answered, "There is nothing our eyes can't say, is there?"

The second time she again had broken the silence. "I don't believe this."

He said, "Maybe no one would notice if we stretched out on the floor here and made mad, passionate love for a few hours." They had been unable to laugh.

The third time they danced he said, "Do you want to see me again?"

She had seen the pain in Bruno's eyes when Peter had come to claim her for a third time, so she answered the only thing she could: "I don't believe I could handle just seeing you." For the next two years she didn't see him. She would never know how hard he had worked to make sure their paths didn't cross.

At the funeral they hadn't talked, but again their eyes never left each other. His eyes held her up as surely as his arms could have done. When he started to approach, she shook her head and nodded toward Nona. Ruth's father had come, but Nona had no male family with her, and Ruth knew Nona needed Peter's presence. He didn't leave Nona's side. The next day he and Nona drove Ruth and her father to the airport. The talk was all superficial. The only honesty was the long goodbye embrace. Peter walked her to a quiet corner of the waiting room and held her, wordlessly, for maybe ten minutes. If Nona or Ruth's father found it strange that the dead man's cousin and his new widow should be embracing, nothing was ever said or insinuated.

Ruth stayed in the United States living with her father and substitute teaching until Nona's cable arrived. "Peter Morelli offers me managership of *guanteria* on Condotti. Can you come?" What a good opportunity for Nona to have the prestige and involvement—but apparently she needed Ruth's support to give her the confidence to accept. Three days later Ruth was back in Rome. She moved in temporarily with Nona, but it worked out so well she stayed. They never missed church or a new movie. Nona's vitality returned, and Ruth's aching loneliness lessened somewhat. They had both blossomed in this year, as if each had known for the other the formula for mental health.

She passed a sign: *Orvieto—4 km.* Now she must confront reality. What if he was all business? What if he didn't forgive her? How could she talk to him in a normal voice when they had never had a conversation in their lives? What if the electricity between them was turned off somehow? What if she had *imagined* the electricity between them? Why did he want to see her? Where had he been all this time?

It was quarter of six when she arrived in Orvieto. His directions were excellent. Five minutes later she pulled onto Via Pietro. (Good God! The street was named after him—or maybe he was named for the street: that would be a little less awesome.) She was stunned when she entered the circular driveway. The villa was a beautiful white brick palace, a mansion in the midst of sculptured gardens. And most amazing of all, Peter Morelli was sitting on the front steps, looking for all the world like a

147

little boy waiting for someone to come home. Then it all seemed to happen in one fluid movement: he was down the steps, leaning in the car and kissing her once, hard and purposefully on the lips, an American greeting instead of a cheeky European hello, grabbing her with one hand and the suitcase with the other, and rushing her up the steps and into the villa, talking all the while.

"We are going down by the lake for supper, Lago di Bolsena. You have heard of it? How beautiful it is? Do you feel like dancing beside a lake tonight? Do you have something long you could wear? Bring a sweater or shawl, since there is often a cool breeze blowing off the lake. Just get ready as fast as you can. Yes? We'll go when you are ready. The bathroom is in here."

He had led her up the front steps and into the cool, dark villa, and she had fleeting glimpses of chandeliers and antique furniture and Oriental rugs, and now here she stood in a beautiful blue and white bedroom, and Peter was rushing into the adjoining bath. "I'll just turn on the water for you; it's a little hard to get a decent temperature sometimes. I'll be waiting downstairs. As quickly as you can, yes?" He put his hands on her shoulders. "You have been a long time in coming." He gave her another of those kisses, but this time it wasn't so fast. This time his lips traveled the boundaries of hers, and his tongue and teeth explored, demanded, and invited. And then he gradually pulled back, and his mouth simply surrounded hers. Luckily he was holding her up, or she would have collapsed, for her bones melted, threatening to form a puddle at her feet.

When she opened her eyes, she was staring at a closed door, and the water was pounding away in the tub. She turned around and leaned against the door for a minute. It had been over a year since any man had touched her. She felt both exultant and unbelievably calm. She was grinning as she stripped off her red sundress and headed for the bath. When the water engulfed her, so did the realization that she had not said a word, not one damn word. All she had done was let herself be kissed and nod her head.

He was standing in the hallway when she descended the

red carpeted stairs. He held out his hand and walked her out to the car. She looked at them both as they fitted themselves into the white Fiat, and for a minute, she couldn't assimilate what she saw. They matched. Or at least they looked like they had tried. She had on a long white skirt and a navy blue halter top, a navy blue scarf tying back her shoulder-length hair, a navy shawl over her arm. He wore white slacks and a navy blue silk shirt. As he was starting the car, he felt her eyes and returned her look. A giggle escaped Ruth's lips. Then she gestured with her hand to show him what she was laughing about. Whether he, too, thought it was funny or whether he was merely captivated by her delight, she didn't know. They laughed, hard, almost hysterically.

"We can't go out like this. We look like a damn magazine ad. This is embarrassing—people will think we planned this."

He kissed her mouth. Warmly. Hungrily. Again. It was getting to be a habit.

"You're beautiful. I'll be right back."

While he was gone, she dried her eyes with a handkerchief she found in his glove compartment. And then laughed some more. She was getting out of the car as Peter came back down the front steps, wearing a brown plaid silk shirt and tan slacks.

"What?"

"I forgot my purse."

"That's all right. Dinner will be my treat."

He said it with such grave gallantry that she had to look hard to find his black eyes twinkling.

"I'm sorry I was gone so long. I had to change my socks, too. You wanted me to match *me*, even if you didn't want *me* to match *you*, right?" He exposed the brown socks.

"You look wonderful . . . wonderfully different—from me, I mean. Thank you for changing." Her words were coming out so jumbled. She tried once more. "Thank you for changing your socks for me."

The drive to the sea was occupied with a travelogue and questions. Where before they couldn't talk, now they couldn't stop. They talked about growing grapes and making pottery and raising sheep. They talked about white Italian stucco and stones versus sand on a beach and the isle of Capri.

The restaurant was delightful, cozy, and unpretentious. He had no reservations. He was treated like a common man instead of the head of Morelli Enterprises, Finest Italian Leather Goods. She loved it. Especially she loved the music of the three-piece band—piano, violin, and bass. They ate in the open air and danced on a board platform built out over the water. They danced between the *zuppa di cozze* and the *fettuccine al prosciutto*. They danced between the *fettuccine al prosciutto* and the *melanzane ripiene*. They danced between the *melanzane ripiene* and the *pollo alla diavola toscana*. They danced between the *pollo alla diavola toscana* and the *coppa di mascarpone*. They danced between the glasses of *vino bianco*, and they danced between the cups of espresso.

When they sat, they talked. They discussed whether Bayern, Munich, or Juventus would take the Winner's Cup in soccer, and they worried about the fate of Aldo Moro. They talked about gloves going out of style in the United States and about the latest Lina Wertmüller film. While they ate across the small table from each other, he enclosed her knees with his own. When they didn't need both hands to eat, he held her hand. When they danced, they said not a word. His hand moved across her back, up her side, under her hair. Hers caressed his neck, slipped inside his shirt. Their dancing was one long, swaying embrace. There was no air between their bodies. She was intoxicated by the smell of his soap, the roughness of his chest where his shirt was unbuttoned, and the hardness of his thigh between her legs. He was entranced by the lemon scent of her hair and the fact that she was braless.

On the way home they spoke only in murmurs and sighs. He drove slowly because he didn't want the night to end. She felt utterly content, her head back against the seat, her body turned toward him, his hand holding her leg against his. They walked into the house holding each other up. At the bottom of the steps, their kiss was tender.

"Do you think we would drown if we tried to swim now?"

She nodded.

"Then you have five minutes to get into bed and fall asleep."

She nodded.

He tried to hit her on the bottom to speed her on her way, but the smack turned into a caress.

She slept in her panties, under a pink satin sheet, and was asleep in three minutes.

When Ruth awoke, she discovered she was clutching a warm, hairy chest. Peter was outside the sheet and she was inside, but they were curved together, her breasts against his back, her arm snuggled inside his, one of his feet pinning both of hers. She sighed and went back to sleep.

She woke up again. This time Peter sensed it and rolled over, pulling her head onto his bare chest, one arm under her head, the other arm rubbing her back. "Go back to sleep, baby." She smiled and slept.

Later, she opened her eyes and focused on short, black hairs. Experimentally she brought her hand up to touch the virile chest on which her cheek rested.

"It's polite to say, 'Good morning.'"

His voice startled her. His breathing had been so deep and even, she thought he was still asleep. She started to struggle out of his arms, but the grip tightened. She was amazed by the early morning intimacy and didn't know what to say, so she said, "Good morning."

"I came to see if you'd like to swim, see?" He motioned to the black bathing suit he was wearing, dropping his hand to the waistband and snapping the stretchy material. "But you wanted to sleep. Now are you ready to swim?" he demanded.

"Yes, sir." She tried to sound meek.

"Ah, I approve of a woman who knows her place."

She raised her arm to pound his chest, but he caught her fist, opened it, raised it to his mouth. His lips and tongue went to work on her fingers then, sucking them one by one, licking between them, and she turned to jelly. But he surprised her by hopping out of bed.

"Down the stairs, to the back of the house, you can't miss it. I'll go warm up the water."

"Peter?"

When he turned, she was flustered because the thoughts were jumbled in her head and she didn't know which ones to let out. She wanted to ask him to come back and ravish her, and she wanted to order him out of her life. "Do you think we can do it?" She had no idea what she meant, but he seemed to understand.

"Si, bambina, si. We will." He paused, searching for the words, this black-haired Roman god standing in her doorway. "You don't travel around the world only to get lost in your own village." He blew her a kiss.

Ruth brushed her teeth, washed the sand out of her eyes, and put on the dark brown, two-piece bathing suit. She must have tried on thirty-five suits, as though he would accept or reject her on the basis of her taste in swimsuits. Seeing Peter's face when she walked out to the pool satisfied her that she and Nona had spent their time wisely that bathing suit afternoon. She was pale after a winter indoors, and her white skin was set off and warmed by the charcoal hues in the suit.

She sat down primly on the edge of the pool. Peter swam over and stood up in front of her. With his hands on the insides of her thighs, he separated her legs where they dangled in the water and fastened them around his waist, his fingers first running up her smooth, soft legs to touch the crotch of her suit, fleetingly, making her want more, and then trailing liquid fire down her thighs to her knees, exerting pressure to manipulate her limbs.

"Sunday afternoon, before you are due to leave, we'll talk about it, yes? Until then we just go with it. What do you say?"

"Yes," she croaked. How could he excite her so and remain so cool and casual himself? His hands came around behind her and pulled her to him, holding her above the water. He smiled a slow, promising smile and kissed her gently on the lips and over her wide, sex-shocked eyes. He lowered her into the water then, and they swam together.

After completing twelve laps, they ate a huge breakfast, prepared by Peter in the vast kitchen. She knew, without asking, that he had dismissed the servants so that they might have the weekend alone. (She didn't know until much later what other arrangements he'd had to make.) Then they toured. In Orvieto's four historic churches they lit candles. For Bruno, Ruth thought, feeling blessedly free of guilt for what she knew would happen. They meandered through the shops of pottery and leather and handcrafts, and Peter bought her a large red straw donkey. For an hour they sat on the wall of the city, looking down over miles of Italian countryside, her head on his shoulder, his arm around her waist, her hand on his thigh. It was a heady view. Later, they deposited the red donkey at the villa and drove to Todi to see some of the summer carnival. Hand in hand they strolled by the amusements and the games, amused only by each other and their own game of chance.

Back home they swam to remove the dust of Todi. Then they laughed and refused to tell each other what they were going to wear when they got dressed for dinner, just to see if it would happen again. It almost did. They both wore dark brown pants, but while he wore a tan silk shirt, she wore a frilly pink blouse with, Peter complained, a bra under it.

"It's a see-through blouse. I can't go braless with a see-through blouse."

"Then what's the purpose of a see-through blouse?" he asked with simple logic.

"Maybe when we get home we could conduct an experiment and see which way you like it better." What was she saying? The last thing Peter Morelli needed was encouragement!

A little after ten o'clock they returned from a rather formal dinner at Orvieto's finest hotel. When Ruth came back downstairs after taking off her bra, she was surprised to find Peter in the wood-paneled study, sitting at a card table. A bottle of Italian champagne and two crystal goblets waited beside the cards.

She was embarrassed to enter the room. She had gone naked before T.J. and Bruno—but somehow the sheer silkiness of the blouse made her feel more wanton than if she had worn nothing at all. Peter didn't make it any easier. He just sat and watched, his eyes glittering with admiration.

"Your blouse doesn't look any different." He sounded too casual. "But you wouldn't have gotten any dinner if you had shown up like this before. Would you like to play a little of Nona's two-handed bridge while I saturate my parched eyes?" His words were cool, but the intimacy of his desire stole her voice. All she could do was nod her head.

"We'll play for your shirt."

"What?" She sat down.

"I'm growing uncommonly fond of your"—he cleared his throat—"blouse. How about if you unfasten a button every time you miss your bid—and when you are all unbuttoned, you can hand over your shirt."

"And then what?" she asked in a tight voice.

"Then we'll go for a swim."

"Oh." She tried to read him. His voice sounded relaxed again, but his eyes were on fire. She gestured toward the champagne then, trying to cut the sexual tension by changing the subject. "What are we celebrating?"

"We are celebrating the fact"—he enunciated every word distinctly—"that tonight, for the first of many, many times, we are going to make love." Then with infuriating calm he bid. "One spade."

She picked up the cards he had dealt her. She had opening count. "Three clubs." She added quietly, "I'm a terrible lover."

"Five clubs." He laid down the dummy, picked up the two defense hands, and led a small heart. Then he looked at her. "Naturally, you have been bad at sex: you are a female New England-type Puritan. Just as naturally, I have been good at sex." They were both smiling as he added, "Since I am an Italian male." He paused. "But tonight we shall both be excellent lovers. Look how well we have always talked, with words and without. From the first look we understood each other. Do you doubt that our bodies will be beautiful together?"

"No," she answered honestly. He was smiling at her so sweetly she stood up and leaned over the card table to kiss him on the mouth. His hands immediately reached under her blouse, thumbs hardening nipples, fingers caressing satin skin. Feeling faint she straightened back up and almost fell into her chair. His mouth was open slightly, and they were both breathing unsteadily.

Ruth finally drew her brilliant blue eyes away from his burning black ones and looked at the dummy. "Seven points! You opened with seven points! How do you justify that? I'll never make my bid." She sought relief in outrage.

"I want to win, Ruth." He smiled a little-boy smile.

It took Peter an hour and a half, and they had finished the bottle of champagne, before Ruth missed by three tricks the small slam that Peter had bid on the last hand. He leaned across the table to loosen the button that would allow her blouse to fall free. Then he reached out to stand her up. While his hands were occupied with pink silk, she turned to walk out to the pool, flashing a smile over her shoulder. She dropped her slacks in the hall, kicked off her sandals on the patio, and wearing only a pair of lacy white panties, she hurried into the water.

She was floating, bottom up, on an inflated blue raft when Peter sauntered out to the pool. He stood at the edge of the water until she looked up. Then he kicked off his own shoes and took off his socks. He slowly unbuttoned the fastenings of his shirt. The silver moonlight and the dim golden lights around the pool glistened on his bronzed body, and Ruth felt like a dirty old woman as she breathlessly watched him step out of his slacks.

Then he hooked his thumbs in the waistband of his brown bikini underpants. Slowly he bent to pull them off, then straightened up. Squaring his shoulders, he spread his legs and secured his hands on his hips—the master surveying his domain—while his penis rose slowly from the black forest of pubic hair to point straight at Ruth.

She was blushing. She was also dripping moisture, feeling her body reacting, literally panting for his. Unconsciously she raised herself up from the raft, breasts silhouetted in the moon glow, reaching toward him. Their eyes made rash promises across the water. For endless minutes he stood, poised, and then he dove into the warm, blue-green pool and surfaced in front of her.

He pushed her from one end of the pool to the other, while they drowned in each other's eyes. The water lapped gently at their bodies as they glided. The too-sweet smell of fresh-bursting lemon blossoms, hyacinths, lily of the valley, assailed their senses and became confused with the musky animal scent of desire.

"Peter," she said finally, needing to break the spell, "you spent a lot of time planning this, didn't you? You arranged everything so well. Did you arrange for that moon, too?"

His finger traced patterns on her lips and cheeks and shoulders. "My dear Ruth, you should recognize by now our standard, fantastically gorgeous Italian love moon."

"And are you"—her voice broke—"just the standard, fantastically gorgeous Italian lover?"

He stopped swimming and stood up in the five feet of water, pulling her off the wet blue plastic and into his arms. Her legs wrapped themselves around his thighs, her body closed into his. "You provocative Puritan—are you asking to go to bed?"

"I was getting a little cold." She snuggled in a little deeper. "Will you warm me up?"

"*Si, carissima.*" He ran his tongue around her lips and then rammed it deeply into her mouth. Her legs convulsively tightened, tucking him in. "We have made love so many times in my dreams, I feel like I know exactly what you like."

And he did. In fact, she discovered she liked things she never even knew existed. He taught her exactly what he wanted her to know. And he quickly discovered how to please her. (The only other thing she would have liked was the return of her favorite pink blouse. He never gave it back, and, although she sometimes wondered about it, she never asked. The President's secretary and the janitor at the Rome Headquarters of Morelli Enterprises occasionally wondered, too, why Signore Morelli kept a frilly pink blouse in the back of his bottom right-hand desk drawer. He could have told them he kept it there for times when he was feeling cold.)

After eleven o'clock mass, they sat at the black wrought-iron table beside the aquamarine pool, still in their church clothes, drinking Chianti. The sun's glow was as radiant as Ruth's. They were companionably silent until Ruth said, "We should talk." It was exactly what she had said to Peter when he had first asked her to dance at her own wedding, and she wondered if he would remember. Her question was answered when he replied just what he had replied almost four years before.

"There is nothing our eyes can't say, is there?" He swung his chair closer to the table, putting his legs against hers, reaching for her hand. "Ruth. Listen. I would never have approached you if Bruno had lived. You are nobody's mistress. But you are the woman I have been waiting for. You are just right. I would like you to be my wife."

"Oh, Peter . . . I don't know."

"What don't you know? Whether I can support you?" His arm swung in a wide arc. "Whether we would be good in bed together?" His gaze was so intimate that she was forced to lower her eyes. "Whether Bruno would want it for you? I'm his cousin. Even the Bible approves. And you know, of course, that Nona set this all up. So you know she approves."

He pulled on her arm, then, to pull her out of her chair and over onto his lap. Very thoroughly he kissed her mouth and her neck, and when she pulled his head against her chest, he unfastened the inhibiting buttons on her dress and pushed aside her slip and bra and very thoroughly kissed a breast, until once again he took her breath away and she had to slide off his lap and walk toward the pool, rearranging her clothes.

She tried to rearrange her thoughts as well, and when she turned back to the table, she demanded: "What do you mean Nona set this up?"

"I asked for her help and advice. I have called her at least once a week for this last year. I told her everything: how I felt, how I thought you felt, that I wanted to marry you."

"You mean she already knew?"

He nodded and reached for her hand to pull her back on his lap. She came.

"She never told me. How wise that woman is. What did she say to you?"

"Oh, she told me how you were"—he rubbed a shoulder—"and what you were doing"—he touched a breast—"and then she'd usually say, 'Not yet,' or 'Soon,' or something like that. But last week when I called she said, 'I think now, Pietro.' So I got everyone away for the weekend, canceled my trip to London, and Nona and I decided on the phony excuse of the papers."

They kissed. Ruth broke away. "But, Peter, I really did bring you the papers for the *guanteria*. Oh, and Nona said to tell you that of course we don't believe any of those vicious rumors, either."

He kissed her soundly. "Thank you *bambina*, for believing in me. I hope you can always say that. And, Ruth, I don't know what you brought, but there are no papers for the *guanteria*."

"Well, Nona packed a briefcase in the trunk, and she said to be sure to give you the papers inside."

"Now I'm curious, too. I'll go get the case."

Ruth handed him the car keys and sat staring into the water, remembering, blushing, while Peter walked to the car and back.

He deposited the briefcase on the patio table and opened it while Ruth leaned her head against his side. There was only one paper inside, a note from Nona.

My dear Pietro and Ruth—

I have the greatest faith in you both and in the rightness of your good love. Congratulations.

Love,
Nona

Under the note, were two crystal glasses, wrapped in tissue, and a bottle of *asti spumante*.

8

"Nona." Ruth called her name as she got off the elevator and unlocked the door. "Nona." Ruth stepped into the apartment, onto the shiny marble floor. The entrance way was mirrors and candles, and it always looked dramatically welcoming. "Nona." Off to the right were three bedrooms and a spacious black and white bath, and it was in this direction that Ruth headed now. "Nona."

"In here, Ruth." Nona was in bed—the largest, lowest, softest bed in the world Ruth always thought—under the covers, playing solitaire bridge, a bed tray over her legs.

Ruth laughed. "Nona! You played bridge last night, and you had your usual game Friday night, didn't you?"

"Yes, but one must practice if one wants to be good."

Nona set aside her bed tray and patted the bed for Ruth to sit down.

"I'm so glad you're back, *carissima*. My curiosity is killing me."

Ruth sighed. "Oh, Nona, it was perfect. It couldn't have been better. I wouldn't change a word or a look or—anything."

"So?"

"So?" Ruth teased.

"Don't test an old lady's patience too far, Ruth." Nona warned with a smile.

Ruth grinned. "Okay. Three weeks."

"What three weeks?"

"*In* three weeks."

"*What in* three weeks?" Nona was impatient.

"You get to be mother of the bride in three weeks."

"Oh, Ruth," she said quietly. Then she reached out to

160

embrace her with a strength that amazed Ruth and made her lose her balance so that she ended up falling across Nona's legs.

Laughing and crying, too. Nona helped Ruth pick herself up and then leaned against the pillows. She retained her hold on Ruth's hands and said, "Oh, Ruth, that's wonderful."

"You old schemer." Ruth touched the ruffle of the old woman's blue flannel nightgown. "I had no idea you were sending out reports. You're no better than the CIA."

"What's this CIA?"

"Oh, never mind. Only there you sat on Friday afternoon, listening to me pour out the story of my nightmare— mine and Peter's—and he had already told you. Thank goodness he did, Nona. Obviously we needed some help. And I'm so glad it was you." Ruth leaned over and kissed the parchment cheek. "I'm glad I found you, Nona. I need you so much. And we'll have so much fun. We will go shopping and have lunch, and you'll have to help me plan all my entertaining, and then later you'll have to help with the babies. Oh, Nona, I do so want babies. But Bruno wanted to wait—we thought we had so much time." She fell silent for a moment, then, "We'll have to buy a really pretty pram and dress little Peter up in his finest bunting and take him walking in the park. Oh, Nona? Can you believe it?"

Tears were streaming down Nona's cheeks. "No, Ruth. I can't believe it. It would be too wonderful, wouldn't it? To have all that before us? Oh, I did so want to leave you in good hands. And now you're going to be Peter's wife, so you will be safe."

"Of course I'll be safe, Nona. What are you talking about, leave me in good hands? Where are you going?"

"Oh, cara, we're not going to talk about my plans tonight, we're going to talk about yours. Where are you going to be married?"

Ordinarily Ruth would have caught the innuendo and pressed Nona further, but tonight she was too caught up in her own joy. "Peter is going to try for the Sistine Chapel. He knows a cardinal who will perform the ceremony—and he hopes maybe procure the chapel as well. That's exciting, isn't it? We decided we'd be married any day the chapel was available."

"But, Ruth, you haven't formally converted. You can't be married in the church, can you?"

"I don't know." Ruth shrugged. "Peter seemed to think it could all be arranged."

Nona stretched out a hand and smoothed Ruth's shining yellow hair back from her face. "Oh—there's the phone, Ruth. Will you get it?"

Ruth leaped off the bed and hurried down the hall.

"Hello."

"I think this sexy voice belongs to a sexy lady. Lady, would you care to drive back to Orvieto tonight? I don't want to sleep alone ever again in my life, now that I've slept with you."

"Oh, Peter. I can't talk now," she replied in a stage whisper. "I'm on my way out to the car to drive to Orvieto to meet my Italian lover."

"*Bambina*, listen." He had a plan. "I can't wait until next weekend. I'll be in Rome on Tuesday. Plan to be busy Tuesday night. And don't plan on going out for dinner, because I have no interest"—he lowered his voice to a make-believe slur—"in eating anything I can't eat in bed."

"Oh, Peter," she moaned. "I'll bring some pretzels along. Are you really coming Tuesday?"

"I'm going to have to—just for the night."

"Oh, Peter." She ached. She grabbed the gold chain she was wearing and unconsciously started stroking it.

"If you don't stop saying 'Oh, Peter,' I'm going to be there tonight."

"Oh, Peter," she taunted in her mellow voice. She ran her stockinged foot up and down the wall opposite.

"Are you happy, Ruth?"

She pictured him sitting in his swivel chair behind that massive oak desk in his study, feet propped, quizzing her. "I am happy, Peter, are you?"

"Yes. We had a good weekend, didn't we?"

"It was perfect, Peter, just perfect." She felt so damned turned on, it seemed like weeks instead of merely hours.

"I have a wonderful idea."

"What?" she groaned. Her body quivering, she curved into a ball on the floor, her legs pressed tightly together.

"I'll call the concierge on Tuesday and ask him to let you in so you can be there waiting for me. I can't get there until about seven. Would you like that?"

"I'd love it. Shall I have dinner ready?" She wanted to hear him say it again.

"No. Definitely not. Just be in the apartment, and . . . be ready."

"Oh, Peter! Why aren't you coming tonight?"

"Ruth, I have to cancel an interview with *Viva* and postpone a production distribution meeting to make it on Tuesday."

"Oh, Peter." She sat up straight, ashamed.

"Ruth, are you excited?"

Peter Morelli wanted reassurance? "I don't think I'm going to sleep tonight, Peter," she reassured him.

"Me, either. Listen, Ruth, I forgot to give you my private number. Call anytime, okay? Really, anytime! It's seven-five-four-one-two."

She stood up to write it down.

"And now," he continued "I'm going to go crawl into that bed we shared last night and cuddle that pillow that I hope will still smell like you."

"I hope it smells good."

"The sweetest smell I have ever smelled," he said softly. "Sleep tight, *bambina*, and be waiting on Tuesday night."

"I will be." She put her palm flat against the wall, as if touching him. "Oh, what's the address?"

"Via Cordova, fifty-four—what you call in English the penthouse."

"Oh, Mr. Morelli, I'm not sure I'm ready to share your poverty."

She could hear Peter laughing. He sounded tired.

"Good night, *bambina*. See you on Tuesday."

"Good night, Peter." She gently cradled the phone and leaned her head against the wall, momentarily unable to move.

Shaking herself back into action, Ruth walked dreamily

to the kitchen and put on the copper teakettle. It was amazing! She knew, because of Bruno's death, that when things got too bad, her mind went into a sort of catatonic shock, and now she felt as though the same thing was happening when things were too good. Thank goodness her body didn't do that, she thought. The sex. Good God, the sex. She hadn't had sex like that since... well... since T. J.

I'm sorry, Bruno. She felt disloyal. But it was exhilarating to feel so alive again, so aroused. She was tempted to go into the bathroom and lock the door.

Instead, she fixed a tray with a pot of tea, cups, milk, saccharine and some cookies and headed off down the hall to Nona's room. When she got there, she stood transfixed. The bed tray over her legs, the lights on, and the candle in front of the statue of the Virgin glimmering, Nona was asleep. It was only about ten-thirty. Nona was usually such a night owl—and to get sleepy tonight of all nights, when she and Ruth had so much to talk about.

Ruth moved the bed tray and extinguished the lights. Nona moaned in her sleep, but didn't waken. Ruth carried the tea tray out onto the balcony. There were doubts nibbling at the corners of her heart, but they were such vague stirrings she couldn't identify them. What she overwhelmingly felt was wonderful—better than she had felt for years. Fresh from her weekend of pampering, she felt loved and protected.

Why me, God? Why would he choose me? Why has he waited for me? He's so old to be married. Thirty-seven. I hope it's not too old. What if he's a confirmed bachelor—or a confirmed playboy. My God—what do I really know about him? Well, I know how it felt. His hands never stopped. They were everywhere at once. His hands on the inside of my legs while we made love. I can feel it now. I wonder how many hours it is until Tuesday night? Less than forty-eight—about forty-three.

She looked around. The stars were glowing in a blue black sky, and the moon was almost full—it should be full by Tuesday night. And the scent of the lemon and lime trees in their buckets on the balcony mingled with the richness of the flower smell. Five floors up, the city lights and sounds were gently muted.

How far away, Pittsburgh, PA! How lucky she was. Her closest high school friend, Marie, was home on the farm with her four boys, never having left the county. Another, Julie, was married and divorced and married again, never having found someone to care. And here she was. Handsome, charming Peter Morelli, rich and famous Italian businessman, wanted to marry her. Saints preserve us!

With that thought she went inside to bed.

"Ruth." Nona was standing above her, face washed, hair brushed, wearing a soft, blue-striped robe; Nona's hand was shaking her shoulder. "Ruth, Susan is on the phone. She called Friday evening. I forgot in the excitement last night to tell you."

"Oh, thanks, Nona," Ruth struggled to sit up. "What time is it?"

"A little after eight."

"Wonder what could be so important?" She rubbed at her eyes and shook her head, trying to wake up. Groggy, she stumbled out to the phone, shivering in her bare feet and flimsy yellow nightgown.

"Hi, Sus."

"Ruth, are you sitting down?"

"No. Why? What's up?" Nona was standing behind her with robe and slippers, and Ruth mouthed a thank you as she slipped into the thongs and bundled into the old pink terry robe.

"You are not going to believe it—at least I think it's good news."

"You're not going to believe my news, either." Ruth winked at Nona as the old lady shuffled down the hall into the kitchen, smiling.

"What?"

"Oh, no. I'm not telling you this over the phone."

"Ruth! I've been dying all weekend with this letter burning a hole in my pocket—"

"What letter?" Ruth was definitely awake now.

165

"That's my news—a letter. Friday afternoon I passed Mrs. Mayberry's desk in the office." Ruth and Susan had taught together at the American School and Susan was still there. "I saw a letter sitting there addressed to you. Mrs. Mayberry said she was just about to forward it to your home in Pittsburgh. I told her you were back in Rome and that I'd take the letter because I see you a couple times a week."

"Who's it from?" Ruth was afraid to ask.

"Now are you sitting down?"

Ruth sat down on the floor. "Yes."

"Somerset, Maine."

"Oh, my God," Ruth whispered.

"Don't you think it's from him?" Susan was pleased with herself. She had been touched when Ruth had told her about T. J., and now she was obviously pleased to have a part in the present developments.

"How's it addressed?"

"Ruth Tyack Sevini—care of American School—Rome, Italy."

"I don't believe it." Ruth felt shell-shocked.

"Now can your news top that?" Susan gloated.

"I don't know," Ruth answered honestly. "I knew a few minutes ago, but I don't know now. Can we have dinner together?"

"No." Susan moaned. "We have a dinner meeting at school tonight, but my free period is after lunch. Want to meet me at the little place near the school?"

"I sure do. You will have the letter with you, won't you?"

"*Certamente*. After holding this darn thing since Friday afternoon, trying to resist the temptation to steam it open, I think I'm more anxious than you are."

Four hours later they sat across from each other at the window table that Pere Diablo's proprietor usually held for foreigners—foreigners, for some reason, always liked to sit at the window—and ordered the Monday special, pasta with clam sauce, veal, and salad.

Susan waited until the waiter brought a carafe of wine,

then reached in her handbag and set the letter on top of Ruth's goblet.

Ruth stared at the familiar handwriting. "Oh, Susan. I'm scared." She held the envelope up to her cheek and closed her eyes for a moment before she slowly tore open the tan paper.

Ruth,

I know the chances of this ever finding you are slim, but I wanted to try. The U. S. Information Agency's Cultural Exchange Division just scheduled me for a reading tour at eight different American embassies, and Rome is on the agenda. I'll try to find you when I get there, unless you find me first. Rome is scheduled for June 11–13. If you are interested, write and I'll send you the schedule and times. I'd also like to know if you want me to try to fit any extra hours into the Rome visit. If I don't hear from you, I'll use the extra time anywhere other than Rome. I have no desire to be in the same city and apart.

You know why I was offered the tour? Someone from U.S.I.A. heard me read at Columbia last year. They said I read like a man inspired. You inspired the poet!

Yours,
T. J.

Ruth passed the letter to Susan without a word.

"Oh, Ruth. He's coming." Susan was ecstatic.

"Susan." Ruth grabbed her hand. "I'm getting married on April twenty-fifth. Peter called just after you did, and he made the arrangements with Cardinal Rosselli this morning. The Sistine Chapel—April 25th."

"You spent your weekend with Peter, Bruno's cousin?"

"Yes. We're getting married. Susan, Tom is a married man. His wife is in a mental institution. Divorce is out of the question—he can't desert her." She stopped and absentmindedly rearranged her silverware. "But of course I'll see Tom. I'll explain to Peter. Tom and I don't have to continue having a physical relationship—but we do have to

167

keep up the . . . emotional . . . support of each other." Ruth appealed to Susan. "Now what could possibly be wrong with that?"

"Nothing," Susan answered positively and added just as positively, "But don't do it."

"Don't do what?"

"Don't talk to Peter about it," Susan said emphatically.

"Why not?" Ruth took a sip of wine.

There was a momentary lull in the conversation as the waiter brought the linguine. Then Susan leaned across the table, her voice low and intense.

"Now you know that I am devoted to Raphael. Right?" Ruth nodded.

"Well, a couple months after we were married, I had an after-school drink one Friday with John. It was the end of the marking period, and you know how that feels. Well, anyhow, when Raphael came home, I mentioned it. And he slapped me." She jabbed a forkful of linguini and stuffed it into her mouth.

"Raphael?" Ruth was aghast.

"Raphael!" Susan chewed her pasta for a moment. "And he kept slapping me. I had embarrassed him, you see. How could I possibly do that? He was so ashamed. I was a loose woman! All that over a drink with John!"

"What'd you do?"

"I walked out the door." Susan gestured with her fork.

"And?"

"And he came after me." She grinned. "He carried me back into the apartment, gave me a bath in cool water,"— again she leaned across the table—"and we made the juiciest love we've ever made. Every once in a while he threatens to slap me around again—just so we can make up."

They ate for a moment in silence. Then Ruth said, "So you just gave up drinks on Friday afternoons?"

"What do you think?" Susan stared hard at her friend.

"I guess you had to." Ruth sighed.

"I have a drink with whom I please," said Susan, squaring her shoulders, "whenever I please. I just don't tell my husband. I'm not suggesting you don't see Tom or that you don't continue some kind of relationship with him. I'm just recommending you don't talk it over with Peter."

The veal and salad arrived, and the waiter refilled their wineglasses. Throngs of schoolchildren passed by on their way back to classes after lunch. They looked like rows of identical bugs in their navy blue uniforms.

"Italian males have the most blatant double standard I've ever seen," Susan continued as she cut her meat. "A man can not only have a mistress, he can flaunt her. A woman can't even have male *friends*. I'll bet, if you wanted to have lunch with Tom and you told Peter about it, either he'd forbid it, or he'd insist that Nona be there, too."

"Are you serious?" Ruth was appalled. "Bruno wasn't like that!"

"Bruno was a saint," Susan stated flatly. "A nicer, more tolerant man I never met in my life. Bruno was the least Italian Italian I ever met."

Ruth shook her head, still unconvinced. "I love Peter. I'm crazy about him. And what in the world could Peter Morelli have to be jealous about? He's got everything." Her voice took on a warm richness as she said, "But Tom—I love him, too, in a very special way. But I can marry Peter, and I know Tom will understand and encourage me," she assured herself. "That's what our love is like. It has nothing to do with people and places and restraints. It's been physical, but I think it could not be. Oh, Susan, help me." Ruth's face was contorted with uncertainty, and Susan reached out to grab one of her hands, almost spilling the wine in the process.

"I will, Ruth." She paused in thought. "I think you're right. Tom will understand and encourage you. You have a chance now, a second chance, for happiness of your own—and you really should take it. You love him. Who wouldn't? And he loves you, who wouldn't?" She smiled affectionately at her friend. "Grab it, Ruth. When Tom comes, we'll work out some way for you to get to see him."

"I think you're right. This is my chance—I should take it. I just feel like reality came crashing down on me. I

certainly don't feel as jubilant as I did last night. I thought,
if I thought about it at all, that Tom and I would just sort
of continue like we were. That maybe he'd eventually
just . . . fade out of my life. But my heart absolutely stopped
at the mere sight of a letter from him. I will *have* to see
him. I will just *not* tell Peter."

The waiter came to ask if they wanted dessert and
coffee. Susan had to get back to teach advanced algebra,
but Ruth ordered tea.

"Good girl. Now, don't worry—and for heaven's sake, be
happy. Wouldn't *Tom* be upset if he thought *you* were
upset because you heard from him? He wrote to make you
happy—not to . . ." Susan stumbled for the right words.

"Yes, you're right. He would be disappointed in me. We
talked about this once, how bad it would be if I let myself
sit around and mope and get my head all bent out of
shape." She was feeling stronger, more confident. "I've
heard from him. That's great! I'm getting married. That's
great! I'll just take things as they come and enjoy the
present." Her confidence faded. "Easy enough to say."

"Yes, but you can do it." Susan patted her mouth with
the napkin and put some money on the table.

"Right." Ruth smiled a crooked smile.

"I've got to run, Ruth, but if I had time, there's one
thing I'd love to know." She stood up and leaned over to
whisper in Ruth's ear. "How'd you inspire the poet?"

"How did I inspire the poet?" Ruth said softly, smiling.
"That'll give me something to think about while I drink
my tea. Goodbye, Susie, and thank you so much. What
would I do without you?"

In answer Susan patted Ruth's cheek and then flew out
the door, hurrying back to her thirty-three eager young
minds. Ruth Tyack Sevini was left with her tea and her
memories.

She had last seen Tom in January of 1976. Bruno had
died on October nineteenth, and Nona, husbandless, losing her only child, had thought of Ruth's grief and had
cabled Ruth's father. Ruth wouldn't have bothered. The
man who wouldn't leave Pittsburgh, Pennsylvania, for

graduation ceremonies in Akron, Ohio, certainly wasn't going to leave for a funeral in Rome, Italy. But he did. Death he could understand. He was a fortress when it came to sharing other people's grief. It was happiness that was difficult for Ben Tyack to bear. Graduation ceremonies were for parents—and since he couldn't go with his Annie, he wouldn't go at all. He always ended up making flimsy excuses, and Ruth had never understood. She thought he didn't care, which wasn't true at all; Ruth was the only color in his black and white life.

Nona knew when she opened the door for Ben and saw Ruth's amazement and gratitude that she had been wise to send the cable. Father and daughter fell into each other's arms in their first spontaneous display of affection and concern for nearly a quarter of a century. Ruth cried for Bruno and his severed life, for Nona and her barren life, and for the injustice of her own fate. Ben cried for his helplessness in shielding Ruth, and he cried for his Annie. The closeness that was established between Ben and Ruth in that late afternoon of tears would never leave them again.

Ruth returned to Pittsburgh, and the months from October to January were filled with discovery and sharing for the two Tyacks. They became friends. Ben would come home from school as early as possible, and he and Ruth would plan their evenings. They went to Pitt's basketball games, the opera, the Pittsburgh Symphony, a Maynard Ferguson concert, a Russian ballet, and a few departmental parties. But mostly they stayed home, talked, and ate elegant dinners. During the day Ruth cooked, trying every bread, pie, and cake recipe she came across. The meat was never plain—it was always sauced. She mastered béarnaise, bordelaise, and Madeira. The vegetables were creamed, souffléed, or hollandaised. The potatoes were puffed, the eggs were quiched. Ruth gained five pounds a month, and Ben was reduced to having only coffee for breakfast and a small tossed salad without dressing for lunch, to try to counteract the effects of the calorie carnival at supper.

They survived Christmas by going home to the family farm in Allegheny County. Agnes's eight grandchildren in the house for four days required the attention of every adult present. Aunt Ruth became once again the favorite storyteller, bath giver and cereal fixer. Ruth was aware of the relatives' whispers: "It's so good for her to have the children to think about." But she enjoyed it anyway. There was no arguing the point: it *was* good for her to have the children to think about.

If only they had all stayed together for New Year's Eve, as well, but they didn't. When Ben went to bed around nine-thirty, Ruth's defenses fell apart completely, and she, too, went to bed, turned on the radio, and cried, remembering the New Year's Eve that she and Bruno had first made love. She missed him desperately. She was so lonely, so hollow. She felt as if she had died, too. A part of her had.

By January Ruth seemed, in her father's categorical mind, to pass from her cooking phase to her puzzle phase. So on Sunday, January 13, Ben came home with the usual Sunday papers plus the *New York Times*, telling Ruth that he thought she might enjoy the challenge of the Sunday Magazine puzzle. She didn't; it was too hard for her. Which is how she happened to be leafing through the *Times Book Review*, and saw the notice:

POETRY READING—FRIDAY AFTERNOON

January 18 at 4:00
All invited—Free Admission
Sponsored by the
English Department of Columbia University

Tom Jeffers, *American poet,*
reading in
McMillin Theater.

She knew she would go. Her father was pleased that she would have a long weekend holiday in New York. She told him she would be visiting a friend named Jill (who happened to reside in Seattle, Washington) and felt only small guilt over the lie. She flew from Pittsburgh to La Guardia airport early Thursday afternoon and, from the airport, called the Columbia English Department to explain that she had made plans with Dr. Jeffers to do an interview for her local paper. He had suggested she come to his hotel this evening, but she had forgotten which hotel it was. The well-meaning secretary was glad to provide the answer.

Ruth thought she would completely surprise T. J. and so, after she had checked into the Algonquin, she went to his room. Trembling with excitement and grinning like a madwoman, she knocked. The door was opened by a black-haired young woman wearing a beige herringbone pants suit and a ruffled white shirt. Ruth could not have been more stunned if a furry green monster or an Indian in a turban had stood there.

"May I help you?" The girl smiled. She looked like a student—looked like Ruth had looked six years ago: fresh faced, intelligent.

"Oh, no, I'm sorry. I'm afraid I have the wrong room." She glanced down the hall toward the elevator, as though it were at fault. "I must have gotten off on the wrong floor. I'm sorry." Her voice was calm, but she was shaking from head to foot. Was this a repeat for T. J. of the night *they* had spent together? Was he even now performing the Zambigadan Festival Ritual? Ruth felt the color leave her face and feared she might faint. The girl seemed not to notice. "No problem," she said and closed the door.

Only then, as Ruth sank against the wall, did she realize there had been noise behind the door. A party. Or a bull session. But there were people in that room, not just a person, not just T. J. and some young girl, but a group.

Relief soared through her as she walked slowly down the hall to the elevator. She thought, then, of calling and asking to talk to him, but she was still shaky. She decided to leave a note in his mailbox at the hotel desk. Acutely aware that he might not be alone when he read it, she was deliberately casual:

T.J.,

Would be glad for a short interview if you have any spare time. Your old friend,

R. Tyack Sevini
Room 697

She ordered dinner from room service, afraid to go out for fear she'd miss him, and sat despondently waiting all evening. Eventually she went to bed, tossed and turned, and finally slept.

At eight-fifteen there was a knock on the door. She had been awake since six and had ordered tea and rolls. Expecting room service, she opened the door immediately.

"Ruth." He said it softly, a statement.

She registered nothing except his eyes: those marvelous, laughing, caring, loving gray eyes. Then Ruth opened her arms to him, and with a moan he was in them, crushing her.

They might have stayed like that forever, but Tom heard people coming down the hall and moved to get the door shut. His back to her, he locked it, then he turned slowly. He was having trouble with control, his mouth unsteady, his teeth biting his lip, his eyes wet. She burst into tears and crumpled into a heap on the floor.

He was beside her immediately, on his knees, arms around her shoulders. In slow motion he eased himself back, lying flat, and pulled her on top of him. Cradling her face, he said huskily, "My sweet, dear girl."

She hiccupped the end of her tears, smiling now, half laugh, half cry. "Hello, love."

She lowered her head to his, and warm lips closed around her salty ones in reassurance and renewal. They both stayed still, afraid to move, to break the spell. They rediscovered the feel of the other.

Ruth lifted her head and said inanely, "You taste like toothpaste."

He smiled at her, his arms tightening around her, his hands moving on her back. "So do you."

"I've been brushing my teeth every five minutes since

six o'clock last night," she said seriously. Her hands were all over his face, feeling the cheekbones, the nose, the ears, the forehead: a mother doing an inventory of her newborn baby.

"You have been here since six o'clock last night?" His gray eyes were appalled, sad for the wasted time.

She nodded solemnly. "I came to your room, but there was a party, and I got scared."

"Dr. Ranson's poetry class. Oh, damn it. To have not seen you sooner. I didn't find the note until I went down for breakfast." The corners of his eyes crinkled, and the spark of annoyance was replaced by devilment. "We'll have to make up for that." His hands strayed down her back to her bottom. The blue nylon nightgown had slipped up around her waist. He caressed the curve of flesh, his hand traveled gently up and down her ridges and valleys.

Ruth's body responded to T.J. in a way she had forgotten possible. His hands on her skin were orgasmic. The organs inside her shifted and shuddered. Flashes of warmth replaced the blood in her veins, and from her heart to her ankles and up under her scalp, the nerve endings danced on her flesh as she clung to Tom, hugging him, grasping him like the lone tree on the mountainside breaking her fall.

Her mind was busy with messages of its own: *this is what life is all about, being with Tom. I am alive!* Aloud she said, "Oh, dear God. I love you."

Her spirit sighed.

The sun spun myriad images over their bodies as they lay on the pale pink carpeting of room 697. The light rays picked up the gold thread of the pink and gold bedspread so that even the Aztecs would have looked on in awe. Ruth and Tom had abandoned reality and were floating in space.

She wanted to ask how he was but instead found her hands busy with the dark brown zipper that was denying her access to his body. When she had that zipped down, the belt still needed to be unbuckled, and then the snap exploded while her hungry fingers pushed at the textured brown material and the smooth white material underneath so that it was out of her way. She grasped him roughly, in a frenzy to fill her hollow spaces, and then she had trouble getting him inside her. She had to sit up, kneel over him. Then she simply descended on him, fitting herself over him, the mitten on the hand.

T.J. swiftly yanked the fluffy blue material over her head, and his hands moved wildly over her body, squeezing her breasts, pulling her down against him to get the feel of the hard nipples and the soft skin, pushing her back up to see the beauty of their union, to fill himself with her womanliness. She was rising up and down on him, closing her muscles, contracting and expanding, in and out, up and down. Their mouths were joined, tongues driving deep, trying with all their might to swallow each other, to climb completely out of their separate skins and into the same comforting cloak of love.

Then her rhythm became too slow for him, and he had to pull her down and roll her over; on his knees, he thrust into her, as though only the most driving pressure could save their lives, and her hips rose up to join his beat. His hands grasped her bottom, and then inside her, pushing her together, pulling her apart, an absolute fierce abandonment of need. She lowered her hands, and her fingers mirrored his moves. She was sure her insides would momentarily pour out on the rug. Famished, he took a breast in his mouth, and at that moment he exploded within her and bit the pink skin between his teeth. She yelped, then moaned. Then, while his lips and teeth devoured her breast, her mouth, his hands were busy between her legs. He could feel the scream of climax starting deep beneath her, and he covered her mouth with his before the noise escaped her throat. And then he was back inside her, full and fierce again. Skin slapped wet and hard against skin. Finally while her body trembled its series of smaller earthquakes, he shuddered in climax and collapsed on top of her.

After a time he pushed himself up on his elbows. "My beautiful, beautiful Ruth. How I have thought about you and dreamed about you. I would awaken, wet or the bed damp, and the memory of your moving body under mine would be so vivid that it would take me a while to realize I had been dreaming." His hands held her head in tribute, his fingers ran through the short blond curls. His lips touched hers, every sentence, every other move punctuated by kisses.

"Oh, T.J. Never, never in the world was there anyone like you." A last rippling tremor ran through her body, and Tom tightened his hold. Suddenly he rolled off her, pulling her along so they were side by side on the floor, still united, no space between their bodies. But a frown creased his already wrinkled brow, and he said very softly, "Ruth, did I hurt you?"

She lifted her head off the carpet and bent over him. She gently kissed his brow. "I feel so good to know that you needed me so much. This hasn't been sex, Tom, this has been something else—catharsis, maybe, I don't know what else to call it. What we just experienced—"

"Are experiencing." He winked at her. "I'm not done."

She laughed and then bit her lip. "You know what I mean?"

"Yes, darling girl, you are so right." She laid her head down on his arm, and while one of his arms held her bottom firmly, the other hand was busy stroking, petting. "I love you, Ruth. My need of you is unquenchable and eternal. I had no idea it was quite so strong, although I know that since I met you, you haven't been out of my mind or my heart."

"Oh, my dear love. Whatever shall we do?"

She looked so solemn, he became tuned to her need. "Let's go lie down in bed. We can have some good hugs and some good talk."

"Okay, but I'm so wet—you, too; we're just drenched with sweat and other secretions." She smiled wantonly at him. "Let's go get dried off."

"Maybe we should hop in the tub for a minute."

"Yes. Together."

He pulled her to her feet, and they walked, arms around each other, into the bathroom. Tom got the tub going, adding some bath oil that the hotel provided, while Ruth sat on the toilet seat staring at him, treating her eyes to the sight of curly gray hair.

"It's all gray now—no brown left anywhere," she observed.

"It's had some rough moments. When did you get yours cut?"

"When I got married. It seemed more suitable."

He was squatting down beside the tub, his hand under the faucet, and when he looked back over his shoulder, Ruth gave an inarticulate cry and crouched down beside him on the floor, her arms around his waist. He cradled her head, and they rocked back and forth a little, each shedding some private tears for the last four years.

He put a finger against her lips then: "Later."

She nodded her head, gave a wobbly smile, and they stepped into the tub. Tom sat down, leaning against the back of the tub, and turned Ruth to face him so that she sat on his lap. She gazed hungrily at his wonderful face: the wide, sexy lips, the rugged complexion, the high, intelligent forehead, the thick gray eyebrows over the liquid gray eyes. Her legs were uncomfortable, but she gladly endured cramped muscles to sit on Tom's lap in a tub of warm, steamy, pine-scented water. There were two washcloths hanging on the rack over the tub: they each reached for one and started washing the other, dribbling water over each other's chest and legs.

Ruth had to get out of the tub to use the john, then got back in, sitting so that he could wash her back. He pulled her up on his lap and hugged her hard from behind, and she felt him growing under her. Water splashing over the side of the tub, she turned around to face him and kiss him and run her hands down his back, pulling him against her, gray curls caressing swollen breasts. They teetered and leaned, and finally he knelt, and eventually Ruth perched on the edge of the tub, leaning into Tom as he came, with gentle firmness, inside her.

They sank back down in the water then, sitting at opposite ends this time, knees touching, holding hands, feeling so exhausted and lethargic they finally decided they'd better get out before they slid, insensate, under the surface.

He dried her with the fluffy white towel, and then she took it from him and patted the moisture from his chest and crotch, admired the muscles in his legs and thighs, leaned against his back.

He pulled her into the room, straightened out her nightgown, and pulled it down over her head, then shrugged on his T-shirt and shorts. They lay down in bed, her head on his chest, and he pulled the covers up around them, elaborately tucking her in.

"This is heaven." She sighed, her fingers roaming slowly over his cotton-clad chest and side.

He gave her a squeeze and said, "Now tell me."

She sighed, again, bestowed a kiss on his chest, and moved her head onto the second pillow.

"Teaching was wonderful. I loved the school. I loved the kids. It's this little red brick schoolhouse in the midst of tan, stucco Rome."

Tom leaned up on an elbow to look at her. Ruth reached her hand out; he grabbed it. She pulled his hand against her cheek and held tight to the comfort.

"My second September in Rome I met Bruno at a bridge party. He was everything you would have wanted for me. Immensely kind, gentle, a very good man. Falling in love with him was easy. He was very steady—an accountant, a good one. He encouraged me to keep on teaching. We were so comfortable, Tom." She looked over at him, imploring him to understand.

He smiled a sweet smile and stroked her cheek a little, where his hand rested. "It sounds wonderful, Ruth."

"It was." She sighed and looked away from Tom to continue her story. "He died in October. A woman crossed the median strip on the autostrada between Rome and Florence. He had been in Florence for three days. I don't know why I didn't go along. I had quit teaching that year. We thought we could travel together and maybe have a baby." Ruth sighed and clutched hard at Tom's hand.

"Bruno got out of her way—he apparently saw her

coming, and he avoided her—but the car, Bruno's car, hit a rut in the grass. It rolled over and over and broke into flames. Nobody got him out." Tears were starting down Ruth's cheeks. Tom moved over on top of her, covering her body with his, as if to protect her.

"How could they not get him out, Tom?" she whispered into his hair. "How could they just let him die like that? A freeway jammed with cars, and nobody got him out." She clung to Tom, crying. He just held on. When the tears subsided, he rolled off and pulled her onto his chest and rubbed her back.

Later she sat up beside him, Indian-style, while he lay with his hands under his head.

"It just tore me apart completely. This sensible, wonderful person dying in a senseless tragedy. And my whole secure, planned life thrown out the window. I could not get my act back together. I just couldn't.

"So, I came home. I love Bruno's mother, but I simply couldn't stay and expect her to help me out of this. So I returned home with dad. He's been great. So patient. He'll walk in, and my eyes will be red, and he'll just sit down and start telling me about his day. He has been so good at just being there.

"But when I saw the notice about the poetry reading in the *New York Times*, I knew I was alive again—you were my first step toward getting back. I had to see you! Was I wrong to stir things up again?"

"Ruth." He pulled up his T-shirt and hoisted her over on top of his stomach, her bare crotch straddling his belly. "This is the nicest thing that has happened to me in four years and four months and twenty-six days."

"You know exactly how long it's been." She was filled with wonder. "I don't believe you." She leaned down to kiss him, her lips moving on his, over and around his mouth, and then she started biting his lips, her bottom moving seductively on his body.

His hands crept under her nightgown, and as he touched a breast with each palm, he said against her lips, "I could eat you up."

She moved back an inch from his mouth and replied

with great seriousness, "Please don't let anything I've said or done discourage you."

T.J.'s eyes reflected the shock of his innocent Ruth sounding so worldly and sophisticated. He loved it. His eyes crinkled with laughter, and he kissed her on the lips before sliding down under her, positioning his mouth between her legs. His hands held her hips, rubbing, keeping her from escaping as his tongue excited her. His lips found that secret place, and while she moaned, he licked inside and around, returning always to the most responsive spot. He needed more room, and he pushed her on her back and grabbed her feet, and his mouth returned to finish its journey. He could feel the little pebble softening, expanding, ice becoming water, his lips licking the newly formed moisture, his nose greedily sniffing the musky female scent, his taste buds devouring the salty sweetness. He couldn't get enough of her. She came and shuddered and begged him to stop, and he kept on. Spasms of ecstasy rocked her body.

When finally he rested his cheek against her pelvis, she tucked a cushion under his head. He could barely open his eyes to smile at her.

From the waist down she felt paralyzed, but she made herself move because she wanted him to feel the ecstasy she had. She held him and kissed him and rubbed him and bit him with her lips, and when she started sucking on the rounded tip of his penis, she felt the response and knew she had enough love in her heart to make up for any lack of expertise.

"Signora. *Prego*, signora." The waiter from Pere Diablo stood before Ruth's table, holding her bill.

Ruth lifted her head from her hands and fought a terrible battle inside herself. She wanted to be in New York with Tom in January of 1976—not alone in a Roman *ristorante* in April of 1977. She shook off the memory and reached into her handbag for money. Outside, she walked down to the nearby square and sat on a wooden bench, staring into a fountain, her thoughts going back again to that January with Tom.

* * *

They had spent that entire weekend together. He had indeed read as a man inspired that Friday afternoon. And then they had practically barricaded themselves in Ruth's room.

Once again Tom was adamant that the weekend be simply a period set apart from the rest of their lives. Helen was in a mental institution, he told Ruth, and he was not innocent of helping her get there. He wouldn't divorce her.

"Ruth, I realize it may be crazy, a pointless sacrifice that may make sense to no one but me. But I can't desert her now. Even if it's only symbolic. Even if she'd never know. I'd know."

"T.J. It doesn't matter. I'll just move close to you; we'll have a forty-year affair." She had been pleased with her solution.

"No! Absolutely no, Ruth. You are twenty-seven. I won't tie you to a parttime love affair. You should get married and have children, not fool around when *I* can get away, for however long *I* can get free, always on the sly, never able to claim each other."

"Tom, please. Any part of you is worth three of anyone else."

"No. All that does is compromise us both and cheapen what exists between us. We'll come to each other whole and free someday—or we'll continue this leap-year business of once every four years." He had stopped talking, then, and had looked through her eyes into her soul. "I love you, Ruth. I adore you. We are part of each other. That's enough."

She cried, begged, bargained, threatened, and cried some more. He was inflexible, immovable.

They had a beautiful weekend, crammed with sustaining memories. And then they had gone to La Guardia, and Tom had put Ruth on a westward-bound plane while he headed north.

Ruth got up from her park bench and walked to her car. She was oblivious to the bursting buds, the fresh greenness, the flowers popping through the ground. Her mind was seeing only gray curls and laughing gray eyes.

"Tom Jeffers," she whispered, "wherever you are: I love you."

And then she drove back to Nona's to make arrangements for her wedding to Peter Morelli.

9

Half hidden by foliage, Tom Jeffers stood in the doorway watching his son and Stanley Ellis putter about the greenhouse. They compared opinions on which cactus was growing tallest, which begonia had the prettiest pink flowers. Tom thought back over the last four years and the progress his son had made since the move. Obviously it had been the right thing for Tommy—in fact, the situation was so perfect that it seemed impossible to imagine it was planned by other than the hand of Providence.

"Evenin', Mr. Jeffers," Emma Ellis said softly behind him.

"Mrs. Ellis," he acknowledged her, smiling. She turned and walked into the kitchen and he followed her, sniffing the mingled scents of a pot roast cooking, apples stewing, and cinnamon bread baking.

She opened the refrigerator and handed him a bottle of dark beer.

"Nice to see, isn't it?" Her weathered head tilted across the brick floor in the direction of Tommy and Stan Ellis.

"You will never know, Mrs. Ellis. Words can not express the debt I owe you and your husband for the way you have taken Tommy to your hearts. *Never* has he thrived as he has here with you two—with the love and security you both offer him."

They leaned on the wide blue Formica counter, Tom sipping his beer, Mrs. Ellis's hands supporting her wrinkled chin.

"It's we who owe you, Mr. Jeffers, sharing that boy the way you do. We were floundering, the man and me, just adrift and anchorless from the time our Harry got killed until you drove in the road that summer day with Tommy." She paused, a tremor ran through her mind, across her lined white face. "We were dead, Mr. Jeffers, just hopeless, tired-a-livin' dead. Then that young fella got out of the car and smiled at us, and Mr. Ellis and I were struck exactly the same minute. I'm not saying he could replace Harry, mind you, isn't any living body could replace any other, but it was like our second chance. Oh, we talk about it, the day Tommy came and smiled at us, the day we started livin' again."

Tom patted her arm, then carried his beer into the den. It was a ritual he and Mrs. Ellis repeated almost every night. The words changed from night to night, but the theme was the same: both were unable to believe their good fortune. Seldom had an arrangement been so balanced; rarely had each side needed the other the way Tommy and the Ellises did.

Tom sighed as he sat down in his brown leather lounger. He pushed the lever to raise the foot of the chair, then ran a hand through his hair. His fingers caught in a tangled curl, and he thought about the color. He had been surprised how fast it had gotten gray. Less than a year after Helen had been committed, he had become totally gray. Amazing. Hair, mustache, beard—he looked ten years older than he was. Yet he was beginning to feel young again. He was lighthearted about Tommy and the Ellises. And he had this room.

As he did every night, Tom raised his beer in salute to the lady on the wall across from his chair. It wasn't a big wall—ten feet long and eight feet high—but every inch was covered with pictures—many of Ruth. He had shot a couple rolls of film of her when they had been together in New York last winter. He had had some of the pictures enlarged and had picked out from his album other shots he had always loved, the Maine coastline, New York. He'd gathered and arranged everything into a giant collage, fixed it all to the wall with wallpaper glue, then applied six coats of shellac over the entire surface. Some of the pictures were huge, some tiny, some were in color, some were black and white. It was startling, interesting, restful all at once for Tom.

Oh, lady . . . I'm waiting for your letter. God, I'll bet she'll be surprised to hear from me. You can always count on old Jeffers. No, Ruth, no communication—nothing! Then who lets down? Good old reliable T.J.—hardhearted old . . .

"Hiya, dad." Tommy bounded into the room, a twenty-two-year-old child, and leaned over to give Tom a kiss. "Mr. Ellis and Mrs. Ellis just went home—she said supper is all ready."

"Then let's go get it." Tom pulled himself out of his chair.

The table was in the kitchen—a huge round wooden table adrift on a sea of red bricks. A blue and white Early American print papered the walls, white Cape Cod curtains curled around the windows. As usual Mrs. Ellis had the red quilted place mats out, the table supplied with the white ironstone dishes, supper simmering. The very first time that Tom had gone off during the day, leaving Tommy to the Ellises, he had returned home that evening to supper waiting. He had been appreciative but admonitory. "Now, Mrs. Ellis, this is delightful to come home to, and I can't wait to taste this supper, but you mustn't do this. It's too much trouble for you." All to no avail. Every time he was away during the day his dinner was ready when he returned home. She would not hear of money. But Tom quickly learned she loved books, and now every time he was anywhere near a book store, he would stock up for her. It was an arrangement that suited them both perfectly. He had marvelous taste in books—she had a novel way with food.

Tom shook his head again, listening to Tommy chatter about the afternoon in the greenhouse. Mr. Ellis had never tried growing things before, and neither had Tommy; the mutual journey was exhilarating. Now there was always a ripe tomato for the salad or a fresh green pepper and sometimes something more exotic, like an eggplant. The flowers were delightful, too—geraniums, marigolds, tulips, whatever Mr. Ellis and Tommy felt like trying. When Tom had read the ad for the house and seen the item "greenhouse attached" he had thought of Ruth and her garden in Pittsburgh. He hadn't even thought about the possibilities for Tommy.

Secluded Maine farmhouse: living room, large country kitchen, den, 3 bedrooms, 2 baths, greenhouse attached, housekeeping available.

He wasn't even sure why he had followed up the ad—housekeeping available had been the charm, probably. The farmhouse was located about two hundred feet from the Ellises' house, the Ellises' home acting as a sort of buffer between the world and the farmhouse. Tom and Tommy would be on up the lane. It worked beautifully.

After supper the two men put the dishes in the dishwasher and retired to the den to play rummy for an hour. Four years ago Tom would never have dreamed that Tommy would get so good at rummy, but the combined efforts of Mr. and Mrs. Ellis had wrought miracles. Tommy was retarded, and he would always be retarded, but in the four years with the Ellises, he had learned an amazing number of things: to count, to recognize his letters, to dial a telephone. It took constant repetition to keep the knowledge in his head, but the Ellises seemed tireless in their efforts. He still couldn't learn to tie shoelaces—it was simply beyond him. And Mrs. Ellis, so fastidious in the kitchen, hadn't the patience to teach him to cook. But, on the whole, there was so much good, so much to be thankful for.

After an hour Tommy was bored with rummy and decided to watch "Happy Days" while Tom looked through the mail. On the top was a letter from Dr. Jeffrey Holmes of Buffalo, New York.

Tom went out to the kitchen to fix a bourbon and ginger, a double, then returned to the study and settled down in his lounger. To the accompaniment of the "Happy Days" laugh track he read about his wife's condition.

Dear Tom,

I wish I had some good news for you concerning Helen's progress. Unfortunately, there is *no* progress. She continues to deteriorate. She no longer does anything for herself—she doesn't dress herself, comb her hair, or brush her teeth. All these things are done for her. Each day they get her up and get her fixed up. She looks fairly normal, but she is as withdrawn as possible—recognizes no one, seemingly hears nothing, won't even flinch if a tray is dropped beside her.

I personally believe her case is hopeless, and as you know, I am not one to easily give up hope. She has no idea where she is. If this sanatorium is a financial strain, I would suggest having her transferred to the state institution. She'll never know the difference.

Tom looked up in time to see the Fonz trying to teach Richie how to be cool. Then he made himself return to the letter.

Physically, Tom, she is very weak, weighs less than ninety pounds. I must warn you that a heavy cold or a bout with pneumonia could kill her. She exhibits no will to live.

I don't tell you all this to depress you, but to try to encourage you to get on with your life. Divorce her, Tom. She won't know and won't care.

I promise you that I will see to it she is humanely and tenderly cared for. In our eight years of sessions before the night in the hospital I had grown quite fond of her. As you know, she was a witty and sophisticated conversationalist—and she was a good listener. Sometimes the therapy sessions seemed to do me as much good as they did her.

But that Helen is gone, Tom. She exists no more. The empty body that is left I will care for, but I have buried my friend Helen. I hope you will do the same with your wife. You are being unfair to yourself and

Tommy to let this shell of a life keep you immobilized and manacled.

This may not sound like a compassionate letter; it may not even sound morally or medically ethical. It is written more in concern for you than anything else. I will continue to have Sister Theresa write you monthly reports as long as you so desire. But please think about all I have said.

Read some of your poetry in *The New Yorker* last month—all this pain certainly has made you into a fine poet.

One piece of hospital gossip. Sally Maye Williams had twin girls last fall: Tabatha and Tomasina.

God speed,
Jeff Holmes

That Jeff Holmes! Leave it to him to find some happy news! Twin girls and one of them Tomasina. He wondered. . . . He knew Sally Maye would make a fantastic mother. A lucky guy, Williams, and a smart guy to realize all the good in Sally Maye.

He sighed and closed his eyes on the hurt.

I will not divorce her. If she lives to be ninety in her catatonic state, I will not divorce her. But how can her mind have gotten so screwed up? And how can I have been so much of an ass that I never even noticed?

"It's really funny, isn't it, daddy?" Tommy looked back at Tom, saw him wipe a tear from his eye, thought he was enjoying "Happy Days," too.

"Yes, son, it sure is." Luckily Tommy could never read anything into voices, so he didn't hear the pain and self-condemnation in Tom's voice.

Tom was pleasantly surprised by the contents of his second letter. It was from his agent, Michael McGrogan, suggesting an endeavor Tom had never even considered.

K.C. Barkley would like your collaboration on a movie. K.C. will write the music for it, feels sure from reading your poetry and essays and introductions that you could handle the text of the movie. K.C. has organized the project—secured producer, etc., and advances from Paramount, asks for you for the script.

How about coming into New York for a week or so and we'll hash over the possibilities, meet the people, etc.

Michael went on to say they were waiting for his agreement before accepting the publisher's offer on an anthology of Tom's poetry. Also, he had signed two new poets, and he would appreciate Tom doing the editing for their collections.

Tom really had better get himself to New York.

A week later he was in the big city. The Ellises had been overjoyed at the prospect of having Tommy for a week or two. They had fixed up Harry's old room, and before Tom had left, he had watched Tommy pack his suitcase and walk merrily down the lane for his adventure.

"Tom! Tom Jeffers!" sang a high voice, distinguishable through the noise of La Guardia, because it was recognized.

Tom swung at the sound of his name and saw the smiling dwarf approach him. Michael looked dapper, as always, in the finest tailor-made clothes and shoes. Today he wore charcoal gray flannel pants, a snowy white button-down collar shirt with gold cuff links blinking in the afternoon sun, navy blazer, red club tie, Gucci loafers, all perfectly scaled down. He was three feet, ten inches of immaculate cheerfulness.

"Michael." Tom reached out to grasp the short shoulder. "You didn't have to come meet me. I know you have a million things to do—I'm not your only client."

"Ah, but Tommy-me-boy, you are my favorite client, and by the Blessed Virgin I finally got ya to New York, so now we'll have ourselves a fine time, don't ya see?"

Michael's specially designed Corvette was waiting in the nearest no parking zone. They hurried off, Michael waving brightly to the on-duty policeman who simply saluted. Tom wondered what Michael had told the cop to secure the parking spot. He also wondered what he himself had done to rate this personal attention. In the twelve or so times writer and agent had met, they had gone out to lunch to a few swanky places, but that was the extent of it. Now he was being treated like Norman Mailer! His questions remained unanswered. Michael had set himself out to entertain, and entertain he did, so that Tom was only partially aware of arriving at the Waldorf-Astoria, leaving his bags, going to 21 for lunch, and then returning to Michael's Fifth Avenue office.

It was close to four o'clock, and Tom's sides ached from laughing; he was glad that a lithe blond had Michael's attention in the elevator and he could relax for a moment.

They walked into the office, and Peggy, very pregnant, tried to lean across the reception desk to shake Tom's hand but found it a hard lean.

"Peggy, how nice to see you."

"I was delighted when Michael said you were coming."

"When did all this happen?" he inquired, eyes encompassing her round tummy.

"Oh, about eight months ago." Peggy smiled at Tom, then nodded over her shoulder to Michael. "She's in there."

Michael grimaced, "How long?"

"About an hour."

"Okay. You keep Tom entertained here, and I'll go settle her ladyship's hash with a bit o' blarney."

As Michael entered his office, they could hear the piano being played by an expert, and then suddenly the concert stopped, and an unhappy voice pouted, "It's about time."

Michael turned on the brogue and softly closed the door.

"Uh-oh," Tom shuddered. "I gather our lunch lasted a little longer than it should have."

"Don't worry. Michael can smooth much more ruffled feathers than those."

"Peggy, you look wonderful. But why are you still working?"

"Oh, I don't want to sit home and worry. And you know

how accommodating Michael is. If I get too tired, I go lie down for a while, or I go home early, or I come in late or something. There are four other women who work here— they're in another office. I'm just the window dressing."

"I should say."

She was blushing prettily when the door flew open and a striking, tall, slim, black-haired woman strutted out, followed by Michael on his abbreviated legs.

"Dr. Jeffers." She extended a well-manicured hand.

Tom rose. "How do you do." He extended his hand, only to have it grasped between both of hers.

Michael managed to place himself between the hand holders.

"Dr. Tom Jeffers, it is my pleasure to present Ms. K.C. Barkley. K.C.—Tom."

More nods and smiles all around. Then K.C. tucked her hand inside Tom's arm and led him into Michael's office. Michael obediently followed after.

As the door closed, she said silkily, "I believe I have some propositions that you will have no desire to refuse."

By five-thirty Peggy should have been long gone, but she was reluctant to depart before she saw Tom's reaction to Ms. K.C. When the door finally reopened, the woman was again holding Tom's arm and cooing, "Now, darling, where shall we go for dinner?"

Tom's eyes frantically focused on Peggy, who smiled up at him from her desk. He disengaged his arm, saying, "I'm so sorry, but I'm tied up this evening."

"Oh, but surely you can get out of it."

"No, I'm afraid not. You see she's sitting right here waiting for me. Aren't you, Peggy?"

All eyes focused on the eight-month-pregnant reception- ist in time to see a demure smile and blush appear.

"Yes," she answered daintily and dutifully.

"Well, in that case I'll see you bright and early tomor- row morning, and we'll get started on the script." K.C. kissed Tom full on the mouth, called "Ta, ta, Michael," and sauntered out, her silver jewelry clinking a fanfare.

Michael said, "Lock up, Peggy, will you like a dear, I'm late for a party. See you on the morrow, Tommie-me-boy."

As the door closed, Tom looked at Peggy apologetically. "I'm sor—" But when he saw she was holding her stomach laughing, he broke up himself.

"You really got her. I never saw anyone get her so good." Peggy's words were punctuated with an infectious laugh.

"She was certainly shocked that I was able to refuse at least one of her propositions."

"The idea that you, of all people"—Peggy was laughing so hard she could hardly talk—"would prefer an eight-month-pregnant whatever-I-am to her!"

"You looked shocked, yourself; I was afraid you were going to have the baby on the spot."

"Oh, it hurts to laugh." She laughed.

"*Would* you like to go out to dinner?" He perched on the edge of her desk. "I would be delighted to take you."

"Thank you *very* much, but I can't stand clothes and shoes anymore today. I have to get home and get comfortable." She smiled up at him, her lips extracting the sting from the refusal.

"Oh, sure. I understand. Besides, what would your husband say?"

"There is no husband, Dr. Jeffers." Her head bent over the blotter in deep concentration. "The Mrs. Abbott on the sign here"—she motioned with the top of her head—"is purely Michael's Irish invention to prevent scandal. The father of this baby is a quite-married man. He and I had a three-week affair, and I haven't seen him since. Nor do I want to see him. All I want is the baby."

"I'm sorry. I didn't mean to put you in a position of having to tell me that." Tom turned to the edge of Peggy's desk to see her better.

"That's okay." She was straightening the already straightened desk, rearranging the paper clips.

"Well, I'll see you tomorrow, then." He broke the awkward silence, cursing himself, and rose to leave. "Shall I wait and walk out with you? I'm not in any hurry."

"Okay. I'll just lock the doors."

Peggy pulled herself up and walked purposefully from door to door, locking up. As he watched, he thought that if he were a painter or a sculptor he would try to catch and immortalize her special grace and dignity. As it was, he would merely write a poem for her: "Mama Bear."

"Okay."

He was pulled out of his trance by her soft voice. They walked to the elevator and rode down to the street. It wasn't until he had said, "Well, then, goodbye," and was turning to walk away that she called to him, "Would you like to come home with me and have supper?"

"Yes," he answered eagerly. Turning, he took her by the arm.

At that moment a miracle in New York transpired: a taxi cruised by slowly. Tom hailed it and handed Peggy in. She gave her address and then sighed and leaned back against the seat. Five minutes later they were entering her apartment. She crossed to the kitchen and opened the refrigerator.

"We could have an omelet and a salad, or there's some frozen fried chicken or some corned beef and Swiss cheese that we could do something with."

"What sounds good to you?" he asked.

"Oh, I don't know."

"Look, I tell you what." He walked over to her and put his hands on her shoulders. "Now, first of all, I am not pregnant. Right?"

"Right." Eyes down; chin down.

"Secondly, I got us into this. Right?"

"Right." Reluctantly. Chin down; eyes up.

"Third, I would like to do something nice for you, to thank you for going along with me in the office. Right?"

"Right. I guess." Eyes and chin up—she was intrigued.

"So. How about if you go change your clothes and I'll get some supper started, and then you can have a little rest, and I'll read the paper, and then when you feel like it, we'll eat. How is that for a flawless plan?"

"Flawless." She was entranced.

"Good."

He dropped his hands and turned his back on her, opening doors and drawers. Feeling superfluous and not a little bit tired, she went to do as she was told.

In the bedroom she stripped naked, put on a cotton print caftan and, barefooted, went out to the couch and laid down. He smiled at her through the window between the kitchen and living room.

"I found a bottle of bourbon and helped myself. What can I get you, my lady?"

Smiling broadly Peggy said, "A little of that ginger ale on ice, please."

Tom served her drink, scowled at something, disappeared into her bedroom, and reappeared with two pillows, which he propped, one under her head, the other under her feet. Then he smiled and bowed his way back into the kitchen. The next time he looked in, Peggy was fast asleep, a small smile on her lips.

He made a chef's salad with the corned beef and cheese, found some bakery rolls in the freezer and set them out to thaw, and mixed together a small can of tomato juice and a can of beef bouillon and put it on to simmer with some parsley and cloves. Pleased with himself, he stretched out in the chair beside the window and read *The New York Times*.

She awoke, embarrassed, wiping the moisture of sleep from her lips, trying to get up, saying, "Oh, my God, I'm so sorry. I had no idea I'd actually fall asleep, and for so long."

"Greetings, my lady. You feel refreshed from your sleep, I hope?" he inquired, putting the paper down.

"Dr. Jeffers, something smells wonderful."

"When you call me Dr. Jeffers, it makes me feel like your obstetrician. Do you think you could try Tom?"

"Yes. Thank you. And what a treat, to have supper made when I get up from my nap. And you even have the table all set. This looks so inviting."

He helped her get up, took her arm, and seated her with great show at the table.

"Now, my lady would like what to drink?"

"What is all this 'my lady' stuff?"

He stopped and looked at her seriously. "Geez. Did I let myself into the wrong apartment? Someone ordered a waiter/cook/butler for the evening in repayment for a favor. I thought it was you."

"But of course it was, Thomas. Carry on." She haughtily waved her small hand.

"And to drink?"

"Oh, I think water on the rocks, please."

They enjoyed their supper, she smiling shyly, he at ease, as if their roles of host and guest were reversed.

"Peggy. Why do you think Michael was so secretive about K.C. Barkley's sex?"

"What do you mean?" She was taken by surprise at the tone of his voice as well as the content of the question.

"Did you see the letter he sent me?"

"Un-huh," corned beef half chewed, "I typed it."

"Well, it was K.C. this and K.C. that. No 'she' anywhere, no mention of her womanness."

"Womanness?"

"Well, I didn't want to say ladyhood or femininity." He choked on some lettuce and his own wit and washed it all down with water.

She was inordinately pleased by his lack of attraction to K.C.

"Well, I don't know. But I think Michael maybe wanted to interest you in the project before explaining that you would be working with a woman. Gee, this consommé is terrific, Tom."

"Thank you. I've never cooked for a sleeping pregnant woman before—it's fun."

She giggled.

"I think he wanted to trap me."

"But why? How? You're married, aren't you?"

"Well, yes and no. My wife is in a sanatorium. She is insane—they don't expect her to recover." He tried to be matter-of-fact, but his voice failed him and cracked on 'insane,' there being no matter-of-fact way to say your wife is insane. He drank some more water.

She reached her hand across the table. "We both have some heavy things to bear."

"Yes." He squeezed the pudgy fingers and for the first time really looked at her as a woman. All he had ever guessed was that she was Jewish. She was short, dark, and chunky, but stylish and pleasant. And now he saw her beautiful black eyes and her flawless complexion and the way she tilted her head to the side when she listened. Probably young men wouldn't consider her particularly attractive, but with his older, wiser priorities, he found her lovely. He felt a surge of desire he had not felt since he had last seen Ruth.

"Could we have some hot tea, Thomas?"

"Certainly." Except that he was afraid to stand up for fear of a telltale bulge. "Just tell me first if you are Jewish."

"Half and half. My father quit the priesthood and married my Jewish mama. When I was six, he hanged himself in the basement and my mother got a job as a seamstress for Lord and Taylor."

He was stunned. "Is she there now?"

"No. My brother teaches philosophy at Strassburg College in Indiana, and he found her a job as a dorm mother."

"You sound like a soap opera."

"You haven't heard the clincher. My brother is a homosexual—but luckily neither my mother nor Strassburg College have found out yet."

"Do you have other brothers or a sister?"

"Nope. Just us two. Thank goodness there aren't others, considering how well we're doing."

"Oh, I don't know. You seem to have your head on straight." He got up to make the tea, skillfully keeping his back to Peggy. "Are you going to quit your job when the baby comes?"

"No. I couldn't. I have a friend with a three year old who's going to take care of her until she's old enough to go to nursery school. And Michael, of course, is wonderful. Did you see the baby's room?"

"No."

"Come on. You won't believe this. Come here."

She rose awkwardly, reaching for his hand. The hallway led back to the second bedroom. Tom was immediately transported to a fantasy land.

The walls were painted a soft pink, pink and white gingham curtains billowed at the windows and skirted the white wicker bassinet. The cherry crib was covered by a canopy of pink and white gingham, and on the floor lay a pink plaid carpet. Everything any baby could possibly want or need adorned the walls, the floors, the shelves.

"See the little pink bear in the crib?" He nodded. "I bought that," she went on. "Everything else—everything—came from Michael. For weeks, every day I came home from work there was something else sitting by the door in the hall. One day I came home from work, and the doorman said, 'I had to open your door this morning to let the workmen in. You forgot to tell me they were coming.' I came up, and found that the whole room had been transformed. Somehow in one day they had painted the walls and laid the carpet. They must have measured the windows, too, because the next day there were the curtains, sitting in a box outside the door. I don't know who is looking forward to this baby more—Michael or me."

"How do you know it's going to be a girl?" He leaned against the doorjamb. She sat in the cherry rocker.

"I just know. One day Michael stopped at my desk and said, 'Girl or boy?' And I said, 'Girl.' The next day this started. He even offered to marry me—can you imagine?" She looked at him carefully, as if really waiting for his reaction. "The last thing Michael would ever want is a wife!"

"Oh, Peggy, I think you're wrong. I think probably the thing Michael wants most in the world is not only a wife, but you for a wife. Doesn't all this"—he gestured around the room—"say anything to you?"

"Well, yes, of course. It says that Michael is a nice person."

"Peggy," Tom admonished, "no one would describe Michael McGrogan as 'a nice person.' He's funny, entertaining, a clever businessman, a rich fellow. But he is definitely not 'a nice person.' Have you ever known him to do anything even remotely comparable to this for anyone else?"

Peggy slowly shook her head. She had never thought about it before.

"Let's go back in and sit down for a minute." Tom took her arm and led her to the rocking chair in the living room. "Tell me something: do you think of Michael as a midget?"

"Of course not!" She was appalled. The teapot whistled, and Tom continued the conversation while he made them each a cup of tea.

"Well, most people do. Most people think of him as a damn clever midget. Don't you think he would like to be considered 'normal'? Don't you think he hungers for the natural things in life? Don't you think he probably would love to have children?"

"Tom, I don't know. Thank you." She accepted her tea. "I just never thought about it. Maybe I ought to—think about it, I mean. Maybe I've been insensitive not to notice—I feel like a fool!"

"No, never," he said from the armchair by the window. "And I don't know—I could be entirely wrong. But I don't think so. Wouldn't you say you and Michael make a good team? Don't you understand each other?"

She sat there spellbound, nodding and rocking.

There was a silence of almost five minutes, interrupted only by the sounds of traffic, the slurp of hot tea.

"Listen, Peggy, I think I'd better be on my way. If I'm to keep pace with Michael tomorrow"—he got in one more plug—"I better get a good night's rest."

"Okay," she answered, still lost in the maze of new thoughts. "Thanks."

He left the apartment, quietly closing the door, and rode down the fifteen floors, smiling to himself. It really was delightful to participate in matchmaking. Good grief, what else could that million-dollar nursery possibly mean? Maybe Michael was too vulnerable and sensitive to say it, but he certainly had let the cat out of the bag by showing it. *Now,* Tom mused, *whether he wants Peggy or just the baby is open to discussion. Who knows, maybe he wants both. Why would he not want the things any other man wants? Just because he's three feet, ten inches tall? Rubbish!*

At that moment Tom stepped out of the apartment building and sniffed in the warm spring air of New York. It was a perfect night—low sixties, full moon, clean air, and drifting across the breeze the smell of an uptown bakery. That scent of yeast, the cacophony of sounds from the cars and buses and subway, the shine and sparkle of primary-colored lights vying for attention overhead, passersbys laughing to each other, ignoring everyone else—this was New York: alive, exhilarating, strong, exciting.

Tom walked the twenty blocks to his hotel room, lost in thought, senses alive to the challenge of New York. He stopped at a liquor store for a bottle of bourbon and then bought a paper from a small Jewish grocer in a small Jewish grocery store. Tom had a small cross-cultural conversation with the grocer. Mr. Meyer was not feeling very well this evening, thank you very much for inquiring, because his wife had bought some crazy new fruit from California that was green on the outside and red on the inside, and she had had no rest, absolutely no rest at all, thank you, until he had tried it. Well, in fact not only tried it, but had eaten the whole thing, although it really didn't taste too bad, but it certainly didn't agree with him, and he couldn't wait until ten o'clock and it was time to close the store. Thank you and goodnight.

Tom was tempted to say, *"Mazal tov,"* as he left, but not sure it was appropriate, he decided he had better confine himself to an innocuous WASP 'Goodnight.'

Back in his hotel room, Tom would have given anything to have been able to pick up the phone and brag to Ruth about his matchmaking and share his big-city-euphoria. Lacking that, he alternately worked on "Mama Bear," and some scene ideas for the movie.

Around eleven he called the Ellises and was told that Tommy had just gone to bed. They had enjoyed the day. Stanley and Tommy had gone fishing and although neither had caught anything big enough to keep, they had had a good walk and a nice companionable time. Tomorrow they were going to cut the grass in the morning and go for a sail in the afternoon.

"The early spring apples are ripening real nice, Mr. Jeffers," Mrs. Ellis said just before they hung up, "so by the time you are due back I think I should be ready to make that deep-dish apple pie you find so satisfactory."

Smiling, Tom replaced the receiver. The salt of the earth, might be a trite phrase, but it was apparently coined with the Ellises in mind.

The two weeks in the city sped by, the days falling into a productive but exhausting routine. Tom decided K.C. must be taking uppers or No-Doz or something because she had such vitality. Twice he had been hammered into having dinner with her; she was so relentless that she ended up outlasting him when they disagreed. As the days passed, he formed a most grudging admiration for her.

"Tom," she said petulantly.

"I was just thinking." Defensively.

"You looked as if you were just sleeping."

It was their last full day. Tomorrow they would work in the morning, and then he would return to Maine. They had worked well together, but K.C.'s time was running short.

"Look," she said very reasonably, "it's so warm and muggy today, and we have been cramped in this office all week. (Cramped in Michael's luxurious quarters?) I think what you need is a change of scene."

Silence was taken for submission.

"So," she continued, even more logically and reasonably, "we'll go to my place and I'll make us some nice, tall, cool drinks, and we'll get all productive again."

More submissive silence; Tom couldn't think of an excuse.

"Let's go." K.C. rose and gathered her things together, and Tom apathetically followed suit. She ta-taed Peggy on the way out and chattered merrily during the taxi ride uptown.

Tom halted, mouth agape, when she led him into her apartment. It was huge and gorgeous. The living room spread out around a grand piano, and furniture was grouped attractively at the edges. Surely she could entertain seventy-five people in here and have space left over. Amazing. She must really have money. It was a new thought to him, and he looked at her to see if it was true. A quick survey of shiny black hair, understated makeup, chic clothes showed him it was true, and he was disgusted that a poet could be so unobservant.

"You sit down." She waved a diamond-watch-clad arm in the general direction of the corral-sized living room. "I'm going to make us a secret family recipe bourbon cooler." She patted his cheek and sauntered out to the kitchen.

It was difficult to imagine anyone who would seem less at home in a kitchen than K.C. Barkley; Tom tried to picture her in an apron, but he soon gave up and focused his attention instead on the unbelievable environs. There were two original Chagalls, a Duchamp, and a Klee on the walls, as well as a number of other original paintings, less impressive to Tom because he had never heard of the artists. On the tables and bookshelves were pieces of sculpture, knickknacks, and bric-a-brac of every imaginable type and description. Only the enormous size of the room kept away a feeling of clutter.

He had just found a friendly round table settled inside a window seat and decided to sit down and spread out some of their papers when K.C. returned and introduced Tom to his first bourbon slush. It was a mixture, she told him, of bourbon, tea, orange juice, lemonade, lots of ice, and then some more bourbon. Tom was an immediate convert.

Drinks in hand, they launched into their project, quickly picking up where they had left off, making steady progress. Around six o'clock she left for a few minutes and returned with a tray of hors d'oeuvres and a second batch of bourbon slushes. They worked for another hour and a half. A little before eight she stretched and said she thought she'd go freshen up for dinner, why didn't he do the same. She led him to her guest room, which just happened to be outfitted with another pitcher of bourbon slushes and the latest edition of the *New York Times*. He showered and then stretched out on the bed with a drink and the paper.

She obviously was bathing and changing because she left him alone for a long time. Too long a time. In boredom Tom finally flipped through some of the sections of the paper he didn't usually read, including the society section. There on page seventeen of section B of the

Thursday, April 26, edition of *The New York Times* was the story of the Wednesday, April 25, 1977, wedding of Italian leather king, Peter Morelli, to American schoolteacher Ruth Tyack Sevini. Tom's world stopped. For a moment he was totally aware of the tick of the clock and the hum of the air conditioner and the soft, piped-in music of a Beethoven symphony. And then he was aware of nothing—the time on the clock was ten minutes later than when he had last looked. He could only account for this strange phenomenon by assuming that he had fainted, simply closing his eyes, his head already being on the pillow.

When he awoke he was suddenly and violently ill and barely made his way into the bathroom, regurgitating his entire supply of bourbon slushes. After a few minutes he was able to sit up and reach for a wet washcloth for his face.

He staggered back to the bed and lay down, closing his eyes, praying that what he had seen was simply drunken imagining. Not so. As soon as he was able to focus his eyes on the page, he saw what he had missed the first time: the picture. Beside the article stood Ruth, in a magnificent gown, smiling into the eyes of a handsome Italian.

Oh, Ruth . . . no! He looks all wrong. How could she have married him? How could she trust herself to a man who looked as slick and suave as this bastard?

Come on, Jeffers, you know who the bastard is. She was willing to settle for a forty-year affair, remember? But, no, you didn't want to do that to her. You and your goddamn standards. Now look what she did to herself!

And look what she did to you.

Tom poured himself a large glass of bourbon slush and started all over again.

The bottom had fallen out. He was suspended over a volcano hanging on by a violin string. He was under a tree in the midst of a thunder and lighting storm. He had just plunged into the bathtub carrying a plugged-in radio. In short, his heart stopped.

At that moment, feeling deader than anyone alive can feel, he saw K.C., who had been absent from his mind entirely, slither into the room. She was wearing some pretense of a robe, crooning in her pretense of a voice that supper was ready, and wouldn't Tommy like a little steak and salad and wine.

Wordlessly, he gave her what she had been asking for for the last thirteen days. She leaned over the bed to blow in his ear, and he reached up and ripped the flimsy robe from her shoulders, yanked her on top of him, unzipped his pants, and shoved himself into her tight vagina.

She loved it. She slid and slunk and cried out in pain and bit his shoulder, and they fought at sex the way they had been fighting at words. There was no softness, no tenderness. They didn't kiss. They didn't stroke or rub or caress each other's bodies. He was simply a beast, ramming into her time after time. At one point he came partially to his senses and tried to withdraw, but she quickly maneuvered him back inside, and she thrust and parried until he got caught back up in the rhythm.

For over an hour, while the cook tried to keep the steaks at a point of readiness, K.C. kept Tom at a point of readiness until she was stretched and bleeding and they both lay insensate, untouching on the covers.

Her snoring woke him, and he silently rose from the bed and dressed and left the room and left the apartment building and left the city. At her lobby door he asked for a cab to the airport and caught the first plane to Bangor, Maine, where he had left his car. He paid the bills as he went, signing things like an automaton, anxious only to put it all behind him.

From the Bangor airport he sent Michael a cable saying he was withdrawing from the project. Never would he do anything other than poetry and editing—not to ever ask him—and that he would be unavailable for a few months. Michael was to use his discretion in all things, including cancelling the European tour.

Tom stopped only once on the two-hour drive home, at an all-night discount store on the outskirts of Bangor, where he purchased one thing: two rolls of the ugliest wallpaper he could find—a gray and black plaid. He arrived home around two-thirty in the morning.

He stopped dead when he entered the den. There on the very top of a stack of mail was an airmail letter.

Well, at least she wrote to warn me, he thought, as he ripped it open.

Dear Tom,

I am delighted to know of your honor. An eight-country tour should indeed be exciting. I'd love to hear from you when you're in Rome. You can always reach me through Susan Cerrera—793980—a permanent resident and friend.

My life is in a state of flux right now. Please understand. But my heart and soul belong to you, T.J. Always.

Love,
Ruth

I think you're wrong, Ruth. I think you sold your soul. Goddamnit!

It was five before he had the den wall, with all its pictures of Ruth, covered. Only then did he lie down, fully clothed on his bed, and give way to the tears that he thought he had left behind when he started grade school. As the sun came up, Tom Jeffers sobbed himself to sleep.

He withdrew from everything then, the way he had withdrawn from the movie project. He wouldn't answer the phone, he acknowledged no mail, and if, by chance, a car stopped, the Ellises were to say he was away. Tom would have withdrawn from life, as well, but Tommy wouldn't let him. They spent every minute of every day alone together or with Mr. Ellis. Stanley and Tommy simply welcomed Tom into their world, and Tom planted and harvested, fished and sailed. He did not look at a book, a newspaper, or a magazine. If he could do it with his hands he was interested; if it required his mind, he was unavailable.

And then, when Tom thought he could not be any more depressed, when the Ellises had spent night after night trying to figure out what to do for him, he received a telegram from Jeff Holmes saying that Helen was dying of complications from pneumonia and that if he wanted to come at all he had better come now.

So he packed a suitcase and drove to Bangor and waited five long hours for a plane to Buffalo and by ten o'clock at night was in the hospital section of St. Luke's Sanatorium. Helen had originally been transferred from the hospital to the Bethel Hope Nursing Home. But when her condition continued to deteriorate, Jeff Holmes had asked that she be moved to this Catholic sanatorium, where he felt Helen would stand the best chance of recovery.

"Sister, excuse me, my name is Tom Jeffers. I am here to see my wife."

"Yes, Dr. Jeffers, this way." *You can never take a nun by surprise*, he thought. The sister walked serenely from behind the nurses' station and led him down the sparkling white hall. "Dr. Holmes is resting, but he left instructions to wake him as soon as you arrived." In her long white skirt, she led the way, her step quick and sure, and he felt better just to know she was in charge.

"No, please, sister, don't wake Dr. Holmes. I would just like to sit with Helen if I may. I'll be there when Dr. Holmes wakes up, but I'm sure he needs his sleep. Please, don't bother him."

She stopped and looked Tom over. Then she smiled a sunlit smile and said, "Thank you, Dr. Jeffers. That is very considerate. Now, here is your wife's room. You will be very careful not to touch anything at all. We have all the instruments monitored in the nurse's station, so we'd know immediately if you did, but we might lose some valuable time getting to the room to get the tubes connected again."

"No, sister, believe me, I would not dream of touching anything."

Her wise blue eyes smiled. "I do believe you, but it is unusual to leave a visitor alone in a patient's room, that is a patient who is this ill, and I felt I had to warn you."

"I understand."

She opened the door and placed her hand on Tom's arm as he walked by. "God is with you."

It was very dark in the room, only the dull nightlight on top of the bed glowing a pale gold. He got close enough to see Helen. The covers were pulled up to her chin, so he was saved the sight of her bony arms and legs. But he could imagine, from what he could see, what the rest of her body looked like. He stood stock-still and started shivering violently while his eyes filled with tears. It did not seem possible that the *thing* lying in this bed could have been his wife. She had been so lovely—short, fluffy brown hair, intelligent brown eyes, always so well groomed and subtly made up. He hoped with all his heart that she was totally out of her mind and had no idea what had happened to her. Thank God there was nobody but him to see her like this.

On the bed before him lay a concentration camp victim. Every bone in her face stood out. The hair on her head was pitifully thin and straggly and was streaked with gray. Fuzzy brown hair surrounded her mouth, as though when the hair on her head died, it had come to life somewhere else. She lay absolutely still, the machines doing the work for her body, making her breathe, keeping this travesty alive. Tom could understand why the nun had warned him that they would know if he touched anything. The temptation to pull the plug was overwhelming. No one could possibly want to "live" like this.

He sat down in the chair by the side of the bed and bowed his head. *Why, God? Why? Why? Why?* It was the only thought he could muster. *How could a God let this happen? How could anyone have to suffer like this? Is this punishment? Then you are no God of mine.*

He sat there, bitter and resentful, cursing, swearing, forsaking, forsaken.

Much later Jeff Holmes walked in, nodded to Tom, looked Helen over, and motioned Tom to follow him outside.

He put his arm around Tom's shoulder and led him down to the coffee shop. As he walked in, Tom had a sudden vivid picture of another coffee shop in another hospital years ago. He straightened his shoulders and removed Jeff's arm as they went over and bought sandwiches and coffee and sat down together.

"I just didn't know whether to call you to come or not, Tom. But then I realized it should be your decision, and not mine, and I should just tell you what was happening."

"You did the right thing, Jeff. I'm very glad you let me know."

Jeff Holmes had aged ten years since last Tom had seen him. The small bald place on the top of his head had grown larger, and now Jeff had merely a smattering of light brown hair around the lower edges of his head. He had new silver-framed glasses, which made him look quite distinguished, and his blue eyes were as alert and compassionate as ever, but there was a stoop to his shoulders that was newly acquired and a wisdom-of-the-ages look that he hadn't carried before.

"Jeff, these must be very trying days for you."

Dr. Holmes looked up in surprise. He had expected Tom to ask about Helen, not about him. He answered honestly. "These are horrible days, Tom. I have never in my thirty years in medicine seen anything like it. I am losing patients right and left. People are simply giving up, withdrawing from life. I have seen more cases like Helen's in the last two years than I did in the previous twenty-eight. I can't understand it. What are we doing wrong? Kids are blowing their minds away on drugs; married people are blowing each other away with guilt; old people are blown away by feelings of uselessness; people of all ages are simply unable to handle trouble. What are we, the weak-kneed generation, or something? I am really depressed by what I see around me." Jeff looked up at Tom from the midst of his lecture and realized what he was doing. "Oh, Tom, I'm sorry. What a crummy thing to lay my burden on you."

Tom smiled for the first time since he had arrived in Buffalo. "No, Jeff, it was just what I needed—a shot of gumption. I've been a little low on it myself."

"Well, I am feeling a lot of doubts. I hope I did the right thing to call you."

"You absolutely did, Jeff." Tom straightened up a little more still.

"Well, I don't know, she'll never know whether you're here or not."

"But I'll know. I think I need to be here—for me. I just wouldn't want to think of her being alone at the end. I want to be with her."

For the next two days he sat and slept and read in the chair by Helen's bed. He never touched her. He rarely looked at her. But he hoped that if she were conscious of anything she would sense she wasn't alone. When he and Jeff had gone back up from the coffee shop that first night, Tom had asked Sister Martha of the compassionate blue eyes for a Bible. She produced one and opened it for him to Job. In the last two days and nights he had read Job twice, Psalms once, and the entire New Testament, with the exception of Revelations—and the Book of Ruth.

Now it was eight o'clock on the beginning of his third night with Helen. Every day they told him she was getting weaker, although how they could tell was beyond him. All he could see was the monitoring equipment; all he could hear was a constant beep and hum.

Tom was reading the paper in his chair when he suddenly caught the change in tone of the constant sounds in the room. He threw down the paper and rose to try to figure out what had happened. For the first time since he had been there, Helen moved and opened her eyes. She looked up at him, smiled faintly, and said, "Jan." Then she closed her eyes and shuddered. A nurse flew into the room. It was Sister Martha, again on her evening shift.

"Go have them page Dr. Holmes and Dr. Winslow."

Tom rushed out to the nurses' station and when he returned to the room, was told to "Please wait outside, Dr. Jeffers."

Jeff Holmes flashed by, and soon another tall man in a white coat hurried in also. It was only a few minutes later that Jeff came out alone and took Tom's arm to walk him down the hall.

"She's gone."

Tom was as prepared for the news as one can ever be, yet still it came as enough of a shock that he didn't remember anything about the next few hours. He was, in fact, surprised to wake up in a hotel bed the next morning. He really didn't remember getting there or checking in—it was all a blank.

He called down for breakfast and a newspaper, and then over successive cups of coffee made lists of things he needed to do before leaving Buffalo. He was just emerging from the bathroom, tying his tie and trying to get up the courage to embark on his day, when there was a knock on his door. He found Sally Maye Williams standing uncertainly on the threshold.

"Would you like to see me?"

Tom pulled her inside the door and took her in his arms in a warm hug.

"It is wonderful to see you," he said. "All my life, I will always be glad to see you."

"Well, Jeff Holmes called this morning, said he happened to remember that you and I were friends, and did I know that you were in town; that Helen had died last night, and perhaps you could use my help in doing some things today. So I called the friendly neighborhood babysitter, and here I am."

"That's right, congratulations. Twin girls! Who would have thought? I'll bet your husband is in seventh heaven."

"He is. He loves it. And they are beautiful. I won't let you leave town without coming to see them."

"Great."

They looked at each other with the affectionate scrutiny of old lovers and mutually decided that she had weathered the years much better than he had. She looked terrific, taking to the matronly role with style.

He looked horrible. His total grayness would have been enough of a shock without the additional wrinkles and lines of the hellish last few weeks, the sleepless last few nights. Tom looked like a sixty-five-year-old man. Everywhere they went that day they were mistaken for father and daughter; finally they just stopped correcting people and let them assume what they would.

With Sally Maye beside him, things were easier. When Tom felt incapable of another decision, Sally Maye just took over, saying, "I think this probably, Tom, don't you?" and he would nod his head yes, and they would proceed on. By dinner time the arrangements were made for cremation the following day. The lawyer had been seen, the new white floor-length nightgown had been selected and delivered to the funeral home, and arrangements had been made with the newspaper regarding the notice of her death "after a long illness," with donations to Westerbury College.

One of their stops had been at the sanatorium to settle the account, which Tom was staggered to find he was incapable of settling. The outstanding bill was for $42,643.94. The nuns would be glad to have him pay what he could when he could, but he felt the financial burden in addition to the other strains.

At dinner time Sally Maye drove him back to the hotel. She wanted him to come home with her for dinner, but he was simply unable to face a happy family situation.

He had a solitary meal in a remote corner of the hotel dining room, then went back up to his room and just sat for over an hour. Finally he picked up the phone to call Tommy and tell the Ellises what had happened.

"Emma, it's Tom."

"Oh, honey, is she gone?" It was the first term of endearment Tom had ever heard her use—the first time, in fact, that they had not referred to each other as Mrs. Ellis and Mr. Jeffers—and it almost undid him. "Yes. Last night. I just couldn't face talking to Tommy before now."

"No, no, Tom. You don't need to tell him—and not over the phone. Stanley and I will do it. It will be easier if he can look at us. And we'll explain about our Harry. Oops, here they come. They were reading stories upstairs, but they wanted some pie now, before bed. Listen, you just tell Tommy how soon you'll be back, okay? He's been worried because he thinks you've been gone too long."

"Has he been bad about it?"

"No, honey, now don't you fret. We'll handle it all at this end. You just hurry home. We all miss you. Now here's Tommy."

"Hiya, daddy." His childish voice was so enthusiastic, it was a balm to Tom's wounded spirit.

"Hiya, sport. What are ya up to these days?"

"Oh, I don't know. Daddy, when are you coming home?"

"Very soon, Tommy, very soon."

"Well, I want you to come home now. I want to sleep in my own bed now, and I want you to read me some more about Robbing Hood."

"You mean Robin Hood?"

"Yes. Now."

"Tommy, I can't, but I'll tell you what I can do."

"What?" Suspiciously.

"I'll bring you any surprise you ask for."

"Anything?"

"Anything. You ask for it, I'll bring it home with me."

There was silence on the line.

"I promise. Now what shall it be? What surprise would you like?"

"A dog."

"A dog?"

"A dog!"

"You mean a big stuffed animal?"

"No. I mean a real live friend."

Tom was silent for a moment, smiling at Tommy's description. Yes, that really was what Tommy needed most—wasn't he smart to realize it and ask for a "friend."

"Okay, sport. I promised you any surprise you wanted, and you shall have it."

The phone thumped to the floor; in his excitement Tommy had forgotten all about Tom on the other end. "Oh, boy, oh boy, daddy's gonna bring me a dog, daddy's gonna bring me a dog," Tom could hear Tommy singing in the background. Stanley came on the line.

"Are ya still there, Tom?"

"Yes. Hello, Stan."

"I'm mighty sorry."

"Thank you." There was a pause. "Stan, you and Emma wouldn't mind a dog, would you?"

"Not rightly, we wouldn't. I think it's a fine notion. Our Harry had a dog that used to keep an eye on him when mother and me was busy. Think it'd be a fine thing for Tommy."

"You wouldn't know of a place, Stan, would you, where I might get a trained dog—a dog that we could trust with Tommy."

"Yes, sir, I would. But it wouldn't be cheap. There's a kennel right outside Bangor, 'bout a mile off of Route Ninety-two, where they train 'em mighty good, so as you can really trust 'em, train 'em to take care of their master, they do."

"That would be perfect Stan, just perfect."

"Would you be wanting me to give them a call?"

"Could you do that? I'll be by Friday afternoon or Saturday morning. If they could have a dog for me to take home, I know Tommy would really be pleased."

"I'll take care of it first thing in the morning."

"Thank you, Stan. Goodnight, now. And thanks again."

"Night," said the brusque Maine voice.

Tom took a shower, went to bed, and slept a calm and dreamless sleep. But it took Stan and Emma two hours to calm Tommy down enough to fall asleep. He couldn't believe that at last he was going to have a real live friend of his own. Mommy would never let him have a dog.

Jeff Holmes and Sally Maye Williams went with Tom to collect Helen's ashes the following afternoon. The memorial service was held in Jed's Cafe. When they were seated and the first round of beer had arrived, the two men raised their steins and stared at each other. It was Sally Maye who finally had to say, "To Helen." They sat, for almost an hour, consumed three beers apiece, and said not another word. Then, as of one mind, they rose and walked out to Sally Maye's car.

Tom had dinner that evening with the Williamses and met his namesake, Tomasina, and her twin sister, Tabatha. As he might have suspected, Sally Maye ran a loose and loving ship. The patrician doctor proudly boasted to Tom that Sally Maye was pregnant again and that they were hoping for twin boys this time. Tom escaped as soon as he could, borrowing Sally Maye's decrepit car.

The next morning he drove to his and Helen's former home and asked the new owner if she would mind if he walked around the grounds for a little while—just for old time's sake. "But, of course not, Dr. Jeffers. Anytime. Anytime at all. We are really enjoying your lovely home."

Tom went to the trunk of his car, pulled out a package, and walked in the woods until he came to the little creek that meandered through the property. He found the big sitting rock where he had once chanced to come upon Helen stretched out nude, basking in the sun, humming to herself. They had made love there, that afternoon. It was one of the few times he could ever remember *finding* her happy and *making* her happy. He stood on the rock and scattered her ashes over the water.

Without stopping for lunch or thought, Tom drove to Jamestown to see Helen's college roommate, Janice Strepp, these twenty years a university physical education instructor. The university faculty directory gave him the address, and he found the apartment without problem.

A thin, nondescript young woman answered the door.

"I would like to see Janice Strepp, please."

"Who are you?" she asked bluntly, no attempt at manners or friendliness.

"Tom Jeffers."

"Just a minute." She closed the door in his face.

It was two or three minutes before the door was reopened and Janice, a tall, athletic woman, stood looking him over, no more friendly than the first woman.

"Well, if it isn't Dr. Jeffers himself. To what do I owe the honor?"

"Helen's death."

He was glad to see the shock register, the sarcasm and hostility abate somewhat. "Come in." She led the way into a much-used brown living room.

"Have a seat." She gestured to the least cluttered of the

214

chairs. Her young friend was sprawled on the sofa. "Go get us some coffee, Cindy."

Cindy looked up disdainfully. "Get it yourself."

"Okay," Janice said in a conciliatory voice, "but get lost. This is a private conversation."

Shrugging, Cindy strolled from the room, and a minute later a door was heard slamming.

The coffee, which had sounded good to Tom, was apparently forgotten.

"When?"

"Tuesday, around eight at night. You knew she had been in a sanatorium?"

Negative shake of the head.

"She quite literally went crazy. Started attacking me, telling me Tommy wasn't my son . . ."

"He wasn't," she said matter-of-factly.

"How the hell do you know?" he practically screamed.

"Because Helen told me. We kept in very close touch for a number of years. Until finally she became somewhat of an embarrassment to me and I had to break it off."

Tom sat dumbstruck, trying to assimilate the meaning of her words.

She seemed lost in thought. Finally she said, "It's hard to lose your first lover."

He thought she meant him. And then it dawned on him what she was really saying. In a voice that sounded completely different from his own he asked, "You and Helen were lovers?"

"Of course. You mean she never told you?"

Now it was his turn to shake his head, but he just stared at her and couldn't get his head to move.

"It started our freshman year. Neither of us had any idea we were lesbians until they put us together as roommates. Then we really became roommates." She gave a mirthless laugh. "The difference between us was that I could accept it and Helen couldn't. That's why she had so many affairs the first couple of years you two were married—she kept trying to find some guy who would turn her on. She never did—so she came back to me. Finally she came one year and found me living with somebody and got all bent out of shape. Like I was supposed to just sit around waiting for her to come see me a couple of times a year. No way, baby."

He had made himself sit, and he had made himself listen, and now he made himself ask, "When was this?"

"Christmas time, a few years ago—four years ago, I think. She and the kid came to surprise me. Well, the surprise was on her. She left the kid sittin' down in the cold car for over an hour while we screamed at each other. Finally I just kicked her out."

That was all he needed to know. He could have asked her whose child Tommy was, but he didn't care to know the answer. After all these years, it really didn't matter. Tommy was his. Wordlessly he got up and walked out of the apartment. He had gotten a hell of a lot more answers than he had ever wanted.

The Blenner Kennels on Old Furnace Road were easy to find. Mr. Blenner acknowledged that Mr. Ellis had called and they had a little something that they thought would just suit the purpose. Now, Robby was not what Tom would have called "a little something" but he certainly did seem like a wonderful dog. He was an eight-month-old Labrador, coal black, intelligent and gentle, and delighted to get in the car with Tom. He tried to lick Tom's face, but when Tom said, "Stop! Sit!" he obeyed immediately.

They arrived home at about one o'clock Saturday afternoon. The Ellises and Tommy ran from the house when Tom sounded the horn, and Robby bolted from the car, dashed up to Tommy, and sat down before him wagging his tail. Tommy dissolved into four-year-old giggles, demanding to know his friend's name, immediately throwing sticks for Robby to catch and running, only to be literally dogged in his steps, to his utter delight.

They collected all of Tommy's things from the Ellises' house and arrived home to find a large chocolate cake waiting on the kitchen table. After Tom, Tommy, and Robby each had a generous serving, Tommy and his new friend went outside to play.

Interesting mail was waiting for Tom. K.C. Barkley and Michael McGrogan were very anxious that he reconsider the movie project, and to show their sincere interest in a script by him they were upping the offer to fifty thousand dollars. Only a hospital bill of forty-two thousand dollars could have changed his mind. He was relieved to know he had a way of getting out of debt with the sisters.

He made his acceptance phone call, and life settled down into its quiet Tommy-centered days in Maine, punctuated by hair-raising, K.C.-avoiding trips to New York.

❧ PART IV ❧

Orvieto, Italy: Spring 1980

❧ 10 ❧

Ruth stretched in her sleep and reached out to the far side of the bed. Feeling nothing, she came slowly to consciousness. Her listless blue eyes reaffirmed what her nervous hands had discovered: Peter had not come home again last night. She sighed and tried to focus her gaze on the bedside clock. Eight-thirty. Little Pietro would already be up and playing in his breakfast mush. Too late for her to feed him; it only upset the nurse when she asked to, anyhow.

"Oh, Lord," Ruth mumbled sleepily. "Nona, you would be so disappointed in me if you knew how things have fallen apart these last three years. I couldn't even make it with Peter." Ruth folded her hands under her head and laid back against the fluffy white pillows. The attraction had been so strong. She really had believed their marriage would work. If only she hadn't gotten pregnant so fast. If only, if only . . .

For eight months their marriage had been blissful. Peter had delighted in how quickly she had gotten pregnant. Ruth spent over three thousand dollars on maternity clothes. That also thrilled him—nothing was too good for the wife of Peter Morelli, the Leather King. Once her stomach started protruding, though, he wouldn't take her anywhere. She was moved out of the penthouse on Via Cordova and installed in the villa in Orvieto.

How she hated it here! God knows, she had tried. At first she thought it would just take some getting used to. Ultimately, she was so alone. No Nona waited here, eager to help. Only Peter's mother, Peter's two maiden aunts, Peter's sheltered playgirl sister, Peter's two orphaned female cousins—women, women, everywhere, and not a friend among them. How could they all be so mean and self-absorbed? Surely someone would have time to teach her Italian. Surely someone could show her the routine of the household. Surely someone could find something she was needed for.

Wrong! She was the fish out of water, the odd person out. She was totally superfluous. She had but one function: to be a brood mare. The young American wife was treated with politeness and respect. Never had there been a glance or a gesture that was other than correct. Never, either, had there been a glance or a gesture that was intimate or caring. It was incredible—she was simpatico with no one. The odds were enormous against being stuck in a villa with six women and finding none of them liked you. But it had happened. Here she was.

And there went Peter. As soon as her stomach started growing, so did the distance between them. First there were the evening meetings: "*Cara*, I must stay in town tonight." Then there were the week-long conferences in Madrid, Tokyo, New York.

"But, Peter, let me come with you."

"No, *cara*, but of course not. This baby is just too precious. You must stay in Orvieto and rest. Just rest and grow fat and enjoy the easy life at the villa."

"But at least let me take Italian lessons." Not for the first time she cursed her own laziness in not having studied the language before: but Bruno's eagerness for English had amounted almost to a mania—and with Nona, there were always too many other wonderful things to learn. Besides, languages had never been Ruth's strong point; she had barely scraped through high school German.

Now she not only had so much spare time, but she had the motivation as well: the very real need to understand what people were talking about, what was happening around her. But...

"Not now, *cara*; not now. It is better you stay in the villa and not put yourself under any strain."

Then she had to recuperate.

"Now you must supervise the baby's care, *cara*."

"But, Peter, there is nothing to supervise. The nurse is raising him with the able help of the six Italian women who live here. He doesn't even know who the hell I am. When he calls 'mama,' eight people answer him. Please let me raise our son myself."

"He is my son, too, Ruth, and he must be raised an Italian. He is the Morelli heir."

They had had the conversation so many times she could recall it verbatim. Always she got excited. Always he remained calm and condescending. Afterward he would do one of two things: either he would tease her, telling her she must be pregnant again to be so excitable and unreasonable and he would take her to bed and make wild love to her, or he would become exasperated and stomp out of the room, downstairs to the six women who were never excitable or unreasonable.

It was no wonder he was coming home less and less. He had put her in a jail made of feathers, and all he could see was how soft and sweet the feathers were. All Ruth could see was that if you interwove feathers tightly enough, they made a jail, no matter how soft and sweet.

Then the pictures had started in the newspapers. She could barely read the Italian, but she could recognize Peter. Usually he was photographed by himself but sometimes with official-looking men. Often he was caught in unflattering poses, looking stern and uncompromising. The articles seemed to be headlined with exclamation points: "Peter Morelli Defies Government Order!" or "Leather King Under Investigation!" She spent two afternoons translating one article, only to be left with innuendo and insinuation. Apparently the papers thought Peter was doing some shady things—violation of government safety standards was mentioned. There were threats from workers about unionizing. There were threats from Morelli top management about firings and layoffs. Some of the problems had to do with the chemicals used in the leather tannery. Was he or wasn't he violating government standards? No one seemed able to prove anything one way or another.

"Peter, what in the world is happening? I read this article. Is any of this true?"

Peter stared at her long and hard for a minute, his face unreadable. And then he broke out laughing and motioned her to come sit on his lap. But she stood her ground, shaking her head.

"*Bambina*," he said softly, persuasively, "come here. I want to tell you something."

Grudgingly she went, sitting straight-backed on his lap, looking straight ahead.

"I promise you," he said, his fingers moving inside her blouse, tracing circles on her breast, "there is nothing for you to worry about."

"Honestly, Peter?" she stared down at him.

"*Si, bambina.*" He buried his head in her neck, unbuttoning buttons, nibbling at tender skin. And the moment for discussion passed in a haze of passion.

So it went. He was usually able to deflect her; she was willing to be reassured. But when she was alone, as she so often was, the doubts and worries came creeping back. She laboriously translated an article about workers dying. And she understood the statistical charts revealing that Morelli Leather was the lowest paying company in Italy. Was he taking advantage of the terrible unemployment problems?

Sitting there, staring at the clippings spread out on the desk—the almost incomprehensible newsprint and the puzzling, tension-filled photographs—she suddenly noticed another figure in one of the pictures: a sleekly handsome woman with dark hair pulled back in a severe chignon and wearing an expensive-looking tailored dress. She was standing slightly behind and to the left of Peter. She looked vaguely familiar, and Ruth quickly sorted through the other clippings—yes! there she was again, this time in sharper focus, and Ruth recognized her as Mariella Gatti, one of the partners in the firm that handled Peter's legal affairs. Ruth had met her at several semiofficial functions in Rome and had always admired this woman who had succeeded in breaking through the sexist barriers in Italy's world of big business. In the picture Mariella appeared to be doing the talking, pointing to a sheaf of papers held by one of the angry-looking officials.

Ruth felt a jab of pain: it wasn't jealousy, she was sure of that. Although she supposed she would be jealous if Peter were having an affair, she wouldn't have been surprised, given the standards of Italian men, and Peter being very much an Italian man. No, this was much worse than a sexual affair: Mariella was obviously included in an important part of Peter's life, one from which Ruth, his wife, was so consistently excluded.

More and more he stayed away. When he was home, the "six" monopolized him so that Ruth was rarely alone with him except for late at night when he slipped into their bed and into her body.

As Ruth's moments with Peter grew more and more rare, so her discomfort with the women grew more acute. It was becoming hard to smile. How she would love to put him, for just one evening, in the position of sitting at a table with six other men, have them speak a language he didn't understand, punctuated by polite giggles and glances. She'd like to see how long he'd last.

She had tried. She had really damn well tried.

But she wasn't allowed to take Italian lessons. "There is no one in Orvieto who speaks English well enough to teach you."

She wasn't allowed to walk around Orvieto. "Signora Morelli doesn't walk—it isn't done. If you want something Giovanni will get it for you. Surely the grounds of the villa are large enough if you merely want exercise."

She was allowed to play tennis on the villa courts, but mysteriously no one ever had time for a game with her, although minutes later they would be out playing with each other.

No, she wasn't allowed in the kitchen—"wouldn't want to upset the staff."

"Of course you can't do the marketing. *Ladies* do not do their own shopping."

"No, you can't give English lessons. Signora Morelli does not work!"

And Giovanni almost had a heart attack and threatened

to quit when she tried to help him with the gardening. He thought he had done something to displease her.

No, of course *ladies* didn't walk their own babies—that was what they had nurses for—nor did they change their own babies or feed their own babies. Although for half an hour before his afternoon nap and for a half an hour after his supper, little Pietro was brought to his mother so that she could play with him. But they didn't know each other—they didn't know what to do with each other. And the moment he started crying, nurse came to put the little *signore* to bed.

Talk about the poor little rich girl!

At ten o'clock one morning, Ruth opened her eyes again and decided she'd better get up, although she couldn't for the life of her think of a reason to do so. She could always go sit by the pool and read—that's what she did most of the time. She had subscribed to every American magazine she could remember the name of, and she belonged to four book clubs. Ruth Morelli was the best-read woman in Orvieto, by far—perhaps the most widely read, best informed woman in all Italy. If only someone other than her knew it. Any time she expressed an opinion to Peter, he patted her cheek and told her to buy a new dress. On the rare occasions when she met someone who spoke English, she had to restrain herself from dominating the conversation. Twice now, wives had taken her aside and told her it was unseemly to show up the men in conversation, even to talk with them instead of with the ladies. The women thought she was flirting; the men thought she was competing; everyone was upset with her. Shit!

Would that Nona were here. But Nona was in Pittsburgh. Dying.

Three months after Ruth and Peter had married, Nona had announced that she was giving away all her things, selling her apartment, and going to live with Benjamin Tyack in Pittsburgh.

Ruth couldn't have been more shocked if Nona had said she had suddenly taken an interest in African sculpture and was going to spend her remaining days in Chad. Nona hàd neglected to mention one pertinent detail that Ben had let slip: Nona was dying of blood cancer. Pittsburgh's University Hospital had some of the most sophisticated equipment and modern techniques for treating leukemia. Nona was in and out of the hospital all the time—now a little better, this time not quite as good. Both she and Ben wrote to Ruth each week, combining their letters in one package so that once a week Ruth had a better day than usual because she heard from the outside world, heard from two of the three people in the world she most loved.

Her letters to Nona had to be cheerful. Nona's great joy was that she had gotten Ruth so well established with Peter before leaving for the United States. So Ruth invented a fictitious life for herself, complete with made up friends and made up personalities for the women in the house, who, thank God, Nona had never known intimately. Ruth's letters were filled with imagined trips, imagined conversations, imagined kindnesses. What else could she give the dying Nona but some peace of mind?

Nona's notes to Ruth were filled with what Ruth knew were real conversations and real kindnesses.

Ruth reached over to the nightstand for yesterday's letters from Ben and Nona and reread them.

Dear Ruth,

I am sorry to report that Nona is not good at this writing. Yesterday's chemotherapy treatment was terribly hard on her. It's only a three-hour session, but then she spends the next thirty hours throwing up. Poor Nona. She somehow manages to wait until we are home, before she lets loose. I sometimes wonder what Mrs. Milbourne thinks of Mr. Tyack and "that woman" getting all these sheets dirty. Nona and I have had some good laughs about the gossip we are supplying to the neighborhood.

I have started working up the ground in the back and will put in a little garden. Nona says she is hungry for fresh vegetables, so we thought we'd plant some tomatoes, spinach, lettuce, and Italian beans. We have been poring over the seed catalogs. But that's about all I'll plant. If Nona is here, I won't have much time, and if she is gone, I won't have much heart for the garden we planned together.

The school called yesterday, asking if I wanted to teach summer school. I said not as of now. I am afraid that I will be going back this fall. She is getting weaker all the time. I now carry her everywhere—in and out to the car, up and down the stairs, anytime she feels she wants a change of scene. She loves my rocker in the dining room because it looks out over the back yard.

Keep writing, Ruth. Nona lives for your letters, and we spend the whole time until the next letter rehashing the contents of the last one. You have made your life so vivid for us; we can picture your world.

We don't really understand why you can't come for a visit—but if Peter won't have it, then he won't. And maybe it's better anyhow that you don't see her again, but just imagine her always as the lovely, energetic Nona you knew. In spirit she hasn't changed.

Your father

Carissima,

Thank you for the pictures of Pietro. What an angel he is—those large brown eyes. You are quite a good photographer, Ruth, to have caught him at such cute poses. We love to hear the reports of what he says and does. And we love to hear about all your social activities. Such a busy life you lead, Ruth. I hope you find some time for contemplation and prayer.

Never forget God, *cara*—such miracles can happen! But I sometimes feel guilt over what I have imposed upon your father. For the last three years he has had to be my full-time nurse and companion. Oh, it wasn't so bad at first, when we could still go out. Why, did you know he had even taken me to see his precious Pittsburgh Pirates play baseball? Now we listen to all the games. We even listen to the ones from Florida. I don't mind at all. It's good to see Ben excited. He has such a beautiful, youthful face.

But now, Ruth, now it is bedpans and basins and messy sheets and sweaty nightgowns—we have such trouble keeping my temperature stabilized. He is marvelous. Does it all in such good humor. He says his only disappointment is that I have never felt well enough to try his chili. (I'm not sure I ever felt that well!)

I would love to write more, but I get tired so easily.

We love you dearly, Ruth, talk of you constantly, and pray for your continued happiness.

Love,
Nona

P.S. Always follow your heart, Ruth.

Always follow your heart. Now what the hell could she mean by that? Surely that foxy Nona couldn't have an intuition that things weren't as Ruth portrayed them, that everything wasn't rosy? Could she?

Ruth turned to look at the clock. Good grief! Twenty after eleven. Well, they'll really have something to titter about at lunch, won't they? Lazy Ruth stayed in bed all day.

She got up, went into the bathroom, and much to her amazement leaned over the toilet and threw up. Damned Italian cooking. All that oil and grease. Nona's cooking was never like that. Oh, shit! She flushed the toilet, closed the lid, and sat down and cried for almost ten minutes. Then she got up, washed her face, and stared at herself in the mirror. Never had she looked worse. There were huge black circles under her eyes, and her whole body looked puffy and bloated—she had gained twenty pounds since her marriage. Her hair was cut in a new French style, which was very mod but not very flattering. She felt rotten. Her body was like an anchor she had to drag around all day. She had no energy, no enthusiasm, no purpose. She would have liked to lose some weight, but she didn't even have the will to try. It sounded, she reflected, as if she had a textbook case of depression.

She bathed and dressed and went outside, seeing no one on her way through the house, and walked. She wandered around for over an hour, oblivious to the beautiful surroundings, the new buds and spring flowers. She thought about everything and nothing; her mind was drugged by inactivity.

When she went back inside, the women were gathering for lunch. Midday was the big meal here, and if there was anything Ruth didn't need, it was a big meal: more weight to add to the anchor. So she sat and picked and knew they were surreptitiously watching as she pushed the food around on her plate. It smelled so awful to her. She ended up eating almost nothing except the salad and a piece of plain bread. After that ordeal, she retired to the garden to wait for the nurse to bring Pietro to her, but Sophia came by first. Sophia's English was excellent, but she usually chose not to use it. Why speak to her brother's wife in English and make five people not understand, when she could speak to those five people in Italian, and only Ruth would be left out?

"Ah, there you are, relaxing, I see." Dig, dig.

"Hello, Sophia. Would you care to join me?"

"No, thank you. Giorgio is coming, and we are playing some tennis. I came to tell you that Pietro called this morning and said you are to be ready to go out tonight. He will be home around seven and wants to leave by seven-thirty."

"For where?"

"He didn't say," Sophia answered carelessly.

"Well, how am I supposed to be ready, if I don't know what to be ready for?" Ruth hated to hear the whine in her own voice.

"Suit yourself. I am just relaying the message."

"Well, didn't he ask for me?" Ruth humbled herself.

"No, I don't think so. It was this morning, and someone mentioned you were still in bed." She turned, calling over her shoulder, "*Ciao.*"

"*Ciao,*" Ruth managed to say between gritted teeth.

Damn him for calling and "telling" me to be ready to go out. Well, he is going to have a little surprise in store for him this evening.

Ruth spent ten disastrous minutes with Pietro, the child

fussy and cranky the whole time. Then she changed into her bathing suit and went out to the pool. She did five laps, rested, did five more, rested, did five more, and then fell asleep in the sun. By the time she returned to her room before dinner she found a much better-looking Ruth staring back at her from the mirror. The circles under her eyes seemed diminished, and her body had a little tingle and glow from the exercise and the sunshine. She took a bath, washed her hair, and feeling more like herself, went down to the patio in sundress and sandals to read the magazines that had come that day.

When Peter came home, he found her with a cool glass of white wine and some crackers on the table in front of her, her shoes kicked off, her legs propped up on the table.

"I thought I asked that you be ready!" He stood before her, immaculate in his gray serge suit, looking like a Greek god or a cigarette ad—she couldn't decide.

So much for her good mood. "Well, good evening to you, too."

"What are you doing—how can you sit there that way?" His eyes were disdainful.

"What do you mean 'that way'?"

"You're sitting there like some cheap call girl," he sputtered.

"There is absolutely nothing wrong with the way I'm sitting. American women sit like this all the time." She was ready to forget it and move on. She laughed. "Good heavens, Peter."

"You are not an American woman." He leaned over the table, glowering. "You are an Italian wife, and I'll thank you to maintain some propriety and dignity in your demeanor. You embarrass my family."

"*I* embarrass *your* family? That's rich!" She picked up her glass and took a long sip of wine.

"I think we had better have this discussion inside, in some privacy."

"Why? No one else here speaks English, anyhow—no one can understand us."

"Oh, so you think they're stupid because they don't speak English!"

"No, I think they're rude because they won't teach me Italian." She picked up her glass again and threw the contents off to the side, barely missing Peter.

"How can they when you spend the day in bed, eh?" He was gesturing angrily.

"What else do I have to do?" She gestured back.

"You could try making yourself useful here, instead of sitting around like"—his arms flailed—"Cleopatra, waiting to be waited on."

"I have *never*"—she sat up straight—"in my entire time here"—each word was distinctly spit at him—"which seems like a thousand years, sat around, 'waiting to be waited on.'"

"Let's go. We're going to be late." He gestured her into the house.

"You go." Ruth leaned back in her chair and picked up a cracker. "I have no intention of spending another evening smiling at things I can't understand and being nice to dirty old men and supercilious young whores." She bit on the cracker.

Peter walked away a few steps and hit the side of the house in anger. Then he turned back to Ruth. "Maybe you should have thought of that before you married me."

"Yes," she said, spraying cracker crumbs, "maybe I should have. If I hadn't been so head-over-heels in love with you and if you hadn't been so sweet and sexy to me, perhaps I would have given some of these things a little thought. But it seemed to me you were quite the international fellow. And besides, *you* speak English. I didn't know I was going to be imprisoned with a house full of Italian-speaking, rude, mean women."

"Get up to your room." He was idling, like a car waiting for a mere touch on the gas pedal.

"Why, so you can beat me?" She challenged. "Why not do it here. I'm sure all six would enjoy seeing me get what I deserve."

"Get out of my sight." His voice was cold and hateful.

"Gladly." She rose with what dignity she could muster. "I'm sure someone will be along momentarily to smooth your ruffled feathers."

He made a threatening gesture, but she hurried inside and didn't look back. Upstairs she locked herself in her bathroom, turned on the water, and sat on the edge of the tub, staring off into space. She just didn't even care anymore. She felt lifeless and empty, unattractive, unappreciated, unmotivated.

It was about a half an hour later that she noticed the tub wasn't filling. She turned off the water, not realizing she'd simply forgotten to put in the plug.

She went and sat on the wide windowsill, then. Someone came to knock on the bathroom door. She ignored them. She simply sat on the wide ledge, legs pulled up, head on knees, watching the sun sink in slow motion behind the mountains.

It was dark when she finally unlocked the bathroom door and went out to her bedroom. Throwing her clothes nonchalantly on the floor, she crawled into bed. She was too tired to bother with a nightgown, so she slid naked between the sheets.

Much later she was awakened by the smell of liquor and the sound of the bed creaking. She opened her arms to him immediately. "Oh, Peter."

He said nothing, but moments later was inside her. She was uncomfortable, emotionally and physically unprepared for sex, but determined not to ruin their one effective means of communication. However, moments later, ruin it she did.

"Oh," she cried in pain. "Peter, my leg."

"What?" he asked from a sex-crazed distance.

"My leg, Peter. There's such a horrible cramp. Please, rub my leg for me. The pain is so strong."

"Goddamn it." He sat up, engorged, unfulfilled, frustrated. "Rub your own damn leg. That does it. You are impossible. I've had it."

Ruth was out of bed, on the floor, moaning in pain, trying to rub some circulation back in her cramped leg. All those laps in the pool this afternoon!

Peter stomped out of the room and slammed the door.

Ruth spent the night on the floor, dry-eyed, sleepless. At dawn she crawled into the bed, lest someone find her in an "undignified" position.

* * *

Her days became a blur of inactivity and repetition. She slept, she read, she swam, she threw up, she picked at her food, and she retreated into herself. Every day she fought a battle with herself to keep from writing to Tom. Only by reconstructing their last encounter and wallowing in the guilt of what had happened could she keep from picking up her pen and emptying her heart to him.

She had been married a little over four months and was feeling terrific, loving their life. She and Peter were very social, were out maybe five nights a week to parties and receptions and premières, everything Italian society had to offer. Peter and Ruth Morelli were the golden young couple of Rome.

The only flaw in her happiness was that she had never heard again from Tom. She had written him that little note, but he hadn't answered. June came and went, and she felt forlorn that he hadn't bothered to get in touch with her. She kept scouring *The Daily American* for some mention of an American poet in town, but never found any.

And then in September Susan called her with a message. He had written to invite Ruth to lunch that coming Thursday. Ruth was to leave a message at the Grand Hotel, telling him if she was available and when and where.

Ruth had suggested they meet at one at the Rome Hilton. It was a beautifully warm September day. She felt poised and confident in a deceptively simple lavender dress from de la Renta. She was looking forward to a nice lunch with an old friend.

He was waiting in the lobby when she got to the hotel, and she saw him immediately. Good God! He was gorgeous. All in gray. Gray suit, gray beard, gray curls, and those damnable laughing gray eyes. It was astonishing that the mere sight of someone could effect another person so strongly, so quickly, so timelessly.

She stopped momentarily. Her heart seemed to stop, too, then began to pound, drowning out the hotel sounds, the traffic, everything. She felt her chest burst. Then a wave of hot, sweet emotion coursed through her as his eyes crinkled in an older, wiser version of that dear, familiar smile, and her legs propelled her closer.

They stopped perhaps two feet apart; she was conscious of her body straining toward his; his rigid stance suggested he, too, was struggling.

"Hello."

"How are you?"

"Fine!" Each sounded very cool to the other.

Then Tom nodded toward the dining room and put a hand under her elbow to propel her forward. As his fingers curled around her bare arm, she felt an electric current surge through her body, and she jumped. They stared at each other in amazement—and knowledge.

The hostess motioned them to a window table overlooking the Tiber and the sunlit vistas of Rome. They saw and were aware of nothing.

The waiter was there, asking if they would care for a cocktail. Tom looked at Ruth, and she stared back blankly, so he ordered two bourbon sours on the rocks.

Still she said nothing, just looked at him, her face reflecting pain. Finally, in typical Ruth fashion, she started in the middle of the conversation: "I thought I loved my husband."

Four months ago in Maine Tom had vented his hurt, his disappointment, his unreasoned rage on a wall. Now he could be compassionate, for he sensed her bewilderment, her lack of security beneath the veneer of glamour. Had sensed it, he realized with shock, since the impersonal little note she'd written in April. She had not mentioned her marriage plans at all! He shook off this startling discovery, tried to reassure her. "I think it's possible to love more than one person at a time."

"I suppose so. But, Tom," she whispered, "I can't even remember what he looks like. Not now. All I know is I want the world to stop right now." Her eyes filled with tears, and she made comic faces to try to keep them from spilling over. "I'm going to cry."

"No, you're not!" He forced a cool tone into his voice, forced his body into a casual pose, elbows resting on the table, eyes feasting on Ruth. "You are going to sit up and drink your drink when it comes and tell me all about your life."

The waiter set down the sours, and Tom held up his glass. As Ruth reached her glass out, he said simply, "To you." Her mind raced over replies: *To you! To us! Let's go to your room. Please hold me in your arms. Please explain these horrible feelings.* But she only answered, "Thank you," in a small and humble voice.

Once again he took charge. "Come on, I'm waiting."

"Tom. Don't do this to me. You know very well there is nothing to tell. Five minutes ago, I thought there was. But now, nothing—nothing without you. Oh, God—tell me what to do." Again her eyes filled with tears, and a few spilled over and down her cheeks. She dug in her handbag, found a handkerchief and wiped at her eyes, trying not to smudge her mascara, but not quite succeeding. Tom just stared at her, wondering at the injustice of fate that it should be too late when she realized. He was angry at her for not knowing before, angry at himself for letting her out of his sight last time. And angry now that she looked to him to take the mess she'd made and make it all right.

He knew why she had insisted they meet in a public dining room at lunchtime—a place and time that would maintain her propriety and insure that he wouldn't get out of hand! Now she could damn well just sit here and eat lunch and see how comfortable she felt.

The waitress came to ask if they were ready to order. Ruth's eyes pleaded with Tom, but he said, "Yes, we'd like to see a menu, please." However, by the time she returned with the menus, Ruth was so obviously near breakdown, unable to meet his glance, he murmured, "We've changed our minds. We'd just like the check for the drinks."

He stood up, flung down a 5000-lire note, and held out his hand to Ruth. She grasped it, eyes shimmering with gratitude, and they left the dining room.

In the tradition of lovers, they were drawn to the river, and they wandered along it until they came to a fairly secluded spot, and there they sat, not talking, not looking at each other, just holding on. They sat so close together on the ground that they were practically sitting on top of each other, in touch all along the sides of their bodies, their four hands intertwined and resting in Tom's lap.

"Tom, I thought it was fine. I didn't see how empty it was. I'm existing in a vacuum."

"I know what you mean."

"You do?"

"Yes. Remember that first night when you said you finally understood the term turned on? I've always remembered that. You know I think in pictures a lot. Poets do." He dismissed any pretension with a self-effacing smile. "Well, I've always pictured myself as a lightbulb. And you're the only one who knows how to screw me in properly."

She started to laugh, but the laughter died in her throat. They reached for each other in desperation. They simply held on until they regained their composure.

Later, he described Helen's death—talked of his unreasonable rage when he saw Ruth's picture in the paper. She told him about her nourishing year with Nona, her busy, empty days since.

They fell silent, aching over their loss. They spent the afternoon like that, in an agony of love. They knew very well how they felt. They knew very well what they wanted to do about it. But once again they felt they weren't free to follow their feelings.

Finally Tom, with a teacher's perception of time, made himself look at his watch and said mournfully to Ruth, "I have to go. My dinner meeting at the American Library starts at six, with a lecture and a question session afterward. But I don't think I'll be very good tonight. What do you think?" Little boy gray eyes looked at her with love, waiting for praise.

"You're excellent. You hold me spellbound by the magnetism of your body and the intelligence of your gaze." She felt her body becoming liquid.

"When will I see you?"

"When is your free time?"

"Only tomorrow morning. Tomorrow I have lunch with the American Academy and give a lecture for them in the afternoon, and then I leave on the evening flight for Geneva."

"What time in the morning?"

"As early as you can get away."

"He usually goes to work at around eight-thirty. I could probably meet you somewhere at nine." She looked at him for the words she knew would come.

"My hotel room," he said simply, telling her, not asking.

"Yes," she agreed.

His eyes were naked with longing. "Right. Grand Hotel, Room 406. Nine o'clock."

"That will be something to look forward to." She grinned her understatement.

"Yes. I think I might be fairly good this evening after all."

They kissed, then, for the first time that afternoon, and the moment their lips met, their body chemistries went haywire. Tom stood up quickly and reached to bring Ruth to her feet, but she remained sitting.

"I have to just sit here for a little bit after you go and try to collect myself. I can't tell you how unprepared I was for this. I was more prepared to have the love of my life get off United 417 in Akron, Ohio, July 16, 1971, than I was for the fact that it is all here, six years later, more alive, stronger, more compelling, more impossible than ever."

He stooped back down beside her, took her face in his hands, and gently kissed eyes, mouth, nose, cheeks, and then again, mouth. But she was unresponsive, afraid to respond for fear she would drown. He looked at her questioningly.

"I have to try to figure this out. I have to try to understand this, to understand what to do about it."

"Well," he said, kneeling before her, "the thing is, there are two of us. Now, you're going to have to come to some decisions by yourself, take the ultimate responsibility. But I'll be there for you. We'll talk about it tomorrow morning. And you can write to me. Here." He handed her a card with his agent's address in New York. "Or all you have to remember is Somerset, Maine."

"Somerset, Maine. Sounds like Somerset Maugham."

"Yes, but he was someone else's writer. I'm yours."

"You sure are." He was relieved to see she could smile again.

"So, don't try to figure it all out on your own. We'll get started in the morning."

"Okay. Nine o'clock. Grand Hotel. Room 406."

"Right."

Once more the mouth needed to be kissed. And then the eyes and then the nose and this time she needed to kiss him back.

Suddenly she sobbed and broke away. "Maybe we should just jump in the river together and end the torture."

"And forgo the pleasure of ever again getting"—he lowered his voice to whisper—"my body inside your body? Forgo the pleasure of ever again kissing those beautiful breasts?" He ran a hand lightly over the outline of her dress. "Forgo the pleasure of ever again eating a cold dinner, naked on the floor, or sitting in church together or talking about a book we've read or lying side by side in bed on a Sunday morning and reading *The New York Times* or hitting you on the fanny with the towel while we clean up the dishes after dinner. My God, Ruth, what do you take me for, a fool?"

"I love you, T.J.," she whispered.

"Oh, my angel-girl, I love you." He looked at his watch again. "I am going to be so damn late. I'll see you in the morning." One last kiss. He was off and running, literally. He was due in the lobby of the American Embassy in ten minutes, shaved and calm and ready for an evening's work.

Ruth sat for about half an hour more, thinking, praying, trying to calm herself and put things into perspective. Then she rose and walked a few blocks to a cab stand, got in, and gave the penthouse address. It was six-thirty, and Peter didn't usually get home until around seven-thirty, so she should have an hour to take a long leisurely soak and to pull herself together.

She let herself into the apartment and called to the live-in maid that she was home. Sevi, who had been

Peter's maid for years and who was fiercely loyal, said in rather an undertone, "Signore," pointing with her elbow toward the bedroom. Ruth gasped out loud. She was unprepared for the *signore* at the moment.

The bedroom door was tightly closed, and as soon as Ruth opened it, she understood why: Peter was stretched naked across the bed reading *Figaro*. He looked up indolently as she walked in, reclosed the door, and called hello. He didn't answer the greeting at all but merely said, "Take off your clothes."

She had been standing with her back to him, unloading her purse on the dresser, checking her hair in the mirror, but she spun around at his command. Was he joking? Why that tone of voice? She could see by the sternness of the expression on his face that this was no joke. Then he flung the newspaper on the floor and clenched his hands at his sides, as if in readiness to pounce on her.

Uncertain, but to avoid confrontation, Ruth complied, unzipping and sliding out of her dress, pulling her pale slip over her head, kicking off her sandals, pulling down and off her panty hose. She halted in bra and panties, and Peter merely said, "Keep going." So she did, peeling off her underwear and throwing it down on the floor. And then Peter said, "Come here."

She felt embarrassed and ashamed and puzzled. What was he doing? She sat down on the bed and said, "Did you have a good day?"

"Not as good as yours, apparently."

And then she understood. Someone had seen her and Tom. . . .

"Lie down," Peter commanded. Further humiliated, she did so, and his piercing black eyes searched every curve of her body. "Roll over." He searched her back, thighs, and legs. "Well, at least he didn't leave any marks."

Ruth tried to roll back over, but Peter was suddenly on top of her, pinning her down, trying to enter her from behind. Her body was dry and tight, but he went on, ramming into her, hurting her, and then he rolled her over and hurt her more, leaving bruises, black and blue marks, and the indentations of his teeth in her soft skin, but doing even more damage to her spirit and her self-image.

Her last conscious thoughts were of Peter dressing, then stomping out, and slamming the door. For three days she was aware of nothing more. During the night a fever started, and for forty-eight hours it raged out of control. Peter stayed home from work and nursed her himself. The doctor said he could find no cause for the fever, but he did dress the superficial wounds. Peter had told him that someone had broken into the apartment and raped his wife, and the doctor was well paid to believe that and remain silent.

Strangely, then, the fever broke, and Ruth awoke on the third morning to see Peter sitting by the window, head in his hands. She croaked, "*Ciao*, Pietro."

He walked quickly over to the bed, leaned down beside her, and whispered, "I have been so worried about you."

She was puzzled. "Have I been sick?"

"Yes, for almost three days now."

"Oh, Peter, my head hurts so much."

"Here, *carissima*, I'll give you some medicine the doctor left."

"The doctor came?"

"But, of course. You have had the very best of care."

Her head was bursting. She had so much to do. She had to get up. She didn't know what she had to do or where she had to go, but she knew she was late, and she knew she wanted to get there. Peter gave her the drug, then rubbed her back and talked soothingly to her until she once more fell into a deep sleep. He was relieved. She seemed to remember nothing.

Tom, meanwhile, had spent the longest morning of his life. He was filled with doubt and terror. Finally, about noon he steeled himself, got the Morelli number from information, and called. The maid answered and was able to convey that Mrs. Morelli was sick. But he had no idea whether to believe the Italian woman or not. Was Ruth really sick? Was she faking it because she had decided not to meet him? Could she be so sick that she couldn't call him? Unlikely. Had her husband found out they had had lunch together and forbidden her to see him again?

Unhappy and worried, he kept his luncheon appointment, gave his lecture, and left Rome on the evening plane. Even the tranquil beauty of Switzerland was unable to penetrate his cloak of preoccupation. "She nearly was mine." What happened to change that? Damn her for doing this to him! Goddammit all to hell.

Peter had gone to the office that next morning after his abuse of Ruth. She was home writhing in fever and pain, alone and unnoticed. But the first person to enter his office that morning was Raphael Tersico. It seemed he was with Eduardo the day before when they had had lunch at the Hilton, and he had learned that Eduardo had told Signore Morelli about having seen his wife and the handsome American leaving the dining room "in a hurry." Well, Raphael hated to dispute Eduardo, but really Eduardo had been exaggerating. They had had a drink together. That was all. It didn't look like an assignation or anything. He really thought Eduardo had been unfair, and he wanted the *signore* to know that. Peter thanked him and sat at his desk perplexed for a number of minutes before he picked up the phone and called the apartment.

The *signora* was still in bed.

He would call back.

An hour later the *signora* was still in bed.

He hung up, seriously concerned now.

Five minutes later he called back. "Please check on her and make sure she's all right," he said to Sevi.

The wait seemed interminable. Then—

"No, signore. She is burning up, she is so hot, and she has marks all over her face and neck."

"Do nothing. I'll be right home."

Peter called the doctor as soon as he felt her head. For two days he feared that he had killed her.

Ruth's body recovered quickly, but she remembered nothing of the last week or so, and Peter didn't try to press her. He was relieved that she didn't remember the incident; he felt guilty enough. He still wasn't clear in his mind whether she was innocent or guilty, or just how far her lunch with the American had gone. But whatever had happened, he had a gut feeling that she would never try it again. For the next few months their marriage was idyllic again: he was the master, the strong one; he led, she followed—docile, subservient, willing to live through Peter. She wondered later, after she remembered, whether in her subconscious mind she had merely been taking her punishment (she had been disloyal to Peter in thought) and loving the punisher.

It was nine months almost to the day before she remembered Peter's brutality. It was only when she was once more wracked with pain and loneliness and, seemingly, betrayal, that the memories of that September day came flooding back.

She had apparently conceived little Pietro during Peter's wild punishment of her, because it was over a month after that before they made love again. Although he held her sometimes and caressed her body, he sensed her new fear of sex, and he went slowly and gently.

Gradually they got things back together. They established a new relationship based on Ruth's repression and Peter's guilt. It was a mutually satisfying relationship even after Peter had moved her into the country villa and Ruth felt herself cut off and isolated. She assumed that all pregnant women experienced the same sense of depression, that it was a symptom of having to slow down when the time for the baby neared. She didn't know it was the beginning of the end.

All during her pregnancy she consulted with a well-known obstetrician in Rome. He was an old man, white haired and kindly. Best of all, he spoke English. Nothing upset him, and he seemed to have endless patience for the questions of a first-time mother. The plan was that she would come into Rome the week she was due and he would deliver the baby at one of the large maternity hospitals in the city.

Unfortunately, the baby was early. She pondered time and time again how different things might have been if there had been someone with her who spoke her language. As it was, her water broke on a Thursday afternoon: much to her distress, she was in the dining room when it happened. She had just risen from the table and was on her way to the bathroom when she felt a flood descending her leg. She was embarrassed, thinking it was her weak bladder, when she saw the light brown stream of bloody fluid and knew. Her embarrassment vanished, and she said triumphantly, loudly, "My water just broke." Only Sophia, unmarried and inexperienced with such baby-related things understood her English, but Peter's mother saw, without hearing, and quickly led her to the living room sofa and made her lie still while the car was fetched. She was driven to the small community hospital in Orvieto.

At first she just had cramps, and while they were uncomfortable, they were mild, and it was a bearable pain. She laid back in the bed and enjoyed the private, sunlit room, the clean, crisp white sheets. But her peace was short-lived. A nurse walked in, smiled at her and explained in Italian what she was going to do.

"*Non capisco*. English, *prego*," said Ruth.

"*Non capisco Inglese. Scusi.*"

Ruth's slacks, blouse, and sandals had already disappeared, and she was wearing only a hospital gown, slit in the back so that it was easy for the nurse, with no more than another "*Scusi,*" to roll her over and insert a tube into her rectum. Her intestines were flooded with water. Would that someone had been able to explain to her that an enema was routine for a woman in labor.

Water creating unbearable pressure in her bowels, the baby trying to slide down into the birth canal creating strong pressure in her uterus, Ruth felt as if bullets were exploding inside her. The nurse simply stood there, holding Ruth's buttocks together with her hand, looking at her watch, shaking her head. Three long, painful minutes dragged by and then, too quickly, the nurse pulled out the tube, and Ruth was powerless to stop the contents of her digestive tract from following. The nurse shouted, "*Non,*

non," and pointed across the hall to a bathroom. Ruth mutely stumbled to her feet and walked drunkenly across the hall to be sick in every way possible. Never in her life had she felt more nauseated.

When she returned to the room, there was a clean bed waiting for her, a fresh nightgown stretched out on the sheets. Ruth took off the used gown, put on the clean one, and fell weakly into bed. But when the nurse returned to the room she barely listened to Ruth's *"scusi."* She had decided that Ruth wasn't trying. Ruth realized that having made the nurse angry was not going to help her any.

The cramps were getting more and more painful, and Ruth tried to remember the breathing exercises she had read in the natural childbirth book. She wanted to get herself started on the routines, but, first of all, she had only read about them, no one had ever shown them to her, and secondly, she needed help, needed someone to remind her to concentrate, and Ruth was alone.

She was still trying to get herself under control when the same none-too-happy nurse walked in with a dishpan of warm sudsy water, a towel, and a razor. Ruth had never heard anyone mention being shaved before a delivery, and she was in a panic to know what the nurse was going to do with the razor. Her question was soon answered. The nurse touched Ruth by the shoulders, pushing her from her side, where she had been fairly comfortable, flat onto her back, which was extremely uncomfortable. Then she yanked down the sheet and pushed Ruth's hospital robe up onto the mound of her stomach, exposing most of her body. None too gently she moved Ruth's feet, bending the knees, placing the soles together, flattening the pelvic region as much as possible. The water felt cooling and refreshing, but the pull of the cold steel razor came as a shock, as did the nonchalance with which the nurse removed all the hair from between Ruth's legs. She then washed the newly shaved skin with an antiseptic, then, mercifully, covered Ruth back up and marched out of the room.

Ruth had yet to see a doctor. She was hoping that, whomever he would be, he would speak English and take away some of her terror. She had an additional hour of mild contractions, before he walked in, and when he did, she was extremely disappointed. He was a middle-aged Italian man who spoke no English, did not even smile, and had the thickest glasses Ruth had ever seen. He patted her hand a little, pulled down the sheet and up the gown, donned a plastic glove, and slid his fingers inside Ruth. He said, "*Quattro*," shook his head negatively, patted her hand again, and walked out.

She was left alone then, with her ignorance and her insecurities, and she watched the sun go down and the night grow black. When the nurses changed shifts, a young Italian girl with short, curly brown hair and gray eyes walked over to Ruth's bed and said, "Hello. American?" Then she got a cool washcloth and wiped Ruth's face and neck and moistened her lips with a special swab dipped in ice water. Those two words apparently had exhausted the English vocabulary of the young nurse, but Ruth had never been so grateful for anything or anyone in her entire life. And so the night passed with a friend. Most of the night the young nurse stayed by Ruth's bed, or if she was gone, she didn't stay away too long, and Ruth got herself back under control and decided she might make it through this birth after all. She dozed off and on, then would awaken to the same dull, passing pains.

The curly brown hair and the gray eyes had brought more than just the comfort of the girl herself. The physical likeness had brought Tom into the room, and Ruth spent many of her waking hours recollecting conversations and glances, touches and groans. She would groan in pain and think about the sounds T.J. made during their lovemaking. She would find herself sweating and remember the dining room floor in Pittsburgh, when they were both drenched with sweat, their bodies liquid on and in one another. She would grasp her friend's hand and hold on for strength and dream that it was T.J.'s hand instead, and that he was there with her, helping her, sustaining her.

At first when they had brought her in, she had asked frequently about Peter. Where was he? Did he know? But then sometime during the night she had awakened from a dozing sleep, and in a flash of memory she had known what had happened the night of September 22. And now she no longer cared if she saw Peter—ever. Too tired even to hate, she longed only to see Tom and explain. She tortured her mind over whether or not he would believe her, but finally her heart knew he would and she began to feel him with her, and that knowledge helped the suffering.

As the sun rose Ruth's young friend got busy elsewhere on the floor. Ruth's pains were becoming stronger and closer together. Finally, for only the second time, the hand-patting, nearly blind doctor came back in the room. He repeated his procedure exactly, this time saying "six" in Italian, instead of "four." By this time Ruth was groaning out loud with every contraction, and she was feeling exhausted. It almost finished her to see the same unfriendly nurse from yesterday come in, and Ruth realized in a haze of hurt that the nurses must work twelve-hour shifts. That at least gave the nurse some justification for her bad mood.

The morning consisted of strong pain punctuated by loneliness. The ache in her spirit was mild only in comparison to the ache in her body. Between the uterine contractions she had contractions of fear. The pain continued. When she felt she couldn't stand it any longer, the pain mounted. Finally her groans became audible, and soon they became screams. The nurse walked in and said "Shh!" Ruth answered her by screaming louder. The nurse ran for the doctor, and he repeated his ballet of hand patting, glove donning, cervix measuring, glove removing, hand patting. Only this time he barked an order at the end of the ritual, and a stretcher appeared. Ruth was moved from the bed to the stretcher and rushed down the hall into a freezing cold room of steel and chrome, white walls and white lights. Then again she was moved from the stretcher to another table.

Now she was made to sit upright and lean forward. Sitting up and leaning forward in the midst of contractions is like leaning into a sword, walking into a fire. Every instinct urges against it, and Ruth tried to fight, understanding nothing. The back of the gown was opened, and there were hands on her back, counting vertebrae. She didn't realize, again, what they were doing—she had never had a spinal before—and was shocked and frightened by the sting of the needle in her back. But moments later the excruciating pain stopped, completely, and she realized they had finally given her some anesthetic.

Once again she was made to lie flat on her back, and this time her feet were raised into the stirrups. She thought, *What an ungodly, unnatural position*. They kept repeating, *"Spingi,"* which even as inexperienced and monolingual as she was, she realized must mean "push," but it seemed impossible. There was no way to gain leverage. The position was so awkward! She thought she could have done better going out into the fields and squatting over a hole like the peasants, because then, at least, she would have had nature and gravity on her side.

Nature took over, anyhow, and she got a second breath, a tiny spurt of energy, and she pushed, three or four times, with all her might. She prayed, silently and fervently, that this labor might be ended—at that point she didn't care what the outcome, her death or the baby's—she just had to be finished with the isolation. And then she heard a smack, followed by the most miraculous sound in the universe: the sound of a newborn baby filling its lungs with air. Tears poured down her cheeks, and all she could think was that it was over and she was so tired and she might never feel good again and that she would definitely never have a baby again, ever. Nothing was worth that kind of pain.

They laid him on her stomach, and she reached up with her hand to touch him, but a nurse whom she had never seen before pushed her hand back, gently, saying, *"Non,"* and so Ruth simply stared. He looked terrible: he was red and blotchy and covered with a mixture of blood and mucus. His skinny legs were bent up and in; his arms flailed uncontrollably. His eyes were pinched shut against the shocking white lights, and his mouth was open, protesting. His black hair was wet and matted. There was an ugly rope of skin and membrane extending from his navel. His penis was disproportionately large and was shooting a spray of urine all over her belly.

She had never in her life seen a more beautiful, more moving sight. Overcome with emotion, she started mumbling the "Ave Maria" in Latin, and for a fraction of a minute the operating room listened to the young American woman lying in an Italian hospital, praying to their God in their language, and the sympathies shifted. For the rest of her stay in the hospital, eight days, Ruth was treated with a respect and kindness that she would have given much for during the labor.

She glanced up and saw a mirror in one corner near the ceiling. In the mirror she saw the doctor sewing up her incision. She felt badly that she hadn't noticed the mirror earlier, or had it pointed out to her, so that she might have watched the delivery.

She was cleaned up; the baby was taken away to be polished and shined; she was returned to her room. Peter was there waiting for her. Vaguely, she was aware of his kisses and praises for what a good job she had done and how happy and proud he was to have a son.

Ruth shook off her lethargy, and her book fell to the ground. It was still Wednesday afternoon. It looked as if nothing in her present life would change. Peter was in his own angry exile. Ruth was in her impersonally polite prison. After Pietro's birth, she had tried to begin their marriage anew; for the last two years she had hoped and prayed that somehow it would work out. She had tried to be patient, tried to be optimistic. But for almost three years now she had had no emotional support, and she was feeling utterly disheartened.

The pool still lay before her, beckoning, patient. She spent so much time these days thinking about the past—it wasn't healthy. She forced herself to get up. She stood for a moment at the edge of the water, looking at the reflec-

tion of the heavy-set woman with unattractively short
blond hair and listless blue eyes. The image shattered
when she dove in. She swam eight laps, then went up to
shower and dress for dinner with the half-dozen vultures.

❧ 11 ❧

Ben called at about two o'clock on Thursday, May 7. Nona had died—she had simply stopped breathing. She had been in a coma for three days; Ben hadn't been able to wake her on Monday morning. All Sunday night he had slept with his arms around her, but Monday morning he awoke to find her in a coma, and he called the ambulance. She had left explicit legal instructions that no life-support systems were to be employed, no extra measures taken, and Ben made sure her wishes were followed. Early Thursday morning she simply stopped living. Ben was sitting beside her, his hand on her arm. He didn't even realize she was gone until he felt her arm growing cold and stiff. She had died as peacefully as she had lived.

Ben would be arriving in Rome on Saturday. He was bringing Nona back to be buried between Bruno and her husband. Nona had told Ben to bury her in Pittsburgh, but he'd guessed she had just wanted to please him. They both knew her place was in Rome.

Ben's voice sounded calm and composed. Ruth fell apart completely. For over two years she had been living a lie to Nona, the one woman in her life who had meant the most and been the most to her. Nona had taught her about faith in God, but lately Ruth had begun to doubt not only herself but God as well. And Nona was no longer there to help her. Now there was a whole list of defections: T.J. had just walked away without a fight; Peter's love had proved shallow and temporary; Pietro preferred the half-dozen and the nurse—or at least couldn't distinguish her from the others; Ben had never been wholly there for her;

Bruno had been killed; and now Nona had died. There was no one left.

Ruth hung up the phone that Thursday afternoon and walked out of the house. Peter was in Tokyo for two weeks. It would be asking too much for him to be home when his wife needed him. Ruth would have to make the arrangements—she and Ben could stay in the penthouse. No doubt her father would want to go back to Pittsburgh right after the funeral—on Monday, probably. He would need to get his life in order again. How could he sound so good? Lucky Ben, to have had three years with Nona. Ruth cherished the one year she had lived with her.

Ruth walked around the villa looking for a refuge for her grief, but there was none. Everything was so cultivated, so civilized—there was nowhere primitive, nowhere to lie down in tall grass and weep. She needed a stream or an ocean, not a cosmetically perfect pool.

She found a stone wall to lean on. Her elbows supported her as she bent, head in hands, and cried. "Oh, Nona, how could you die? I need you so."

Then she chided herself for thinking about herself when she should have been thinking about Nona. She sniffled and looked out over the Italian hills remembering the Nona she had loved so much. What a lady. All of five-foot-three, totally undistinguished physically: brown hair liberally streaked with gray, ordinary blue eyes, a large Italian nose, a wide mouth with a gold tooth on one side (which had disconcerted Ruth at first). But, oh, how remarkable she was inside. Nona had possessed that rare ability to work completely and to sit completely. Most people look right either working or sitting—Nona could do both: work hard or sit still.

Nona, more importantly, was the best listener Ruth had ever met. When she talked to Nona, the woman did nothing but look at her and listen. Ruth could talk in a crowded restaurant, and Nona's eyes never traveled over the crowd. She could talk in the car, and Nona never noticed the scenery. She always had Nona's attention and interest.

And Nona was objective. Even when talking about

Bruno, she wasn't partial or nearsighted. "Bruno waited all his life for you; he wanted a girl with lots of heart. He would have been devoted to you if he had lived to be ninety. Now, you, Ruth," Nona had continued, "I think would have tired of Bruno. He was such a patient, conservative person. I think you needed, need now, someone with more spontaneity, more vigor."

"Oh, but, Nona, I loved him," Ruth had protested.

"*Cara*, I know, I know. I'm not criticizing. You were wonderful. You gave him the happiest years of his life. Never had he been so confident, so fulfilled. Always hold that in your heart, Ruth—that you were the best thing that ever happened to him."

They had had a hundred conversations like that, and another hundred on God.

"How do you *know*, Nona?"

"How do you know there isn't a God?" Nona countered.

"I don't. But you don't know there is," Ruth persisted.

"Do you want the truth, Ruth? Do you know why God exists for me? Because I want Him to. I want to live my life with a God. I want to have some standards to live up to, some power to get down on my knees to. I want to live a life that has meaning—and a life with God has more meaning."

"But Nona there is no explanation for things like Bruno's death."

"That's right. There is no *explanation*. There is only faith. Go read Job."

Another time Nona had said, "I think Christianity is like life—which is like a good book. There is vitality, adventure, mystery—and not *all* the loose ends are tied up. There is hope and mercy and destruction and devastation —and then building out of the ashes."

"Building out of the ashes." Ruth's memory drudged up that phrase; she could even hear Nona's soft voice saying it. *That's what I feel like*, Ruth thought. *I feel like everything is in ashes around me*. What was it that Browning's poem said? Ah, yes, "Leave the fire ashes, what survives is gold."

That's true of people. People who have come through

traumas and crises are the ones who have found the gold within themselves—the strength. God was Nona's gold. He was her strength and courage. What's mine? If I have any. . . .

She sat down, back against the wall, knees up, head resting on knees, and let herself drift. It was a long time later that she became aware of Giovanni humming to himself not far away as he pruned the olive and date trees. She waited, very still, until he had gone to carry away a load of brush, and then she rose and went inside. She changed into her swimsuit and did fifteen laps without stopping. Then she had supper with the six, played with Pietro, a little more successfully than usual, and went to her room.

She bathed, washed her hair, and packed a suitcase, thinking that in the morning she would ask someone to drive her into Rome. By eleven she was in bed.

Around four in the morning, she awoke feeling alert and rested. For almost an hour she lay there, unable to get back to sleep, before she had the most wonderfully awful idea. The Maserati Bruno had given her was out in the seven-car garage, and just the other day she had noticed—when straightening drawers, for lack of anything better to do—where Peter kept the keys. She would simply drive herself to Rome! And what better time than right now? Feeling marvelously alive, she dressed in slacks and a sweater, picked up her suitcase, and crept down the stairs and out the back door.

The night was at its darkest, but Ruth's spirits were lighter than they had been for a long time. *No one in this house will miss me,* she thought without self-pity. *I'll just call from Rome and tell them where I am.* She was relieved to see there was a full tank of gas in the Maserati but was worried when she had trouble starting the engine. At last, on about the fifth try, the car purred, and she drove out, stopping to close the garage door.

On the drive to Rome Ruth had an exhilarating sense of freedom that was tempered by an almost forgotten feeling of serenity settling within. Perhaps it was being in Bruno's car, but she sensed a control and a self-confidence that had eluded her for years. Perhaps driving had something to do with it; she hadn't been behind a steering wheel for over two years. Someone else had always driven her—and she had always let them. There was a lesson in that, somewhere. . . . The night was beautiful, still and dark—then the sun broke on the horizon. Ruth remembered the night she and Bruno had shared on the beach at Ostia, and the memory buoyed her. *I can do it. I can be whomever I want to be. I can be me. Me is a good person. Bruno loved me. Nona loved me. They might be gone, but the person they loved isn't gone. I am here. And I will make something worthwhile out of me!*

The sun rose all around her, breaking forth in a symphony of yellows and oranges as she drove slowly and carefully into Rome. She was getting stronger by the mile, and she would work on getting stronger still. She was not insignificant. She was Ruth. T.J.'s Ruth!

The thought stung her like a mosquito: it sneaked up on her and got under her skin, catching her totally unaware. She couldn't brush it aside—she had to keep examining it. Why was she T.J.'s Ruth? Why not Bruno's or Peter's? What was the difference?

Of course she was not Bruno's because he was dead, and belonging to something dead, clinging to it, negates life.

But why not Peter's? What was she to Peter? She was his wife, for heaven's sake—the mother of his child. She was also sexy and witty, his companion and conversationalist. At least . . . used to be. Okay? What did they talk about even then? Well, where to go and who to see and architecture and history. Nothing wrong with that.

What about T.J.? What did they talk about? Well, themselves and each other—and hurts and pains and pleasures. They talked about reading and writing—about poetry. And T.J. always wanted to know what she thought. And she wanted to know what he thought. They bounced ideas off each other like two people playing tennis.

But if she and Peter played anything, it was more like golf: they were together, and the ideas went down the fairway side by side, but they didn't intersect. Neither of them kept the ball bouncing for the other. Even when things were good, they weren't essential to each other for the game of life. And, Ruth thought, that was just how Peter treated her—as nonessential. She was an extra in his life. A trifle. Something to enhance his life. The icing on the cake.

But she was bread to T.J.—at least she could be. They nourished each other. They expanded and grew and bloomed in each other's presence.

She drove into Rome, down the brick streets that had lasted two thousand years, past the walls that had repelled barbarians and infidels, into the splendid city of Raphael and Michelangelo and Pope John Paul II, and she felt her shoulders growing straight, and she felt capable.

I can do it. I can make the arrangements for Nona, and I can place her tenderly in the ground, and I can see to it that her friends are there and that there is love abounding at her funeral.

I can comfort my father, and I can reassure him that he did a beautiful and caring thing for Nona, and that her letters revealed a youthful, vivacious Nona who hadn't existed before she met him. I can put myself on the shelf and take care of these things. And when they are done, I am going to bring me down from the shelf and get myself dusted off and cleaned up, and the stagnation is going to end, and I am going to resume being a worthwhile and useful person. Maybe I'll teach again or volunteer or write or something, but I will not sit around like some hothouse orchid and get smelly. And if I can't be worthwhile with Peter, then I will be worthwhile without him.

She looked in the rearview mirror and saw eyes still smudged with shadows but also flashing with determination and purpose. She smiled and nodded in recognition at her old friend.

With strong resolve and a ramrod back, Ruth parked the car in the underground garage. She was surprised to see Peter's car there; she assumed he had been driven to the airport. She took the service elevator to the top floor, where she quietly let herself in the back door.

"Sevi," she called softly to the maid. It was only a little

after seven-thirty; Sevi might not be up. Ruth didn't want to wake her. And then she heard voices in the dining room. Thinking that it must be Sevi and some friend, and not wanting to walk in on something, Ruth tiptoed to the little two-way mirror on the kitchen wall. Peter had had the mirror put in years ago when Sevi had complained that she never knew when to clear the table between courses. From the dining room one saw merely a charming little silver-framed mirror. From the kitchen one saw the dining room.

Ruth walked softly to the mirror and was astonished to see Peter and a man she knew to be Dominique diGuro. She instinctively pulled back from the mirror, waiting for Peter to come stomping out to the kitchen, exploding. Why was she there? How dare she stand there eaves-dropping.

Come to think of it...why was *he* there? He was supposed to be in Tokyo.

She gained courage when the flood of Italian continued unabated, and she was apparently undetected. She peered into the mirror again, trying to understand.

Dominique diGuro was "the enemy."

And it *was* Dominique diGuro, she was sure. She had heard them all talking about him often enough and had tensed at the scornful tones as the six women bashed his name about. She had seen his picture in the paper, the name obvious under the bad snapshots. And once, when she and Peter were dining out in Rome, in the early days of their marriage, diGuro happened to be in the same restaurant.

"That, Ruth," Peter had said pointing from the dim alcove where they sat in privilege to the brightly lit, large main room, "is the enemy. DiGuro is a government serf. He sits on this committee and that committee, talking of safety regulations—of which he knows nothing—spouting union ideology. Incredible. Don't ever waste your pretty all-American smile on him."

She had wanted to know more. She still didn't under-stand exactly why the gray-haired, mild-looking man with his elegant young wife was the enemy. But Peter had reached beneath the table and started stroking Ruth's leg, pressing it against his, and she soon lost her concentration in a haze of sexuality. The moment was lost.

And now the two of them were sitting in the penthouse dining room. There didn't seem to be any animosity between them. They were sitting at the table looking both relaxed and animated, a pot of coffee between them. To all appearances, two friends were having an early-morning get-together. They were each leaning back in their chairs, Peter with his legs crossed, diGuro with his stretched out. Every once in a while Ruth heard what certainly sounded like a laugh. Maybe they had worked out their differences.

She was just getting up her nerve to go in and say hello when she noticed the open briefcase on the table.

A shiver ran the length of her spine so that for a moment her whole body shook.

She had never seen so much Italian lire in one place before in her life. What the hell was all that money doing on the dining room table? And what the hell was she witnessing?

She would have tried to make an escape, so certain was she that she should not be where she was, but fear immobilized her. And then she heard the men rustling about, the briefcase snapping shut; she watched with amazement the handshakes, the pat on the back from Peter to diGuro. She saw diGuro pick up the money-heavy briefcase.

Oh, dear God! What have I just seen?

She watched them walk toward the front door, then leaped to the stove and put on the teakettle. Then she sank down in a kitchen chair and tried to understand the Italian melodrama she had just witnessed. Peter was paying off diGuro, that much seemed clear, and instinctively Ruth knew it to be true. That explained why there had never been any *proof* that Peter was disobeying government safety standards. Yet the rumors must have been true. Innocent men do not hand out lire like it was—cookies.

"What are you doing here?" Peter's voice broke harshly on her thoughts.

"Nona died. My father is bringing her body back to

Rome. I came to make arrangements." She knew she sounded horribly distraught.

"When did you get here?"

"I just walked in the door. I just put the teakettle on. When did *you* get here?"

"Last night. I finished things up in Tokyo earlier than I thought." He walked over to the stove and seemingly absentmindedly felt the side of the kettle. Satisfied, he came and sat down at the table with Ruth. "I'll take care of everything for Nona—don't worry about a thing."

"No," she said quickly and forcefully. "I'm doing this. All of it. Nona is mine—was mine—and I am doing this for her, making the arrangements, making the decisions. I don't want your help, Peter. I am absolutely adamant about this. Do you understand?"

"Of course I don't understand. Why should you have to go through all this when I can do it perfectly easily and probably do it better?"

"Peter, I don't care if you could do it twice as fast and twice as well. *I'm* doing it. Period. *Basta*. *Finito*." Her voice was firm and angry.

"Okay, okay. Call me if you need anything." He shot up and stalked into the bedroom to dress for the office.

She sat at the kitchen table and started making lists of all the things she had to do; she didn't have time now to think about what she'd just overheard. Half an hour later she set off to see Father Barista. She didn't know if Peter had left yet or not, and as she walked down the street, she decided she really didn't care.

Father Barista was saying mass when she got to St. Mary's, so Ruth knelt in the back and prayed. When the priest led the congregation toward the exit, she was feeling much calmer.

"I need you," she mouthed as he passed, and he nodded his head. She kept her seat, knowing he'd return when he was free. About ten minutes later he slid into the pew beside her and grasped her hand.

She smiled at him, and his answering smile was the warmest thing she had seen in years. Paulo Barista had gone to school with Bruno and had been a neighborhood priest at their boyhood parish for almost fifteen years now. He had said the funeral mass for Bruno; Ruth knew he would say it for Nona.

"She died, Paulo," Ruth said after their greeting.

"I hope it was quick and painless," he said squeezing her hand.

Ruth nodded. "My father is bringing her back tomorrow. Can you help me make the arrangements?"

"But of course. Come on." He stood up and pulled her along. "We'll go back to my office. I'll need to cancel some things for this morning, and we'll want to make some phone calls."

"You do have time to do this now, don't you?"

"Ruth." He stopped and surprised her by grasping her shoulders in his big, warm hands. "Bruno and I were boyhood friends, schoolmates." He lowered his voice to a whisper. "Later we even went drinking together. I spent a lot of time at their house when I was young. Always Nona had cookies and juice for us, and always she had time to listen to our young opinions and ideas. When I started here, she had a little supper for me, and my first Sunday here she had the church packed with friends, just to make me feel welcome. Before she left for the states, she told me in detail what she planned to do in Pittsburgh with your father. She asked my blessing and my forgiveness. I give her only the blessings. Nona rarely needed forgiveness, and certainly not for her plan for dying. I think she lived a worthwhile life, and I think she died in Christian grace and with dignity."

He studied Ruth's wide, somber eyes. "I see we have something to talk about, too, don't we?" he asked.

"What?"

"What indeed? Something is definitely amiss with you. I never saw such pain in your eyes before." He paused, and she nodded. "But do you understand now about Nona?"

"Yes. Thank you for . . . for caring."

"Let's go." He took her arm and led her back to his office. His secretary canceled his morning appointments, and he and Ruth closeted themselves, making arrangements for the mass, the hearse to be at the airport, the burial permit, the arrangements for the opening of the family vault, and finally notifying a few of Nona's closest friends. They were finishing up all the details they could think of when the secretary knocked and handed Paulo a message. "Oh, no. Signore Garnetto has sent for me. Knowing him, he waited until the last minute. He is the most considerate ninety-six year old I have ever met." They exchanged a smile.

Ruth rose quickly. "Thank you, Paulo, from the bottom of my heart."

"*Prego*, Ruth, *prego*." Once again he grasped her hand, held it between his two, and then he pulled her into his arms, and she closed her eyes and held him tightly. Then, without looking at him, she pulled away and walked quickly toward the door. She had her hand on the knob when he said softly, "Let us have dinner tonight."

She turned in surprise to scrutinize his face and saw only sincerity and support. Paulo was there to help. He sensed that Ruth needed help, and needed it now. For Bruno and for Nona he wanted to help her. He reluctantly admitted that he wanted to help Ruth because of Ruth, too.

Ruth nodded her head.

"Can you pick me up here? About eight-thirty?"

She nodded again, and he turned back to his desk as she walked out.

She spent the afternoon walking, drinking tea, shopping for flowers. She ordered a mammoth bouquet of wild flowers from her and Peter to be sent to the funeral home. From Pietro she sent some tiny pink tea roses. She also asked for three perfect yellow, long-stemmed roses to be sent to the funeral home. Nona had asked for three such flowers to be placed in the coffin with Bruno, explaining that she had done the same thing for her husband. Now Ruth would do the same thing for Nona.

When Ruth got to the penthouse, Sevi was there, but not Peter. Ruth greeted Sevi, then walked into the master bedroom. She picked up her suitcase from where Sevi had set it and carried it into the smaller guest room. There she bathed and changed, and by six o'clock she was gone again. She went down to the garage for the car and drove up to Trastevere, one of the seven hills, where she sat, watching the city, thinking and planning. After about an hour and a half she parked and walked to a nearby *trattoria* and ordered some Campari. There she remained for another hour until it was time to pick up Paulo Barista.

To her surprise he came to the driver's door and said, "Would you mind if I drove?"

"Of course not."

They walked around the car, and he opened and closed the passenger door for her before climbing in under the wheel, zooming off with a roar of the engine.

He laughed in sheer delight. "Dear Lord, I love this car. My one wish is that I would be allowed to have a car—but one corruption leads to another, they say." He grinned wickedly at her, and she laughed in response.

He drove to a tiny seafood restaurant in Ostia, where he had dined with her and Bruno many times.

"What a nice idea, Paulo. I haven't been back here for years. Bruno always loved their scampi. I think I'll have some."

"Yes, me, too. And pasta to start, and a nice dry, white wine—Orvieto, I think." He did not notice Ruth wince at the name of the wine that was also the name of her prison. "This is a treat for me. I get out so seldom, I always feel like I have to do it all when I do get out."

They gorged themselves while Paulo entertained her with stories of schoolboy escapades. She had heard them all before, but it was fun to hear them again. He was charming and bright and demanded nothing of her, but she found herself telling him about teaching and how much she loved and missed it, and he urged her to get back to it.

"I will, Paulo. I have to. I feel so insignificant and useless without something like that in my life."

"I know. Do what you have to do, Ruth."

She nodded. Their dinner over, they stood up and were

walking toward the car when he suddenly grabbed her hand and pulled her quickly in the other direction.

"Come on. Let's go walk on the beach instead of going right back."

But after a short time the long day took its toll, and Ruth collapsed in the sand. "Oh, Paulo, I'm too tired to go another step."

"Okay. Listen, would you mind if I went for a quick swim?"

"Are you kidding? It's only May. You'll freeze."

"No, I won't. Would you mind?" He was a child asking permission, and she remembered that part of being a priest was the rule of obedience.

"No, of course not. Go right ahead. I'll just sit here and watch."

He stripped down to his shorts and ran into the water. She admired his athlete's body, then lay back against the sand, her purse under her head, listening to him splashing and laughing.

She awoke gradually, stiff and confused. He was sitting right beside her, his head on his knees, but he heard her move, and his head jerked up, his eyes and mouth immediately smiling.

"You were tired."

"Oh. Yes, I really was. I didn't even realize. What time is it?" she asked, stretching and sitting up.

"About eleven-thirty."

"Oh, that's not too bad. Paulo, I'm sorry, I'll bet you had things to do. You should have awakened me."

"No way. I just spent the most peaceful hour imaginable sitting here, listening to you and the surf snoring in counterpoint."

"Snoring?" She laughed. "I'll have you know ladies don't snore."

"That's what I always thought, too."

They laughed and rose to walk to the car.

"Shall I come with you to the airport tomorrow? I'd like to if I won't be intruding."

"We would love to have you. Thank you."

He drove back to Rome in silence, stopped the car, got out in front of the rectory, and squatted down on the curb while Ruth moved awkwardly back over the gearshift to the driver's seat. "That was a beautiful evening," he said softly.

"Paulo, it was wonderful. I feel so at peace. Thank you."

"You're welcome. Thank *you*. What time will you pick me up tomorrow?"

"Let's see, the plane's at three, isn't it?"

"Yes, that's right—so two?"

"That should be plenty of time. Thanks again, Paulo. I'll be back here at two."

"Okay, *cara*. *Ciao*." He winked at her and stood up and vanished into the rectory.

She was driving back to the penthouse, worrying about what lay before her, when she passed the Grand Hotel. Impulsively she pulled into the circular driveway. Her car was parked for her, and she was ushered to the main desk. In a flash of memory she inquired, "Would you by any chance have Room 406 vacant tonight?"

The desk clerk smiled a knowing smile and said, "I'll be glad to check, signorina."

She put on a haughty face, and he turned away, swinging back around a moment later to say, "Yes, Signorina, by some incredible fortune the one room you want is free this evening."

"Good. I'll take it."

"*Prego*, signorina. *Prego*."

She signed in, took the key, and received a strange look when the clerk inquired if she had any baggage. "No. None," she answered, pleased with herself for not blushing or offering any explanation. She turned and went to the elevator.

The moment she entered the room she felt T.J. was with her. She quickly went to the bathroom, brushed her teeth with her finger and some water, and snuggled into bed in her bra and panties, grasping the second pillow to her breast. In moments she was asleep.

Saturday dawned warm and sunny, but Ruth didn't realize it. The drapes were shut, and she slept late. When she awoke she called room service for breakfast. The strange reaction to her request indicated it was late for that meal, so she asked the time and was surprised to learn it was 12:20. She kept her order toast and tea, anyhow.

Then she called Peter.

"Where the hell have you been?" was his response to her hello.

The urge to hang up was overwhelming.

"I'm at the Grand Hotel."

"Why?"

She ignored the question.

"My father is bringing Nona back today. Should he and I stay at the penthouse, or should we stay here in the hotel?"

"I think you should both come here," he said in a suddenly humble voice.

"Okay. I'll be home in about a half hour to change. Then I'm going to the airport to pick them—I mean dad—up."

"I'll drive you."

"No, thank you. But you could take us both out to dinner tonight if you want to. The viewing is from seven to nine."

"All right." He sounded resigned.

"See you in a little bit—if you're there. *Ciao.*"

"*Ciao.*"

He wasn't there, and she felt only relief. The day went smoothly. Ruth and Ben had an emotional greeting and then a quiet ride, Paulo driving sedately to the funeral home.

They got things arranged in the room, the flowers as they wanted them, some chairs set up, and then Paulo took Ruth and Ben out for a drink. By seven o'clock they were in place at the door to greet the other mourners. Nona had been very popular in her small circle and in church, and it showed in the attendance. Almost a hundred people filed through in the two hours, everyone giving Ruth a warm kiss and their condolences, treating Ben with great respect. They knew that if Nona trusted herself to this man for the last years of her living, he must be a good man.

Around quarter to nine Peter arrived, staying in the background, waiting for the people to clear out. Then he offered to take everyone out to dinner, and Ben and Paulo both accepted, much to Ruth's relief. The four of them had a quiet, comfortable time, Ruth saying almost nothing, no one pressing her.

When they got back to the penthouse, Peter made no comment when Ruth went into the smaller guest room and closed the door. He and Ben had a Scotch before bed.

Monday it rained, and the mass and the burial were over much too soon. The finality of the last moments before the vault door was closed and locked hit Ruth with an intensity for which she was unprepared. Back at the penthouse, where Sevi served a buffet meal for Nona's relatives and closest friends, Ben shooed everyone else aside and led Ruth into the kitchen. He took a box from his pocket and handed it to her.

"This is yours, from Nona," he said. And he walked out, leaving her alone.

The tears came out in a gush as she opened the box and looked at the contents. Inside were Nona's most special treasures: her engagement ring, a large, beautiful diamond set in a simple silver setting; Bruno's baby bracelet from the hospital; a story Bruno had written about her as a schoolchild, telling that she was the best mama in the world; a wedding picture of Bruno and Ruth with Ben and Nona; and her favorite blue-flowered bridge cards. So little and yet so much, so vividly Nona. For long minutes Ruth put her head down and sobbed.

When she felt cried out, she unfolded the letter that had been on the top of the box.

Carissima, carissima,

Don't cry. I can feel you crying already. Don't, please. You break my heart. I had so much, Ruth. My childhood was so happy, my husband a good man, my son an absolute saint, and I love my daughter-in-law completely. She has brought me immeasurable happiness. And, then, when I would have been well satisfied to have lived a life with love and friendship abounding, along came your father. What a surprise—at sixty-eight, to feel like sixteen. We laugh, we whisper secrets, we even write notes in church. What bliss, Ruth, to blush as his eyes caress me, to tremble with joy at the feel of his hands.

I have read that you never feel more alive than when you are dying. Rubbish, Ruth, total rubbish. I would feel very dead dying, were it not for the love with which your father has bathed me. That is what makes me feel alive Ruth, love. Not sex! Don't mis-understand me.

No, dear, the love I am talking about is the eyes that smile into one another, the hand that holds my head over the toilet after my chemotherapy, the arms that cradle me at night when I am scared, the wink from across the room, the anticipation of need, the reaction to mood, the feeling of peace and well-being in another presence. It is this love that allows one to feel most alive, and it is this love that allows one to look death in the face and smile. Because love like this can only be God-given. And if God can give love like this, I have faith that he knows what he is doing in other areas as well. Things like life after death are beyond my scope, Ruth. And, frankly, I don't have to know the answers. The recipient is in no position to demand of the Giver.

Do not fret, sweet child, do not doubt, do not despair. I wish I had the energy to give you pages and pages of advice—to tell you everything I have learned. Alas, I cannot. And it would be useless anyhow. Each of us must walk different paths and must learn differ-ent lessons and will have different teachers. So I have only two things that I want you to remember and practice. (1) Be of good faith. God cares. (2) Take any risk, risk any challenge, to keep your heart open to love.

> I love you, dear child of my soul—
> on earth and in heaven—
> Your Nona

Again the tears streamed down Ruth's pale cheeks. "Nona," Ruth moaned, "you have told me just what I needed to know." *Thank you, God, for Nona. I know you are taking good care of her.*

Peter and Ben were in the study, no doubt having a drink. Ruth slipped into the bathroom, washed her face with cold water, took four aspirin, and went to bed. The box spent the night on the pillow beside her.

She became aware of someone shaking her and looked up into Peter's closely shaven face. It must be morning!

"Your father needs to leave for the airport in about half an hour. Do you want me to take him, or do you want to?"

"Thank you, Peter." She was able to smile at him for the first time in days. "No, I want to take him. I'm so glad you woke me up."

"All right."

She bathed and dressed as quickly as she could, hiding her lank hair under a scarf, swearing at herself because all her pants were too tight. Then she sat and drank a cup of tea with her father.

"Are you better this morning, honey?"

It was the first endearment she could ever remember hearing him use, and it almost undid her.

She nodded. Then she looked up to study his face. He looked calm and peaceful. "How can you be so together, dad?"

He sighed as he buttered a breakfast roll. Then he put his knife down and looked calmly at Ruth. "I knew she was dying when she came to Pittsburgh. She came under that understanding, that she needed a place to die. We had been writing ever since your wedding to Bruno. First it was funny little notes, or some unusual stamp she would have found for me or something." He picked up the knife and rebuttered the already buttered roll, then put the knife down again and sighed, as though in resignation. He had decided to be honest with Ruth—to tell her everything.

"Then the notes changed and became letters. And then the letters became more frequent. Then they became daily, and we apologized if we missed a day. We went from innocent pen pals to close friends to"—he stumbled for the word he wanted—"intimates. When I came over for your wedding to Peter, I stayed with her, you know. We were together all the time." He couldn't bring himself to say to his daughter, "We slept together." He hoped she understood.

"I asked her then to come back to the States with me. She couldn't do it. She said she wanted to, but was afraid of pulling up her roots. Then, when she found out for sure about the leukemia, she knew her roots were going to be pulled up anyhow. She said she was much more scared of dying without love than she was of dying in a strange place. So, she said, she'd come if I would have her under those conditions. I said, and I meant it, I would have her under any conditions.

"It came as such a surprise to us. We knew we could get along. We knew it would be companionable. But it was so much more. We had the most wonderful time, Ruth. We understood each other so well. You should have heard her teasing me, bullying me, bringing me to life. She changed my existence.

"All the friends in the hospital became 'our' friends—and I have to get back home and visit them. The neighbors—you wouldn't believe the neighbors! I came home for a little while that first night, after the ambulance took her away, and the back porch was full of food. Mrs. Mullins had made a chocolate cake, and Mrs. McBride had baked me an apple pie, and old Miss Stewart had a huge pot of beef stew plugged in and simmering there on the porch. It was incredible. And they have been right there since. Jane Mullins was going to get rid of the wheelchair for me before I got back, so I wouldn't have to see it anymore. Annie McBride said, 'Give me your keys. I'm going to clean this house for you before you return, and Tuesday night you're coming to dinner.'

"I don't know if you can understand, Ruth. It's not that they are taking care of me. It's that they care. Over thirty years I've lived there, and most of them as long, too—and we've never cared about each other before. All of a sudden I know that Janie's daughter has twin girls and that Annie's sister is dying of cancer. I never knew that, but you know Nona. She had them talking. And, I guess they figured that if Nona thought I was worthwhile, then maybe they should pay some attention, too. And now I live in the midst of friends. So it's easy to go home.

"And, besides, Nona has me completely convinced that God is in his heaven and all's right with the world. She said: 'Now, Ben, why should God have to explain and justify to you what He's doing in the world?'"

They reached out and held hands over the table. His mouthing of Nona's words had brought her right into the room, and touching each other, they touched her as well.

In the hall the clock chimed, and Ruth said, "Oh, dad—we better go, we're going to miss your plane."

"Okay. I'll get my suitcase."

When he emerged from the bedroom, he was carrying a small leather portfolio, as well as the suitcase. As they drove to the airport, they chatted companionably about Ben's sister Agnes and all the family news, as well as Ben's plans for the summer and his resumption of teaching in the fall—but on a part-time basis.

Only when Ben was turning to leave for the plane did he hand Ruth the portfolio.

"Nona was insistent that you get this in private, so I decided to wait until now. Maybe you can go out to the car and see what it is. I don't even know. She was absolutely secretive."

"Thank you, dad. I love you."

"I love you, Ruth. You have always been a source of great happiness to me. I hope you're okay, honey."

"I'll be fine, dad," she said, moved by the new openness of her taciturn father.

A final kiss and hug and he was off.

She stood and watched until the plane was safely in the sky, and then she carried her gift from Nona out to the car and opened it. Inside was a check for ten million Italian lire.

Ruth drove back through Rome, stopping at the International Bank of Rome to deposit most of the check into a new account for Ruth Tyack, taking the rest in cash.

From the pay phone in the bank lobby, Ruth called Peter. He was in a meeting but had left instructions that if she called he was to be disturbed.

He came to the phone quickly. "Hello."

"Peter, listen," she said, as though she didn't already have his attention. "I need to get away for a while by myself. I'm going to fly to Greece for a few weeks, I think. Okay?"

There was a long pause. "Of course, *cara*, it will do you good. But I'll come join you. Tell me where you're going to stay—or better yet I'll call and make the arrangements for you. I'll meet you back at the penthouse tonight, and we'll go out for dinner. I'll stop at the travel agency and get some brochures and ask around for the names—"

"Peter, listen," she interrupted, "I have to go now. I'll be in touch."

Ruth hung up and walked slowly out to the car. She drove north, taking the small roads instead of the *autostrada*. She didn't know if Peter would try to find her or not, but she wanted to avoid the possibility. She didn't get out of Italy that first day, but stayed in a small *pensione* near Parma. She ate a lonely dinner and attended evening mass before retiring to her small room. She fell asleep immediately. The next morning she was up early, stopping only to buy some dry toast crackers. She drove for a couple hours before she was ready for food, then a ham omelet and toast sustained her to her destination.

She had once heard Nona fondly remembering a place where she had vacationed in Switzerland. The unusual name had stuck with Ruth: Schloss Zwingli. But when, after much trouble Ruth found the town, she was disappointed. Zwingli was nothing—a village of about ten houses, no stores, no restaurants, not even a post office. Finally she found an old woman, sitting on her front steps, crocheting lace, and Ruth stopped the car.

"Hotel?" she tried the international word.

"*Ya.*" The white head nodded, the worn teeth smiled, the arthritic finger pointed down the road in the direction from which Ruth had just come. "*Fahren Sie zurück,*" she intoned slowly, and Ruth said, "*Ya,*" and smiled her understanding so far. *"Da ist der kleine Weg,"* the woman put her hands close together to show Ruth something small. *Weg* sounded like way, road—a small road. Okay. *"Hinter dem See, da ist das Schloss."* See? Sea? Water? Lake? Nona had extolled the beauty of the lake. *"Dieser bringt Sie zum Schloss Zwingli."*

"Danke schön," said Ruth; somehow she always learned how to say thank you in a language—though little else.

"Aber bitte, aber bitte." The old woman nodded and smiled politely.

Ruth walked to the car, turned around in the little rut that was the woman's driveway, and headed back the way she had come until she came to a small dirt road running in the direction the gnarled finger had indicated. She followed this track until she came to a large and beautiful lake. Perched by the water's edge was a dream castle— long and high and resplendent with flowers. The water and air at Zwingli were the cleanest Ruth had ever seen or breathed, and she was overcome by the sheer physical beauty of the Swiss countryside.

As the car crawled up the lane toward the *schloss,* a robust middle-aged woman emerged from a side door calling over her shoulder, "Heinrich, Heinrich." She walked purposefully toward the car.

"Willkomm, Fräulein."

"Danke schön," said Ruth. Then, "Do you speak English?"

"Englisch? Nein." The woman smiled, showing perfect white teeth and warm blue eyes. *"Je parle Français."*

"Je parle Français un peu."

"Très bien." She smiled, again.

Ruth took a deep breath. "May I stay here?" Ruth asked her in French. "Do you have room? Is the hotel open?"

"Je comprends. Mais oui. Bienvenue. Ah, Heinrich!" The woman had swung around to call to him and almost hit him in the stomach. Engrossed in their conversation, they hadn't noticed his approach; perhaps eighteen years old, he was glowingly, Germanically healthy. He held out

his hand, saying to Ruth in heavily accented English, "If you give me your keys, I will get bags."

"Oh, you speak English!" She was relieved.

"I speak English, French, German, Italian, a little Russian, a little Polish. Plus I have a very strong back, and I am the guard-of-life."

"Lifeguard," Ruth corrected smiling.

"And, incidentally, I am her son."

He was disarmingly charming.

"I have no bags."

"Nothing?"

"Nothing."

"Well, if there is nothing to carry, perhaps you would let me save your life?" He cocked his head and winked at her, and she laughed. But then his mother started talking to him in quick, staccato German, and he stood up straight, clicked his heels together, and very politely said, "How do you do, madam." In an undertone, "My mother warns me to stop being impertinent. So now I will be formal and proper."

"Please tell your mother that I like impertinent better."

He turned to his mother and opened his mouth, but Ruth reached out a restraining arm. "On second thought, perhaps it had better be our secret."

"Yes, madam," he said in a most somber tone, then brazenly winked at her again. She laughed in delight. His mother frowned but had trouble maintaining her pose. Obviously she, too, found him irresistible.

With much fanfare Ruth was ushered into the castle, around the castle, around the edges of the lake, back into the dining room where the three of them, Mrs. Schiesser, Heinrich, and Ruth, ate together, Heinrich translating for the two women so that no one missed anything.

A box of beautifully washed and ironed clothes was found—things guests had left behind from time to time and never bothered to reclaim—and Ruth was outfitted in slacks and shirt, a bathing suit and nightgown. They even managed to find a beat-up pair of Mrs. Schiesser's canvas shoes that would do for the time being.

After dinner a fire was lighted in an upstairs parlor, and Mrs. Schiesser sat down to knit, Heinrich sat down with schoolbooks and paper, and Ruth was offered her choice of four English novels, all of which she had read. She chose one and sat with it open on her lap, letting the good feelings sink in, feeling the tensions float out on the lake with the mist.

At nine-thirty Mrs. Schiesser yawned, put down her knitting, and stood up. In any language or no language the message was clear. Everyone said good night and retired to their own rooms. Ruth was no sooner in the door, however, when there was a stealthy knock.

Since she was still dressed, she opened the door, knowing full well who stood there but unprepared for what was to follow. He was holding in his hand a large, warm jacket, a twin of the one he himself wore. His finger was to his lips, and he held out his hand.

"Where are we going?" she whispered.

"For a canoe ride. I haven't saved your life yet today," he answered.

It was delicious fun to sneak down the stairs, halting when a step creaked to see if there would be any reaction from inside Mrs. Schiesser's room. But they got down and out without being challenged and walked the distance to the lake. Heinrich got the canoe, and they pushed off from the shore just as the moon broke through the trees. Ruth had never seen a more tranquil sight than the Swiss lake in the moonlight, empty but for the canoe, bordered by tall pines, smelling like clean wash. They rode in silence. Not a word was spoken during the half hour or so that he paddled her around the lake. When their glances met, they merely smiled. Ruth leaned back against a cushion and closed her eyes, trailing her hand in the water.

When he pulled the canoe up on shore, she said, "Heinrich, thank you." She hoped he understood.

"With great pleasure, madam," he said, hamming it up again. Then wordlessly, without touching her, he delivered her back to her room, smiled good night, and went down the hall, to his own room, closing the door softly.

For a week she had the castle and the Schiessers to

herself. During the day she did nothing but eat and sleep and walk and canoe and swim and eat and sleep and walk some more. Evenings were cosy gatherings in the upstairs parlor, with sewing, studying, and reading.

Friday night there came an influx of visitors: all week-end there were twelve people at the castle, and Ruth saw little of her new friends. But Monday morning the last of the interlopers left, and Ruth had her serene situation back again. Every night she and Heinrich sneaked down for a canoe ride. One night he handed her the paddle, and he laid back. She didn't get very far, though, and they laughed out loud at her clumsiness with the canoe. He took over again, and they continued on their journey. Still they didn't talk, as if the rides were somehow sacred. During the day, and especially during the homework period, they talked nonstop. Ruth, the teacher, corrected themes, checked spelling, and suggested new organizational patterns. He was studying for exams for university and before long Ruth was actively in on the studying: quizzing him, drilling him, helping him devise reviews and memory aids and fact sheets.

Tuesday of her second week at Zwingli she wrote to her father, telling him where she was and that he was, under no circumstances, to give her address to anyone except a man named Tom Jeffers—should he want it. She explained as concisely as she could that she had left Peter for good, relinquishing little Pietro, too, and that she wasn't sure where she was headed, but she knew it wasn't back to Orvieto. She hoped he would try to understand, to not condemn; she loved him and would be in touch.

She waited two more days before she wrote her next letter. On Thursday she spent the entire day writing ten drafts of the letter she would send Peter. She had left permanently, she said. She would never, under any circumstances, come back. She didn't want to tell him she had overheard the conversation with diGuro, so she simply said the differences between them were too great to be bridged and were, in fact, irreconcilable. She was so terribly sorry. She had some exquisite memories of their time together. She thanked him for those. She was dismayed

for the difficulties that had arisen, things that she simply
could not have foreseen, and she thought he couldn't have,
either. Pietro was his. The child belonged in Orvieto as
she never could, and she would not ever try to take the
boy away from his father. She was not running out on her
duty to her son; she was instead giving Peter full custody
of the child who was completely his, culturally and biologically.

It was a hard letter to write. She showed up for dinner
Thursday night with very red eyes and a very stuffy head.
But she valiantly helped Heinrich with his studies, and
then they had their customary canoe ride. Later, she went
to bed and slept dreamlessly, waking to still puffy eyes,
but a more settled heart.

Another weekend passed, again with an influx of visitors; this weekend they were fifteen. Monday morning she
sat down to write her third and final letter. The answer to
this one would determine the rest of her life.

My darling T.J.,

I am taking a terrible risk by writing to you in this
way, but these days there is such poignancy and
passion in my missing of you, in my absence from
you, that I have no choice but to make myself
completely vulnerable to you, to just lay myself wide
open (if you will pardon the sexual innuendo, which I
hope you will not).

You are my darling. I have never called you that
before, but now it is the only term that seems strong
enough. You are mine, and I am yours, as you so
correctly realized in "Possession" so long ago. Can it
really be that nine years have passed? Have we
wasted nine years, by spending them apart instead of
together?

She stood up and went to the window, looking down at
the lake. She breathed in the cool, pine-scented air, trying
to fortify herself for what she knew she must write. The

fresh green mountains looming in the distance seemed to help her gain perspective. She returned to the old wooden desk.

I realize that this letter may come too late. As you said nine years ago, "If you have gotten your life back together, then just disregard this letter." Except, please, don't disregard it—please tell me if I am too late or if I have simply disappointed you and not been there for you one too many times. You may not be able to trust me enough to want me to come.

If you are free emotionally, I ask you for the chance to make up to you for any pain I have caused. I promise you, nothing and no one will stand in the way, ever, of my devotion to you.

Now that I have said that, I have to immediately qualify the statement. As usual there is one hitch. Or there might be one hitch from your point of view. I think I'm pregnant. I haven't been to a doctor, but I think I'm about three months pregnant. Under no circumstances will I have an abortion. (Well, under some circumstances, I might, but not under these. I believe this baby is healthy.) I also believe this baby is a girl. So, while I am ready to come to you under your conditions—marriage, living together, living near, being available, whatever suits you—I do not come alone.

I have left Peter for good—or for bad—but I have left forever. I will not go back. I have given up any and all claims to Pietro. The child is completely Peter's son. I did nothing but carry him for nine months. Already this pregnancy feels different. Already she is my little friend.

Someone who works for Peter saw us in the Hilton that day. When I went home late that afternoon, he was lying naked on the bed waiting for me. In short, we had a most unpleasant scene, physically and emotionally. That night, I suppose in repression, I got a high fever and I was delirious for three days. When

I finally came to, I didn't remember anything, about you or about Peter's abuse. Only in labor with Pietro did it all come back.

It took me until now to be able to write to you. I am so sorry. I don't understand why you left without putting up a fight, but I recognize there are a million possible explanations, and you owe me none of them.

Again Ruth went to the window for sustenance. She felt she must say something to him that would give him a choice, that would not make him feel obligated. She tried a prayer before returning to the desk to finish her letter.

I am presently in a very pleasant situation. I am living with a family on a Swiss lake. I can stay here indefinitely. Nona died, Tom, and she left me money. No matter what you decide, my child and I will eventually come back home. I must settle down to a job and a feeling of usefulness again.

Oh, my love, I hope this makes some sense to you. I'm afraid to write any more. I'm afraid to tell you how much I am longing for you because I don't know that you are free and willing to hear.

But what I started to say before is, that I am fine where I am. If you want some time to make up your mind, I understand that, too.

But, please, let me hear from you, one way or another.

Love from
your Ruth

Ruth explained to Heinrich, "I wrote to a man in the States, the man I love, to ask him if he wants me to come to him. Now I have to wait for him to write back. How long do you think it will take?"

"From the United States? Mails are very slow—probably about three weeks."

So they settled down to wait, the Schiessers and Ruth, and Heinrich decided to help fill her days. One a day, it seemed, another university candidate would drift by to ask the teacher for help. It was soon customary to find Ruth in the little parlor with at least one student morning, noon, and night. She loved it. She taught, she cajoled, she encouraged, she corrected—and for a good part of the day she kept her mind off her own troubles.

Three days after writing to Tom, Ruth drove herself into Zurich. Her first stop was a maternity hospital, where she had a pregnancy test and was assured on the spot that she was indeed going to have a baby. She was then ushered into the clinic obstetrician's office, where she was examined, pronounced fit, and stocked with vitamins. She became an instant convert to socialized medicine.

Then she went shopping. This time, instead of three thousand dollars in maternity clothes she spent about one hundred dollars and felt she was well outfitted. Her special purchase was a ten-dollar maternity bathing suit so that she could swim in the daylight and not be an embarrassment to the Schiessers or herself.

Driving back to the lake, she felt calm and confident. She was going to make it, and the little girl growing inside her was going to make it. They would make it on their own if Tom didn't want them, but she hoped to God he did. She waited, she hoped, she prayed and she thought up reasons why she hadn't heard from him yet.

One week passed, then two, then three.

The Schiessers wanted her to stay. They loved her company, had taken her to their hearts. The students wanted her to stay. She was an invaluable help to them. Thanks to her they were going off to university with an edge, an advantage.

So Ruth promised that, no matter what the answer from the States, she would stay at the lake until September. And no matter what, she would leave September first. That was her deadline.

She knew she could move home with her father, he would be glad to have her, but she really wanted to try it on her own, if her first choice of trying it with Tom didn't work out. She thought she'd go to the East Coast somewhere—Boston maybe. Surely she could find a job. Perhaps not what she wanted right away, but she could find something.

She would get an apartment and find a good obstetrician and settle down to wait for the baby. After the baby was born, she would find a job and find a good situation for... she was trying not to name the baby. She really wanted Tom to name her. That would be his part. No matter what he chose, she would love it. And his naming her would be like his setting his seal on her. If she never heard from Tom, then she would work on a name.

And so she made her plans, her contingency plans, and she waited.

Three weeks and one day, three weeks and two days, three weeks and three days. The Schiessers watched her grow bigger in the stomach, more introverted in spirit. She still smiled, laughed, participated in the conversations, and helped the students. She and Mrs. Schiesser were teaching each other English and German respectively. They became good friends. The Schiessers were delighted with the coming of the baby and hoped Ruth wouldn't leave before the baby was born.

But she was determined to. She had set aside this summer to enjoy, relax, and get strong. September first she would be starting the rest of her life. By then she would be as strong as she was going to be. She tried to think of all the advantages of Boston.

Three weeks and four days, three weeks and five days, three weeks and six days, and then four weeks.

Three days into the fourth week it was time for Ruth to go back to the obstetrician in Zurich for her monthly checkup. This time Katrine Schiesser went along. They had a delightful day. They had lunch at a lovely little restaurant on Lake Geneva, owned and operated by friends of Katrine's. They bought Ruth a few more maternity clothes, including a lovely blue dress of dotted swiss, which seemed so appropriate in Switzerland. Katrine purchased some supplies for the castle and some pants for Heinrich for university. Ruth bought him a very Ivy League-looking sweater. They got home late and very happy. And they both secretly knew a letter would be waiting for Ruth when they arrived.

But Heinrich shook his head sadly and offered Ruth a canoe ride right then and there—in front of his mother. Ruth was so upset she accepted. For over an hour he rowed her around the lake.

She cried and died a little inside and then stiffened her resolve and decided she would live through this, too. Only damn him for not writing back at all, for ignoring her plea completely.

When Heinrich finally beached the canoe, Ruth stood rather awkwardly and almost fell getting out. He caught her in his young, strong arms, and when she looked up at him in surprise, he gently lowered his lips on hers. It was an incredibly soft and loving kiss.

"You're a beautiful woman, and if he is too stupid to realize it, then the hell with him."

"Heinrich, you have been so good to me." She touched his face and stood up on tiptoe to kiss him on the cheek. "I can never thank you adequately for the way you have understood and comforted me. You are the one who is a beautiful person."

"But madam"—he resumed his mock-gallantry and they were back on safe ground—"it would be impossible not to be good to you."

"You clown." She laughed at his outlandish accent, his crazy bow. In companionable silence they went inside and found Katrine waiting for them with peach pie and milk.

Another week and five days went by, and every day Ruth came more to terms with life on her own with the baby. The routine continued, the guests flowed in and out of the castle, some now coming for the entire week. Katrine was busy, and Heinrich was rushed, providing all the handyman services needed. Ruth slowly expanded her role in the household, helping more and more in the kitchen. Katrine hated to see her on her feet, but Ruth was able to convince her that she felt fine and that it was much better for her to be active than to sit around moping. Katrine agreed with that, and soon Ruth was in charge of lunches for everyone.

Saturday morning dawned bright and clear. It was the end of June, and Ruth was enjoying each day and looking forward to September. She had accepted the fact that she would never hear from Tom and that she would survive without him. She had accepted that—yet in the back of her mind there glowed a faint ember of hope.

The ember became a forest fire when Ruth stood on the porch and watched the Western Union boy ride up on his bicycle. She knew before he asked for Ruth Tyack that it was for her. And she knew before she opened it what it would say. But she had underestimated the poet's ability for brevity. She smiled as she read the words, then ran in screaming for Katrine and Heinrich. And then, in the middle of a working day, Heinrich rowed both women out in the middle of the lake, and they opened a 1948 vintage bottle of champagne and drank to Ruth and Tom, passing the telegram from hand to hand, admiring his message.

My darling Ruth—
    When are you and Beth coming home? Letter follows.

Love,
Your T.J.

❧ 12 ❧

Tom Jeffers smiled all summer. One letter from Ruth was all it took to make a believer out of him. "Darling T.J.," he kept hearing in his mind. To realize that he had almost missed the letter because of the damn mailman. The jerk had stuck the letter and the electric bill inside that copy of *Poetry Northwest*!

Thank God the electric company sent him that nasty second bill, with a penalty because he had missed the date. He was bound and determined to prove to the utility bigwigs that he had never gotten the bill. He had tracked down the mailman.

"I recollect that electric bill, Mr. Jeffers. Came the same day as that fancy foreign airmail letter ya got."

"Airmail letter? What airmail letter—I never got an airmail letter." His voice was immediately out of control, his heart fibrillating! The mere mention of airmail had brought with it a certainty that the letter was from Ruth. Ruth had written. He had to find it.

Slowly the mailman "recollected" a magazine that day, too, and then later "recollected" sticking the letter and bill inside the magazine so that they wouldn't get wet in the rain. Tom had driven home like a maniac, shaken each and every magazine that had come in the last few months until the precious letter and electric bill finally fell out from the pages of the June issue of *Poetry Northwest*. He stared at the handwriting. Without opening it, he knew what was inside. He knew, somehow, deep inside him, that she wouldn't have written unless she was ready to come.

He sat back in his leather chair, holding the letter to his chest, and said a prayer that the contents would be what he thought they would be. It was over two years since he had seen her, since their afternoon together along the Tiber. Would this letter explain what had happened? Would it be an explanation he could accept?

Still clutching the letter, he went to the refrigerator for a bottle of dark beer, which he opened one-handed, spilling a little because he refused to put the letter down. He returned to the den and sat for a moment more. Tommy came in and asked him something. He nodded his head, not realizing that he was giving Tommy and Robby permission to go ask Emma for some cookies they had smelled baking.

Slowly, reverently, he opened it, savoring the anticipation the way a lover holds back on a climax, and when he saw "My darling T.J." he said out loud, "Thank you, God." He read the whole letter. Then he went back and reread the whole thing. Next he downed the entire twelve-ounce beer in one lifting of the bottle. Then he read the letter three more times, paying special attention now to the things left unsaid, reading between the lines to catch the pain and the humiliation, the lack of self-esteem and the shattered self-confidence.

He felt saddened. To love someone is to want them to be intact. It was clear that Ruth was mutilated, bruised in spirit. He hoped that Switzerland was healing her. He had waited this long; he could wait a little longer. He wanted her to be able to come whole and strong, wanted her to come as an equal.

He would gladly take care of her the rest of her life if she had a physical problem. But they could never have a satisfying and fulfilling relationship if one of them was emotionally dependent of the other. It was her mental health that he had always cherished; that had been one of the strong forces drawing them to each other. They were each fairly strong and secure within themselves, and they wanted much the same thing in a relationship. They each wanted someone else who could stand on his own, but who *chose* to stand with a partner. They would both be vulnerable, both sensitive, both leaning sometimes on the other, but in a nonmanipulative way.

He had observed so many married couples who controlled each other with guilt or fear or insecurities or even sex. He hoped and prayed he and Ruth would never do that to each other. There had to be room for each to be a separate person as well as room for togetherness, to provide encouragement, sustenance, romance, and adventure.

He reread the letter once more.

A baby. She was bringing him a baby. He couldn't wait to see her pregnant—those beautiful breasts swollen with milk, that rounded tummy a mound of kicking, punching, gymnastic baby. That was such fantastic news. My God, how Tommy would love a baby. He could close his eyes and picture Tommy's rapt expression. His son would sit and watch and watch the tiny hands and feet in absolute astonishment. Tommy had never been around a baby; he was going to just love it. He would be the first to notice every little thing. Tommy would no doubt be rewarded with the first smile and would probably learn the fine art of diapering before he would.

I will tell nobody, Tom decided. *I am going to keep this in my heart, and I am going to savor every drop of it, as though I were a child with a hidden stash of candy.*

Once more he read the letter. And then it came to him in a flash. Beth. Elizabeth Jeffers. He didn't know if Ruth had a name picked out or not, but he would lobby for Beth. Beth and Ruth. Simple, solid, feminine names. Baby Beth. He could feel her in his arms right now, weightless in her pink plaid blankets, cuddling into his chest to sleep. He had adored Tommy as a baby but had never thought to have another.

He composed his telegram reply and dispatched it over the telephone to Schloss Zwingli. Then he sat down and wrote a six-page letter, explaining about the mailman, chattering some of the three years of build up of chatter—and telling of his love. Then he drove into town and asked for the fastest way of sending a letter to Switzerland. The postal clerk was surprised that anyone would be willing to spend six dollars and thirty-nine cents to send a letter airmail, special delivery, priority mail. But Tom Jeffers would gladly have spent sixty dollars or even six hundred. It was only important to him that he get his answer across the water and get an answer back.

On the way back home, he stopped at Emma's and told her to get the stew off the stove and into the refrigerator and to get on her dancing shoes—he was taking her and Stanley and Tommy out to dinner at the Lobster House down the coast. She smiled and came across the room and kissed him on the cheek. He pulled her into a hug and twirled her around the kitchen.

Emma finally escaped to plop down in a chair, out of breath yet laughing like a young girl. She asked no questions, and it was probably the very lack of inquiry that caused Tom to burst out, "She's coming."

Emma nodded her white head and brushed off her warm brow with her apron. "The woman on the wall."

"Yes. I don't know when. Maybe not for a while. She's been sick. But I found the letter today." He explained about the electric bill and the *Poetry Northwest*. They laughed and oohed and ahhed the ironies of life, the coincidences, and just how remarkable miracles are. And then Tom went to tell Stanley and Tommy that they were going out for dinner. He didn't explain why.

They had a delightful night, cracking lobster shells and sipping white wine. Even Tommy was allowed to have some white wine, and his angelic face soon became flushed, as much from the delight of being out in a fancy restaurant as from the wine.

They drove home, Tommy's head resting in Emma's lap in the backseat, and then when everyone else was in bed and asleep, Tom sat up and drank successive cups of tea and plotted and dreamed and planned and lusted. For once in his life he let his fantasies and fancies roam free. Elizabeth had just graduated from college first in her class when he finally fell asleep.

Saturday Ruth got her telegram.

Sunday Tom received the reply.

Darling—
September 1. Who's Beth?

Your Ruth

Sunday night he sent his answer. Monday the same young man on the bicycle pedaled up to the castle.

My darling—
Elizabeth Jeffers is our daughter.

Proudly,
T.J.

Wednesday she finally succumbed and sent a reply to that.

TJ—
Buy the cigars, darling. We love you.

Ruth

From then on they relied on letters. Each wrote every day; neither ever missed a day. Even when Ruth fell and sprained her ankle, she wouldn't let the doctor give her a shot to numb the pain. She said it was because she was worried about the baby feeling any effects of the medicine. That was true. It was also because she had not yet written her daily letter to Tom and was not about to be put to sleep until she did.

Somehow, while writing to him, the pain diminished enough, all by itself, that she was able to get by with no drugs whatsoever.

Tom wrote even when he was in New York. The team of K.C. and T.J. had done four movies now, and were about to begin their fifth. K.C. would find the material, usually a novel, once an operetta, and while Tom converted the original into a script, K.C. scored the action, providing a lively musical background for the words. Then they sold the finished product, scored script, to a production company. It was an unorthodox, backward way of doing things.

But it worked and was proving extremely lucrative. And money was very important to Tom. Since he had a son who would never be able to support himself, Tom, at fifty, wanted to be certain he would be leaving Tommy an established, adequate trust. He was willing to work with the talented K.C. because he simply couldn't pass up the opportunity for such generous amounts of money.

The pattern that he and K.C. had fallen into was that he would check into a hotel upon arrival in New York, but one or two nights he would stay overnight with K.C. Their sex was wildly exciting—passionate, lustful, and erotically ambitious. It was also romanceless and loveless. It was alien to Tom's soul, but his body craved it. He looked on it as a sort of drug addiction: when he was getting his dosage, he relished it and felt like a king; when it was over and the immediate effect had worn off, he felt depressed and met his own eyes in the mirror a little furtively.

After their bouts, they would doze off exhausted, and the instant Tom awakened he would head for the shower, staying there for long periods of time. He finally realized he was trying to wash away any lingerings of their time in bed. K.C. teased him about his long showers, calling him fastidious, telling him she thought he really didn't like sex at all, that he must be a Puritan at heart. He finally realized she was right: he didn't like "sex"—it left him feeling hollow and unsustained.

He couldn't talk to K.C. about it. It was insulting to her the way he felt. He wondered if she were satisfied by their acrobatic maneuverings. Obviously he was not the only one she took to her bed. She received dozens of unaccounted-for phone calls, had even turned a gentleman or two from the door while she and Tom were working or eating or screwing. He wondered if she had a deeper relationship with any of them than she did with him. He hoped so.

Despite his interest in the story for the fifth book, he had great hesitation about starting work on this new project. He had written K.C. about Ruth—about his plans to be married. Now he worried that K.C. was going to give him some problems about their personal relationship.

It was a reserved and cautious Tom who walked into her apartment that Monday morning in July.

His fears were ungrounded. She had gotten his letter, wanted to congratulate him on his marriage-to-come, and now let's get to work. When the day passed and she seemed to accept his new status, he started relaxing. For four days they worked in their usual pattern, which was one of trial and error, throwing ideas and tunes and scene structures to each other. They always got a lot accomplished, although they fought over every detail, which left them irritable and frustrated. Each day they started around nine and quit around four, eating lunch while they worked.

Their base of operations now was K.C.'s apartment—usually the round table Tom had selected the first time he visited. He had never gone back into the guest bedroom suite. Realizing it held bad memories for him, K.C. had maneuvered their sexual encounters to other parts of the house—sometimes the terrace, sometimes the living room rug, sometimes her bed; once she followed him into the bathroom and attacked him while he was standing over the toilet. He had struggled minimally.

Now each day around four Tom made some excuse and hurried out the door. He would go for a long walk, stopping by the zoo or at a museum or bookstore on his way home to eat a solitary dinner before settling down to poetry and writing to Ruth.

Friday morning the vibes were different from the start. The maid/cook answered the door and told him Ms. Barkley was still in bed. She ushered him into the living room and left him to his round table. Ten minutes later K.C. entered in a plain pink cotton nightgown. Her hair was disheveled, and she was wearing no makeup. She walked to a sofa near the table and sat down, pulling her feet up under her, the nightgown around her feet.

"Hi," she said in the softest voice he had ever heard her use.

"What's the matter?"

"Oh, I'm just feeling so blue this morning." She certainly looked like she was feeling blue. She turned her head away from him, staring disconsolately.

From the distance of maybe five feet, he saw a tear run down her cheek, and he was touched. Never before had he seen her without makeup and without her defenses intact. Somewhere deep inside him warning bells were ringing, but he ignored them and went over and sat beside her on the sofa.

"Anything you want to talk about?" he offered, sitting back against the cushions, primed for listening.

She threw her head down on his lap, crying quietly.

He stroked her hair, wondering what the hell was going on. This was so out of character for K.C. She snuggled deeper into him, and he could feel her wet cheek moving on his pants, rubbing him at strategic points. He felt himself responding and turned her around on his lap to kiss her. But he surprised her and caught a gleam of triumph in her eyes, a small smile she didn't erase quickly enough, and he knew then that he had been set up. This was, as he had first suspected, a little girl act, with the emphasis on act.

He slid out from under her and stood up. She could tell from the bulge in his pants that her ploy had been successful, and thinking he had stood to strip, she held her arms open and shifted her legs, drawing her nightgown up around her waist, exposing moist, black curls, warm inviting thighs.

His body leaned toward hers of its own volition, and he cast his eyes about for help. His glance riveted on a piece of modern sculpture at the end of the sofa. It had always intrigued him, this abstract object of shape and texture, and he had often wondered what it was suppose to represent. He had decided that it looked like a tree, swaying in the breeze; except now, for this one moment in time, he saw with stark clarity that it was a pregnant woman. He halted, and his body temperature dropped three degrees, as though someone had thrown him into a cold Swiss mountain lake.

He straightened, tucking in his shirt, and walked over to the window, where he stood, leaning on the frame, trying to give her time to get herself together. She gaped at him for a moment, unable to fathom what he was doing, then did the first thing that came to mind. She threw the piece of sculpture at him. Unfortunately it was made of metal. Also unfortunately, her aim was very good. It would have hit him in the back of the head, but he heard the noise of her movement, and her indrawn breath, and swung around, moving a bit to the side, so that the heavy sculpture merely grazed him on the cheek instead of knocking him unconscious. As she watched, eyes filling with horror, a long gash across his cheek turned bright red.

He barely felt it. All he knew was that he had closely escaped an even greater danger than the pain of the metal. He drew out his handkerchief, held it to his face to stem the flow of blood, and said to her, "You understand?"

She nodded yes, mutely.

"We can work together. But that is it. Nine to five. Nothing more. Ever. Under any circumstances. You try one more thing like this, and we're through."

"I understand. My God, Tom. I'm really sorry."

"Shall we work tomorrow to make up for losing today?"

Again she nodded, silently, and he turned and walked out of the room and out of the apartment. She laid back on the sofa and cried real tears because she knew she had lost him for good.

They worked together for the next six days straight, and got more accomplished and had a more comfortable relationship than ever before. The balance of power had shifted: whereas she had been the one in control and in command, now it was Tom who held the reins. He decided when to start and when to break. The sexual tensions that she had worked to establish and keep burning, he would have no part of. Now they concentrated on work.

He was relieved to return to Maine on Saturday—and enchanted with the letter Ruth had waiting for him.

My darling T.J.,

I was just thinking about sex, and I want to tell you what I realized.

Sex with Bruno was like classical music to me. It

was slow and beautiful and very patterned and programmed. I never went out of my way to seek it, but when it came, it was never unwelcome. It was just nice. Sometimes it didn't keep me awake—do you fall asleep during symphonies, too?—but I could always rouse myself to be appreciative when the concert was over.

Sex with Peter was like rock and roll or disco. It was wild and animalistic and caught me up in it. I could dance the rhythm, and sometimes I would seek out the music, but sex with him was surface. Do you know what I mean? It never really touched me. The world could stop, and the stars could explode, but it was illusionary. I would wake up the next morning feeling that I'd made him happy, but there was never the fullness within my own heart. It was like eating a candy bar—for an hour afterward I had energy, but there was no real nourishment.

Now, sex with you, my darling, is jazz. Sex with you is from the soul and reaches not only from the tingling of my scalp to the twitching of my toes but from the back of my kidneys to the bottom of my heart. Sex with you is spiritual, sensual instead of only sexual, commitment instead of involvement. I awake the next morning and the next morning and the next morning even unto nine years later, knowing who I am because I can define myself in terms of you.

I love you, T.J.

Your Ruth

He wrote back in the same vein:

My darling Ruth,

You have delighted me completely, as usual, with your analogy of sex to music. I would like to go a step further and tell you that most of the sex I have had since last I held you in my arms has been performed on a Moog synthesizer. Have you heard of that? It is like music on a computer. Sounds sort of like music, but it is all really pretend. Resemblances are only surface—there is no depth, no character, no soul (to use your well-chosen word).

How about food, while we're on the subject of sex? Can you think of a food analogy? I thought of one a few years ago, at a time when you were, sadly, very peripheral to my life. I walked into Emma's kitchen one day, and she was making bread. The whole kitchen was permeated by this musky, musty, warm, moist smell of yeast. And I felt so sexually stimulated. (I knew immediately it was not Emma, whom I love as a mother. So I searched around for other explanations.) You flashed into my mind. I saw you, I could feel you. I could smell the very special, very private smell of you. It was the smell of rising bread. Then Emma made some coffee and covered up the smell with the smell of coffee beans. But the analogy went further, because she sat down across the table from me and started kneading a second batch of bread. I had never before watched anyone doing that. You need a very light and gentle touch. You have to work all the flour granules in just so. And you keep kneading until you feel the certain stickiness and elasticity that tells you that the bread will rise. And I thought of you, and my hands on you and in you and drawing circles in your hair until you feel elastic and smooth and your skin rises up around my fingers and I feel myself dissolving into you.

My God, Ruth. I'm not sure any number of cold showers will help tonight. September 1 seems very far away. I'm not complaining, mind you. But I am a little anxious to get on with my baking and on with my nibbling.

You are, in the words of William Gass, "bread in my mouth."

Love and lust from your lonely T.J.

The summer was a haze of activity for Tom. Afraid that, with the nervous anxiety and anticipation he would get nothing done, he had rashly promised K.C. the fifth script by September 1. That of itself would have filled every waking hour in August, but one night while getting ready for bed, he looked around his bedroom and realized that it needed to be refurnished and redecorated. He decided not to do the painting and wallpapering himself, for he wanted it to look professional, but he did the shopping, more than he had ever done in his life. He had the woodwork painted white and chose a bright, small-flowered print paper for the walls. Emma helped him hang white ruffled curtains at the windows. He bought an early American bedroom set of substantial maple and a magnificent white quilted bedspread. When all was in place, he decided they needed a warm, bright carpet underfoot, and he found a bright green shag that matched the leaves on the flowers in the wallpaper. The room was finished on August 25.

The on-going project that sapped his energy during the warm days of August was reading and studying Ruth's letters so as to answer them as honestly and compassionately as he could. He could sense her getting stronger with each letter. Earlier there had been a great deal of worry over little Pietro.

I can't understand it, Tom. I really worry about myself and wonder what's lacking in my character. How can a mother give up her child? How can I have walked away from him? Long periods of time go by, hours, I mean, and I don't think of him at all. And when I do think of him I can bear the thoughts. What kind of monster must I be, to be able to do this? I'm not sure you want me.

He thought about it, trying to see from her point of view, to feel with her emotions, trying to find honest words and thoughts that would bring comfort.

It's a strange thing about children. Tommy is not mine biologically, and Elizabeth will not be, either. But both children are totally mine. They are mine in spirit. I could not love either more than I do, more than I will. (Already Elizabeth is a very real presence to me. I wake up sometimes at night, and my arms are cradling her. Isn't it amazing? The only better news I have ever had in my life was that you were coming home. Next to your presence, I seek Beth's the most.)

There is a strong matter of need that binds people together. Now you and I need each other for completion. We need each other to fill the empty spaces that we have discovered cannot be filled by another.

I believe it is the same with children and parents. Tommy needs me, has always needed me. He needs the unique things that I am capable of bringing to him. I try to fill his life with color and imagination and warm security. I try to provide what he needs to be happy.

We will do the same with Elizabeth. We will try to provide for her an environment of love and security. We will try to prepare her for the world so that she can hold her head up and say proudly, "I am Elizabeth Jeffers, and I am a unique and very special person. At least that's what my daddy always tells me."

Sadly, oh, so very, very sadly, you were unable to do any of this with Pietro. All the things that parents want and need to do with and for their children were denied you in his case. You were allowed to establish no intimacy with him. You do not know his body intimately, for you were not allowed to care for it. You do not know his mind or his spirit intimately, for you were never close enough to watch him develop and grow.

I am no psychiatrist, my darling, but I think it is very natural that you do not miss Pietro. It would be like missing a stranger. You gave birth to him—he came out of your body. But a great many women do that every year and then put their children up for adoption. That is in essence what you did—except that you lived with the family that adopted him and you watched him from a distance for two years. You had the worst of both worlds. No court in the land would allow a mother who was forced to give up her child to continue to live in that child's presence.

I know you well enough, my dear, dear Ruth, to know that you will always carry some guilt around about this. Each person has his own devils to deal with. I certainly have mine. My wife went insane. I am not blameless for that. But I hate guilt, Ruth. *Guilt is the most destructive emotion*. We simply can't let it destroy us. Our love for each other, I hope will work as a cure. We *can* make the world a better place. We have to. Our past guilts get in the way of that, so we must find the strength to resist the downward pull of guilt and concentrate instead on the upward pull of life.

By July her letters had dealt with both past and present, as she exorcised her ghosts and came to terms with who she was. And in August the tone changed, and the content changed again. Mentally, she was already in Maine and was getting herself geared up for her new life. And Tom, too, was busy looking ahead, reacting to the hints in her letters. She wrote,

Someday, my darling, I am going back to the classroom. I *feel* like a teacher. Do you know what I mean? My essential being is Ruth, your Ruth, Tommy and Beth's mother, teacher. Does that sound crazy? Well, it doesn't really matter if it does. That's how I think of myself.

The day after receiving that letter, Tom sat in the office of Ted Handler, the principal of Somerset Consolidated High School.

"Tom how are you?" Ted greeted him. "Say, can we count on you for another fine assembly program this year?"

"Glad to, Ted, glad to. By the way, I have a question for you, too. You don't have any vacancies in your English department, do you?"

"For you?" Hopefully.

"No, for a friend. One of those people who is a born teacher."

"Well, I have a woman who is retiring in January. Would that help?"

"That would be perfect. I'll have my friend get in touch with you."

"Great. Finding a good teacher who wants to come to Maine in January is not all that easy. I'm glad for the good lead."

Tom went home and wrote to Ruth that not only could she get into the classroom someday but she could probably get in very soon, if she was feeling up to it:

Believe me, darling, I'm not trying to get you out of the house, but if you would like to teach, I'd like you to. Tommy and I will watch Beth while you're at school. And if I'm off or in the midst of a heavy deadline, I'm sure Emma will be delighted to sit and rock. And if that doesn't work out (although I'm sure it will), we'll find some other way for you to do what you and I both know you should be doing. I'm not trying to get you organized or to run your life in any way. But I will do everything in my power to see to it that you are free to be you.

Ruth was awed by the letter; he could tell from the way she replied:

Only you could do it that way. You offer me exactly what I want on a silver platter and then make some dismissing comments like, "Here's a little trifle for you." You are the most amazing man! I love you, Tom, I just adore you.

As for the offer of you and Tommy taking care of Beth—what can I say? I'm sure I would have some guilt to handle if I leave you to be responsible for Beth while I spend my days teaching. But it is a situation I do think could work. Imagine how good Beth and I would both feel as I drove off to work, knowing she was going to spend the day with "daddy"—she will so adore you. I think you're wrong. You mentioned that you thought Tommy was going to get the first smiles—I think you will. I think our little girl is going to be daddy's girl.

As for running my life—nothing could be further from the mark. I am not coming to you to be a clinging vine—although there are times when I certainly intend to be clinging. (Do you think you could possibly stay with me in the hospital some of the time? I know Beth will be easier and will feel different, but after last time—and the strength of the pain and the strength of the fear—that is not as much of a consolation as it should be.) Nor do I intend to come and take over your life. I don't even intend to take over your kitchen. After all, you have been there for five years now, and I'm sure you have things down to a fine science. I'm sure, too, you have gotten to the point where you really enjoy your solitude. Are you sure two girls in the house won't be too much?

He read all the words and between the lines, and laughed at her doubts. But he did not laugh at the part in parentheses: he spent twenty minutes on the phone talking to Fred Marshall, a friend and a doctor of gynecology and obstetrics. He then sat down and wrote a factual and, he hoped, reassuring letter:

I had a very interesting conversation with Fred Marshall today. He is a good friend and a fine obstetrician. He said he would be glad to have you come to him and that it would be easier but not essential for him to have your records from the doctor in Switzerland. There is a Lamaze course starting September 15 and lasting for six weeks. He says we could come learn the breathing techniques. Of course, whether or not to do natural childbirth is up to you. Lamaze or no, Fred says I would be allowed to stay with you the entire time, labor and delivery, that I will be able to watch the actual birth, as will you. I will sit by your head in the delivery room and hold your hands and wipe your brow, since you are the laborer. And I promise you, I will never leave you. I will be there, hanging on to you and having all the sympathetic pains I can muster. We will do it together, darling. I promise you, this will be a different experience entirely. Do you doubt it?

Now, as for taking over my kitchen—I can't wait to have you in this house. I want the house to look like you and feel like you and smell like you. I fixed up our bedroom for us. It is all bright and shiny new. But everything else is waiting for you.

I just can't wait to get my hands on your body. I want to feel you—up and down and in and out. And you better come ready to do some feeling yourself, because I have been missing a lot of strokes, and I want all my strokes to come from you. Put on your thinking cap, Ruth, and your feeling cap. Devise in your mind every kinky and straight and crooked and lopsided fantasy you can. Think of every erotic pose you have ever heard about or read about or imagined. Because we are going to try them all. Twice. The good ones three times.

I hunger for you like a man with a broken jaw hungers for bread. And the day you arrive they will take the wires off of my jaws, and my appetite will be insatiable. And if that scares you, so be it. Because it scares the hell out of me how much I want you.

He worked doggedly on the script and established a schedule by which he would finish his work on August 30. He was on schedule as the last days of August came around. This longest, happiest summer was finally coming to a close, although Ruth refused to tell him what plane she would be on . . . refused to tell him exactly what day she would be arriving.

I don't want you to worry about me, Tom, I will be there. If the plane crashes in the middle of the Atlantic, Beth and I will swim to Maine. If there is one thing I am these days, it is unsinkable—in many ways.

I don't want you to meet me. I want to come to you. I want to come on my own two feet, in my own good time, in my own way. You were right in saying I want to come as an equal. I want to be your partner.

And, no, your appetites don't scare me. There is nothing I want more, nothing I hunger for more than you.

And Tom wrote to Switzerland.

This is my final note. If you want to hear from me again, you will have to get close enough to hear my voice. Or better yet, close enough to simply feel the beating of my heart.

I want you to know, pregnant lady, that I have listened to and resisted your hints about marriage all summer. And I will tell you exactly why. When and if I ask you to marry me, I do not intend to take no for an answer. So bring your chubby little body home here, and we'll see what happens. We'll see if you still make as good an apple pie as you once did, and if you still give as sweet a kiss. I make no promises, but I will try and do the honorable thing.

I adore you, beautiful, sweet heart. I got the license July 18. All I lack is the bride. These fucking details! I LOVE YOU—COME HERE—NOW. I CAN'T WAIT ANY MORE—I NEED YOU.

Ruth stopped in front of the white Cape Cod, sure from Tom's explanation that this was the Ellises' house. She was tired from the successive plane rides, cramped from the two-hour drive, and more exhilarated than she had ever been in her life.

Maine in the fall has to be seen to be believed. September of the changing leaves boasts sunlight drifting through the trees. The tourists have all returned to the cities, and Maine once again belongs to her own people.

A peacefulness had settled over the countryside, and as

Ruth drove she felt it invade her spirit; she knew with absolute conviction that she was on the right road.

She walked slowly, uncomfortably, from the car to the wide front porch. The door was flung open even before she raised her hand to knock. The short, white-haired woman looked at her as if she were a ghost.

"I'm looking for Tom Jeffers," Ruth said nervously, forgetting to say hello.

"Praise the Lord," answered Emma Ellis. "Stanley! Come here. You won't believe it." She turned her attention back to the woman in front of her. "Hello, Ruth," she said very gently, her hands on each of Ruth's arms. "You are here to stay?"

Ruth nodded. "Yes, Mrs. Ellis. I am here to stay. But how did you know it was me?"

At that moment she heard a firm step and a tall, white-bearded caricature of a Maine fisherman rounded the corner.

"Ruth!"—he broke out a rare smile, then immediately sobered. "You're home, ain't ya? Here for good." Ruth nodded. "Cause I for one just ain't taking ya on up the lane if ya ain't planning on remaining."

"Yes, Stanley, she already told me—she's come home. And, Stan," Emma added somewhat shyly, not wanting to embarrass Ruth but unable to contain her excitement, "look what she's brought along."

"What?" Puzzled.

Again shyly, Emma reached out and lightly touched Ruth's stomach. "A baby, Stanley."

"Oh." Weathered face turned crimson. "Guess we wouldn't mind a young 'un around the place, would we?"

Ruth laughed out loud in delight at the obvious Maine understatement and walked the two steps across to give Stanley Ellis a kiss on the cheek. He patted her arm awkwardly. "Glad you come, girl."

"I have never felt so welcome anywhere."

Stanley and Emma looked at each other and laughed. "Oh, you got the three most welcoming welcomes yet to go, don't she, Emma?"

"Indeed she does," Emma took her hand. "Come on."

"Tommy's planting those new marigold seeds," Stanley called after them. "I just left him."

"And Tom and Robby are out walking, aren't they?"

"Yup. Want me to go try and fetch him?"

"No." Ruth said, after a pause, "I think I'd rather meet Tommy alone."

Leaving Stanley in the doorway, Ruth and Emma proceeded up the lane in companionable silence.

As they walked in the front door, Emma called out, "Tommy, come see. I have a surprise for you." And around the doorway came a handsome brown-haired, brown-eyed young man, as tall as Ruth, but with the innocent, searching gaze of a small child. He paused momentarily and then bounded across the room, throwing his muddy hands around Ruth's shoulders, singing, "Ruth is here, Ruth is here. Oh, you finally came. You finally came."

Her arms flew around him to hug him tight, but he felt something between them and stepped back. "You're kind of fat, aren't you?" He looked down at her stomach and saw a bulge. She looked at her tan blouse and saw muddy fingerprints all over her shirt.

"No, Tommy, that isn't me being fat—do you know what that is? That is a new friend for you." She unconsciously said Tommy's magic word: friend. "I'm going to have a baby. A little tiny baby." She showed him with her hands how little the baby would be. "And we can take care of her, and we can feed her bottles of milk, and then later we can teach her to walk and teach her to talk, and you can teach her all about flowers and plants."

He was enthralled, and so was she. Neither of them noticed Mrs. Ellis back out the door and softly close it behind her.

"May I see your greenhouse?"

"Oh, yeah, yeah." She smiled at how he mimicked Tom.

Taking her hand, he led her into the warm, fragrant sunlit room and gave her a detailed tour of each and every plant. She listened carefully, for she loved growing things too, and knew gratefully that Tommy and she had an instant rapport.

Tommy paused for breath, and Ruth said, "Tommy, do you know what?"

"What?" His eyes sparkled.

"I'm awfully hungry. Are you?"

"Mrs. Ellis says I'm always hungry." His face fell. "But I don't know how to make anything."

"Oh, that's okay. I know how. I'm a good cook."

Tommy's world righted itself, then he said wistfully, "I wish you could teach me."

She grabbed his shoulders and looked him in the eye. "I promise I will teach you how to cook."

"Really? Oh, I'm so glad you came." Another muddy hug.

Ruth closed her eyes, savoring his innocent welcome, then laughed. "Now, let's you and me head for the chow wagon, partner."

Tommy led the way.

Planning the menu required delicate negotiation. Ruth rejected peanut butter and jelly sandwiches, and Tommy rejected scrambled eggs. They settled finally on toasted cheese sandwiches for their first cooking lesson. Tommy explained they needed to make four: one for Ruth, one for Tommy, one for Tom, and one for Robby—whoever the hell Robby was. Ruth showed Tommy how to butter the bread and put the cheese inside. She was demonstrating the fine art of flipping the sandwiches so that they'd cook on both sides, when the door was flung open and a very large black object hurled itself across the room, settling itself at Ruth's feet with a "ruff" and an enthusiastic wag of tail.

"That's Robby," said Tommy proudly, and since Robby was sitting politely, Ruth squatted down to say hello. And that is how Tom found her: down on her haunches beside the dog, the cheese sandwiches slowly toasting on the stove, Tommy standing by with spatula in hand.

"Daddy, Ruth is teaching me to make toasted cheese sandwiches. Isn't that great?" And he carefully explained each step of the process while Ruth and Tom stared wordlessly at each other.

Tom felt paralyzed, unbelieving. Ruth in his kitchen doing so ordinary and so beautiful a thing as making toasted cheese sandwiches. Ruth trying to get up but having trouble; Ruth saying with a self-conscious giggle, "I seem to be stuck."

He crossed the room in a flash, kneeling beside her. Purposefully he placed a hand under each arm, touching each breast, and smiled in delight at the muddy fingerprints on her blouse. Their bodies rose in unison, and he just held her, feeling her warmth, her laughing breath, knowing she had never looked so good as she did at this moment, almost dropping from fatigue, hair disheveled, blouse dirty, shoes kicked into a corner. She had invaded his home, she had charmed his son, she had come to him.

He leaned slowly to kiss her forehead and then, gently, her lips. The kiss was a seal—no searching, no passion, no lust, no questioning in it, but an establishment, a bond, warm lips held on warm lips. He raised his head, still holding her securely in his arms.

"You are staying." It was a statement. But he must hear it from her lips.

"I am staying. You can kick me out, you can run away, you can escort every award-winning songwriter to every event you would care to go to, you can holler at me, you can beat me black and blue. I am staying. Come rain or come shine. I have come home. I only wonder that it has taken me so long."

"Ruth, is it time to turn the sandwiches?"

"Let's see, honey." Grasping Tom's hand in a death grip, she walked heavily over to the stove and slid the spatula under one of the sandwiches. It was a warm brown. "Sure is, Tommy. Your timing is perfect. Let's see if you can turn the other three." In silence Tom and Ruth stood and watched Tommy, Tom behind her, she leaning back against him, his hands on her big belly, his cheek next to hers.

"Come here." He led her down the hall to the study. "You're sure you're here to stay?"

"My darling T.J.," was all the answer she gave.

Inside the study, he again folded his arms around her. "I can't wait to get my hands on your body." He held her cautiously, with restraint. It was Ruth who threw her arms around his neck, and they both felt all the old passions flare, along with new passions, born of absence and longing. Lips clung, souls stretched, hands roamed freely; they might never have stopped except for the voice in the doorway demanding, "Are you two just gonna kiss all the time?"

Tom answered him, only fractionally releasing Ruth and looking straight into her eyes, "Not *quite* all the time."

"Oh, brother!"

"Never let me go, Tom," she whispered.

"Never. Nothing between us." At that moment, as he tightened his hold, the baby kicked, and he stepped back—an expression of astonishment and utter delight on his face.

Ruth laughed, and he patted her stomach tenderly. "I'm sorry, little daughter. I didn't mean to crowd you." He looked at Ruth. "We'll let *almost* nothing come between us—babies don't count."

"I think the sandwiches are done," said the voice of reason.

"Okay, son, I just have to show Ruth her wall here." Tom pulled out the desk chair, placing it beside the lounger and led Ruth to it. He yanked on the desk to pull it away from the wall. Then while Tommy stood in the doorway, the spatula thumping his hand in impatience, while pregnant Ruth sat in the straight chair, not believing what she was seeing, but loving whatever it meant with all her heart, Tom began to strip away the ugly gray and black plaid wallpaper.

ABOUT THE AUTHOR

SUSAN ROSS was born and raised in Bucks County, Pa., earned her degrees at Ohio colleges and traveled extensively in Europe for three years. She and her three sons now live in Akron, where Ms. Ross teaches English at the university. *Heart* is her first novel.

CIRCLE OF LOVE

Step out of your world and enter the Circle of Love.

Six new, satisfying and beautifully written romances every month.

Look for them beginning March 1982.